Matchmaking a Grump

Highland Hills

Angela Casella

Denise Grover Swank

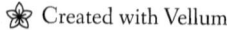

To all the grinches out there. This one's for you.

Chapter One

Kennedy

"Don't be alarmed. It's not that bad."

"Harry!" I snap, horrified by my reflection in the vanity mirror of my temporary bedroom. "This self-tanner's turning me orange! How is this *not that bad?*"

"People like oranges. Oranges are popular. They have a lot of Vitamin C." After saying it all in a rush, he sighs and lifts a hand to his head, scrubbing his buzzed hair. "I don't even know what I'm saying right now. I hate oranges. Some are too sweet, some are too sour, and you can never find one that's just right."

He's as pale as a sailor with scurvy, so maybe he should rethink his stance on the whole Vitamin C thing. Then again, maybe he's pale because he's as panicked as I am.

Okay, don't freak out, Kennedy. You can solve problems. You're good at solving problems. You're here, aren't you?

The non-profit I work for needs to keep its doors open, and although I have a trust fund, the money won't be mine, really mine, until I'm thirty. That's more than a year away, and I'm afraid we won't make it a year unless a miracle happens. It's less than a month before Christmas, so it's the time of year for miracles.

The thing is, sometimes you need to *make* the miracle happen.

1

I'm a Littlefield "of the Littlefield Bank fortune," or so my parents always put it. My father would give me an advance on my trust fund to pay for any material things I might want—dresses, an apartment, a lavish lifestyle—but I'm not allowed to give the money away. I'm particularly not allowed to give it to my boss.

I know what you're thinking. *Poor little rich girl.* But I don't *want* to be a rich girl, poor or otherwise. I've never wanted my parents' money. They're despicable people—something I realized at age six when my mother threw away my old winter coat rather than give it to my nanny, Rose, whose daughter was my age and also my friend.

"We don't want to give her ideas, Kennedy," my mother said, tsking. "Then she'll be stealing all your dolls and nice things the second your back is turned, won't she?"

So I started giving my things away to other kids in secret. Nanny Rose wouldn't accept my gifts, but others did. Kids at school. People I saw out on the street. I gave away anything I could get my hands on. Of course, my little kid logic didn't understand that other people would be blamed for my largesse, and the instant my mother accused Nanny Rose and our housekeeper of stealing, I let the truth tumble out. After that, my parents always kept a careful eye on me.

They still do.

In their minds, I'm the weak link—the one who might just let the revolutionaries in the back door.

You might be wondering why someone who doesn't want to be a rich girl would agree to be the star of a reality dating show called *Matchmaking the Rich.* I wouldn't blame you for wondering if I'm a hypocrite. But consider this: millions of people will be watching me on TV—millions of people who'll have to listen to me mention my non-profit in every episode. Despite what my father thinks, I've inherited something from him besides his money and the Littlefield blue eyes, because I made the producers put that into the contract. I get at least one reference to Leto's Hands per episode. Signed, sealed, and delivered.

This is the best fundraising coup I could have engineered, and my boss was happy to give me a month off work—no email contact, no phone calls, no anything—to film the show.

"Maybe you'll come back with a husband," she'd said with a wink.

I'm not opposed to it. That's the purpose of the show, after all, to see me engaged.

If being rich isn't important to me, then maybe it won't be important to one of the men whom Nana Mayberry, the matchmaker behind the show, has picked for me. Maybe these guys would just prefer to be with someone else who has money so they don't always have to wonder if that's the only thing the other person sees in them.

It's not pretty, being used.

It's the ugliest thing there is, maybe.

My gaze lands on the mirror and lingers, taking in the distinctly orange hue of my cheeks, which clashes with my dark hair and blue eyes.

Okay, so maybe being orange is worse. Especially in a peach-colored dress.

I lift a hand to my cheek. "How could this happen? She's a professional makeup artist. Everything looked fine before she left."

"I don't know," Harry says with plenty of agitation. "A lot of free makeup samples were sent in, though." He loses more color, if that's possible. "I don't want to alarm you, but are you feeling dizzy or nauseous?"

"Harry, no one poisoned me," I say, holding back a laugh. It's adorable how concerned he is on my behalf.

Harry's the co-host of the show, but he also happens to be the best friend of my future sister-in-law, Tina.

Tina and my brother Zach live in Highland Hills, where we're shooting the show, and Tina's the one who got Harry to audition for this job. Of course, she didn't realize at the time that I was going to be the first contestant. She didn't realize because I didn't tell her, or

Zach, or anyone other than my best friend, Olive, that I was applying.

The producers called me last week to tell me they'd hired him. They said they'd done it because they thought it would be best if we had two hosts—male and female—to appeal to both demographics. But I didn't need my brother, Zach, to tell me that's bull. They hired Harry because he's funny and sweet, and Nana Mayberry is a cold, dour woman who probably spent her last life as an icicle.

I know her type. I was birthed by a woman just like her.

I don't question their decision, I'm just happy for it, because they've assigned Harry to personally handle me, which means I won't have to spend much time with Nana. She'll be hanging around with the men, I guess.

Peering into the mirror, I turn my face from side to side. Yes, still orange, especially against the peach of the dress. "Okay, well, obviously we need a different dress." I lift a finger. "Let me ask Olive for advice." I give him a plaintive look. "Can I use your phone?"

Mine is in a drawer somewhere, and it won't be returned until filming is done. Still, I know her number by heart. He sighs and looks around the room, which is unnecessary since the door is closed and it's just the two of us in here, before unlocking his iPhone and handing it over.

I snap a photo and send it to her, along with the text. *This is Harry's phone. No time to explain, but I'm orange. The premiere starts filming in half an hour. HELP.*

Bless her, she answers within thirty seconds, while Harry paces the floor nervously, nearly tripping on a navy rug with a border of unicorns.

Black dress. Wear a veil. Maybe they can make it a whole thing where they're hiding your identity until the second episode? HIDE THE ORANGE.

I glance at the time on Harry's phone. Twenty minutes. We have twenty minutes before I'm due to film my TV debut. We're staying in an enormous mansion that I've visited before but don't know well. For the production, we're calling it Labelle Manor, though the title seems too noble for the house. My first meeting with the eight guys Nana Mayberry has hand-selected for me will happen in the ballroom, because of course it has to be something "appropriately glamorous," to borrow her vocabulary. She's probably with them right now, making sure they have perfectly aligned pocket squares, little suspecting her leading lady has turned orange.

Even though the holidays are fast approaching, and it would be wonderful if this place were decorated with enormous trees and velvet ribbons and nutcrackers as tall as Harry, it's not. It's like Christmas forgot to visit this one corner of Highland Hills, North Carolina, because the small town we're nestled in has its decorating game *down*. I had a day to visit and soak in the holiday cheer before I was locked away in my castle like the heroine of a Disney movie. The show won't be airing until March, and it would look strange if the holidays were represented, so the joy will be kept to a minimum.

I love the idea of Christmas, although it's always been about gift cards and one-upmanship with my family, not hot chocolate, sleigh rides, and caroling.

I shake off the thought because I have a mission to accomplish, and mooning over the holidays, or lack thereof in this house, won't make it happen.

"Harry, we need the black dress in the wardrobe. Is there some kind of veil or something?" I show him the text from Olive because it's easier to do that than offer an explanation, and he brightens like someone lit a bulb inside him.

"Yes, yes, I like the way she thinks," he mutters to himself, taking the phone from me and tucking it into a pocket. He hoists me up from my chair at the ornate vanity table and, to my surprise and delight, gives me a twirl. "You, Kennedy Littlefield, are going to be a woman of mystery. We won't tell them who you are in the first episode. They'll be guessing. God knows they'll guess, but they won't guess correctly. Then you'll make your big, non-orange debut on the second episode after we send two of the guys packing tonight."

I laugh, delighted by the thought. "Okay, but where are we going to get the veil?"

His expression turns fierce, that of a man on a mission. "My roommate helped get this set up and running. He'll know where Evelyn Labelle stored all her things before they rented out the house. That woman looks like the kind of person who'd own a black veil. I'm sure he can help me find one."

The Labelles are the owners of Labelle Manor, a place that is over the top to the point of tackiness. The guest rooms where the men and I will be staying all have themes—there's a rooster room, a cupid room, and so on. I have the distinction of staying in the princess room, which must have belonged to one of their daughters decades ago, because, at the risk of sounding like the princess from *The Princess and the Pea*, the four-poster bed has a mattress so lumpy that I had to have someone special order a mattress pad just so I could get more than a few hours of sleep. Still, it's huge, and there is an enormous head-to-toe mirror showing me that I look like someone who spent hours being naughty in Willy Wonka's chocolate factory, only I've been turned orange instead of blue.

"Nana Mayberry's grandson?" I ask with a frown, because I know Harry lives with two of the Mayberry grandchildren.

Don't get me wrong. I'm not judging the guy. I'm the last person who'd blame a person for their relatives. But I wasn't under the impression that any of the Mayberrys were involved in the production. In fact, Tina is friendly with a couple of them, and they made it very clear to me that they want nothing to do with their grandmother.

Again, I can't blame them, but why would a Mayberry be helping with the show if they all find it, and their grandmother, so objectionable?

"Is he here?"

"He is!" Harry says, rushing over to the wardrobe to retrieve the black dress. I take it from him. "It's worth a try, I guess, although I can't think Mrs. Labelle would appreciate it."

It amuses me to think about Evelyn Labelle recognizing her veil on television. She probably would. Maybe she has a motion tracker sewn into all her things.

"I'll be back in a jiff!" Harry says. "Wait...is that something people still say?"

Laughter spills out of me, probably partly from nerves. "I'm not sure anyone's said that ever. Wait, though. Can you unzip me? I'm not sure I can get out of this thing by myself."

It's a mermaid-style dress, tight enough that there's not a whole lot I can do mobility-wise.

He does the deed graciously, then exits the room in a flurry of motion.

I work on extricating myself from the dress. It's a dance I know well enough, and before long, I have the peach dress on the hanger. It's too bad, really. It's a confection of gold and peach that did all kinds of things for my natural complexion.

If I didn't know better, I'd think someone was trying to sabotage me, but I can't imagine why the makeup artist would do that. After all, she'll see me again soon enough.

The only reason she left when she did was because one of the guys got himself punched at the local brewery last night, on our final day of freedom. He has a black eye that desperately needed her attention. Being orange is more of a problem, obviously, but the transformation happened gradually, and by the time I'd noticed, she was probably halfway across the house. Given the size of this place, looking for her would have been like searching for one particular pin in a box of them.

I pull on the long-sleeved black dress, which is equally stunning. The design and cut are simple but flattering, and the sleeves help ensure the self-tanner mishap stays my little secret. I wait for Harry to show up to save the day because I'm no more able to zip myself into this dress than I was to zip myself out of the last one.

There's a knock. "Come in," I call out, then I shriek at the reflected sight of a stranger barging in through the door. This particular dress has a long zipper that goes down past my butt, so he's just seen my entire backside and my lucky underwear.

He's a big guy, a few inches over six feet, and muscular, with a short dark beard.

What the hell? Did one of the contestants from the show decide to barge into my room before filming to make a case for himself in private?

If he tries anything, I'll slap him in the face and show him just how well this particular silver spoon girl can defend herself, but after a second, I register that he looks as horrified as I must—probably from the combined shock of finding me not quite dressed and also orange.

"What are you doing here?" I ask, reaching back reflexively to try to hold the gaping fabric together.

"Fuck," he says, stepping back. "I...fuck."

"Eloquent," I say coldly, channeling my mother. Melinda Little-field isn't the kind of woman who'll let any man ruffle her, however large, unexpected, and masculine.

He works his jaw. "You should have said you were changing in here. You told me to come in. For all you knew, you could have been inviting anyone in here."

The nerve!

"I was expecting someone," I say primly. "And that someone was not you."

"Yeah, no shit," he says, lifting a hand to his mouth. He tilts his head. "Who were you expecting? Prince Charming? Which one is he? Number Six?"

"It's rude to come into a woman's room without introducing yourself," I say. I'm a little intimidated by him, to be honest. First, I have no idea who he is. Second, I'm still unzipped. Third, he's just... so big. So masculine. There's this energy around him that's untamed. I'm not used to men like him.

His mouth works into a wry grin, and he lifts his other hand, which is when I finally notice it. A black veil.

"I guess in this one case, I *am* Prince Charming," he says. His gaze moves over my body again, settling back on my face, and by then I'm sure pink has joined the orange of my cheeks. "It's not that bad," he says. "If Harry hadn't told me, I might not have noticed."

I hold back a snort. "Well, there you have it. I'm about to be filmed for a national broadcast, and I don't look 'that bad.' Thank you for the vote of confidence."

He lifts his eyebrows. "You could have just said thank you."

Crap. He's kind of right. Although I'm surprised Harry passed this job on to someone else after leaving my room with the intense focus of a knight on a sacred quest, there's no denying this man was helpful. I take the veil from him, admiring the quality of the lace. It's dark enough that they'll be able to see my features—or at least that I have them—but not any details. The orange will go unnoticed.

"Thank you," I say. "It *was* kind of you."

Is it my imagination, or is he rolling his eyes? I ignore it. "What happened to Harry?"

He snorts. "He'll be here in a minute. My grandmother cornered him into a conversation, but he seemed to think this couldn't wait." He nods to the veil.

Grandmother. So...this must be the roommate. I'd imagined him differently.

Maybe Harry had to convince Nana Mayberry to go along with our strategy for the episode. They'll probably have to run it by the producers too, and now we're down to—I glance at the carriage-shaped clock mounted on the wall—ten minutes.

That's not good.

"Well, have fun," the guy says, turning to leave.

"You're going?"

He stops and turns to look at me, raising one eyebrow. "You want me to stay, Princess?"

Something shivers through me, although I'm not sure why. I'm not intimidated by him anymore. He's rude and gruff, but he's no danger.

I tip my head over my shoulder, silently indicating the zipper. "I could use a little help."

"Oh," he says, looking taken aback, and for some reason I'm pleased to have done that to him. "I shouldn't do that."

"You have two hands, don't you? I'll bet you know how to use them."

I didn't mean it like *that*, but he looks slightly flustered, and I can't deny that's how it sounded. I open my mouth to apologize, realize there are certain situations not improved by words, and shut it again.

He heaves a sigh like I asked him to do something hugely objectionable, but comes closer, his scent engulfing me as he does. He smells like campfires and pine, just like the Christmas candle I used to light in my room when I was a kid. The memory makes me smile.

"What are you so happy about?" he asks as he circles around me. His presence seems to crowd me, but it's not unpleasant.

"Thinking about Christmas," I say. "I like Christmas much more than this house does."

"You're not mooning about your eight suitors?"

"Leave it to a matchmaking family to use the word suitor." It's a glib response, but I feel a surprising amount of anticipation. Soon, he'll reach for the zipper, then it will slide up my back. He'll probably do it quickly enough to catch skin, a man like this.

He snorts. "You're the one on the show, *Princess*."

I decide I don't like that name just as his hand clasps around the zipper. It's probably too small for him. I can feel the warmth and rasp of his fingers. I can tell from such a slight touch that they're callused. The zipper slides up slowly, surprising me. It's a sinuous movement, bottom to top. He surprises me further when he finishes by fixing the clasp at the top of the dress.

"There," he says, circling around me, the warmth at my back going with him. "It'll do."

A laugh escapes me. "A true king with the compliments."

He shakes his head slowly, his mouth tipping up on one side. "Nah, your prince is going to be in that ballroom. I'm just the court jester."

He turns to walk away, and as he steps out the door, I realize I don't actually know his name. Just that he's a Mayberry.

"What's your name, Jester?" I ask.

Swiveling back a little, he gives me another half-smile. "Rowan."

"And I'm Kennedy."

"No shi—" he starts before course-correcting. "Yeah, I know. Break a leg, Kennedy." He makes a face. "Non-literally, of course."

Then he's gone.

Chapter Two

Kennedy

"You're orange," Bachelor Number Seven bellows. He staggers back into the champagne fountain and is immediately soaked. Priceless crystal glasses tumble to the floor.

This is a *disaster*.

For one, there's something screwy going on with the heating system in the house. The grand ballroom has a beautiful polished parquet floor and floor-to-ceiling windows with mountain views and gorgeous maroon velvet curtains, which I strongly suspect were purchased by the producers. In every corner, there's an elaborate trellis stretching from floor to ceiling, woven through with plants that are either real or really good knockoffs. It would be even more pleasant if it weren't freezing, probably no more than fifty degrees. Even though the dress I'm wearing is long-sleeved, the fabric is thin lace. The guys, all dressed in suits or tuxes, got lucky...and not one of them has offered me a jacket. I've kept away from the champagne fountain because the last thing I want right now is something that's going to make me colder.

Rowan Mayberry has been in and out of the room for the last

hour, presumably trying to fix the problem, but it only seems to get worse.

The other issue is that the bachelors are all terrible.

Well, maybe that's not fair. Rowan was right about Bachelor Number Six—Marcus is as much of a Prince Charming as I'm liable to get. He's a hedge fund manager with golden hair, blue eyes, and a personality that might be less impressive if it weren't ranked against the seven other frogs Nana Mayberry chose for me.

They were brought in one by one through a double doorway in the side of the ballroom, introduced by Harry, who carried a scroll as if we're in some sort of Regency movie. It would have been fun, actually, if any of them other than Marcus appeared to *have* a sense of fun. Okay, maybe I'm jumping to conclusions. I admit I haven't spoken to them enough to know for sure—each one had a memorized speech, most of them revolving around money and how they got theirs. I'd listen to a minute or so of monologuing, greet the guy, and then he'd take a seat on one of the thrones set up across from mine. It didn't help that one of the men kept flubbing his speech. We had to repeat his entrance five times, with Nana Mayberry telling me to look more pleased until it felt like my face hurt from all the fake smiling. I wish I could say it was the first time it's happened, but I've spent my life being told to smile.

And, yes, I said there were thrones. Mine is even on a mirrored pedestal. In the middle of the thrones is the champagne fountain, which had an elaborate stack of crystal champagne flutes next to it. Yes, I said *had*.

After the cameras got footage of us all sitting around smiling at each other for what seemed like an eternity but was probably only about twenty minutes, Harry announced it was time for the champagne cocktail party to begin. I'd talked to most of the men, or rather they'd talked *at* me, making sure the cameras were capturing them (one of the men even told the cameraman to walk around to get his good side). Then, as Bachelor Number Two—Deacon—finished telling me about his family's vacation home and started to walk away,

Bachelor Number Seven, Jonah Highbury the Fifth, walked over and flipped my veil with a laugh, asking what I was hiding. Which was when he backed into the champagne fountain and broke all the glasses.

"Rowan," Nana Mayberry screams, waving a hand at the cameramen set up around the room. They keep right on filming. According to Harry, the producers have informed them they don't have to answer to her and her mercurial whims. There's no sign of Rowan, so presumably he's off working on the heating problem.

Harry hurries forward from where he was standing to one side of the thrones and flips my veil back into place.

"There's no rewinding time, Harry," I say with a laugh, flipping it back. A ring on my finger got caught in the netting and nearly ripped the hat and a bunch of pinned hair off my head. "Yes, Jonah." I, disentangling it and glancing around as I take in the others. "Everyone. There was a mishap, and I'm currently a lot more orange than usual."

This is already a nightmare, so I might as well own it.

"Rowan," Nana shrieks again, as if she's unaware that he might be out of hearing in this sprawling house.

Miraculously, he steps into the ballroom seconds later. His gaze goes to me first, and his lips tip up. "So, your big secret's out, huh?"

"Rowan," Nana Mayberry says with pinched lips, gathering his attention. She points to the pile of broken crystal on the ground as if he's a paid servant and not her handyman grandson who appears to be helping her out of the goodness of his heart.

"Your wish is my command," he jests, then leaves again, presumably to get a broom.

"Were you exposed to radiation?" Jonah asks. Based on the way he's eyeing me, it's not the first time he's said it.

I give myself a mental shake. "Nope, no radiation. Bad self-tanner."

He takes two big steps back, as if bad self-tanner is contagious, and his shoe cracks a piece of the already broken glass, prompting him to jump back farther and bump into Bachelor Number Three, who gives him a disgusted look and shuffles away, nearly mowing down Nana Mayberry. She'd hustled up closer to evaluate the broken glass situation.

Number Three, who calls *himself* Meathead, is the most fit and muscular of the contestants—the son of a man who started a hugely successful fitness program—so she doesn't seem overly upset. In fact, Nana reaches out and touches his back.

"Steady there," she says, in no hurry to move her hand. "A man like you could knock me down without a second thought."

There's a hearty dose of implication behind the words. I'd feel worse for Meathead if he hadn't already told me that I should cut dairy, gluten, and refined sugar from my diet. I don't need someone stepping into my mother's shoes on the first night of filming. The only other thing of note about him is that he's clearly the guy who got punched in the eye. The makeup artist is good, but there's a slight purpling of flesh that can be seen through his foundation.

Jonah wipes his face with a kerchief from his pocket, seemingly oblivious that the kerchief is as wet as his suit. He gives a shiver, and it occurs to me that hypothermia isn't fully out of the question given the temperature in here.

I glance at Harry. "Shouldn't we get him a change of clothes?"

The words have barely left my lips when Rowan returns to the room with a broom, dustpan, a purple robe, and towel.

I can't help but smile. He has it more together than anyone else involved in this production, myself included.

He gives everything to Jonah, who is instantly affronted. "I'm expected to sweep?" he asks, as if being asked to clean up after himself is more hideous than any of the demands made on Cinderella.

"And I thought you were stupid," Rowan quips.

Jonah bristles, then stalks toward Rowan, but he almost immediately retreats, having correctly deduced he'd lose any fight between the two.

"I'll do it," I say, holding out a hand for the broom.

"No, you won't," Rowan says, his brow furrowing. He seems pissed off by the suggestion. I remember him calling me "princess" and internally bristle.

"I can sweep."

"Yes, most of us have the ability to sweep," he says, his expression still severe, like he should be out chopping wood instead of helping on the set of a reality dating show. "But you didn't make the mess. You shouldn't volunteer to clean up after other people."

I'm annoyed by his high-handedness. Shouldn't I be allowed to volunteer my help however *I* want? His words remind me of my parents, which probably isn't fair. They don't like it when I volunteer my help to people who genuinely need it; Rowan is telling me not to do the dirty work of Jonah Highbury the Fifth.

The stare down between them continues for several seconds, then, to my shock, Jonah shrugs on the robe and starts sweeping.

A glance shows me the cameramen are soaking it all in. This is definitely going to make it into the first episode.

"Well, this is exciting," Harry says, almost manically, clapping his hands three times. Then he pulls a face. "I guess we'll have to skip the champagne social though."

Darn it. That would have been the perfect opportunity for me to talk about my non-profit, although I already know that at least six out of eight of the guys would have such little interest in the topic their eyes would glaze over.

I've only brought up my job once, briefly, with Marcus, mainly because he's the only one who asked me anything about myself. I feel another glow of warmth toward him.

"Aren't you going to ask us how we feel about this?" asks Deacon.

Jonah finishes sweeping and stacks the dustpan full of glass against the wall, relinquishing the problem to someone else. Rowan rolls his eyes but doesn't say anything. A couple of production assistants move forward and roll the thrones, which are apparently on wheels, flush against the wall.

My gaze follows Rowan as he leaves the room. Presumably, he's off to tackle the heating situation again.

"Are you talking about missing the champagne social?" Harry asks Deacon. "It *is* disappointing, but I'm afraid the sponsor only sent over a certain amount for tonight, and the crystal people..." He pulls a face as he glances at the crystal graveyard, propped against the back wall.

Something tells me they won't be pleased that we've highlighted the breakability of their product.

"I'm talking about the *lies*," Deacon says darkly, glaring at me. "I don't like being lied to. It brings up a lot of buried trauma for me. My ex-girlfriend told me she was related to the Washingtons. She never said she meant George Washington, but we all know that was the implication. I told everyone in my family. They bring it up every Thanksgiving dinner. Every last one."

"Well, sorry," I say, playing with the edge of the veil.

"Don't you recognize her?" hisses Colton, Bachelor Number One. "She's a Littlefield, you idiot. Of the *Chicago* Littlefields."

I guess that still means something to some people. Then again, Colton's from a banking family, just like me. For him, the Littlefields mean something. He doesn't know—and probably wouldn't care— that my father disowned my brother. I'm pretty sure my dad would have disowned me too for pulling, and I quote, "this little stunt," if it wouldn't be such a public relations nightmare. Because everyone is going to know their daughter is on this show. Because it's not such bad publicity for them, honestly, unless I make a fool of myself.

I've received a dozen messages from my mother warning me not to make a fool of myself.

"Of course," Nana Mayberry says. She's still standing next to Meathead, her hand pressed to his back. "You're all crème de la crème." She rubs his back. "I wouldn't accept anything less."

Harry has a tortured look on his face, as if he knows this isn't going well but isn't sure how to right the ship. "How fun that you've guessed the bachelorette's identity!" he tells Colton.

"Isn't that a different show?" someone asks in an undertone.

"My name is Kennedy Littlefield," I say, sweeping a glance around to take in all the guys. It's hard to do with eight. I'll be glad to send two home tonight, and I'm pretty sure I already know which two. One of them is wearing a purple robe with tiaras on it that almost certainly belongs to Evelyn Labelle.

"You're beautiful, Kennedy," Marcus says, giving me an appreciative head-to-toe glance. He's stepped forward from the group of guys. Someone grunts in annoyance, but I don't look up to see who. I don't need to. Something deep inside me knows it's Rowan Mayberry.

Marcus reaches for my hand and lifts it to his lips, staring into my eyes as he kisses it. It's the kind of move that should make a woman's heart race, but to my disappointment, my heart continues to beat at its regular pace.

Maybe he'll grow on me. My brother and his fiancée love each other more fiercely than any other couple I know, and they met because she was posing as his fake girlfriend. In the beginning, they weren't even *attracted* to each other. So, yes, it's totally possible that this time next month, Marcus will be my everything.

The thought gives my stomach a little flutter. Hopefully, my heart will catch up soon.

"She *is* pretty, but she'd look even better if she *weren't* orange," Jonah mutters, adjusting the tie of his robe.

"This is very exciting, very exciting," Harry blurts. His color has risen, and he looks like he's a paper bag away from a panic attack. Poor Harry. "Well—" he claps his hands and looks at the grandfather clock across the room. "It's time for the thirty-second waltzes."

"Waltzes take longer than thirty seconds," says Colton. He's pretty attractive too, actually, easily a second to Marcus, with dark, slightly curly hair and big brown eyes.

Harry taps his watch. "Yes, well, we have to make accessions for our runtime."

It's a ridiculous notion, flouncing across the floor with each of them for just thirty seconds apiece, but then again, this is what I signed up for.

"At least the exercise will make us warmer," I say, smiling at Colton, who just offered me his hand. I take it. Once again, I'm hoping to feel something—a spark, a zing, a zip—but it's a hand, and it feels a little clammy actually, despite him being a very good-looking man.

"You're cold?" he asks.

"A little," I admit, fully expecting him to offer his jacket.

He doesn't.

Neither do the next three men.

They may be thirty-second waltzes, but we have to repeat a few of them multiple times. The room isn't getting any warmer, and although the exercise has helped, I'm relieved when Marcus finally does offer me his jacket. The gallantry is on point. So is the slightly spicy scent it carries as he arranges it over my shoulders. Only...I can practically feel the cameras zooming in on us. The show is the whole point of being here—making magic happen for millions of viewers— but I still find myself wishing this moment could be just for me.

Jonah is still wearing his robe for our waltz, and I'm still wearing Marcus's jacket. They'll definitely ham that up in production—

Jonah's a rude klutz, and is Kennedy still wearing Marcus's jacket? Gasp! It's funny to imagine but slightly surreal.

After the waltzes end, Harry grins maniacally at the cameras and says, "Well, it's not easy to say goodbye, but it's almost time for the first Rolex ceremony, folks."

"Of course," Nana Mayberry cuts in, stepping in front of him, which would have been more effective if he weren't so much taller, "We're going to need to consult with Kennedy first, Sweet Tea."

That's her nickname for him, although I can't pinpoint the reason for it. Harry likes his tea half sweet and half not, so maybe she doesn't think he's properly Southern. Whatever her reasons, they're probably not kind. I've come to realize there's very little kindness about her. She's certainly not the warm, fuzzy kind of grandmother who gives hugs and offers fresh-baked cookies. If there are blankets in her house, they're probably like the ones my mother purchases—for show.

The guys are sent off, probably to somewhere warmer, but Marcus insists on leaving me with his jacket. I don't object. Once they're gone, Nana Mayberry and Harry hustle me into a small sunroom attached to the ballroom. It's still cold. The cameras crowd in with us, and Harry ushers me over to the couch and fusses over my dress as I get settled. He then sits across from me in a chair, Nana Mayberry in a slightly taller one next to him.

Something tells me she planned that. One cameraman crouches to the side of us and another is facing me.

"Now, before we start," Nana Mayberry says. "Jonah is on the no-cut list. You can't send him home."

"What?" I squawk, my gaze shifting to Harry.

He gives me a sympathetic look, scrubs a hand over his buzzed hair, and nods. "Sorry. I can't believe I'm saying this, but I agree with her. He needs to stay until the bitter end."

Darn it. I was counting on him to be sensible.

"But he's *terrible*," I say.

"Precisely. This is a *television* show," Nana Mayberry says in a withering tone, as if I'm too stupid to understand why there are cameras following us around. "Your future husband is in this house right now, mark my words. Jonah may not be an obvious match for you, but we need to ensure the show stays entertaining. He sticks around."

"He's a wild card," Harry says sympathetically. "People enjoy watching wild cards. It's why we love dating shows. He's already made tonight ten times more interesting. Deacon is petulant, and Jeff, Bachelor Number Four, is a bit dull, poor guy. Listening to him is like watching paint dry. Marcus and Colton are both shoe-ins for this first round, and Meathead is...a grown man who calls himself Meathead. Take him or leave him."

"Take him," Nana says in an undertone. "Definitely take him."

"What about the other two?" I ask, struggling to remember their names.

"Someone needs to fill those chairs, huh?" he says with a chuckle. "Quinn and Ray will do a good enough job of that. Leave them and cut the two you don't want to run into on ice cream runs to the kitchen in the middle of the night. But keep Jonah."

Crap. I have to admit that they're right, but it doesn't make me any more eager to spend more time with him.

Still, I feel like I have to put in a token objection. "So I have to keep him and send someone else home—a guy who might be a good match for me?"

Harry gives me a weighing look. "Kennedy, are you honestly saying you can't comfortably send home a different guy? I think you could probably send home four."

He's right.

"Okay," I say slowly. "Meathead goes."

Nana scowls. "He's very good looking," she snaps. "Having him is good metrics. I was going to suggest we have him lift each of us on camera."

21

I'll bet she was.

"They're *all* handsome," I say. "But I don't need someone around commenting on my dietary choices. It's nearly Christmas."

"Not in this house," Nana Mayberry objects, straightening her back.

"It's still the holiday season. That matters to me. I'm going to eat cookies and drink cocoa, even if I have to make them myself. I don't need Meathead reminding me of the calorie counts."

"Fine," she snaps, clearly unhappy about it. "Meathead goes, but Jonah stays." She sends a withering glance at Harry. "See, Sweet Tea? I'm capable of compromise."

He shrinks away from her a little before nodding to the cameramen. "We're ready."

As soon as the cameras start rolling, Nana tilts her head, studying me with false concern. "

I don't think Jonah is a good match for you, Kennedy."

Indeed. I'm not surprised by her hypocrisy. I'm used to it—my mother and her friends make an art of saying one thing and meaning another. I'd rather not be comfortable with this kind of discourse, but I'm definitely familiar with it.

Harry gives me a quick glance, like he's wondering if I'm going to flip out on her. But I don't. I give her a sheepish smile and say, "Well, he *is* a little clumsy, and he seemed thrown by my self-tanning mishap, but so was I! I couldn't believe it when I looked in the mirror." I tap my chin. "Still, there's something charmingly straight-forward about Jonah. He certainly says what he's thinking."

There's a choking sound, and I look over at Harry, alarmed.

"It's okay," he stammers out, lifting a hand. "I'm just choking on my own spit."

We continue the discussion, and I tell them that I have concerns about Deacon and Meathead. Deacon, because he's still clearly not over his ex-girlfriend's betrayal. Meathead, because he comes off as judgmental and got into a physical altercation the night before filming. After a few minutes, I segue the conversation into a longer discussion of my job, which Nana tries to cut short with a sour look on her face, but I make sure to deliver our mission statement in full.

We return to the ballroom, and while the guys filter back in, having been summoned by some signal, Harry presents me with a glossy wooden case, which I open dramatically for the cameras.

"This is it," he says, glowing, once the men are all seated in their thrones, which have been wheeled back into position. "The Rolex ceremony."

I unclasp the case, revealing six glossy watches, the sale of which would probably keep Leto's Hands running like a well-oiled machine for months.

As I try not to feel bitter about that, the electricity goes out.

Chapter Three

Rowan

This isn't going according to plan.

Then again, I don't have a specific plan. I only know that I can't let this travesty masquerading as a TV show get renewed.

One season? Sure, it's embarrassing to have our family name dragged through mud again—the way it was the last time someone had the dumbass idea of giving my grandmother a power trip and a platform for her bullshit. But if it's a one-season wonder, it'll *go away*. Any longer than that, and my mother will come running back to Highland Hills for her chance at a sliver of the spotlight.

No fucking thanks. Our family doesn't need any more spotlights on it, picking up all the dirt and dust that is *very much* there. And if you ask me, our town doesn't need more tourists barreling through it, looking for small-town charm like it's something they can package and bring home in their suitcases. My friend Oliver's always quick to let out a world-weary sigh when I say things like that. "You don't complain when a new bar opens, Rowan, or when there's a new restaurant. Not all change is bad."

Of course, we both know that's bullshit. I *do* complain when new bars and restaurants open. My sisters call me Old Man Rowan, and maybe they have a point, but even so. Highland Hills needs a hit dating show as much as I need to go antiquing with my twin sisters, Holly and Bryn, this weekend. (Yes, they actually invited me, but I'm reasonably sure it's a joke. Holly's been pulling at least one practical joke a week on me ever since she moved in with me last summer.)

So I take my time going downstairs to look at the breaker that I tripped. I don't want them to finish filming tonight. The longer it takes to film the show, the more expensive it will be. The more expensive it is, the less likely the producers will want to throw more money at my grandmother.

When I come back upstairs, the camera guys have their cellphones out, using them as flashlights—none of the bachelors are doing this, of course. Or Kennedy. They're not allowed to have their phones during filming. Actually, based on what Harry told me, their devices are literally under lock and key, which sounds fucking brutal. Not that I'm the kind of guy who's always texting or calling people—no thank you. But what if they want to sneak out for a night? What if they want to watch YouTube to figure out how to break a heating system—or fix one? There are plenty of TVs in the house, but Harry says those are cut off from the internet, and although the Labelles do have some dusty DVDs stashed in the basement, there's nothing but a box set of the show *Dallas* and several Mary-Kate and Ashley Olsen movies. No need to mess with those. If anyone tries to have a movie night, the DVDs themselves will do the tormenting.

I doubt these guys will be jonesing for YouTube fix-it videos, anyway. That one guy, Jonah, had clearly never used a broom in his life. They're not the fix-it-up types.

My gaze sticks on Kennedy, who looks fine as hell despite the tanner mishap.

I don't like that Number Six put his jacket on her.

Because I'm as capable of hypocrisy as the next asshole, I also don't like that it took six guys to pony up a single jacket.

Of course, I'm not allowed to have an opinion on that, being that I'm also the one who messed with the thermostat.

My grandmother sees me in the low lighting and bustles over. She's in her eighties, but there's nothing frail about her tonight. Her ego certainly hasn't taken any hits. Still, she's getting old. That's why I answer her calls for help, even though she's not the kind of grandmother who'd knit me a blanket or send me a birthday card. Or do anything for me. The fact is, she's family—and if I'm not the one answering her calls, those calls will be made to my sisters, who are not as immune to her bullshit as I am.

"Rowan, why aren't the lights on?"

"I'm a handyman, Nana, not an electrician. I'll have to call one of my buddies to come take a look in the morning."

"But we're filming *tonight*," she hisses. Her hair is still perfectly contained by her bun, and if she's agitated by the shitty bent the night has taken, it doesn't show in the glow of the phone flashlights. Then again, she's never been one to show emotion—or feel it. When she gathered us kids together to tell us our mother was leaving because she'd decided to get married to her fourth husband, who wasn't keen on taking in her five kids from three different men, she said, and I quote, "I'm in the unfortunate position of being stuck with your mother's mistakes, but you *will* be allowed to stay here, so long as you do your duty."

That's not the kind of thing a teenager forgets.

My sister Bryn took it to mean *she* was in charge of us, but I've always felt the gut-deep need to look after my sisters. Call it sexist if you'd like. They probably would. But it's my duty to take care of them, and I go about it in my own way. This is part of that. I'm going to do my damnedest to protect them from this TV show.

"Not anymore, you're not," I tell Nana. "You need someone to come in and look at the heating system too. That's above my paygrade."

Not true. I live in a hundred-year-old house. I've basically rebuilt the heating and cooling system.

"What good are you?" she asks with a scowl.

"Not very," I say. "But I can give my other buddy a call in the morning, have them both swing by. They're *much* more useful."

It's a bit of a gamble, because one of the guys in this room could offer to go down and take a look, but I'm pretty sure none of the bachelors know which end of a screwdriver is the business half. The PAs probably just want to go to bed.

I'm not fool enough to think this little hiccup will cause much of a delay, but if enough problems and incidents crop up, surely these rich assholes will decide the show's not worth their while—it's them and the producers I'm counting on, not my grandmother. She isn't the kind of person who'll ever give up. It's one of the things I reluctantly admire about her.

It's probably the only thing I admire about her.

She heaves a sigh and waves me off, then announces to everyone else that it's a wrap for the night.

I'll have to sneak back downstairs in the middle of the night to fix the shit I messed up, but lucky me, I have a key. My grandmother has appointed me the official fix-it man for the show, mostly because she likes that she can pay me minimum wage.

If my gaze skates to Kennedy again before I take off, then my only explanation is that she's a beautiful woman. Even orange. And there's no harm in looking. Seeing her in her room earlier, her dress undone, showing a stretch of skin leading down the slope of her back to her magnificent ass is up there with the best things that have happened to me this year, even if it wasn't my sight to see. If that's pathetic, then so be it.

My breath catches when I realize she's looking straight back at me. I make the kind of bow that would do any court jester proud.

* * *

27

"You did what?" my sister Holly asks, hitting me with a hard look.

"You heard me."

She throws a french fry at me. I try to catch it in my mouth, and when it hits me in the nose, I scowl at her.

"You deserve it," she says. "You deserve a dozen french fries to the face. That was a crap thing you did."

"The heating system, the electricity, or the self-tanner?"

"The self-tanner, obviously. I couldn't give a shit about Labelle Manor or whatever they're calling it. In fact, if you want to throw a good haunting their way, I'd encourage it."

She has plenty of reasons to dislike the Labelles. Her boyfriend Cole's wife was a Labelle. Okay, that came out wrong. Holly's boyfriend is a widower, and his late wife was Millie Labelle. The Labelles were shitty to him and his wife, and they've continued their trend of being garbage human beings.

Holly and I are currently having a late dinner in a booth at Cole's brewery, which is basically the only place she likes to go now. I'd bitch about it more, except the food is not only pretty good but always free, and so is the beer. Besides, neither of us are much for cooking, so if we weren't here, we'd be at the house we share with Harry, microwaving frozen dinners.

The brewery is already partially decked out for the holidays, and there's holly lining each of the windows. I accused Holly of being responsible for that, but she said Cole did it as a joke. The rest is Cole's daughter Jane's handiwork, although Holly played elf.

My sister shakes another fry at me. "Tina and Zach are our friends, and so is Harry. If you fuck up our rooming situation with Harry, I'll go red on you, so help me God."

The fry breaks in half, the top falling limply. She bites it off.

"You're a savage. But you're also correct. He's hardly ever there, but the house has never looked better." I twist my mouth to the side. "You're never around anymore either, but whenever you are, it immediately gets messier."

"Takes one to know."

I shrug because she's right. About everything. "Yeah, the self-tanner was a dick move. It's just..."

Her lips tip into a sly smile, and her eyes sparkle with it. "Kennedy's too pretty, and you're convinced those rich assholes would never willingly leave unless you turned her orange."

Dammit. Holly's become much too good at reading me. She'd probably phrase it differently and say she's gotten good at slicing through my bullshit.

"Something like that," I mutter, pushing my plate away. I barely mauled half my burger, which is unusual, but my appetite's taken a hit. Everything's taken a hit lately.

I hate that everyone around town is giving me shit about the show. I hate that my last name is synonymous with little cartoon hearts and fat babies carrying bows and arrows. It's always been like that, to be honest—it's your lot in life when your family business is matchmaking—but it's much worse now that my sisters are launching a dating app and my grandmother is the cohost and creator of *Matchmaking the Rich*. Try escaping *that* claim to fame.

My nickname since the first grade has been Cupid, for fuck's sake. The guys at the firehouse where I'm a part-time firefighter still call me that.

"You like her," Holly says, waggling her eyebrows.

I grunt. "You think everyone else is obsessed with love just because you took an arrow."

She throws another fry at me. This one I do manage to catch in my mouth. "Love's not a death sentence, Rowan. I'm still very much alive. So is Bryn. And Willow."

Willow's my little sister, and the first of us Mayberrys to fall prey to the family curse. She doesn't seem to mind much, I guess. She lives in Asheville with her fiancé, Alex.

Maybe it seems dramatic to call falling in love a family curse, but that's the way it seems from the outside looking in. I've seen three of my strong, independent sisters go gooey over a few guys. And yeah, they're pretty solid guys at the end of the day, but they're hardly worth the trouble, if you ask me. It's much better to be alone, to rely on no one but yourself. The only two single Mayberrys left standing are me and our baby sister, Ivy.

I'm not annoyed that my sisters have found partners, obviously, but I like having them to myself every now and then. It's been nice, getting closer to Holly and Bryn over the past year. Growing up, most of the time it didn't feel like I had much of anyone besides Willow. Now, Willow's gone, thank God, because even though I won't quit Highland Hills, it's the kind of trap that has teeth. It's better that she's somewhere else. Even if she's fallen into a different kind of trap.

"I want more from life than just being alive," I say pointedly. "I definitely want more than a legal contract binding me to another person."

She breaks into a song about wanting adventure, which I'm pretty sure is from *Beauty and the Beast*—mock me if you will, but I do have four sisters. Her boyfriend, Cole, pauses on his way back to the bar with a tray of empty glasses and leans down to kiss her mid-verse. My scowl deepens, although I can't deny that I'm impressed he hasn't dropped the tray.

"How's the sabotage going?" he asks me, grinning as he pulls back.

I glance around, annoyed. "Be careful, man," I say in an under-tone. "This needs to stay quiet."

He waves his free hand carelessly. "Those guys can't come in here anymore. After last night, they're confined to the house. Trust me, that Jonah the Fifty-Eighth or whatever told everyone that at least five times."

"Was that before or after your brother punched Meathead?" I ask.

Cole laughs. "Before *and* after. Shit, that was a scene. But if he hadn't punched him, I would have needed to step up."

Holly reaches up to touch his face. "And I owe your brother a cold one for taking one for the team. Your face is too annoyingly perfect to be punched by a Meathead fist."

Apparently, the guys all made a nuisance of themselves at the brewery last night, further proof that I need to do my part to make this go away. Meathead kept aggressively flirting with Brittney, Cole's second-in-command, despite her making it very clear that she was both disinterested and annoyed. When he leaned forward and tried to lay a kiss on her over the bar, Cole's brother took a fist to him. It had led to a short brawl, broken up by Cole and a couple of other guys.

"The sooner those assholes get out of town, the better," I say.

Holly belts out a laugh. "So his solution was to turn Kennedy orange and freeze everyone to death."

Well, when she puts it that way.

I groan. "You're right. Maybe I'm not cut out to be a supervillain."

"Yeah, you're definitely not," Holly says. "You're too much of a closet softy."

"Am not," I say, instantly annoyed at myself for sounding like I'm five.

"You teared up when you saw Bryn's sonogram photos the other day."

"Did not."

But I did. So sue me. It's not every day a man gets to see his niece for the first time.

"Men can cry, Holly," Cole says, surprising the shit out of me by taking my side.

"Well, of course they can, dum-dum," she says, clearly unmoved. "But the ones who do are softies." She lifts her eyebrows at both of us. "I'm not the one acting like that's a bad thing."

"*You're* not a softy," I interject.

"Oh, hell no." She points a finger at me. "But I *did* cry when I saw those pictures." She gives me a pointed look. "I'd also cry if someone turned me orange and locked me in the Labelles' house with a bunch of rich assholes."

I huff out a laugh. "Princess volunteered for the role. You've got no reason to feel bad for her."

Still, even as I say it, I can acknowledge to myself that I do sort of feel bad for her. She's a bit untouchable, like a princess, but there's a certain naive optimism about her, as if she really does believe the shit my grandmother is peddling, or at least wants to.

Tilting her head, Holly says, "So why don't you give her a reason to unvolunteer?"

"For one thing, she's on a dating show called *Matchmaking the Rich*," I say, annoyed, although I'm not sure who's done the annoying. "She's hardly going to throw her panties at a handyman who moonlights as a fireman."

"This is your problem," Holly says. "You expect women to up and throw their panties at you." She eats a fry. "Sometimes you need to work for the good things, bub. They're not just going to climb onto your lap like that one woman I walked in on you with."

"Christ, are you ever going to let that go?" I ask. I've only brought one woman home since she moved in. One. And she's never let me forget it. We were making out on the couch when Holly crept into the room with a baseball bat, thinking I was an intruder. "Besides, what would be the polite way to acquire a woman's panties? Go through her drawers and steal them? Ask nicely to borrow them? Because I'm pretty sure either of those things would make me a sexual predator."

She gives me her *you're impossible* look. Cole watches with us with amusement, then kisses her again—I look away—and takes off toward the bar with the tray.

"I mean it," Holly tells me, and I don't doubt she does. "I'm starting to think you should pillage the show and save the princess."

"You play too many video games."

"Accurate."

My friend Oliver, whom I texted after leaving the Labelles' place, enters through the front and approaches our table. He's wearing a scarf his mother knitted for him and a beanie hat over his dark hair, but he pulls it off as he approaches us. It's a Thursday night, and there's a pretty decent crowd.

Oliver would have been better off if he hadn't come back to town, but now that he's here, he's stuck. His father is sick, and he's not the kind of guy to stay away and watch him die from a distance, even if his dad has made it clear that he'll never approve of him. No, he's the kind of guy who'll chuck his whole life just to support the people he cares about. Lucky for him—or not, depending on your perspective— he works in marketing, and he's talented enough that his boss agreed to let him work remotely. He's staying indefinitely, and that means I'm determined to make things as good for him as possible.

"Hey, man," I say, standing and giving him a backslap when he reaches our table.

"Cupid!"

I make a face. I'm less than fond of my nickname, but what can you do?

"How's the sabotage going?" Oliver continues, grinning as he loosens his scarf.

Goddammit. I take a glance around again, but there's still no one paying attention to us.

"We can't just openly talk about this," I say, as he sits down next to Holly, who scooted aside to make room. "Some people think the show is a good thing for this town." Namely, the people who stand to make money off it.

He shrugs without much concern. "So what do you want to talk about? My mother wants me to chop down a Christmas tree at Ralph's for her this weekend. So that'll be a whole thing." He gives me a pointed look. "You want to come?"

"To chop your tree? No, thanks."

"To chop your own, asshole. I figured you could get one for your house."

"Yes, please," Holly says. "I'm really feeling the Christmas spirit this year. And maybe you can sneak a contraband pine bough over to the Labelles' house so Kennedy isn't completely cut off from Christmas. Tina says she's bummed by the lack of Christmassy things."

"Then she shouldn't have volunteered for the show," I say, trying to sound more severe than I feel. My mind supplies an image of her wistful expression as she talked about Christmas and the way the holiday was completely absent from the Labelles' house. Still, it occurs to me that the tree outing is a potential opportunity.

Oliver has been lonely since returning to Highland Hills. There's not much of a dating scene here for anyone, and there's probably only five or six openly gay men Oliver's age, tops. We met Harry in Asheville earlier this year, while paying a visit to my sister Willow. There were some sparks between them, I thought. Or at least I caught Oliver looking at him appreciatively a few times.

I'm not playing matchmaker. Obviously. I'm *not* a matchmaker.

But Oliver could use some more friends, is all. He just moved back to town a year and a half ago, and his dad has been steadily getting worse. The situation at home isn't easy, and whenever you're in the thick of something not easy, it's better to share it.

"Let's go on Sunday," I say, knowing it's a day off for the people on the production. I'm fairly sure my grandmother wouldn't give anyone a day off if she had her way, but in this one thing, she doesn't. It's in the cameramen's contracts. Harry will be free to join us.

"You got it," Oliver says, although he's giving me a look that suggests he knows I'm up to something, even if he's not quite sure what. That look is mirrored on Holly's face.

"You're really going to chop down a Christmas tree for us?" she asks wistfully. "Isn't that something."

"Let's not make a big deal about it," I grump. "It's not like I'm a total grinch. I go to Ralph's all the time."

Oliver and Holly exchange a look and have a good laugh at my expense.

Chapter Four

Kennedy

"How do you feel about the drama between Jonah and Marcus?" Harry asks me. His head is tilted slightly, his expression serious, and I know—because he's told me—that he's practiced this look in the mirror. We're sitting in that same private conversation room off the ballroom with Nana Mayberry and the cameramen. Originally, they'd set up the Mayberry Matchmakers office for our private interviews, but when the deal with the Labelles was finalized, it was decided we'd be sequestered in this cavernous house for the entirety of shooting, other than a skiing trip we're taking just before Christmas.

It's Saturday evening, and I'm only slightly orange now, the tint having mostly washed away with a special body wash Harry and the very apologetic makeup artist were able to procure. I'm dressed in a very uncomfortable though gorgeous emerald green mermaid-style dress, and I'd give anything to be in the sweats Olive gave me for Christmas last year—the ones with "Santa Babe" written across the butt. Or one of the other holiday-themed nightgowns I snuck onto set, knowing that nighttime would be my only opportunity to acknowledge the season. If I were home in Chicago, we'd be watching a Christmas movie marathon with hot chocolate and gingerbread cookies from our favorite bakery. Instead, I'm here by myself, dressed like a doll, pretending that I don't think Jonah is a garbage human being so people won't suspect we're only keeping him around for the drama.

I sent Meathead and Deacon packing on Friday, after we painstakingly refilmed the Rolex ceremony.

Even Jonah looked surprised when he was asked to stick around. Deacon, who'd muttered that this was just like the situation with the Washingtons, had agreed to leave without any argument, but Meathead had tried to talk me around.

"You're giving *him* the Rolex?" he asked, gesturing to Jonah, who'd had to put on the purple robe again so he'd look consistent, even though he was wearing a fresh suit beneath it. "You want *him* to stay?"

"Yes," I said, "I'd like to get to know him better."

Deacon glowered at me, as if silently accusing me of lying again. He'd be right.

"What do you like about him?" Meathead asked in disbelief.

It took me a solid thirty seconds to find anything to say. "His hair," I finally stuttered out.

It *is* nice—slightly longer than you'd expect in someone named Jonah Highbury the Fifth, chestnut brown and as glossy as if he just got a cream rinse.

"That's shallow," Meathead told me with a glare.

I was tempted to tell him the only thing I liked about him was his muscles, but I'd already eliminated him from the show and felt no need to drag him down farther.

Jonah's been a pain ever since. On Friday afternoon, we had a group date at a nearby vineyard, which the owners closed down for us. They'd even taken down their Christmas decorations, something I found disappointing, other than some delightful fairy lights dangling from the awning of the building.

Despite the lovely setting, the wine all tasted like vinegar, but

Jonah was the only one who felt the need to say so. And he felt the need to say so at least four times.

Marcus pointed out the obvious—that he was being rude—and Jonah challenged him to drink a full glass of the spice wine. Honestly, no one would want to do that. It tasted like potpourri smells. Marcus took him up on his challenge and then ran to the bathroom to vomit. The owner begged us not to include that detail in the episode, but I saw the look exchanged by Harry and Nana Mayberry. This was another of those rare occasions when they agreed with each other.

Afterward, the feud between the two guys escalated. We had a fondue social earlier this evening, and Jonah flung hot cheese at Marcus. Then Marcus loudly accused Jonah of double-dipping. Worse, there was a hole in one of the fondue pots, and no one realized it had been slowly leaking cheese onto the floor until one of the contestants stepped in it. The look of disgust on his face suggested he'd stepped in something much worse.

While Rowan's friends took care of the problems with the heating and electricity, there've been other strange annoyances—a beeping noise no one could locate until Colton finally found a CO alarm at floor level in a dusty room on the second floor. A howling sound that proved to be a window that was stuck one fourth an inch open in another little used room. A leaking sink on the first floor.

I haven't seen Rowan, other than a glimpse of him at the fondue social, standing off to the side with a smirk on his face, his hands shoved into the pockets of his work jeans. There was a slight hole below the knee that looked like it got there by actual work, not the design pretensions of a fashionista.

Something tells me he's not the kind of man who'd dip bread in melted cheese. He's probably the kind of guy who likes steak and thinks potatoes are vegetables.

Of course, I shouldn't care about Rowan Mayberry. He's been very clear about what he thinks of me. *Princess.*

After Jonah stomped off from the fondue social, Marcus shrugged at me. "Sorry, he gets to me."

"He gets to all of us," Colton quipped. "But I'm starting to think this house is cursed." His eyes gleaming, he added, "Think about it. The lights, the heat, the weird incidents."

It was a throwaway remark, but it stuck with me, maybe because it's lonely sleeping in my huge room, without the use of my cell phone. I miss Olive. I miss Tina and Zach. I definitely don't miss seeing my mother's daily reminders of what a disappointment I am, but it's only been a few days, and it's already so strange being here, sequestered from the outside world with a bunch of people whom someone else chose for me. Worse, it'll be six days before I'm allowed to send anyone else home. Two more people will leave on Friday, which'll leave me with four. Then two more will go home the following week. The final two will go on the skiing trip with me. We'll all be together through Christmas, and then I'll spend a weekend with each of them individually before making my final selection.

There's no filming tomorrow, but on Monday morning, I have a horseback riding date with two of the guys. Of course, it's Marcus and effing Jonah, which brings me back to Harry's question...*and* the cameras are probably documenting my momentary mental break.

What did I think of the drama between Marcus and Jonah? What didn't I think of it?

"Kennedy," Harry says softly. "Is this conversation upsetting you?"

I almost laugh. "No, it's not upsetting. I just wish Jonah and Marcus would be a little more mature about their dislike for each other. Of course, they're both men who are used to getting their way. It's natural for there to be some tension."

"We've heard from a couple of the guys that Jonah isn't well-liked in the house," Harry says with plenty of sympathy. "How does that make you feel?"

Like they have sense.

I grimace. "I guess they haven't seen the side of him I have."

"His hair?" Harry teases.

Nana Mayberry's mouth purses with distaste. "We all know why you're jealous, Sweet Tea," she mutters with plenty of ill nature. Harry has a receding hairline and buzzed hair, although he's told me that he misses wearing it longer. He lifts a hand to his forehead, his expression dejected, and I feel a surge of dislike toward Nana.

"We're all jealous," I say, smiling at Harry. "I've heard at least two of the guys ask him about what conditioner he uses, but he's very closed-mouth about it."

Harry smiles back at me.

"Did you know," Nana asks with a slight smile that lacks any joy, "that Marcus has no experience with horseback riding?"

There's an undercurrent of malice to her words, like she thinks this will tarnish him in my opinion.

"Oh?"

"New money," she says with a haughty sneer. "He's one of those bootstraps types."

As far as I know, she's not rich at all, despite the premise of this show, but I don't call her on it. Money doesn't quantify worth, after all. It only impacts what you're able to buy. I just say, "I look forward to teaching him, then."

Deacon could have called me out on that lie too, because it is one. The last thing I want to do is go horseback riding with Jonah and Marcus and listen to them bicker like schoolchildren. Marcus is handsome and occasionally gallant, from offering me his jacket that first night to helping me dip my bread in cheese so it didn't get all over my mermaid dress. But this little Jonah feud has soured me on him, like he's a bottle of table red from that winery. Honestly, I wish this whole thing were over, but I signed up for a reason, and I intend to see it through.

"You know," I say, "one of the things we fund at Leto's Hands is vocational training."

"You teach people to be jockeys?" Harry asks in wonder.

"Well, no. But teaching doesn't stop having value when you age out of school. Our goal is to ensure every woman has a way of earning money for herself."

"Every woman *does* have a way," Nana says crisply. "Marriage."

That dislike I've been feeling curls in around me, tightening its grip. "Marriage is far from the only way a woman can make something of herself," I say, trying not to let her see that she's affected me. Something tells me it would only make her dig her heels in harder. "We teach computer skills, and—"

"I think we're done here," Nana Mayberry says, standing.

"I have the contractual right to talk about Leto's Hands in every episode," I say, getting to my feet too. It takes a lot of effort in this dress, which make me feel like I've been swallowed by a boa constrictor.

"And you have," Nana says. "We need enough material for two episodes per week, dear. No one wants to be bored to death. The men are here to have fun and find love. Which is also why *you* said you were here."

"I am," I say, feeling my heart beating in my throat. I can't help but mentally tally the men. The only standouts in the group are Marcus and Colton, who are both smart and attractive. But I can't say that either of them do it for me.

Yet. I tell myself. *They don't do it for you yet. Love needs room and time to grow.*

Still, I haven't felt any zips of attraction. Nothing compared to what I experienced with the one big mistake from my past. Truthfully, I wouldn't care too much if both of my frontrunners left this week, except then I'd be stuck with the other four. It's disappointing, because I really did sign up for this hoping something would come of it. That I'd be pleasantly surprised. That I'd be swept off my feet. That—

I can practically hear my mother laughing at me. *There you go again, being a Pollyanna. You need to let other people make the important decisions, Kennedy. You've got a pretty face, but God didn't give you enough sense to fill a thimble.*

I straighten my spine, because her voice is the last one I want in my head.

Nana Mayberry's still giving me a look that suggests she also has doubts about my thimble-filling ability, so I say, "Besides, Nana Mayberry, I thought it was *your* job to find me love. If my match isn't here, then isn't it your fault as my matchmaker?"

A gasp escapes Harry, who's the only one of us still sitting, his eyes as large as marbles.

"Calm yourself, Sweet Tea," Nana Mayberry says, but her gaze is on me, as if we're in one of those staring contests Olive and I used to do in high school. Except Olive and I would always break into laughter, and I have a feeling something more sinister will happen if I lose this stare-off with Nana. "Your match *is* here, Kennedy," she finally says. "If you're open to love."

"Of course I am," I say in a voice as sweet as spun sugar. "That's why I'm here after all."

Then I leave and go up to my room. I'm still wrestling with the terrible zipper of my dress, my cozy pajamas laid out on the bed in the hopes that I'll eventually get to change into them, when a knock lands on my door. I'm not sure why, but my mind flashes to Rowan walking through that same door a few nights ago. His eyes took me in for a long moment before he looked away, and it felt like it wasn't just because of the orange tone of my skin.

"Who's there?" I ask, my mind still lingering on the memory. That can be the only explanation for why I'm a little disappointed when Harry says, "Do you need some help with your dress, Kennedy?"

It's thoughtful of him to check. Then again, he saw what it took for the makeup artist to help me get into it.

"Yeah, please," I say, feeling a lump in my throat. It's a sense of longing, but I'm not entirely sure what for, unless it's that image of Olive and the movie fest.

There isn't even any cable or internet here, as if the producers are determined to keep us iced out from the outside world.

Harry comes in, a big smile on his face, but it wobbles when he sees me.

He shuts the door behind him. "What is it? Did one of those jerks hurt you?"

A genuine smile crosses my face. I'm so glad he's here. If it were only Nana, I don't think I could hack it.

"No, nothing like that. I guess I'm just a little lonely."

"Spoiler alert. We're bringing Tina and Zach in for a family visit next Friday, so there's that to look forward to."

Laughter spills out of me. "Zach's going to hate that. He's going to hate *them*."

"Yeah, probably," Harry admits. "You know, you can use my phone again if you want to," he offers immediately. "Just don't tell Nana. That woman scares the shit out of me."

A laugh rips out of me. "Yeah, me too."

"No one would know it," he says, grinning at me again. "You were awesome back there, saying it's her fault as your matchmaker if all the guys suck." He pulls a face. "They're not all terrible, are they? Colton's pretty to look at. And Marcus, although he's too blond for my taste. The winners are almost never blond, huh? It's like there's this universal taste in men, and we were all born liking them tall, dark, and handsome." He pulls a face as he touches a hand to his own pale hair.

I try to smile and fail. "Yeah. You're right. They're both really good looking. It's just...I don't feel a spark, you know?"

He lets out a sigh. "I feel you there. I met a guy who was perfect on paper before I moved here. I mean, a lot of the guys I've dated have had about two dozen red flags each, but this guy had, like, five max. Anyway, I digress. There just wasn't anything there." He makes a face. "You can't make something out of nothing, Kennedy. But that doesn't mean you can't have some fun. Who knows," his smile turns sly, "maybe Jonah Highbury the Fifth will grow on you."

"If I tell you Jonah's growing on me, promise to slap me awake," I say, lifting my mass of hair over my shoulder and motioning for him to go around and free me from the dress.

I'm in front of the mirror, just like I was that day with Rowan, and I feel a weird sense of déjà vu that has a razor's edge of regret. Which is just stupid. The only thing I like about Rowan is that he's direct and real. That he's not one of the egotistical jerks his grandmother chose for me.

I sigh, my gaze falling to the bed and the Santa Babe pants. "You know what, Harry? I wish it were Christmas around here."

He shoots me a conflicted look in the mirror, his fingers tapping the zipper of my dress before he swoops it down in one elegant pull. Turning his back so I can change, he says, "You know, if you were sick tomorrow, I'm betting no one would come in here to check on you. Especially if you said you had something gross, like food poisoning." He pauses. "There's maybe a thirty-five percent chance Marcus would check on you, but if you texted him to say you didn't want him to because it wouldn't be romantic, he'd probably stay away. Or if you told him you had violent diarrhea."

I laugh as I pull on my Santa Babe pants. "What are you getting at, Harry?" The shirt goes on next, and already I feel so much better. I'm more myself like this—more Kennedy, less Littlefield. "You can turn back around," I tell him.

He does, and he gives his buzzed hair a nervous-seeming scrub before he says, "You can't tell anyone."

Now I'm intrigued.

"Tell them what?"

"I'm going to sneak you out. Rowan invited me to go to a Christmas tree farm with him and his friend."

"Rowan?" I say with a gasp.

He gives me a searching look. "Don't you like him? He's kind of gruff, but I've concluded that's mostly bluster. I'm pretty sure they'll have hot chocolate." He purses his mouth to the side while he waits for my answer and shuffles a little on his feet. It strikes me that he's nervous.

"Are you worried we're going to get caught?"

An amused sound escapes him. "Absolutely, yes, and we're going to have to establish a safe word in case either of us gets an inkling that things are going south. But in the Christmas spirit of honesty, I should mention that I wouldn't mind having you there for personal reasons."

I could tell him that I'm pretty sure honesty has nothing to do with the Christmas spirit, but I'd rather find out what he means.

"Personal reasons?"

He makes a face. "Rowan's best friend Oliver."

Oh... "Let me guess, is he tall, dark, and handsome?"

"Is he ever," he says, but he doesn't sound all that pleased about it.

"Is that not a good thing?" I gasp. "Oh, is he not gay?"

"He's definitely gay," he says. "Unless he goes around kissing men for some other reason."

"He kissed you?" If it comes out as a squeak, it's because this is the most exciting thing that's happened since I turned orange.

"Yes," he sighs.

"Why is this a bad thing if he's tall and dark and handsome?"

"It's just...it happened months and months ago, when Rowan and Oliver visited Asheville."

"Full story, now," I say, grabbing his hand and leading him over to what looks like a fainting couch. We both sit, and we probably have identical grimaces when we sink into the upholstery, which feels as comfortable as plastic.

"So," Harry says, shuffling his feet a little more, then he sets his elbows on his knees and cradles his head in his hands. "I went out for a drink with them, and we were all having a good time, except it kind of felt like there was this *vibe* between Oliver and me. Then, when Rowan went to the bathroom, Oliver gives me a look and says, 'We're finally alone.' And I say, 'So what are you going to do about it?' which was a lot better than I usually respond in situations like that. And then he *kissed* me."

"That sounds incredible," I say, getting excited. Even though I'm the main contestant on a dating show, it's way more romantic than anything that's happened to me. Except...

"Wait, why didn't anything happen between you after that? That's a pretty epic build up. It's the sort of story a person would tell at an anniversary party."

He sits back up. "Don't tell anyone this. Not even Tina."

I make the sign of the cross.

"Are you Catholic?"

"No, but it makes for a powerful statement, doesn't it?"

He shrugs. "Okay. So, I'd had fettuccine alfredo for dinner. I'm lactose intolerant, and I have a nervous stomach when I get anxious."

"Harry," I say slowly. "Are you telling me what I think you're telling me?"

He heaves an unhappy sigh that suggests my imagination is on point. "Yes. He kissed me, and it was the best kiss I'd had in I don't even know how long, and then I released noxious gas. *Loudly.*"

"What did you do next?" I ask, completely caught up in the story.

"What do you think I did?" he asks, getting up from the couch and starting to pace. He throws his hands up. "I ran!"

"What'd you say the next time you saw him?"

"I haven't seen him!" he says, pausing to look at me. There's a glint of panic in his eyes.

"What do you mean you haven't seen him? Don't you live with Rowan? I thought this guy was his best friend?"

"He is!" Harry says. "Do you know how hard it's been to avoid him? But I can't avoid him forever, and you want a taste of Christmas, so..."

"So you think it'll be easier if you have a friend with you."

"*Yes*," he says. "And I want you there enough that I'm willing to risk my job to make it happen. Will you come?"

Chapter Five

Rowan

"You asked Harry to come?" Oliver asks. There's a weird expression on his face, like he's not sure whether to be pissed or pleased by my failure to mention that until this exact moment. We're standing at the tail end of my truck in the lot of Ralph's Trees, Oliver having parked his Subaru across from me. He rubs his goatee thoughtfully. "Does he know I'm going to be here?"

"Yeah," I say. "He said he was looking forward to it."

To be fair, he looked like he was going to shit his pants while he said it, but Harry looks like that about a quarter of the time. I've never met someone so tightly wound. He's a good guy, though—a solid guy—and dating Oliver might mellow him out.

I mentally curse myself. I can practically see Holly giving me a knowing look, saying something like *the matchmaking apple doesn't fall far from the tree. Goddammit, maybe she's right.*

"He did, huh?" Oliver says with a slight smile on his face. "Have you noticed he's been avoiding me since he moved into your place?"

I can't say that I have, to be honest, but I've been told before that subtext needs to hit me in the face with a two-by-four before I pick up on it.

"Really?"

"Yeah," he says, chuckling. "When I came over to borrow some tools last week, he practically dive-bombed into his room. I'm surprised he didn't break his nose."

"Huh. Should I not have asked him?" I ask, scratching *my* nose. This isn't going very well. So much for having matchmaking blood. The only other time I've tried to set two people up was Oliver and my sister, Willow, and given that he's gay and she's engaged to a writer, you can see how well that turned out. I make a mental note to never try anything this stupid again.

"No," he says thoughtfully. "If he knows I'm here, it's fine."

"Um, is this where I should ask if something happened between you two," I say.

He laughs in my face. "Shit, Rowan, you're really bad at this."

"I'm trying. Does that count?"

"Sure," he says. "But we don't need to talk about this, man. I can't remember the last time you told me about any of the women you're dating."

"Wait, you're dating him?"

"I'm obviously not doing a very good job of it if he's dive-bombing out of rooms to get away from me."

I tilt my head. "But you want to date him."

"Undecided," he says with a twinkle in his eye. "I find his neuroticism charming, but I'd prefer to date a man who can stand being in the same room as me."

I feel like I should press him for details—I know my sisters would —but truthfully, I'd rather not. After all, he might decide to press *me* for details, and I have a whole lot of nothing to share. The last time I brought a woman home, my sister nearly hit me over the head with a baseball bat, for fuck's sake. That's not an experience I'd like to repeat.

I tell myself that's why I've been on a dating and hookup drought —my sister is cock-blocking me. Truthfully, though, she's hardly been around. I have to acknowledge that part of the problem is that I'm bored of meaningless sex with tourists who'll only be in Highland Hills for the weekend or a week, and the last local woman I arranged a date with gave her number to someone else in my presence.

Holly says I'm too much of a grump.

Bryn and Willow tell me I'm emotionally unavailable.

My baby sister, Ivy, probably has a fucking opinion too, but she keeps herself too busy writing romance novels to bother much with the rest of us. Or maybe she just has the sense to stay away.

"What's got you all broody?" Oliver asks, nudging my shoulder.

"Christmas," I say. "The mayor's paying me to string lights on his house this year. He told me, unironically, that he wants it to look the house in *Christmas Vacation*."

He clucks his tongue. "Make sure you do it when he's not there. He could talk the ear off a dead person. The last thing you need is to go tumbling off the ladder because he's chatting you up about the recycling schedule."

I laugh. "Thanks for the hot tip. I don't want to go out stringing Christmas lights."

"I dunno. It'd be an ironic way for a grinch to go out."

I lift a hand and gesture at the pine trees on display, the log cabin where people can buy hot chocolate or cider. Canned Christmas music is piping from somewhere. "Would a grinch come here?"

"Yes," he says, slapping my arm. "Absolutely. He'd come here, and he'd steal all of it to keep other people from making merry."

Another car pulls in as he finishes saying it. It's Harry's Prius, and I can see his beanie-clad head in the front seat.

"He thinks he's hauling a tree home on that thing?" Oliver asks with a laugh.

"He's not allowed to get one for the Labelles'," I say, thinking of Kennedy and the wistful look on her face when she said the Labelles' house was the one place Christmas would miss this year. Shit. Maybe I *should* send a pine bough home with Harry, except she'd probably interpret it as a taunt. Maybe she'd be right. Maybe not. I don't have time to consider it, because Harry's parking, and my lips part with surprise when the back door of the car cracks open.

She's wearing a beanie and large sunglasses, but it's her—my princess. I instantly correct myself for the absurd thought—she isn't *my* anything. It *is* her, though. She doesn't have the kind of face a person can forget, with her long, dark hair, big blue eyes, and small, pointed chin. I'm not saying I want her. I'm saying what's obvious: she's beautiful. My mother was a beautiful woman, too, and she used her beauty as a weapon, taking down one man after another—using him up and then moving on. I know not to let good looks blind me.

Still, she's the kind of gorgeous that hurts, and I'd be an imbecile if I didn't notice. It would be like failing to notice that the sun has risen over the mountains.

"She's not supposed to be here," I say, lifting a hand to my jaw.

Harry gets out of the driver's seat, practically humming with nervous energy, and herds Kennedy toward us.

"Didn't know this was going to be a prison break," I say as I nod to them in greeting. Oliver stands up from where he was leaning against the truck, his gaze on Harry, whose cheeks have turned red.

Yup, something definitely happened between them.

Kennedy wraps an arm around Harry's back and squeezes before letting her arm drop. "Harry knows I've been missing Christmas, so he was sweet enough to ask me to come along."

"It's been a while," Oliver says to Harry. "Why don't we go inside and get some hot choco—"

"No dairy for me," Harry says. "No dairy for Harry." Then he lifts a hand to his mouth. "I don't know why I said that."

"Because it rhymes, and it's funny," Kennedy says encouragingly.

If she says so.

"There's cider too," Oliver says, seemingly not put off by my roommate's verbal missteps.

"And whiskey," I say, because if ever there were ever an occasion for a drink...

"You want to drink whiskey before you use an ax?" Kennedy asks, her tone a little judgmental if you ask me.

"Yes, Princess," I say. "I'm an ax-toting lumberjack. I'm the person the Christmas trees have nightmares about at night. Should you really be seen out here? Won't Harry get fired if you are?"

Harry removes his hat and scrubs a hand through his short hair. "You wouldn't tell your grandmother, would you?"

Kennedy's giving me a look as dark as if I just shot an uppercut into Santa's jaw and suggested serving up his reindeer as venison.

"I try to talk to her as little as possible," I tell Harry. "Your secret's safe with me." Then, to Kennedy, I say, "Just keep your hat and the glasses on."

She's unlikely to get recognized anyway. Her photo hasn't been released to the press yet. And yet...

I don't really want her to put the full princess effect on display. I'm not sure I can handle it, on top of whatever Oliver–Harry drama is going on.

"Well, okay," Oliver says, as if he's the one normal person in this sea of awkwardness. Actually, I think he *is* the one normal person in this sea of awkwardness. "Let's get some drinks—" his gaze goes to Harry, who looks down, "—of whatever variety we choose, and we can go check out the trees. Rowan was saying you guys can't bring one back to the Labelles'?"

"No, but we were thinking we could watch," Harry says.

You want to watch us chop down trees?" I ask in disbelief.

"I've never seen someone chop down a tree before," Kennedy says staunchly, lifting her jaw slightly.

Well, I believe that.

"Used to having other people do your dirty work for you?"

"What is your *problem?*" she hisses, and I have to admit, that was a bit harsh. To be honest, I'm pretty sure I didn't mean it.

Oliver smirks at me. "Do you have a notepad? Because it might be a long list. Cupid here isn't known for his cheerfulness."

"Cupid?" she asks, with too much enthusiasm for my taste.

"Cupid," he confirms with a twinkle in his eye, the jackass. "It's been his nickname since we were kids. You know, because the rest of the Mayberrys are such dyed-in-the-wool romantics."

"I don't like it when people call me that," I growl.

"We shouldn't call him that then," Harry says, surprising me with his instant support. "I hate it when people call me Twitch, but my cousin George does it at every family gathering. Of course, it only makes me more anxious, and then I actually do—" His eyes go wide, and he looks at me and blurts, "You said there'd be caroling. I'm always up for some good caroling."

"Do you sing?" Oliver asks as we all start to walk toward the log cabin.

"In the shower," Harry says, then stammers. "I mean. I only sing in the shower because I don't want anyone to have to listen to me."

"Harry has a *beautiful* voice," Kennedy says.

"You hang out outside his bathroom?" I ask, lifting my eyebrows.

"Wouldn't that mean I was outside *your* bathroom?" she asks.

She said it as a challenge, definitely not some kind of invitation, but my mind flashes to taking a shower with *her*. What she would look like in the shower, with the hot water coursing down her slick body, her beautiful long, dark hair loose, her—

I trip on some gravel, and suddenly I'm face down in the parking lot, gravel scraping my nose and forehead. Fuck. It hurts, and worse, I'm incredibly aware of Kennedy having watched the whole thing.

"Shit, are you okay, Rowan?" Oliver asks, reaching down for me.

I stand up without accepting his hand and brush off the gravel, annoyed at myself. "I'm fine."

But Harry's not the only one who's red now.

Kennedy takes a step toward me, her hand reaching up to my

cheek. Her fingers brush my skin so lightly, it should barely be felt, but I *do* feel it. "You're bleeding," she says in a low voice.

"I'm fine," I say, "nothing worse than I'd get shaving."

"You have a beard," she says, her lips tipping into a slight smile.

I can't help smiling back, because her smile is like the sun, warming the things it touches. "I hate shaving."

Then, because Oliver is giving me a *you're being really fucking rude* frown, I add, "Thank you."

We resume our trek toward the cabin, none of us speaking again, because my faceplant only made things more uncomfortable.

Ralph himself, a big man with red cheeks that suggest he's been enjoying plenty of his spiked cider, opens the door. He's dressed up like Santa Claus, probably wearing the same coat and beard he used when I was a kid.

"Ho, ho, ho, welcome to Ralph's," he says, waving us in.

"Hey, Ralph," Oliver says.

"Don't destroy the illusion for the newcomers," he says, winking at Kennedy.

"Yes, Ralph." I roll my eyes. "This thirty-year-old woman thinks you're Santa Claus."

I can feel her eyes on me again as she says, "Hey, I'm only twenty-nine. And I hope I'll never be too old for Christmas magic."

"That's the spirit," Ralph says, his delight over-effusive.

The interior has a dusty fake Christmas tree with dozens of empty wrapped boxes underneath, an ax station, and a drink bar in the corner that's brightly decorated with Christmas lights and a sign reading "Ho-ho-ho-hot chocolate." Like everything else, it's seen better years, and that's why I like it. It's nice to have some things stay the same when the world keeps changing around you, pulling away the things you thought you knew.

"Do you want anything?" I ask Kennedy.

"I can order my own drink," she says stiffly.

"Actually," Harry says, still holding his beanie, "you can't. We couldn't risk retrieving your wallet from the office, remember?"

"Oh," she says, biting her lip, and the sight of her white teeth flashing against her plump, pink bottom lip sends blood pumping directly to my dick.

Damn it. My dick would choose to react to a woman I definitely can't have and almost certainly don't want.

"I'll take a hot chocolate."

"How about you?" Oliver asks Harry.

"I have my wallet," Harry says stiffly. "So no need to worry about me. Or Kennedy! I'll buy Kennedy's drink too."

Oliver shrugs. I shrug.

"I have emergency cash," she tells him. "You don't need to buy me anything."

"I insist," he says.

My friend orders a coffee, black. I get spiced cider with a splash of whiskey, and if I partly did it because I have a weird impulse to do the opposite of impressing Kennedy, then so be it.

They're up next, and Oliver gives his head an amused shake when Harry pointedly asks if the spiced cider has dairy in it before ordering some for himself. Kennedy gets a hot chocolate, and the look of joy on her face when she sees the mountain of whipped cream that gets put on top before the lid is applied is cuter than it has any right to be. If this place is less impressive than what she's used to, and I'm guessing it would have to be, it doesn't show. She seems as delighted as a seven-year-old child holding her father's hand and jumping up and down, eager to see a tree get murdered.

Once we've acquired our drinks, Oliver and I approach the ax station, where Ethel, Ralph's wife, is waiting. She resembles Mrs. Claus, with her snowy white hair gathered into a bun and her red house dress, but it would be a mistake to think this is a costume. She looks the same year-round.

"Gonna get a good one, boys?" she asks, beaming at us. "I still have those pictures of you from last year, Rowan."

"You were here last year?" Kennedy asks in surprise.

"Oh, he comes in nearly every year," Ethel says, being far too chatty for my taste.

"Not for myself," I say quickly, instantly annoyed with myself for feeling the need to explain. Despite what Holly and Oliver implied the other day, I *do* actually like this place. I've liked it ever since Jay, my one-time stepfather, used to bring me here to chop down a tree with him. My own father never bothered to do that sort of thing, but Jay was a good man. The only stand-up guy to fall within my mother's clutches. He's my sister Ivy's father, so I still see him every now and then, usually when she's passing through town. He invites me to do things sometimes. Go hiking. Watch a documentary about something we both enjoy, like ice fishing, but I usually don't take him up on it. I feel the weight of knowing that he might feel obligated to spend time with me. "I always come and get one for one of my sisters."

"Your grandmother?" Harry asks.

"No," I scoff. "She'd sooner drink the blood of Santa Claus than put up a real tree."

Ethel scowls at me. "Oh, you." Turning to Oliver, she says, "Nice to see you again, sweetheart. Good of you to come instead of your father. He's always complaining about his back."

Oliver gives a slight nod, choosing not to tell her what very few people know yet. His father has Stage Three cancer, which is why he came back to this shit hole.

"How about you folks?" she asks, beaming at Kennedy and Harry. "What a nice-looking couple you are."

"Oh, no. We're not..." Harry starts, then swallows. "I'm not... I mean, if I were, she'd be on my top five list, obviously. Maybe top two list, but..."

Ethel eyes him strangely. "Are you going to cut down a tree or not?"

"Not," he says. "We're here to watch the carolers."

"You're out of luck. They all came down with food poisoning," she says, shaking her head. "I told them not to trust anything Draper Hiddleston made for them, but did they listen? They scarfed down those cookies he brought in like no one's business, and every last one of them spent the night in the bathroom." She shrugs. "But we're piping Christmas music out back, and you're welcome to take photos with the sleigh. There's a life-sized model of Santa in it."

"Thanks," Kennedy says, seeming to mean it. "That sounds wonderful."

It's not. The sleigh's been there since I was a kid, and the Santa, which used to be animatronic but stopped working about a decade ago, is probably a health hazard at this point.

"Well, you lot have fun," Ethel says, but something in her gaze tells me she finds our grouping weird and will be talking about it to other people. The more people who talk about it, the more likely it is that my grandmother or one of the producers will put two and two together.

Not good for Harry. Or Kennedy.

I shouldn't care about that. I want that show to crash and burn. I need it to. But Holly's right about one thing—Harry's a good roommate—and I also don't want Kennedy to get in trouble. None of this has been about getting her into trouble.

Which is why I say, "Harry's my roommate, Ethel. That's why he doesn't need a tree." I clear my throat. "And this is my friend," I add, setting my drink on the counter and putting an arm around Kennedy's back. She jolts like a shying horse but doesn't throw me off. Still, she seems about as into it as if Ralph had wrapped one of his ham-hock arms around her.

"She's just here for the weekend," I say with a pasted-on smile.

I put the right amount of insinuation behind it, and Ethel grins. "Say no more."

Which is exactly why I did it. Two strangers acting weird with Rowan Mayberry and Oliver Perez might be worth some gossip on a slow afternoon, but if one of them is Rowan's flavor of the week? Who cares.

I drop my grip on Kennedy, and we all head outside after Oliver and I grab our axes and work gloves, juggling them with our to-go drink cups.

As soon as the door closes behind us, Kennedy turns to look at me, her brow wrinkled. Fuck me. She's a knockout like this too. It's like she can't help herself. Everything she does has to be beautiful and graceful, even if it's being pissed off.

"What was that all about?" she asks coldly, staring me down even though I'm several inches taller than her. She's not small for a woman, though. Five eight or five nine, easy.

"Ethel likes to gossip," I say.

"So why did you give her something to gossip about?" she asks through her teeth, clearly unhappy with me. It probably doesn't speak well of me that I find her reaction slightly amusing.

"I did it for your sake, Princess. You should be thanking me."

The nickname was the wrong thing to say, because her glower deepens. Actually, no one seems to be looking at me kindly right now.

"Ethel likes to talk," Oliver says, waving his cup. "Two strangers, one of them Rowan's roommate who works on *Matchmaking the Rich...*"

"So why'd you tell her that we live together?" Harry asks, his eyebrows winging up in a dramatic mask of alarm.

"It would be worse if she found out from someone else," I say. "This way it looks like we have nothing to hide. Like Kennedy here's a tourist who's in town for one weekend, not the runaway bachelorette."

"That's the wrong show," Harry says, but it seems like a rote response. "Huh. You might have a point."

"Of course I do," I say. My gaze shifts to Kennedy, but if I was hoping for an apology or a thank you, I'll be waiting a while. She still seems pissed.

"Won't it be worse if they discover who I am? You just implied that I'm..." Her cheeks flush, and I feel a swell of something.

You're not attracted to her. You're not attracted to her.

"Some kind of strumpet," she finishes.

"Strumpet?" I say, my lips turning up.

It would be incredibly stupid for me to hit on Kennedy Littlefield for real. Setting aside the whole princess thing, she's the lead contestant on a dating show my grandmother is running. *And* I'm friendly with her brother, who would probably be less than pleased with me.

"Who are you? The Queen of England?" I ask.

"Come on, Harry," she says, her gaze still on me from behind those big glasses. "Let's go check out that sleigh."

"You might not want to get on there," I say. "It's been sitting out here for at least three decades."

"Then it's a year older than me," she says pointedly, as if I'm an ass for not knowing her exact age. How was I supposed to? It's not like she has her birthdate tattooed on her arm.

"All right, have at it," I say, lifting my to-go cup in a cheers.

She's already walking away, Harry at her side. He glances back with a little regret in his eyes, as if he's not so sure he wants to get on a sleigh that old but feels the need to be loyal.

"You sure have a way with women," Oliver says with a chuckle.

"You sure have a way with men."

He nudges me with his shoulder and laughs. "Touché. Want to go chop down some trees?"

I grunt. "Yes, please."

Chapter Six

Kennedy

"The nerve," I mutter.

Who does Rowan Mayberry think he is, anyway? He acted like I was an infectious disease from the moment I stepped out of the car, and then he dared to wrap his arm around me and pretend I'm *his*.

Worse, that natural physical chemistry I don't have with any of the guys in the house? It leapt between us like flames traveling across a path of paper.

Darn him.

No, *damn* him. And damn my mother for hardwiring it into me that ladies shouldn't swear, because those words feel right.

"Do you think Oliver remembers what happened this spring?" Harry asks in an undertone, glancing back at them. Harry's still clutching his hat in one hand, his dairy-free drink in the other. I'm grateful for my dairy-heavy hot chocolate. It's exactly the sort of creature comfort I need right now.

There's nothing better for solving your woes than a pillow of whipped cream, Olive would say. I feel a fierce press of missing her. True to his words, Harry let me borrow his phone to call her from the sitting room closest to my bedroom last night, and we watched Mary-

Kate and Ashley Olsen in *The Case of the Christmas Caper* together —the only Christmas movie the Labelles had in their very small DVD collection. It was laughably bad, and we *did* laugh. A lot. But it's not the same as watching something together in person.

"Well?" Harry presses, his eyes so full of hope. "He didn't say anything about it, so maybe—"

"Harry," I say softly, glancing at him. "I'm sorry, but that's not the kind of thing someone would forget."

He sighs heavily. "You're right. I know you're right. It's just... Why are *you* upset? The whole strumpet thing?"

"Yes!"

"I mean, I guess it is kind of an old-fashioned word. The sort of thing you'd read in a poem rhyming *strumpet* and *crumpet*." He lets out a groan as we near the sleigh, and even though the thing looks like it would fall apart if rust weren't holding it together, I'm guessing that's not the source of his distress. "I said 'No dairy for Harry.' I mean, I'm basically sabotaging myself at every opportunity here. Why didn't you clamp a hand on my mouth or stomp on my foot really hard? A kick would have been understood—no, welcomed—in this one situation."

"Huh," I say, studying him. His nerves seem to prickle off him, as if he's become a human hedgehog. "You really like this guy, don't you?"

"What's not to like?" he asks mournfully. "He's tall, dark, and *delicious*, and he doesn't accidentally rhyme words and pretend he did it on purpose."

"He seemed to find it charming," I say, hoping it's true. Oliver seemed amused, at the very least, and he hasn't been trying to keep his distance. I've caught him taking surreptitious glances at Harry, although that might be because he's been behaving peculiarly. Except... "For all we know, he asked Rowan to set this whole thing up." I pause, thinking about it. "I mean, it's a little weird that they asked you, right? You don't strike me as an outdoorsy guy."

His jaw works. "I own a Prius. I care about the environment."

It's not the kind of car you'd go off-roading in, but I don't say so. Instead, I hurry to assure him, "It's not an insult. I'm not outdoorsy either. My mother would never let me play outside if it was muddy. Or rainy. Or really anything except sunny and dry."

He sighs. "I never let myself play outside if it was muddy or rainy. You're right. I only pretend to like hiking because Tina's always going on about all the trails around here." His eyes take on a far-off look. "Do you really think Oliver asked Rowan to set this up?"

"Maybe." The thought carries me away for a second. It would be *so* romantic if Oliver had spent the last several months thinking about Harry as the one who got away—literally, since Harry ran off. "You know, how amazing would your 'this is how we met' story be if you and Oliver end up getting married?"

Harry laughs, some of his angst floating away. "You think I'd tell everyone that I had a gas explosion the first time he kissed me? That's going to the grave with me." He scrunches his features. "Except I did tell you, so I'm already failing at that."

"I think *he* would probably tell people." I grin back at him, then gesture to the sleigh. "Will you take my picture sitting in it?"

He gives it a dubious look. "I know you're not going to like what I have to say, but Rowan might be right. If that were a wounded animal, it would be taken out to pasture."

I pull a face. "What a terrible saying."

"Huh," he says, tilting his head. "You're right. I guess I never really thought about it. But seriously, you might get tetanus or something. It's not a common problem, but if you haven't gotten your booster, you should really have second thoughts." He gives a shudder as he takes in the plastic Santa in the driver's seat. It looks like the eyes are supposed to move, but they're frozen in a grimace. "That thing is absolutely nightmare fuel. I'll be thinking about that tonight when I'm trying to sleep. No question."

"Come on, Harry. I want to send a picture to Olive. She'll get a real kick out of it."

He sighs and gives a solemn nod. "Be careful where you step. I read a story the other day about a woman who stepped in a fire ant colony and was so badly bitten they had to amputate."

"I'm pretty sure that's not true."

He twists his mouth to the side. "You could sprain your ankle though."

I wave him off, consider the sleigh for a second, and decide Olive would be most amused if I sat next to the creepy Santa. I step in beside the mannequin and put an arm around him. "Can you take it like this?" I ask, smiling up at Harry.

He's gaping at me, not making a move to lift his phone. "Oh. My. God."

"What?"

"Don't freak out, Kennedy," he says slowly.

I half expect him to say our safe words—*candy cane*—because he's seen one of the guys or, God forbid, Nana Mayberry up at the cabin, but it takes only a second for me to realize he's looking to the right of me. I glance over and shriek. The Santa's hinged mouth has dropped open, and an enormous spider is crawling out of it.

I try to leap out of the sleigh, but my foot gets caught on something, and I go sprawling next to it. My hot chocolate is a casualty of the fall, but thankfully none of the hot liquid spills on me. I catch sight of someone in my peripheral vision, hurrying toward me. Harry.

But when I look up, it's not Harry. It's Rowan, his forehead sweaty.

"What happened?" he blurts, crouching next to me.

"I..." But suddenly I can't get any words out, because he's so close to me, staring at me with such intensity, like he might chop up the ground if he finds out it tripped me. My lips part, but no words come. His spicy scent is engulfing me and making me stupid.

"*Princess*," he says, reaching out to touch my hair. He runs his fingers through it, and my lips part further.

"It's okay," Harry says, stepping toward us but keeping a good distance between himself and the sleigh. I honestly can't blame him. It's better decision-making than mine. "She wanted to take a photo with the Nightmare Santa, and then its mouth popped open, and it belched out a spider. I'm really having second thoughts about this outing, Rowan. Are you sure this isn't one of those scenarios where they're secretly taping people while they torture them? I know most of those movies are fictional, but if people can think it up to put in a movie, then they can just as easily make it happen in real life."

I'm prepared for Rowan to scoff about princesses and their selfie habits, but instead he looks amused. "You wanted to pose with *that*?"

He nods at the Santa with the gaping mouth just as Oliver emerges from the woods. "Everything all right?"

"Nothing some whiskey can't cure," Rowan says, reaching for my hand. I let him take it, feeling a tingling awareness as his big hand engulfs mine, even through his work gloves, and he lifts me to my feet as easily as if I were a doll. As soon as I'm on my feet, he hands his cup to me.

"You carried that all the way over here?" I ask, stunned. He got to us so quickly he must have sprinted.

He looks a little embarrassed as he says, "I was about to take a sip when I heard you scream." He juts it toward my hand again.

"But it's yours," I say.

"Worried about backwash?"

Maybe. I'm also keenly aware that his lips were probably pressed to the plastic lid, and mine might go in the same place.

"I didn't drink any yet," he says. "I was too busy picking out a tree."

"You're sweating," I say. I have the desire to trace it off his forehead, but that would be demented. If I were to mention such a thing in front of my mother, she'd probably tell me it's a sign that I'm defective and have been since birth.

"I started chopping it already," he says, then swears under his breath. "I shouldn't have left it like that."

"Well, let's go finish," I say, before I can totally think it through.

He glances at Oliver, who's now standing next to Harry.

The woman from earlier pops her head out the door. "What's wrong?" she asks, her face drawn. "We can't afford another accident with one of the axes."

"An ax accident," Harry says, his color worsening. "You could call them ax-ccidents." He shoots me a panicked look, silently communicating that this was another occasion when I should have been close enough to kick him in the shin.

I mouth the word "sorry."

"Just a spider," Rowan tells her, and because he can probably see the righteous indignation on my face, he adds, "You know how I am about spiders."

She chuckles, probably too relieved that we haven't axed ourselves to really care what we're up to, and heads back into the cabin.

"You're scared of spiders?" I ask Rowan.

"Deathly," he says.

Taking him in, his sweating brow, his short beard, and those intense eyes, it's hard to imagine he's afraid of anything.

"We should stick together," Oliver says. "Make sure we're safe from Santa."

Rowan shakes his head ruefully. "I already chose my tree. You're still looking. Maybe Harry should help you, and Kennedy can help me."

"I don't know much about cutting down trees," I admit.

"And here I thought you liked to watch," he says, lifting his brows. There's an undercurrent rumbling under his words, or maybe I'm the one who put it there, noticing that sweat and his scent.

I take a hearty sip of the spiked cider, and it's delicious. It's also nothing like the drinks served at my parents' famous Christmas Eve party—a stiff, joyless affair that's only "famous" for its cold elegance. The trees no one in the family is allowed to decorate. The hors d'oeuvres made by a famous chef. The cookies made to look pretty rather than to be eaten.

I feel a swell of relief that I'm here and not there. Which is maybe why I start nodding. "Okay, let's do it."

The way Rowan immediately glances at Oliver tells me he's up to something. It strikes me that he seems very eager to get Oliver and Harry alone together.

Wait a minute...

I steal a glance at Harry, who looks panicked but not necessarily displeased, and decide this isn't one of those occasions on which he'd like a kick. So I follow Rowan into the trees.

"You left a tree half-chopped?" I ask.

"I know. It's probably a safety hazard," he says, wiping his brow. "But I heard you screaming at the top of your lungs. I figured you'd had an accident."

"Or maybe an ax-ccident," I say with a small smile.

We both laugh at the expense of our friend, which probably isn't very nice, although there's plenty of fondness behind it.

"I guess I'm afraid of spiders too," I tell him. "Or at least spiders crawling out of Santa Claus's mouth."

"I'm not sure I'd want to meet the person who wouldn't find that frightening," Rowan says, stopping in front of a glorious pine, taller than him. His ax is resting against the trunk, business side down.

"How'd you choose it?" I ask.

"I looked to the heavens and asked for guidance, and a ray of light led me to this tree."

"Really?"

He gives me a wry look. "No. It's a good tree. My stepfather, Jay, taught me what to look for."

"And what's that?"

"Well, the first thing to look for is one that's no more than six inches in diameter. You don't want to be out here all day, do you?"

Actually, I'm not so sure I don't. It's better than being cooped up in that house, surrounded by men who are vying for my attention.

Men I don't feel much inclined to give my attention.

"So that's the only factor?"

"It has to look good too," he says, giving me a smirk.

I glance away as he takes up the ax, but I can't keep up my *don't look at Rowan Mayberry* efforts for long. My gaze takes him in as his muscles bunch beneath his shirt and he deals another blow to the trunk. He must have set aside his coat before coming to me, because his arms are only covered by a red-and-black-checkered flannel shirt, his hands in those gloves.

"Are you playing matchmaker with Oliver and Harry?" I ask in a burst.

He lowers his arms before making another strike. "What makes you think that?"

"You seemed like you wanted to get them alone together, and we both know Harry's not the kind of person who'd be interested in cutting down his own tree, yet you invited him anyway."

"Maybe I wanted to be alone with you," he says, tilting his head at me.

"No, I don't think so," I say.

He snorts and takes a swing at the tree.

"You said you come here every year?"

He pauses, glances at me. "Not every year. Last year, my little sister, Willow, was in town. Willow's all about Christmas."

"And you came with your stepfather."

"I did," he says with a nod. "Jay. But he and my mother were only married a few years."

"I'm sorry," I say. "He sounds nice."

"He is...so I'm not sorry. He's a good guy. The kind of guy who deserved to marry someone nice, and he ultimately did. He and his wife have been together for decades now." His face twists into something that's not quite a smile. "You know, they actually met here."

He's usually so closed off and hard to read, but for some reason he's talking to me, really talking, and I sense the hurt under his words.

"I'm sorry you have a hard relationship with your mother."

That earns me another snort as he raises the ax again. "That would imply I have any relationship with her."

"I wish I didn't have a relationship with my mother," I say, then lift my hand to my lips, as if I could shove the words back in. They're true, but it's not the kind of thing a lady would say.

"Oh?" he asks, smiling. He lets the ax hang by his side. "Zach doesn't talk about them much, but we all know what happened."

Actually, he probably *doesn't* know. It's not like my brother goes around telling people that he was disowned because everyone found out he's illegitimate. My father didn't feel the need to punish my mother, but my brother? He couldn't throw him away fast enough. I'll never forgive him for that, or my mother for letting it happen.

Zach and I have another brother, Phillip, but he hasn't bothered with us since finding out the truth. He's my father's heir, the one who's supposed to take over, but from what I can tell, he hasn't been spending much time with my parents outside of work either.

"They're awful people," I say, surprised at myself for admitting it so openly.

"That's okay, Princess," Rowan says, lifting one side of his mouth. "Your fate isn't decided by who your family is. You didn't choose them, and I'm guessing you wouldn't have."

"Why do you call me princess?"

"Because you did decide to go on that show," he says, grinning full on now. "That *is* on you."

Chapter Seven

Rowan

She's looking at me like I slapped her. Or maybe like she wants to slap me. Fuck. I didn't mean for it to sound like that.

Yes, you did, whispers a voice in my head, adding, *you asshole.*

"Look," I say. "I know why you're doing the show. My sister told me about your nonprofit, and—"

"Then you know that there are some things more important in life than looking like an idiot on screen," she says, with so much goddamn nobility, she might as well be a princess for real.

"You're not going to look like an idiot. They're the idiots."

The thought of her kissing any of them makes me want to grind my teeth until a back molar crushes. But that's not because I want those pretty lips for myself. It's just obvious to anyone with eyes that she's worth all six of the remaining men.

"They're not all idiots," she says, looking away, and her words strum something in my chest.

"Oh? Which of them has caught your attention?"

I'm not sure why I'm asking something I don't want her to answer, only I've never been smart when it comes to this sort of thing. It's like I was born with my romance button broken, or so my sisters tell me. Like there was only so much of it to go around between us Mayberry siblings, and my portion was the romance equivalent of a few grains of salt.

"I don't want to talk about the guys," she says. "Why do you spend so much time on set if you think the show is stupid?"

There's an awareness in me—of her, her head tipped toward me, those big eyes soaking me in from behind their dark shields like I'm her Prince Charming—but I muffle it. Because I'm pretty sure she wouldn't be looking at me like that if she knew I'm the cause of all the little accidents and mishaps that have been happening on set. The inconveniences that have caused the guys to grumble. Turning her orange, however temporarily. So I look away.

"She's my grandmother, Kennedy." I take another strike at the trunk, savoring the burn of my muscles, because this, at least, is something I can do.

"So you're loyal to her?" she asks in a quiet voice.

"No, I'm loyal to my sisters. If she weren't calling me, she'd be calling them, and she's already fucked up their lives. She doesn't get to me." I pause, swallowing, and examine the trunk. "Besides, even though she's a battle axe, she's a little old lady. It's our job to take care of her, or at least to make sure she's eating and taking her medication. When our mother walked out on us, she left us with our grandmother. Nana wasn't the kind of woman who'd give us band aids and make it all better, but she did at least keep us."

I can feel her looking at me, a not-unpleasant burn.

"You're loyal."

"I'm pragmatic," I say, making another strike with the ax.

"You don't like compliments."

"Not undeserved ones, no," I say, finally looking at her. She's studying me over the top of my cup, her gaze pointed. A few strands of her hair have escaped the knit cap and are playing in the slight breeze.

"I'm starting to think you're deserving of a few," she says. "Setting aside the whole strumpet thing."

"You can compliment me on my choice of beverage," I tell her. "I'll accept that since you're drinking it."

"Because you gave it to me." She puts a finger in the air. "Takes care of difficult old ladies." Another finger. "Feels sympathy for women who've had close brushes with terrifying Santas."

Before her smile can wash over me and make me lose my will, I turn back to the tree. Another couple of strikes, and it'll fall.

Holly's going to like this one. It's full and tall, but there's a slightly sparse spot in the back that makes it look less than Hollywood ready. There's such a thing as too perfect, after all.

"It's about to come down," I tell Kennedy. "Make sure you're standing back."

I'm hit with an image of her being struck by a branch. It would be a hell of a thing for her to have to go to an emergency room when she's not even supposed to be here.

It's not really possible for her to get hit where she's standing. Even so, I say, "Come over here next to me." There's an unintended huskiness to the words, and I give myself a mental shake.

She hustles over and stands near me, the heat of her like a beacon. She smells slightly of apple and whiskey.

"Aren't you cold without your coat?"

"No," I say, adjusting to her proximity. "Physical work keeps you warmer than any coat."

She makes a little sound, and I realize there's another possible interpretation to my words—one I didn't mean but was maybe thinking about anyway.

"I've always loved fresh Christmas trees, but this is kind of sad," she says in a soft voice.

"Too late to turn back now," I tell her. "Besides, they're grown for this purpose. If you didn't choose one, it wouldn't be fulfilling its purpose."

"But wouldn't it be nice not to have any purpose to fulfill? To just exist?"

There's a thread of longing in her voice, and I look at her in spite of myself. It's on the tip of my tongue to remind her that they're Christmas trees, for fuck's sake, but I know she's not really talking about the trees.

"People are allowed to be wildcards sometimes," I tell her. "Not Christmas trees."

She smiles slightly. "You're right. And anyway, it's coming down. It'll look beautiful." She pauses, but I can tell she has more to say. Those little strands of hair dance under her knit cap. "I wish I could see it once it's decorated."

"Maybe Harry can keep sneaking you out." Reaching over, I tuck the hair back into her cap. "It can be a whole thing." I can't interpret the look she's giving me from behind those glasses. I only know that I like it more than I should. "Of course, your six boyfriends wouldn't like it."

She laughs. "I'm pretty sure there's only one or two who would care."

"Jonah?" I ask innocently, but in my chest, there's an unhappy burn. She's thinking about Marcus probably. Pretty boy Marcus with his millions. How am I supposed to compete with that?

You're not, dumbass.

"You know, your grandmother and Harry made me keep Jonah around," she says, lifting a finger to her lips as if I might feel compelled to share gossip.

I scowl. "Doesn't surprise me to hear my grandmother did that, but Harry's getting the shit chores at the house tonight."

She laughs in apparent delight. "It's okay. They're right. Having characters like him around will make the show interesting. It'll make more people watch, so more people will hear about Leto's Hands."

"Excuse me?"

She shrugs. "It's the nonprofit I work for. Leto's Hands." She makes a face. "My mother always says they might as well have called it Leto's Handouts. Leto is the Greek goddess of motherhood."

"I may not have gone to college, but I'm not stupid," I say, even though I've never heard of Leto or her hands.

She frowns. "I never implied you were. A lot of people don't know what the name means."

"So maybe you should rename it."

The wrinkle between her brows smooths over. "Maybe. But if they were going to do that, they probably should have gotten to it before I had it written into my contract that I get to mention it at least once every episode."

A laugh escapes from me, because fuck, my grandmother must hate that. "What does Leto do with her hands?"

She gives me a chastising look. Okay, fair enough.

"It's a nonprofit that helps single mothers," she says.

I'm tempted to ask what drove her to work at such a place, because when people seek out a calling like that, there's usually a specific reason that compelled them to. But to my surprise she offers up the information without being asked. "My nanny when I was a little girl. She was a single mother. Her daughter is Olive, my best friend."

I study her for a moment, letting this new information slip into place. Kennedy Littlefield isn't anything like I thought she would be.

"You ready to watch a tree come down, Kennedy?"

She smiles at me. "Yes. If I had my phone, I'd even take a video."

"I'm glad it got locked away in phone jail."

Her pretty, tinkling laugh is my accompaniment as I make the last few strikes to the trunk. Well, that and the faint echo of a pretty shit version of "Santa Baby," which I can never listen to without thinking of the dance my mother did at a town party when I was nine, and she was trying to make the then-police chief into Husband

Number Four. She'd crowded us kids into the corner and told Bryn not to let us leave her sight. Bryn was Type A from the womb, and she'd kept us all organized, a snack plate each, but she hadn't been able to crowd out our vision.

That sour thought is in my head as I take those final strokes. Still, there's a certain satisfaction inside me as I watch the tree come down, the smell of pine sap wafting into the air as it thumps to the ground. The knowledge that I've done something special for my sister, something she'll appreciate. The knowledge that Kennedy is probably watching.

I turn to her, and sure enough, she has a look of wonder on her face.

"You're used to having other people cut your trees down for you, huh?" I ask as I prop the axe against the trunk and strip off my work gloves. I could wear them to move the tree, but I don't like the way they feel on my hands.

She glowers at me. I deserve it.

"Sorry, that was a shit thing to say. I was trying to make a joke."

"It's okay." She makes a face. "The truth is, I've never had a real Christmas tree. My parents have this famous Christmas Eve party. Or at least they like to think it's famous, but the trees are never real. They're these super convincing fakes that they spray with pine scent. My mom wouldn't want to get needles all over the floors, even though she wouldn't be the one cleaning them. But it's just not the same."

I have to laugh at the thought of people spraying fake trees with pine scent because they're neater. "No, I suspect it's not," I tell her. "What do they do at this famous Christmas Eve party?"

"It's awful," she says. "There's a lot of expensive hors d'oeuvres and champagne, and every year, they put together these crazy favor bags, but there aren't any presents under the tree, and there's no warm cider or hot chocolate. The only Christmas carols they play are from the philharmonic orchestra."

"Sounds like your suitors would fit right in," I say. Even as I say it, I know I'm closing a door between us—putting some sort of ending to this moment that's felt strangely right. But that's a good thing, because I can't afford to have thoughts about Kennedy, and I shouldn't want her to have thoughts about me.

"Oh shit," I hear Oliver exclaim, followed by a shriek. Kennedy and I exchange a quick look, and then I'm running through the Christmas trees, Kennedy racing after me. It doesn't take me long to find them. Ralph's isn't huge, and I'm good at following noise. Sometimes, before my little sister Ivy went to live with Jay, I'd be left alone with her. I'd have to basically echolocate her by listening to her little grunts and happy squeals. She'd always be engaged in some self-destructive activity—trying to eat my grandmother's bobby pins or pulling thorny roses out of a vase so she could pull the petals off.

By the time we reach them, the shouting has stopped. Actually, Oliver has Harry wrapped into a hug, and they're both laughing. I feel a twinge of regret, like I've interrupted a moment that should have been allowed to play out. They pull apart as we near them.

"What happened?" Kennedy asks. Her sunglasses are still on her face, but her cap is askew from her run, that long pretty hair spilling out.

"I..." Harry starts. Swallows. "A squirrel..."

"When the tree came down, a squirrel jumped on his head from inside the branches," Oliver says through a rumble of laughter. "We didn't even notice it was in there before it happened."

"What'd you do?" Kennedy asks.

"I ran!" Harry says, and Kennedy starts laughing. Harry joins her, and then Oliver, and then me, even though I'm not altogether sure why we're laughing, other than I'm relieved it was only a squirrel that landed on him. If it had bitten him, his short, thinning blond hair wouldn't conceal the mark, so I'm guessing he's good on the rabies front.

"It stayed balanced until I brushed it off," Oliver says at last, wiping his eyes. "I think it was in shock."

"Thank you," Harry says as he reaches out and touches Oliver's arm. "You *saved* me."

"I didn't save you," Oliver says with a grin. "It was just a squirrel. But if that'll convince you to go out to dinner with me, let's pretend I did."

It's starting to feel more like we're intruding on their moment, so I say, "I'm going to bring my tree out to the truck. Will you help me, Princess?"

"Only if Harry doesn't need me."

Harry gives a nervous shuffle, like he still feels a phantom squirrel on his head, but stays put. "Candy cane," he says to Kennedy.

She smiles at him, and he waves and then salutes. We take off, walking toward my fallen tree.

"Will I take one end, and you'll take the other?" she asks, her eyes gleaming a bit behind those glasses, as if she's excited about it.

"No," I say with a snort. "More like I'll take it all."

"But you—" She gestures back toward the guys.

"They were having a moment," I say with a shrug.

Her grin is more contagious than it has any right to be. "You *are* matchmaking."

"No, I'm not," I say defensively, even though I kind of am, I guess. "I'm just letting them work shit out. That's what a friend should do."

"Yeah," she says, bumping her shoulder into me playfully. "That *is* what a friend should do."

And if there's a pleasant hum from the place where her shoulder touched mine, it's probably only because of the moment—the high of seeing Oliver happy, of having cut down the perfect tree, of being with—

"You're going to let me help with at least part of it, right?" she asks as we reach the tree.

"How about you carry the ax and your drink?" I say, nodding to the little cup sitting by the tree. I shrug into my coat.

"It feels like you're giving me a job that doesn't matter," she responds, pouting a little.

Shit. She's cute when she pouts too.

"It matters," I say. "Ralph is very particular about his axes."

"And you?" she asks.

"Am I particular about my axes?" I ask, raising my brows as I study the tree.

"Are you particular about who touches your things?" she asks, lifting her eyebrows in return. "Because you seem resistant to letting me touch your tree."

I laugh, but my mind mentally substitutes another word for tree. The thought of Kennedy touching me, running those small smooth hands over me, sends blood pumping down south, but I think of a dozen different shitty things to get myself back under control. Spiders pouring out of animatronic Santas' mouths. My grandmother stalking around the set of *Matchmaking the Rich* as if she might magically become rich too if she's enough of an asshole. Jonah Fucking Highbury kissing Kennedy.

Clenching my teeth together, I heft up the tree.

"You're really going to carry it by yourself?" Kennedy says, seeming kind of annoyed.

"It's easier," I insist.

She doesn't look convinced...or like she's not in any mood to touch my tree anymore.

"Can you get the other things?" I ask, standing there with the tree in my arms, like I'm giving it a hug.

"Fine," she says with a sigh, collecting them. It makes me laugh a little more when she picks up the ax so tentatively, like it's a dead animal she's lifting by the tail.

"It won't hurt you," I say.

"I'm not stupid," she snaps, throwing my phrase from earlier back at me. "I might not have much experience with axes, but I know which is the sharp end."

"Thank you," I say. "I mean it. Ralph really does care about his axes. And I wouldn't want to litter out here."

She gives me a nod of acknowledgement, but I can tell she's still feeling salty about me not letting her help.

"You can help me get it into the bed of the truck," I offer before I can catch myself. "And get it strapped in."

"Really?" she asks, sounding much more excited than the task warrants.

It shouldn't be charming, but it's goddamn adorable.

"Really." I'm sick of standing still with my arms around the tree like it's my long-lost relative, so I start moving back toward the cabin. I swing around it, while Kennedy ducks in to return the ax.

It takes her awhile to come out. Is she talking to Ethel? The thought makes me smile—*strumpet*—but it's not hard to imagine. Kennedy's the kind of person who could probably draw anyone into conversation just by being herself.

I've already got the tree into the bed by the time she comes out with a little shopping bag.

"You already got it in," she says with disappointment.

"You're going to help me get it strapped in," I tell her. Because I did wait for her to come back for this step. "What'd you get?"

She lifts a long-sleeve T-shirt out of the bag. The slogan says *We Put the Christmas in Tree*, which frankly makes zero sense. I'm guessing Ralph came up with it after drinking too much of his special sauce. It's enormous—large enough to fit two of her at least.

"You like sleeping in big shirts or something?" I ask. I don't hate the thought. My mind supplies an image of Kennedy wearing the huge shirt, her hair down, and nothing else.

She tosses it to me. "This one's for you. I got one in my size too."

I catch it, surprised to feel a knot forming in my throat. "You thought I'd want to remember this?"

A dick question, but she immediately says, "I knew you would."

"Thank you," I say, folding the shirt. I open the driver's door and stick it inside the truck, feeling a little off kilter, like I'm no longer sure what to say or do with her.

When I shut the door, she's waiting for me. "Let's do this," she says.

I show her where to anchor the bungee cords, and there's a strange energy humming between us the whole time—a promise. We've just finished the task when Oliver and Harry emerge, both of them seeming pleased as they heft Oliver's tree over to his blue Subaru Outback. Harry is red enough to match Ralph's old Santa coat when I glance at him.

So that's going well, at least.

I steal a look at Kennedy, and she smiles covertly at me, as if Oliver and Harry's potential romance is a project we're working on together. I like that more than I should, especially since I would strip my family of every last connection to matchmaking if I could.

Kennedy makes a *come here* gesture, and I step closer, crowding her because one step doesn't feel like enough.

She sucks in a breath, then says, "He's letting Harry help with *his* tree,"

Her words make me smile.

"Didn't want you to go back to the house smelling of tree sap, Princess. It would be a tell."

"You didn't think I could carry it," she challenges, tucking some dark hair back into her cap.

"No, I didn't," I agree. Because it's true, and true things should be copped to whenever possible.

"One of these days I'm going to surprise you, Rowan," she says, looking up at me, close enough that I feel the warm puff of her breath on my face and smell the sweet scent of spiked cider.

I don't tell her that she has already surprised me. I don't tell her that I've surprised myself more than anyone else ever could. Because, fool that I am, I have a thing for Kennedy Littlefield.

I lean in a little more, almost close enough to kiss her, and—

"Rowan?" someone says from behind me.

Chapter Eight

Kennedy

For a second there, it felt like Rowan was about to kiss me.

For a second there, it felt like I was going to—very enthusiastically—kiss him back.

But the stranger might as well have thrown a snowball, disrupting the weird heat building between us. The interruption reminded me that I'm here in Highland Hills for a purpose, and while that purpose is supposedly to fall in love, I'm definitely not supposed to fall in love with *him*.

The man's tall, with hair that falls somewhere in the spectrum between white and blond, and has large blue eyes. He looks a little pale and drawn, as if he's been pulling too many hours at work.

Rowan turns to him, all prickles again, and I wonder who he's mad at this time. Himself? Me? This guy?

"Jay," he says, and I remember his stories about the stepfather who was too good for his mother. It's a funny twist of fate that he's here at the same time as us. Then again, Rowan likes this place because Jay used to bring him here, so maybe it's not that weird after all.

"Haven't seen you for a while, buddy," the guy says, coming over and clapping him on the back. "You haven't been answering my calls."

I can feel Harry watching us as he and Oliver get the tree situated on top of Oliver's car. Okay, I'll be honest, Oliver's doing most of the work, and Harry's watching me with a look of concern. He's probably worried we'll get caught.

I'm worried we'll get caught too, but mostly for his sake.

"Yeah," Rowan says sheepishly. "About that. I've been busy."

Jay nods, as if he's not surprised to hear it, then says, "It's too bad Ivy's not coming home for Christmas." A corner of his mouth hitches up. "Hard at work on her next book now that *Naughty Saint Nick* is out. Number five on Amazon, did you see that?"

Rowan smiles back at him. "Yeah, don't ask me to read it, though. There are some things you don't want to know about your sisters."

"I read them all," Jay says, then frowns, lifting a hand to his left shoulder and wincing, before continuing. "She marks the pages I should skip."

"Your sister's a writer?" I ask Rowan, impressed. "Why didn't I know that?"

Even as I say it, I know there are plenty of answers that fit. Because I don't know him all that well. Because Tina didn't tell me, or maybe she doesn't know. Because it's none of my business.

"Maybe I was worried you'd use me for autographed copies," Rowan says. "It's happened before."

It's more of a playful answer than I expected from him. His stepfather must be surprised by it too, because his gaze turns to me with interest. "Who's this, now?"

"A friend," Rowan says. He looks at me, and I half hope he'll put his arm around me again, like he did inside. What does it say about me that I *want* to be treated like a strumpet?

"I'm Kennedy," I tell Jay, reaching for a handshake. Rowan scowls at me, and I can definitely feel Harry frowning at me from a distance, but I doubt Rowan's stepfather is on Nana Mayberry's speed dial, and he doesn't strike me as a particularly gossip-hungry man. He's not going to slap photos of me up on the internet.

"Pleased to meet you, Kennedy," he says, shaking hands. His face contorts slightly as we shake, and I can't help but wonder if something's wrong with his arm. I feel a wash of concern for him. Was he injured? Should he really be picking up an ax right now? I don't like the idea of him going into the woods by himself if a handshake makes him wince...

"Maybe Rowan should help you with your tree," I blurt.

Rowan shoots me an accusatory look. It occurs to me that I might be stepping on toes without realizing it. Rowan sounded nothing but fond of Jay, but there might be underlying family dynamics I don't understand. Or maybe he's reached his tree-chopping quota for the day. Still, he doesn't hesitate to nod to his stepfather. "Yeah, of course I'll help you, Jay."

"How'd you two meet?" Jay asks, ignoring the tree offer.

"Through friends," I say with a smile.

Rowan looks uncomfortable.

I can *feel* Harry's growing discomfort. If a look could reach across a short distance and shake a person, this one would.

Oliver hustles up as if to pop the discomfort bubble, giving everyone the kind of friendly smile Rowan only seems capable of in stolen moments. "Good to see you, Jay. It's been a hot minute."

Jay grins at him. "I was just saying so to your buddy here. He's gotten too busy to answer my calls, I guess, not that I blame him. The last thing kids your age want to do is hang out with an old man."

Oliver laughs heartily. "Rowan's never been a kid. I'm pretty sure he darns his socks at night by candlelight."

"Very funny," Rowan says, but he seems relieved by the interruption, like he wasn't quite sure what to do with Jay before Oliver came up.

Harry hustles up to me and takes my arm. He smells of tree sap and apple cider. It's pleasant, and I'm hit with a pang of sadness.

When we leave, we'll have to leave Christmas behind too. Labelle Manor is all sharp edges and strange embellishments, from the huge ceramic goat in the eastern corridor to the princess bed in my room. It's not the kind of place you can curl up in and feel peaceful.

"We need to leave," he whispers. "Now."

"I know," I say. And I do. But I don't move toward the car or wave in farewell. I'm just...not quite ready. Rowan revealed his vulnerable side, and I don't want to look away. Not yet.

Harry frowns at me, and I'm sure he's about to say something about the show. Then he leans down, showing me his head.

"Did that squirrel leave marks on my scalp?"

There are a few little scrapes, as if made by tiny claws, and I'm about to say something when Oliver says "Oh, shit," his voice full of panic, and there's a muted thump. I look over at them, alarmed, and see that Jay's sitting on the ground, Rowan crouched over him.

"Did he fall?" I ask, feeling stupid even as the words leave my lips.

"Rowan caught him," Oliver says. "We need an ambulance."

"Call the guys," Rowan says, handing his phone to Oliver. His face is expressionless, but his eyes are fathomless depths of worry and fear, and the look in them pierces all the way down to my soul. For some reason, they seek me out, and I find myself removing the sunglasses and stowing them in my pocket so that our gazes can lock, nothing in between us. A second passes before he looks back down at Jay. "I think he's having a heart attack."

I don't even think. I practically leap across the few steps separating us, the urge inside me undeniable: *Go to him. Go to him.*

Olive's grandmother died in front of us when we were little girls. She was there one minute, gone the next, so the first thing I do is look in Jay's eyes. He's still there. Even though he looks groggy and woozy, he's conscious. He's alive.

"I'm okay," he croaks as Rowan unzips his coat and loosens the collar of his shirt.

"No, you're not fucking okay," Rowan says. "But you're going to be. You're *going to be*."

There's ferocity behind the words. The promise that Rowan Mayberry will chase down the Grim Reaper himself if he dares to take this man. Maybe that's why Jay has a slight smile despite the lines of pain surrounding his eyes.

My heart is in knots.

I barely register Oliver making a call. Suddenly, though, he's crouched near us. Then he's saying, "They're coming with an ambulance, Rowan. A few minutes."

Rowan nods, but his eyes are on his stepfather. "Come on, Jay. You've got to hold on. Just a little while. They're gonna be here."

"Kerry's going to be pissed about the tree," Jay says through that slight smile of his. "Hates it when I wait too long after Thanksgiving."

"Something tells me she'll get over it." Looking up, his gaze pleading, Rowan says, "Aspirin. Does anyone have any aspirin?"

I don't, but I'm already on my feet. "I'll ask inside," I say as I race for the door. Ralph's already opening it, a worried look on his face. "We need aspirin," I say, not trying to modulate my voice. "A bottle of aspirin. They think he's having a heart attack."

"Oh my stars and garters. I thought it would be Ralph who had the heart attack," Ethel says, slipping out from behind her counter and hurrying toward us. She has something in her hand, and she juts it out, almost hitting me, and I nearly gasp with relief at the sight of a bottle of aspirin. "Always do believe in being prepared. The boys have called the paramedics?"

I nod, snatching up the bottle. "And they're on their way. *Thank you*."

I bolt out the door and then to Rowan, giving him the bottle. Harry steps forward with a literal case of water bottles, which he must have retrieved from his trunk. "I have water," he announces needlessly.

"He has to chew it," Rowan says, his hand shaking as he tries to open the bottle of pills.

My own shock and panic recede because I recognize I'm needed, and being needed has always helped me gather myself.

I take the bottle from his hands and steadily open it, shaking a few pills out onto his palm.

His eyes meet mine, and he swallows. "Thank you. Thank you." Then he lowers his head to Jay. "Jay, man, you've got to chew these."

"I think...I'd rather...take the heart attack," Jay jokes.

"Well, you're still having a heart attack," Harry comments, then jolts a little, as if realizing he shouldn't have said it. He nudges the case of water, which he set on the gravel floor, with his foot. "Should I sit in the car? Maybe I'll sit in the car. Unless there's anything else I can do, obviously."

Oliver takes his hand. "Thank you for the water. Why don't we keep standing here?"

Jay accepts the pills and chews them, making a face as he munches into them. "Kerry," he says, looking at Rowan.

He'll need to call her, I realize. He'll need to tell her what's happening. But I can tell Rowan is hesitant to move even an inch away from Jay.

"I'll call her," I offer.

"My...pocket," Jay says, and Rowan slides his phone out.

It's unlocked, so I start searching for her number, smiling a little because Rowan is giving Jay crap about not keeping his phone locked. It's obvious he's trying to distract him.

"She's...wife," Jay manages, and sure enough, her number is saved under "wife," which is so sweet, I feel a little flutter in my heart. The photo is of a dark-haired woman with large caramel eyes. Horror starts to seep through my veins, because I'll have to tell this lovely woman that her husband is probably having a heart attack.

"Where will they bring him?" I ask.

"Highland Hills Hospital," Oliver says. "It's the only one."

I feel the burn of Rowan's gaze beating into me, something shining in his eyes besides worry and fear, and I turn away to make the call. Ralph and Ethel are in the doorway, along with a few other people I don't recognize. Shit. So much for keeping this outing under wraps. If there's any hope of doing that, we'll have to leave soon. But I can't stand the thought of leaving Rowan alone with this.

I mean, obviously he's not alone. He has Oliver. But...

But you've never met a problem you didn't want to make your own, Kennedy, I can hear my mother telling me.

Maybe it's true. But that doesn't mean I'm any more willing to run out on him.

I hit the dial button, and Kerry answers on the second ring. "I'm not coming back, Jay," she snaps. "You're not going to make me feel guilty by sending photos of Ralph's and the perfect tree you found there. The past is the past. You can go fuck yourself."

Crap. Well, this is awkward.

"Um, Miss..." I realize I don't know her last name, or Jay's for that matter, so I settle for the "Miss."

"Who are you?" the voice asks, her tone cutting. She releases a bitter laugh. "What, he thought he'd get a little strumpet to call to make me jealous?"

The part of me that's punch-drunk picks up on her use of 'strumpet,' but it's hardly like I can save it as evidence for my argument with Rowan.

"No, ma'am," I say. "Your husband...I'm afraid he's having a heart attack."

There's a pause on the other end of the line, and I expect a more sympathetic response from her this time. I'm shocked when she says, "Well, give his daughter a call. He's no husband of mine. Not for much longer."

"He'll be at Highland Hills Hospital," I blurt, hoping she'll think better of it.

"I'm in California, *dear*," she says. "Taking the first vacation I've had since marrying that man. I'm not going to cut it short because of him."

And then she hangs up.

I tap the phone with my fingertips, tempted to call Olive and ask her what in the world I should do, because that was *brutal*, and I don't intend to tell someone, mid-heart attack, that his wife is a...well, bitch. Sometimes only a swear will do. No matter what he did, her reaction has to be unwarranted. Then again, I don't know Jay. I only know what Rowan has told me about him, and our perception of the people around us is always colored by our own perspective.

That's exactly the reason for the majority of my mistakes.

But I don't have time to describe all this craziness to Olive, so I put on my big girl panties, as she'd put it, and head back over to Rowan and his stepfather. Jay's lying on the gravel now, his upper body reclined on Rowan's lap, and Rowan has the look of a cornered animal. I know he's afraid he'll have to watch someone he loves slip away in front of him. Jay's still conscious, though, which is good. It's even better that I hear sirens approaching.

Unfortunately, I'm not saved by the bell, because Jay's eyes seek me out as I hand the phone back to Rowan, who takes it from me with cold fingers, his thumb brushing the back of my hand in thanks. A shiver shakes through my body from that light, *voluntary* touch.

"Kerry?" Jay asks.

I crouch down next to them. "I wasn't able to get through to her," I lie, feeling horrible about it, but sometimes a lie is better than the truth. "I left her a message to call you."

"Thank you," he says, closing his eyes.

The sirens get louder.

"You and Harry need to go," Rowan says, the words a rumble from his chest.

I barely notice Harry whispering, "Oh, thank God," because pain is stabbing me through the middle. It feels like so much of my life has revolved around me being sent away from important or unpleasant things. From anything at all, really.

"Oh, okay. You're right. Everything's under control, and this moment is for family."

"That's not why, Princess," Rowan says, and with the arm not cradling his stepfather, he reaches over to tip up my chin, his eyes burning into mine. "You're not supposed to be here. Neither is Harry. I don't want either of you to get into trouble. You've helped us. A lot. Now, you need to help yourself."

"But I don't want to leave you," I say, the words spilling out even though I know I'm giving away far too much. I'm not supposed to like him. I'm supposed to dislike him, if anything.

He smiles. "I'll come see you. Now, go."

I get to my feet, my whole body shaky. It still feels impossible to leave him like this, with his stepfather in his arms. And he doesn't even know about the whole Kerry thing. At the same time, he's right. Harry and I aren't supposed to be here, and we'll get in trouble if we're caught. There's something else Rowan's not saying: if it gets out that Harry and I *were* here, the producers might try to make it a storyline for the show. Jay probably doesn't want that, particularly if he's having marital problems.

They're more than problems.

"You'll come to me?" I ask. I hate the note of pleading in my voice, but it's terrible to think that I might walk back into the news blackout of Labelle Manor and hear nothing about Rowan or his stepfather for days.

"I'll come to you," he says, his eyes searing me. "Don't forget your shirt."

I pick up the bag from where I dropped it, and Harry joins me.

"Don't worry about the water bottles," Harry says to them. "Those are yours. Staying hydrated is the best thing you can do in a crisis, and...anyway."

"I'll give you a call," Oliver tells him with a nod. He's smiling slightly, so at least he doesn't mind Harry's verbal flatulence.

"And I'll answer it," Harry says, then gets pink. "Obviously I will."

The sirens are getting louder. It won't be long now before the emergency response vehicles pull into the parking lot.

"Go," Rowan tells me once more.

And we do.

Chapter Nine

Rowan

"He's okay, Ivy," I say into my phone, playing with the seam in the arm of a waiting room chair. It's busted, like most of the things around me. Even the little Christmas tree in the corner has twisted limbs, and the menorah on the table next to it is dented. I guess there's no need to give people perfect things while they're waiting for shit news. Except the news I just got was actually not that bad. "They say it was a mild heart attack. I'm going in there to see him in a minute. A nurse just came and told me he woke up."

"Oh, thank fuck," she says, back at home now. When I first called, she was at a busy bar. The heroine in her next book is a female bartender, I guess, and she's always been all about doing in-person research. Truthfully, I think she's a bit like me, and she doesn't want to settle for one boring job when she could have hundreds of little ones. Except I could barely string enough sentences together to fill out a greeting card, and she's written millions.

I'm impressed by my little sister, even though I really wish she hadn't chosen to write a book about a fireman. The guys doubled down on the Cupid nickname, and half a dozen copies of the book are always floating around the firehouse. People lend them out to their friends, for God's sake.

"I'm sorry you had to see that," Ivy continues, bringing my attention back to our conversation, "but I'm glad you were there with him. Ralph doesn't seem like he'd be good in emergencies."

"No," I agree. "But Ethel had aspirin. That helped, I guess."

"And was anyone there for *you*, Rowan?"

"Oliver was there," I say, even as Kennedy flashes through my mind. She immediately hopped into action, and she didn't stop. She even volunteered to call Kerry. When I first met her, I figured she was the kind of woman who liked to keep her hands clean, but I read her wrong. I wish she were here, to be honest, although it's ludicrous to think the woman starring in my grandmother's matchmaking show could sit side by side with me in this tacky hospital waiting room without drawing eyes.

I tried following up with Kerry, but there was no answer. I haven't been able to get a hold of my other sisters either. Bryn and Holly are both at a big event related to the dating app they helped create, and Willow lives in Asheville. I'll tell her, but not yet.

"Good. That's good." Ivy heaves a sigh, and I picture her running a hand through her short hair. The rest of us have dark hair, but hers is blonde and curly. When we were kids, people would ask if she was a visiting friend.

She feels like one most of the time.

"Well, looks like I'll be up for Christmas, huh?" she says.

"Don't sound so happy about it."

"I'm not, dipshit," she says, but it's not without fondness. "I *have* been meaning to come visit for a while now," she adds. "But I was hoping to wait until after the show. The last thing I want is for Nana to pull me in front of the camera as her romance mascot."

Yeah, you'd rather leave that role to Bryn and Holly.

"That's something she would do," I agree. "But I see no reason to tell her about any of this. Jay's not her son-in-law anymore. *Ipso facto,* it's none of her business. Mom either. You'd be staying at the house with Jay, anyway, I'm guessing."

She always does. Sometimes I wonder if my sisters are hurt by that, by Ivy's closeness to Jay, but they've never said so. I think we all understand.

"Is Kerry there?" she asks. There's a strange note in her voice, like she maybe knows something I don't.

"No," I say. "Kenn—my other friend who was there tried calling her, but she didn't answer. She left a voice message. I left another one just now. I'm surprised she's not here. You know how the gossip mill is in this town. Half the people in Jay's address book probably already know about this."

"Roger that," she says. "Which is why I can't imagine how you think I can keep my presence in Highland Hills a secret for more than five minutes."

"Oh, you think everyone's going to be talking about the famous novelist in town?" I ask, smirking. It feels good, teasing her. It feels a bit less like I've gone six months without seeing her.

I understand why Ivy's kept her distance. At the same time, part of me still thinks of her as the little girl who kept crawling around after me and Willow when we were little. The kid sister I used to keep from swallowing "chokes," as we called them.

I miss her, is what I'm saying.

"You know they will be," she says, laughing. "I was more thinking they'd paint a scarlet A on dad's door. Or at least some people in town would."

She's right. As with any small town, we have our share of prudes. "They're just jealous," I say.

"Thanks, Rowan."

"You know, if you'd consider changing the bar in your book to a brewery, you could do your research right here," I say. "I don't know if you've talked to Holly recently, but she's with Cole Garrison, the guy who owns Ziggy's."

"No shit. I'll think about it," she says. "But about Kerry. I think something's up with her and Dad. I called him the other week, and she was shouting at him in the background. You know how he is, though. Nothing's a problem. Everything's great."

"Huh," I tell her, because I don't care to think about that. I need to get through this current crisis before addressing the other ones lining up for attention. The nurse who came to see me earlier motions to me from the double doors. "I think I can go back now."

"Take pictures. Call me. I want to know everything."

"Will do, Little Bit," I say, using her childhood nickname.

"Thanks, Rowan. Thanks for calling. For being there."

"Of course," I say. "Jay's still family."

In some ways, he is. In some ways, he's not. He *has* been asking me to hang out a lot more lately, maybe because of the trouble she mentioned with Kerry, and now I feel like a real dick for not following up. It's just...he did ask us, and especially me, to spend time with him after he divorced our mother, but the invitations eventually dried to a trickle. It was natural they would, but it also hurt, especially after my own father took off without a backward glance.

Jay did deserve better than our mother, and I never resented him for seeking it out. I just wished all us kids could have gone with him.

"You had to say he was your father to get in to see him, right?" Ivy asks.

"Yeah, I did," I say through a throat that suddenly feels swollen. I swallow back the "what of it," and tell her to get her ass up here.

I hang up, pocket my phone, and follow the nurse through the winding halls to Jay's room. She tries to make small talk, and I answer in grunts. We walk into the room together.

I'm not a paramedic, but I know enough of them to have known what to expect, pretty much. Still, it sucks to see someone you know and care about hooked up to a bunch of machines to keep his clock ticking.

"Rowan," Jay says, his voice husky, as I pull up a chair to his bedside. The nurse checks his vitals, then leaves. "Did you get through to Kerry?"

"'Fraid not, but I just got off the phone with Ivy. She's coming. Bit of an extreme measure to get your daughter home for Christmas."

He laughs a little, then winces, and I feel like an asshole for making a joke. A shitty one at that. If it's going to hurt when he laughs, he needs to make it count. "That's good," he manages at least. "Really good." He stares into my eyes for a long beat, then says, "Rowan, there's something I've been meaning to tell you. That's why —" His mouth purses. He glances at the water on the side table next to the bed, and I bring it over to him so he can reach the straw.

After taking a long drink, he says, "Your mother told me something after the plans for the matchmaking show were finalized. There's something she wanted to reveal on air." He forces a smile. "You know she has a flair for the dramatic. I convinced her not to, thank God." He squirms a little on the bed. "But you know your mother. I don't totally believe she wouldn't try something, even now, so I wanted you to hear it from me first."

"And?" I ask, my tone tight. I shouldn't talk to him with anything but butterflies and flowers in my voice, considering what he's been through today, but it's pretty obvious I'm not going to like where he's going with this. I'm a little tired of bad news. I'm a handyman/fireman nicknamed Cupid who's interested in a woman who's currently living with six other men. I might as well have set my sights on Snow White. Isn't that enough? How much can one man take?

"Rowan, you need to understand that I didn't know this when you were a kid. I may have suspected, but I didn't know. She only told me a couple of months ago."

"What the f... What are you talking about, Jay?"

"I'm your father, Rowan."

"Yeah, I know you said you're still our stepdad after—"

"No," he says, adamant. "I'm your father."

His words and the way he's saying them sink in. Shock roils

through me, followed by a cold, numb feeling. "You're my father. So. What? You were having an affair with my mother when she was still with my dad?" A humorless laugh escapes me. "Well, I guess he's not my dad, not that he ever was much of one."

"Yes," Jay says, his face full of sympathy, like he understands what a barrel of shit he's just unloaded on me and is sorry for it. Like he knows this is going to make me respect him less. "We started seeing each other before she had you, but it didn't last long. She said she wanted to try to be a real family with you and her husband...and Bryn and Holly, of course. I don't have an excuse, other than that I loved her."

"Jesus, Jay. I always knew our family was fucked up, but this adds another layer," I say, getting to my feet. Pacing. It's a layer I could do without.

If Jay's my father, I could have gone to live with him like Ivy did after our mother left. Only, I wouldn't have wanted to leave Bryn and Holly. I definitely wouldn't have left Willow.

Fuck. I'll have to tell her this. Will she think I'm less of her brother once she finds out we're only half-siblings?

"I'm sorry," Jay says.

"Yeah, me too. I can't... I need to go. For a while."

"You take all the time you need, buddy," he says, giving me a slight smile. "Just as long as you come back."

My heart's burning as I stomp off down the hallway, through the waiting room, and out to my truck, where the stupid, fucking tree is waiting in the bed. Suddenly, I'm exhausted. Thoroughly and utterly exhausted. All I want to do is go home, sit in a room, preferably dark, and drink whiskey until I pass out. And if that sounds horrible, then you have a limited imagination. The numb feeling that engulfed me in the hospital room is receding, and I don't want to feel what lies beneath it.

My sister isn't back yet by the time I get home, not that I was expecting her. Her app event is supposed to last all day. The house feels empty, though, and I don't like it.

I find that long-sleeved T-shirt in the front seat, the one from Ralph's. After I bring the tree inside, I go to the bathroom and pull it on. I'm wearing it while I sit in my chair. I'm wearing it while I pour myself the first drink. I'm wearing it when I push the bottle away.

Because it's not the kind of comfort I want.

Chapter Ten

Kennedy

Harry is basically running on adrenaline as he drives us back to Labelle Manor. The ambulance pulled into the parking lot literally seconds after we turned out of it.

"This doesn't feel good," I say to myself. I keep thinking of the look on Rowan's face—the way he was trying to come off as stoic but wasn't quite managing it.

"Which part?"

I give him a look, and he sighs. "My anxiety is at about eleven right now. I'm trying to repress everything." He pauses, and then his lips tip up slightly. "Well, maybe not *everything*."

I turn in my seat to face him. "I could use some good news, so tell me Oliver kissed you. *Please.*"

"He did," Harry says, slapping the wheel. He jumps when the horn goes off. "And it was after that squirrel tap-danced on my head, so I know he actually likes me. He said life certainly seems more exciting with me around." He frowns. "I don't know what could be exciting about the whole gas thing. That was just embarrassing, but everyone always tells me to stop over-analyzing things, so I decided to let it go."

"Was the kiss good?" I ask.

"*Yes*," he says. "But the whole time, I had this phantom itch on my head from the squirrel. When he pulled away, I started scratching it like I was infested with lice." He grimaces. "Can you get lice from a squirrel?"

"No," I say. "You can only get head lice from another person." I shrug in response to his questioning look. "Despite what my mother thinks, infestations do happen at private schools."

He gives a full-body shudder as he continues to drive.

"Do you think Jay's going to be all right?" I ask in a small voice. "That was awful."

"He seemed all right. I mean, he was still moving and talking."

"Yeah," I say, but my mind is firmly fixed on Rowan. I hated leaving him like that, even though it had to happen.

"How'd it go with Rowan?" he asks, swiveling his head to study me quickly before returning his attention to the road. There's hardly anyone out, but Harry's a fastidious driver. "I mean, before his step-father had a heart attack."

I almost laugh, mostly because Harry didn't say it as a joke. But my mind summons Rowan again. There was a moment, before Jay came up to us, when I thought...

Of course, it's stupid to think any such thing. Rowan has made it pretty clear that I'm not his type, and I'm supposed to be dating several other men. Truthfully, I don't feel anything for any of them, but wouldn't it be unethical to pursue anyone else? Besides, while I might have a month off work, I *do* work in Chicago, and Rowan's life is very firmly rooted in Highland Hills.

"Kennedy?" Harry asks, and I glance back at him, lifting my fingers to my lips.

"He's different than I thought," I say, because I don't want to make Harry worry. This show's success is important to him—and to me, although for different reasons.

"I told you he takes some warming up. He comes off as a grumpy jerk..." He pauses. "And he *is* grumpy. But he's not a jerk. At least not most of the time."

I laugh. "A beautiful attribution."

I consider telling him about Kerry and the incredibly awkward phone call I had with her, but Rowan wouldn't want any gossip going around. While I trust Harry, he's someone who enjoys sharing good stories so much he might not be able to help himself.

Once we get back to Labelle Manor, Harry sneaks me upstairs to my room, where I've been supposedly holed up all day with my food poisoning complaint. It feels strange to be alone right now, with five thousand thoughts pounding through my head, but Harry doesn't stay. I know being around me is probably ratcheting up his nerves after everything that happened at the Christmas tree farm, and I'm supposed to be sick. I'm there for all of ten minutes before someone knocks.

Rowan, my mind supplies, even though logic dictates that it's much too soon to expect him. I fly over to the door, but as soon as I start opening it, the person on the other side pulls it shut with such force I nearly fly into it face first.

"Excuse me?" I call out with plenty of attitude.

"I'm sorry, my peach," says a voice that very clearly belongs to Jonah. "I wanted to bring you some gifts, but I don't want to get too close in case it's something other than food poisoning. You might be infectious, and I'm very sensitive to gastric complaints."

I make a face at no one, but at least this means I don't have to open the door and talk to him.

"But we can still talk through the door," he suggests.

My air-scowl deepens. "I'm too unwell to talk."

"Oh," he says. "Oh. You need to use the bathroom. I see. Well. I hope my gifts will make your time on the porcelain throne more pleasant."

A laugh escapes me before I can rein it in.

"Are you crying, Kennedy?" he asks.

100

"Yes," I say, my stomach hurting from the effort of holding in laughter. Then, because I need to get the full story so I can share it with my friends later, I add, "I hate being sick. How'd you get me gifts if you can't leave the house?"

"I paid one of the cameramen to do it." His tone shifts to the tattle-tale singsong of a small child. "Marcus has been paying them to bring in organic supplements."

I couldn't really care less.

"Okay," I say. "Thank you."

Please let him go.

"Be strong," he says, and I can imagine him laying his palm against the door, which fills me with an urge to laugh that's so strong my ab muscles are straining to contain.

"Thanks, Jonah. I will. I'll see you when I'm well again."

It occurs to me that I might be able to keep this charade going for a little while, at least long enough to miss the disastrous horseback riding session that's supposed to happen tomorrow. Harry said my brother and Tina will be visiting later this week. Maybe they'll know what's happening with Rowan.

He said he'll come. Maybe he'll come.

But I don't want to depend on it. Depending on it seems dangerous.

I hear Jonah's footsteps retreating, thank goodness, and I pop the door open to see what he brought me. There's a basket with a bright orange ribbon attached to the handle, and I bring it into the room, shutting the door. Laughter convulses through me when I see what's on top—a framed photo of Jonah. It's a glamor shot, done at what I'm guessing is his desk at work. Did he bring this with him from home? Has it been gracing his room until now?

I set the photo aside and laugh a little harder at the industrial-sized tin of breath mints. Other than that, there's a short biography about Jonah Highbury the First, which I will absolutely be reading, a monogrammed handkerchief like the one he had the other night, and a bottle of Scotch that appears to be from a family company.

That, I make use of right away. It's been a hell of a day. I'd prefer a glass of rosé, but desperate times call for desperate measures. I consider grabbing a glass, but it would undoubtedly scandalize Jonah —and my mother, for that matter—if I drank straight from the bottle. So I do.

I'm only a couple sips in when another knock lands on the door.

I flinch and cap the bottle, hiding it in my underwear drawer as if I'm a high schooler sneaking booze, even though I never *was* a high schooler sneaking booze.

It's probably still too early for Rowan, so I ask, "Who's there?"

"It's me," a man says. It's clearly someone who expects to be recognized by the pitch and timbre of his voice, but I'll be honest, I'm drawing a blank. Still, I don't want to offend him, especially since I don't know whom I'd be offending, so I step forward and give the door an experimental tug. This time no one pulls it shut.

Marcus is standing in the hall, dressed in a dark sweater that makes his blond hair look like spun gold. He's almost too good looking, and yet...I don't feel any desire to tug him into my room by the hem of his sweater. To be honest, I kind of just want him to go away. His presence is only a sliver more welcome than Jonah's—possibly even less, given that Jonah's basket amused me.

"You have a framed photo of Jonah?" he asks, glancing over my shoulder. His tone is half accusatory, half pissed off. Like he thinks Jonah and I are pulling off a long con.

Oh, for God's sake.

"Yes," I say, "didn't you run into him in the hallway? He just dropped off a gift basket *to make me feel better.*"

Maybe it's a little hypocritical to remind him that I'm supposed to be sick, but he presumably dropped by to check on me.

"And he gave you a framed photo of himself?" he asks, amused now.

"Don't take inspiration from that," I say, nodding to the dresser to my right. "There's only so much room for me to display things." The top is covered with what my mother would call bric-a-brac, her lips pursed in distaste, of course. Actually, most of the surfaces in the room are covered with more of the same.

"I was worried about you, Kennedy." He reaches for my arm, skimming his fingertips over my sweater, and disappointment wells in my stomach. It might as well be a cat batting at me. No tingles. No warmth.

When Rowan touched me, it felt like fireworks were exploding beneath my skin.

My mood sours further.

"Well, you don't need to worry about me." I step over to the basket and lift out the book, waving it at him wildly. "I have fantastic reading material. Now, I really have to—"

"Oh," he takes a step back. "Your stomach's acting up again, huh? Sorry. I didn't mean to make you uncomfortable."

Good God, what did Harry tell them, anyway?

"Yeah, I'm feeling pretty lousy," I say, because at least that much is true. "Thanks for stopping by, though."

"Hey, do you think you'll be better in time for horseback riding tomorrow?"

"Maybe."

His mouth stretches into a grin that should be devastating but is only mildly pleasant. "You might not want to miss it. I have a surprise prepared for Jonah."

If he thinks that will make me want to be there, he doesn't know me very well. All the same, I'm ready for him to leave, so I smile and say, "I guess I'd better try to improve, then, huh? I'll check in with Harry in the morning."

He beams at me and waves, then says, *"Parting is such sweet sorrow that I shall say goodnight till it be morrow."*

My smile feels as fake as a Halloween mask. I mean, it wouldn't be surprising if Jonah thought it was romantic to quote *Romeo and Juliet* to a woman, but I'd had higher hopes for Marcus. I can't decide whether it's better or worse that he didn't perform it for the cameras. Actually...

My gaze flicks behind him, and I catch sight of a camera at the curve of the hall.

Did both visits get filmed?

Of course they did. Where did I think Jonah got all that stuff anyway? Either he brought it with him, or the PAs helped him acquire it.

I'm upset, without quite understanding why I'm upset. Wasn't getting filmed the point?

"Well, thanks," I say. "I'll see you soon."

At the last instant, he pulls a single flower from behind his back. My first reaction is confusion. Has he been holding that behind his back the whole time we've been talking? My second reaction is annoyance. Because all of this feels so completely processed, it's like a chicken nugget of a moment. I don't blame Marcus. He's just doing as he's told. It just... I can't say it takes me out of the moment, since I wasn't particularly feeling it anyway, but it's a wakeup call nonetheless.

I take the flower. I smile. I act my part too.

Needless to say, all the guys come by at some point throughout the afternoon. Jeff brings me a contraband holiday romance book, so he is *de facto* my favorite. They all come with offerings, in fact, one of them giving me a heated blanket that is also very welcome. By the time someone knocks just before ten, after I changed into my pajamas and rejected most of my dinner tray—my stomach too twisted up by thoughts of Rowan and Jay to eat much—I'm sick and tired of guests. All of them have come and gone, anyway, so what is this? A group lullaby singalong? I open the door quickly, eager to see them off, only to find Rowan Mayberry behind it.

And he's wearing the same shirt I am and carrying a large reusable shopping bag.

"You're wearing my shirt," I blurt.

"We match," he says, the corners of his mouth lifting slightly. "My sisters would give me so much shit about this."

I glance both ways down the hall, then drag him inside by the arm.

It's also not lost on me that something inside of me has started to glow, like holiday lights flickering into brightness.

It isn't until he's inside, the door closed after him, that I get a good eyeful of him. He looks like crap—tired and sad, almost defeated.

"Oh my God," I say, my hand lifting to my lips. "Did Jay...is he?"

"They think he's going to be okay," Rowan says with a sigh, then paces to the opposite side of the room and leans against the frame of the big picture window. There are low book cases beneath it, covered with more crap. He reminds me of the lion I saw at the Chicago Zoo when Olive's mother brought us there. "They're going to keep him for a few days, though, maybe a week. To be honest, I don't really want to talk about Jay right now. I wanted to distract myself from all that for a little while."

I swallow. I should tell him about Kerry. He needs to know, doesn't he? If I fail to say anything, he'll find out another way, most likely when she brutally tells him herself.

"There's one thing I need to fill you in on before we shove it onto the shelf."

"Oh?" he asks, gripping the top of the short built-in bookshelf with the hand not holding the bag. His knuckles look white. It's obvious he knows this is bad news, or at least that he's had enough bad news in one day that he can't imagine it being anything else.

"It's Kerry," I say in a burst of words. "I did talk to her. I know it's wrong to lie, but..." I swallow. "It sounds like she left Jay, and she's on vacation. I have no idea what happened between them, but she was really dismissive, even when I told her about the heart attack. I don't think she plans on visiting him."

"Fuck," Rowan says, his face transforming into a grimace that's almost intimidating, even though it's not meant for me. "My little sister said she thought something was off between them. Dammit. This isn't good."

"No," I agree. Then, because he should know exactly what he's dealing with, I add, "She didn't seem very nice."

His mouth lifts a little, in a pantomime of a smile. "Guess he's got a type, huh?"

"Don't we all?"

"What's your type, Kennedy?" he asks, his eyes hooded as he studies me. "Suited Man Number...Six, is it?"

"Very funny," I say, feeling a burst of self-consciousness. "I think it's safe to say they're your grandmother's type, not mine. She's the one who chose them."

"For you," he says. But then he gives a nod of acknowledgment. "She does like to think she knows what's best for everyone. Doesn't mean she's right."

He glances around, then does a double take when he notices Jonah's framed photo sitting on the low bookshelf with the other tchotchkes. Eyebrows raised, he says, "What's with the beauty shot? Is Jonah the new front-runner?"

A scowl slips over my face. "Absolutely not. He brought it by because he thought it would make me feel better. I guess Harry told everyone I have food poisoning, but they were all acting like it was giardia. Maybe he figured food poisoning wouldn't be enough to make them stay away, so he implied it was something worse."

He laughs ruefully and shakes his head. "Sounds like Harry." He adds a shrug. "Sounds like Jonah, too."

"All of the guys came by," I say, mostly because he *did* say he wanted to be distracted. When I see the salty look my words put on his face, I rush to add, "For the cameras of course."

Silence hangs between us for a few moments, and it's not the comfortable kind. It's loaded with the strange tension between us, with the knowledge of what happened to his stepfather today. With the question of why Rowan is here and what we'll do now that he is.

I'm the one who breaks it. "I have a bottle of scotch in my drawer. Unfortunately, Jonah's the one who gave it to me."

"I think we can overlook that," Rowan says, his lips lifting. "You know, I didn't take you for a scotch drinker."

"I didn't either," I admit. "But I'm realizing that I like a lot of things I didn't think I would."

It sounds like a leading comment, and honestly, I'm not totally sure I didn't mean it that way. Seeing him now, after spending all afternoon sending away one rich jerk after another, I know that there's one man who holds my interest presently. And it's not any of the six who are vying to be my husband.

I can't keep him. I know that. If nothing else, it would destroy the show, and if the show implodes, then so does my big plan for Leto's Hands. And yet...I can't help wondering if I can give him—and myself—a different sort of distraction tonight.

Chapter Eleven

Rowan

Kennedy Littlefield looks positively touchable tonight, dressed in her Ralph's shirt and a pair of shorts so small you'd almost need a microscope to find them, not that I'm complaining. Her hair is down around her face, her blue eyes soft and sweet, untouched by makeup. Some women I know would have shrieked to have a man show up when they were in their pajamas, but her face is clean for bed, and she doesn't seem fazed. Of course, why would she be? She's even more gorgeous in the moments when she steps down from her pedestal. I've noticed it before now, on a few stolen occasions—her dress unzipped down her luscious back, her head tipped up to look at the tree at Ralph's, her hair captured in that knit cap.

Don't think like that, you dumbass.

I'm not here to ogle Kennedy...except, if that's not why I'm here, why *am* I here?

I'm not totally sure, to be honest. Other than I told her I'd come. Of course, I could have just as easily pulled Harry aside after he came home, passed on what little news I had, and that could have been that. It's just...I wanted to comfort her in person. After all, what happened today was no normal clusterfuck. A woman like Kennedy has probably been shielded from the world. It's likely the first time she's watched a man keel over. Hell, I'm a part-time fireman, and I've only seen it happen once. Most of our calls are for kitchen fires, smoke, or kittens caught in trees.

I watch as she pulls the bottle of scotch from the drawer. I expect her to take out some crystal goblets—I guess my grandmother or one of the producers pulled some sort of partnership with a crystal company, because it's everywhere in this house—but she just sits on a floor pillow beneath the big picture window and nods for me to do the same. I shrug and follow suit.

This whole room is ridiculous, not that I expected anything different. Each of the Labelle's suites has a theme, and this one is a princess room. There are little crystal slippers, a ceramic horse-drawn carriage, and other expensive dust-collectors arranged on top of those short bookcases that line the room, along with every other available surface. It's strangely appropriate yet inappropriate, because Kennedy is most definitely a grown woman.

I watch, my mouth dry, as she opens the bottle and takes a swig. Blood channels to my dick at the sight, and I plop another pillow onto my lap because I don't want to scare her off.

When she holds the bottle out to me, I hesitate, and her eyes widen. "Oh, sorry. Did you want a glass? We can get glasses."

"No," I say, my tone harsher than intended. Part of me is desperate for that bottle—for the comfort of what's inside of it and also the pleasure of putting my lips where hers have been. If I can't kiss her or slide those little shorts off her hips, at least I can do that. I take a slug of the scotch, then make a face. "What the fuck is this?"

She laughs so hard a snort escapes her, which makes *me* laugh.

"I...think...Jonah's family makes it," she says through more gales of laughter. "I didn't think it was very good either, but I don't know what scotch is supposed to taste like."

"Not like this," I say, shaking the bottle, but then I shrug and take another sip. It doesn't improve upon acquaintance. I cringe. "Nope. It's worse the second time around."

"You're right, but I do like the burn," she says, reaching for the bottle. When our fingers brush, another pulse of attraction works through me. I tell myself it's just because it's been too long since I've had a woman. I almost believe it, but then she asks, "What's in the bag?"

"Contraband," I say, smiling at her. "It's for you." My smile fades, though, because I don't like what it implies that I brought this to her. That's the kind of thing a putz would do—a man who's let himself be Cupid's bitch. It's definitely not a smart action for a man who would very much like to no longer be known as Cupid, please and thank you.

"Oh?" she asks, setting the bottle down and reaching for the bag. I hand it over and watch as she pulls the little fake tree out of the bag. When she looks at me, there are tears in her eyes.

Shit, I didn't want her to cry.

"Did I do something wrong?" I ask, straightening.

"No." She lifts a hand to straighten one of the branches, which went askew in the bag. There are little ornaments that came on it, plus battery-operated lights. "You did something exactly right." She flicks the lights on, then looks up at me, the soft glow playing over her features. "Thank you, Rowan. *Thank you*. I can't believe you did this for me after the day you've had."

"It's not a big deal," I say, suddenly self-conscious. Even more so when she sets it on the ground and leans forward to hug me. Her soft cheek and long, silky hair brush against me, but she's leaning back again all too soon. For a second, I'm speechless, then I mumble, "I saw they were selling them over at Wheeler's Market, and it's on the way."

"Well, it's a big deal to me," she says. "I love it."

Her eyes are shiny, and I'm afraid she's going to cry. I'm no good at comforting crying women. It flusters me. It brings out my incompetence. So I blurt, "You'll have to hide it."

She smiles, looking back down at the tree and fiddling with one of the wire branches. "I like the idea of having a contraband tree."

"A contraband tree and crappy scotch," I say. "You're a rebel, aren't you?"

She grins at me with shining eyes. "Maybe I am."

I'm tempted to ask her to rebel with me.

I'm tempted to tell her that I needed a way to forget tonight, and something led me to her.

Instead, I grab the shitty scotch from where she put it on the floor and take another pull from the bottle.

"Maybe you should help me rebel," she says, and I nearly spit the mouthful of scotch out. "Why don't we play Truth or Dare?"

I nearly choke. "What are we, two girls at a sleepover?" I ask, lifting my brows.

"No, we're a man and a woman at a possible sleepover," she says, making a gesture to match mine.

Fuck, I'm glad I grabbed that pillow.

"You know I can't stay over here, Kennedy," I say, trying to sound firm. It's obvious that we've both felt the draw between us, but that doesn't mean I need to listen to it.

"Sure, but it's only just after ten. No one's going to come check on me until morning."

The thought of staying here until morning, of sneaking around with the princess of the show while the male contestants are off bickering and in-fighting pleases me more than it should. So does the thought of spending more time in her company, of watching this other side of her unfold.

I think again of Zach, and of what he'd do to me if he knew I have a boner for his sister.

"Your brother and I are kind of friendly, you know," I blurt.

"I'm a big girl, Rowan," she says with a sassiness that makes my blood boil. "I'm perfectly capable of playing Truth or Dare with another adult."

I don't actually want to leave. I certainly don't want to talk to anyone in my family or to Jay. I've called the hospital to check on him, and they said he's been sleeping a lot but that there's nothing to currently concern them. The news about his wife is shitty, for certain, but it doesn't make me feel more inclined to run back to the hospital. Maybe that means I'm a coward. If it does, so be it.

Ivy has bought a plane ticket, or so I gather from the texts she's sent, and she'll be in town tomorrow. I still haven't spoken with Bryn, Holly, or Willow. I'm guessing my phone is blowing up with messages from them by now, but I don't feel compelled to check. That probably means I'm an asshole in addition to being a coward. I *did* give my sisters the information they need, including where Jay is being kept, and I assured them that both he and I are okay.

I haven't told them about his secret. I'm not sure I'll tell anyone. Except I feel it beating into me like it's a hammer thumping my head.

"Okay," I say, through a scratchy throat. "But you go first, Princess."

"Shouldn't we spin the bottle to see who goes first?" she asks, looking up at me playfully with those big blue eyes.

"Let's not mix genres," I say, moving the pillow in my lap because it's pretty damn uncomfortable at this point.

"Okay," she says softly. "Truth."

"Which of the guys in the house is the front-runner?"

Maybe I want to know who my competition is. I don't know. I probably should have asked her some other shit, like what she'd like me to do to her, because if this Truth or Dare bullshit isn't an invitation, then I've completely lost my touch with women.

If Kennedy's annoyed by my presumptuousness, it doesn't show. "I don't know," she answers. "I'm not vibing with any of them, to be honest. So I'll probably just go with whoever Harry and your grandmother think would be the best choice for the show." She makes a disgusted face. "Even if it's Jonah."

Her answer pleases me more than it should, especially since I have a natural horror for the idea of letting my grandmother do anything.

Kennedy cocks her head, studying me. "There's someone else who's caught my interest."

My pulse thrums faster. My dick twitches. "I don't know how to break it to you, but Oliver's gay."

"You *know* who I'm talking about."

I do. But I'm less certain of why she's calling it out in the open. Isn't it as obvious to her as it is to me that anything between us would be a non-starter? She lives in Chicago; I hate big cities. She's from a rich, cultured family; I'm a handyman and part-time fireman with a high school degree. Then, the kicker—she's the star of a reality TV show in which *my grandmother* has set her up with several eligible bachelors.

This is not the stuff a long-lasting relationship is made of.

But maybe that's not what Princess is asking for...

If she wants a different kind of fun, the kind that comes with no strings, I'm more than interested...

I open my mouth to say something, but she thrusts the bottle of shitty scotch into my hand. "Your turn," she says.

"What if I don't want anymore?"

"Then you're wise. I meant your turn for Truth or Dare." She swallows, and my gaze tracks her long neck. The shirt covers too damn much.

Is she going to dare me take it off? To kiss me?

I want both of those things to happen, but not because of a damn dare.

So I swallow and say, "Truth."

Is it my imagination, or did her face fall?

Definitely not my imagination. Still, I can tell she's thinking hard, really pouring herself into it, like this is an exam she's determined to pass. "What's your favorite hobby?" she finally asks.

"Other than cutting down Christmas trees?" I smile. "I'm a handyman because I like to tinker. Ever since I was a little kid, I've liked building things."

"What's your favorite thing to build?"

"I build car models and give them working motors."

"I'd like to see one of those," she says, and I think she actually means it.

"Truth or dare," I ask, peering at her. Wondering if she'll go for the dare this time. Wondering what I'll ask her to do if she does.

"Truth."

A smile flashes across my face. "What's your Christmas wish, Princess?" I'm not sure why I'm asking, other than that there's something sweet about the way she loves Christmas—the honest and deep joy she takes in it.

She tips her head up a little, giving me a better look at her pink lips, then says, "When I was a kid, I always wished Santa would bring me a puppy. I must have written him two dozen letters about it, like that kid in *A Christmas Story*, but of course he never brought one. My mother thinks dogs are dirty, and my dad thinks there's no point to domesticated animals that aren't eaten."

A dry laugh pulls out of me. "Brutal but not without logic. We didn't have pets either. My mother and grandmother didn't want to have to clean up after us, let alone anyone else."

"Brutal," she repeats, her mouth tipping slightly into a smile. "Did you want one?"

"When I was little," I say, leaning my head back against the shelves. "I used to like Tintin, running around and getting into adventures by himself. He always had that dog."

"I can imagine you like that," she says, "rampaging through Highland Hills with a dog. You know, that's how I knew that there was no Santa Claus," she adds with a touch of sadness. "Because my puppy never came."

"Do you have a dog now?" I ask, wondering about her life in Chicago. Is she different there? If we'd met there, would there still have been this strange energy arcing between us?

"I don't," she says in a small voice. "I guess I don't really trust myself. My parents weren't any good at taking care of us. What if I'm just like them?"

I feel a surge of anger, not at her, but at the assholes who made her question herself. I haven't known her long, but it doesn't take a long acquaintance with Kennedy Littlefield to recognize that she's a nurturer—the kind of person who'd find an injured walking stick insect and try to nurse it back to health.

"They shouldn't have made you feel that way," I say. "You'd do great with a dog sidekick. I can see it now." I nudge her arm, wanting the excuse to touch her. "Here, help me form the picture. You'd want—"

"A bulldog," she says, laughing at my expression of surprise. "What? I always thought all the extra folds of skin were cute. They look like little aliens. But *cute* aliens."

I can't help laughing. I'm surprised I'm even capable of laughter after the bullshit day I've had, but being with her makes me feel lighter. "Okay, you want a cute alien. I'm getting a really good picture of you now." My laughter dries up at the look of longing on her face. "You should get that dog, Princess."

"Maybe I will," she says, smiling. "I've always liked the thought of having one around. It can get so lonely, living by myself. I love the thought
of having a little dog to curl up with when I'm watching movies or reading books."

I wouldn't mind curling up with her, although it would be stupid to say so.

"Maybe you should ask Santa for a puppy."

"Maybe I will," she says. Her expression serious, she adds, "It would be nice if he could act quickly on it, because this house would feel a whole lot less creepy if I had a little friend to keep me company."

"You think it's creepy?" I ask, leaning toward her. I can't help myself, it's as if she's a warm fire in the hearth.

"Absolutely. What would you call it?"

"Self-indulgent and silly. Ugly. Overly large. But not scary."

She laughs. "I guess it's all those things, although I'll be honest, my parents' house isn't much smaller."

"No," I say. "I don't imagine it is." It's a good reminder of how different our lives are, of how unlikely we would be as any sort of pairing, even for a night of fun. Still, when she looks at me with a pointed challenge in her eyes and says, "Your turn" again, I find myself saying, "Dare."

Her smile is radiant, and I feel like a god for being the one who brought it out in her—a real smile. The ones she flashes for the cameras are proper and pretty, but they don't transform her whole face—her whole being—the way this one does. "I was hoping you would say that."

My blood pumps faster, hotter as I wait for her to choose what she wants me to do—hopefully to her.

So her next words surprise me.

"Did you know there's a basement pool?"

"Yes," I say. While I've studied the blueprints for this place, trying to think of the best ways to sabotage the show without potentially hurting someone or causing the kind of damage that can't be fixed, I already knew that bit of information.

"It's in a heated room," she says, grinning. "What do you say to a swim?"

I'd rather stay in here, with her, but she seems so excited by the idea, just like she was about my damn Christmas tree, that I don't want to say no. "I don't have a suit with me."

She gives me a look, then blushes and says, "You could wear your clothes, but it wouldn't be much of a dare if you did. From my understanding, dares usually include the kind of thing a person wouldn't normally do." She licks her lips. "Like skinny dipping."

I've done plenty of skinny dipping in my day, back when we were kids and used to drive out to Waller Creek together to party, but I can tell *she* hasn't. From the way she's talking, I'll bet she hasn't played many games of Truth or Dare either. Beneath the excitement this stirs, because I absolutely want to see this woman naked, I feel a little sting of resentment. I suspect she's using me the way pretty, polished girls have used me before—as their little bit of blue-collar fun before they dive back into their lives. But if I'm going to be used, it might as well be by someone like Kennedy.

"As you wish," I say. Something about Kennedy makes me feel like the farm boy in *The Princess Bride*, maybe because she's so obviously out of my league. "You got towels?"

"In my en suite," she says, her voice breathy, like she can't quite believe what she just said but also doesn't want to take it back. "I'd better hide the Christmas tree before we go."

I have to laugh at that. "Princess, if we're found in the pool together, your Christmas display will be the least of your problems. Especially if we're skinny dipping."

"You have a point." She looks conflicted, though, like she can't stand the thought of the little tree getting confiscated.

I smile at her. "I'll hide it. Get the towels."

When she slips into the bathroom, I tuck the tree into her closet, behind her long, silky gowns. I'll see her wearing them, I suppose, but from afar. She'll probably have one of them on the first time she kisses Marcus or Colton. Jonah or Jeff, Quinn or Ray. I've unwillingly watched dating shows—blame having four sisters—and I know how this works. At least a few of them will kiss her before it's over, a thought that makes me want to beat their faces in the way Cole's brother did to Meatball the other night.

Kennedy's not mine, though. Not for longer than one night, so I don't have any damn right to get pissed about that.

Kennedy comes out with the towels and flinches a little at the sight of me. "Are you okay?"

"I'm fine," I say harshly.

"You look pissed off."

"I always look pissed off."

"Not always," she says, surprising me by balancing the towels in one arm and reaching out to touch my face. Her fingers trace the line between my eyebrows. "You've laughed at least a few times today." Then she blanches. "I mean. Obviously not after what happened with Jay, but…"

"I'm not upset," I say, capturing her hand and holding it. I like the feeling of it in mine. "I'm enough of an adult to know people are perfectly capable of smiling and laughing when something awful is happening in their lives. It doesn't make you an asshole to find good things where you can and enjoy them. There's always a seed of something good, even in a shit bagel."

She smiles at this. "Leave it to you to start with something profound and end with a shit bagel."

I'm tempted to tell her she doesn't know me well enough to make pronouncements like that, but she has a point. Besides, I don't want to argue with her. I want to be good to her—to show her that maybe tonight can be a bright spot for both of us.

I want to believe it can be enough.

"Let's go," I say. She takes a step toward the door, but I stop her with our still entwined hands. "Follow me, Princess. I know which way to go so we don't get followed."

Chapter Twelve

Kennedy

I creep out of the room, following Rowan with my heart hammering in my chest. He released my hand so he could lead the way, and I miss the way he held it—firm and capable, but gentle, as if he was aware of the physical power imbalance between us and wanted to make me comfortable within it.

I can't believe I told him we'd go skinny dipping, but he said he wanted a distraction, didn't he? I don't want to pretend I'm doing this just for him, though, because that would be both wrong and inaccurate. In truth, I know I will have limited opportunities to spend time with Rowan Mayberry, and even fewer to potentially get him naked. After seeing what happened to Jay earlier, remembering what happened to Olive's grandmother, I have a new appreciation for how short life is—and for how much of it I have yet to experience.

And, fine, I really, really want Rowan to at least kiss me. I've never kissed a man with a beard before, and I'd like to know what it feels like.

Another excuse, Kennedy. Admit it, you just want to kiss him.

All right, I do.

"Where are we going?" I whisper to him as he leads the way

confidently through the house's winding hallways, into the back, where we haven't done any filming.

"The servants' quarters," he says glibly. "There's a back stairway I'm pretty sure no one will be using."

"Good thinking," I murmur, hefting the towels in my right hand. "Why do you know this house so well?"

Something passes over his expression, but I can't read it. Possibly because he's peering straight ahead, looking to the left and right every so often, as attuned to his environment as if he's on a top-secret mission.

"I helped out a bit while they got set up here," he says. "And I grew up in this town. Everyone's seen parts of 'Labelle Manor' as they're calling it these days." A small smile flits across his lips. "We used to dare each other to break into the basement when we were high school kids."

"But wouldn't you get in trouble?" I ask, scandalized, even though I know that's exactly what he expects, and maybe wants.

"They used to go to Aspen every winter for a skiing trip. The challenge was to swim a lap in the pool without getting caught, then leave."

"And you did this?"

"I never got caught," he says, glancing back at me with a smile. "You're in good hands."

"I don't know about that. You just admitted to breaking and entering." The look on his face suggests I'm a goody two-shoes, which is probably an accurate assessment, but it also annoys me, so I continue, "If you're going to break in somewhere, it's smarter not to admit to it."

A laugh escapes him before he swallows the rest of it, obviously trying not to make much noise, even though I know the guys are quartered on the opposite side of the house. The production assistants and cameramen are all staying here too. Only Nana Mayberry and Harry are allowed to come and go.

He glances back at me before facing forward again. "I'll bet you've never broken any rules, Kennedy Littlefield."

I make a sound of affront. "Not true."

"Oh, yeah?" He peers around a corner, then nods and motions me onward. "What rules have you broken?"

"My parents didn't want me to come here," I say.

"Them and me both," he says, with a smirk. But he must have seen the stricken look on my face in his peripheral vision because suddenly he's turning toward me and taking my shoulders in his hands. Heat soaks into me from his palms, burning through the thin material of my shirt. "I didn't mean it like that. I just...I wish we could have met under different circumstances. Like, if you came to town to visit Zach."

"You think he'd be cool with you flirting with me?"

"Absolutely not," he says with a smirk. "But we've already agreed that I'm not intelligent."

As if to punctuate the remark, he shifts his hand from my shoulder to my jaw, tipping my chin up to him. I have a moment to take in his eyes—deep blue and full of heat—and then he lowers his lips to mine. It starts out exploratory, but there's an instant spark, like something lost has clicked into place, and I let the towels tumble out of my other hand so I can wrap my arms around his neck and draw him closer. His hand sifts through my hair, using it as a way to grip me closer. His lips are demanding, just like the man, and his short beard rasps against my skin in a way that will probably leave a mark. Is it wrong of me that I'd like it to?

He pulls back, looking at me. "I shouldn't have done that."

"Are you saying you regret it?" I ask, annoyed...because *I* don't regret it.

"No. That brings us back to me being stupid."

"I wish you'd stop calling yourself that."

He kisses me again, softly this time, then lets me go and stoops to pick up the towels. To my amusement, he folds them. "We'd better keep going. Don't want to get caught by the hall monitors."

I nearly snicker because it does feel like we're children being naughty, and I can't say I don't like it. I wasn't given many choices as a child—I was told which schools I'd go to, what I'd wear to them, and who I was allowed to invite over. It's nice to have this stolen experience gifted to me, a present nearly as welcome as the Christmas tree that brought tears to my eyes. I feel them pricking at me again while I look at him. Because Rowan's stepfather had a heart attack today, and he still took the time to think about me.

"You're right," I say, trying to take the towels from him. He holds on. "We don't want to get caught before we even get to the pool."

He gives me a weighing look. "It's my dare. You don't have to do it."

A laugh tears out of me, then my eyes widen, and I lift a hand to cover my mouth. "You want to skinny dip by yourself?" I ask in a whisper.

"There's no point in whispering now," he says in an undertone. "You've already laughed loudly enough to wake up the bones this house is buried on."

I'd be offended, but there's a thread of amusement running beneath his words. Besides...

"Bones?"

He smirks at me. "That's what they say. It might be a scurrilous rumor, but..."

"Wait a second, you got on my case about using the word strumpet, and here you are saying scurrilous?"

His smirk widens. "So I have bad judgment *and* I'm a hypocrite."

"Why would you want to go skinny dipping by yourself? Why would anyone?"

"I don't," he says, "but I'm not going to use it as an opportunity to corner you into it. If you want to skinny-dip with me, Kennedy, then you're the one who's going to get in that water. I'm not throwing you in."

It's half challenge, half vow, and he's peering at me in the dark house with an intensity that makes me wet. I can't remember the last time anyone ever affected me like this—with just a glance. No, that's a lie, I've only ever felt this kind of attraction with my ex, Brandon. So I know just how dangerous it can be. Still, instead of arcing away from him like he's a flame that might burn me, I take a step toward him.

"Okay. But what are you waiting for? I was promised a pool."

"What Princess wants, Princess gets," he says.

I don't quite like the words. It's reminiscent of the way he acted toward me the night we met, after he zipped up my dress, but I don't call him on it. I just follow, feeling the warmth of his big body, remembering the way his lips felt against mine, his scruff. I shouldn't want more, but what harm would it do?

He's certainly not looking for a relationship, at least not with someone like me, and I've already decided that I can't see myself with any of the guys on the show. They're not here for romance anyway. If they were, they wouldn't always be so concerned about the presence—or lack thereof—of cameras. I won't be breaking any hearts if I let Harry choose the "winner" and only act sweet to him on tape.

I follow Rowan to a lush carpet, then into a back hallway that's not nearly so nice. It's quiet back here, almost oppressively so, and I hear every one of Rowan's soft steps—and every one of my own, although I'll be the first to admit that I'm less graceful than the man in front of me. How did a big man get so soft on his feet?

"You don't hunt, do you?" I ask in sudden horror.

His laugh rumbles through me. "No, Kennedy. Not every bearded mountain man is a hunter."

"I wasn't stereotyping you," I say, feeling a touch of righteous indignation. "Though you certainly like to stereotype *me*. It's just…

you're really light on your feet. I wondered if you learned that from hunting."

He stops and turns toward me, contrition and something else in his eyes. "You're right. Do you want me to stop calling you Princess?"

"No," I admit. "I kind of like it."

He laughs, then rubs his chin. "I'm light on my feet because my grandmother didn't like noise," he says. "All of us kids are, except for my sister Holly, who got louder because she doesn't like it when people tell her what to do. And Ivy, I guess, because she didn't have to spend much time at our grandmother's place. The rest of us got left there a lot. Like I said, my mother's not much of one."

Sympathy grips at me, but he's already shaking his head slightly.

"Don't feel sorry for me. I'm not a dick because I had shitty parents. That part came naturally."

Still, I reach out to touch his arm. "I'm sorry all the same. I wasn't allowed to run around either. Kids should be allowed to be kids, don't you think?"

"Yeah," he says, but he's clearly eager to drop the subject because he turns and keeps walking until he reaches a door. Opening it, he reveals the back staircase. It's dark, with only a faint glow coming from the bottom, presumably from some sort of nightlight. It provides enough illumination for me to see the enormous spiderweb waving in the top right corner of the doorway.

I squeal.

"Seems to be a theme of our day," Rowan says lightly, but his expression darkens, suggesting he's thinking of the other part of his day. I wonder if I should encourage him to leave, to go to his stepfather and his sisters, but for all I know, he's not allowed to stay over at the hospital anyway. He's not a blood relative, or even a legal relative anymore, whatever the heart might have to say about it.

Not your place, whispers a voice in my head. Besides, if I'm being honest with myself, I don't want him to leave. I want this moment with him—this distraction for both of us. *Later,* I decide. *I'll tell him later.*

Rowan grabs one of the towels and uses it to brush away the spiderweb.

"That's your towel," I say.

His smile is barely illuminated in the blackness. "We already established that I might be the only one going in."

But we're both going in. He knows it. I know it.

He leads the way down the stairs, and when I close the door behind me, he illuminates the path forward with his phone, which makes the whole undertaking less intimidating. Through another few corridors, we finally reach a closed door labeled "pool room," as if the people who live here need it to identify where to go.

"Ready?" he asks me, his brows winging up.

"Ready," I confirm.

He opens the door and flicks on the lights. I step inside, shutting the door behind me, only to find a pool that's been drained down to the concrete.

"Well, that's anticlimactic," he says.

I'd laugh, but the sinking feeling inside me tells me just how much I wanted to see Rowan Mayberry swim naked.

"Still," he throws the towels down, then shrugs his shirt over his head and throws it to the ground. The sight of his bare chest makes me gasp. A few of the men I've dated have worked out, but none of them have looked like this. He's tan and muscular, his chest sprinkled with dark hair. He's every bit a man. "Dare's a dare." He takes another few steps toward the ladder, toeing off his shoes, then pauses to take off his socks.

"You're not really going to get naked and go in there, are you?" I ask, even though I kind of want him to.

He stops, his hand on the button of his pants, and starts laughing. "No. But you should have seen the look on your face." He retreats to grab his shoes, then his socks, but before he can go for the T-shirt, I grab it.

"You know, I think I've decided I'm taking this back."

"Oh yeah?" he says, eyebrows cocked, his shoes hanging off the fingers of one hand, the socks now stuffed inside. "That's a dirty trick. If a man did that, you'd say he was a dick."

I feel myself blushing, because he's absolutely right, and I hold the shirt out to him.

"I was just fucking with you," he says, waving it off. "I like that you want me to walk around shirtless." He takes my hand—the one not holding his shirt hostage—and tugs me toward the ladder leading down into the empty pool. "What do you say we go sit down there to finish our game?"

"I say yes," I tell him.

I let him lead me to the ladder. He goes down first, then lifts up his arms for me.

"You think you can bear my weight like that?"

He gives me a look that questions my intelligence, and he probably has a point. He has the muscles of someone who uses them for work *and* play, a thought that makes my mind take a deeper dive into the gutter.

So I get down and let him lift me into the pool with seemingly zero effort.

"We should have brought the scotch," I say as he sets me on my feet. I don't particularly miss it, but I want it because my nerves are rubbed raw, being down here with Rowan, remembering his mouth against mine and wanting it to explore other places.

"No, I think we made the right call about the scotch. Jonah's family should have stuck to their generational wealth. Work isn't for them."

I laugh, but I'm very aware that he hasn't backed away from me. Looking up at him to make sure it's okay, I lift my hands to touch his chest. It's hard and hot beneath my palms.

He hisses in a breath.

"I think it's my turn for Truth or Dare," I say.

"Let me guess," he says, making no move to shift my hands as they slowly explore the expanse of his chest. "You want a dare. I can see it in your eyes."

"No," I say as I continue to glide my fingers over his bare skin, unable to stop myself. I look up into his eyes and find them scrutinizing me. There's a flame of need in them, and I feel an answering one inside myself.

You know where this kind of wanting can lead...

Still, I can't bring myself to care.

I hold his gaze, then say, "Truth. You wouldn't dare me to do what I want to do. You'd probably ask me to give Jonah peroxide shampoo or something."

His laughter sounds surprised. "That would be pretty damn funny," he says finally. "But what makes you think I'd ask you to do that and not to take off your shirt? It would be no more than you made me do."

I smile at him. "You're right, but you still wouldn't."

His expression turns serious, maybe even a little annoyed. "I'm no saint, Kennedy. I can't have you thinking that."

"I should hope not," I say, my heart beating out of my chest. Maybe that's why I lay my palm flat against *his* heart. His eyes are like black holes as he reaches up and holds my palm in place. I can feel his heart beating fast too. Relief courses through my veins, a tonic. I'm not the only one who's affected by what's happening between us. I'm not the only one driven half mad by it. *"Truth,"* I repeat.

"What are we doing here?" he asks, his hand still holding mine, his eyes pinning me.

"I know what I hope we're doing," I say. And I reach up onto my toes and kiss him.

Chapter Thirteen

Rowan

I'm being an idiot, and I know it.

There are other words that would also fit: asshole, dick, dumbass.

I don't care.

Kennedy's lips are sweet, soft, and hungry, and it would take a man in possession of an iron will to push her away. After the way she's been running her hands up and down my chest, my willpower is as nonexistent as the water in this pool. There's no question she feels my hard-on through my jeans when I pull her to me, but she snuggles closer, sending more blood pulsing to my dick. This woman makes me lose my grip on reality, and I don't mind one bit. In fact, it might be exactly what I need right now.

I suck in her bottom lip and let myself trail a hand down her back to touch the curve of her ass. It's round and soft, and I keep my hand there as she grinds against my dick. It's obvious she wants to form a better acquaintance with it. Fuck.

I shouldn't be doing this.

I kiss her harder and lift my hand up from her ass, because I'm getting all kinds of ideas about pushing her pants down, and wrap her long hair around my fist. I angle her head to the side and then lean in to kiss her jaw and then her neck, noticing that she must spray perfume there—a soft, floral scent that's perfect for my princess.

Not yours. She can't be yours.

I ignore the voice and nip the flesh there, savoring the way she reacts to me, the small sound she makes from the back of her throat, the way she rubs closer, her tits pressing into my chest, her abdomen against my dick.

"Rowan," she says, her voice breathy and bothered. "I want you."

I make myself pull back slightly, but I keep my hand in her hair, wanting those silky strands wrapped around my hand for just a little longer.

"We can't forget why you're here," I say.

Or why I am. I'm trying to sabotage the show she's hoping will be a platform for the business she obviously cares deeply about. Which brings us back to me being a dick.

Hurt flickers in her eyes, and I can't help myself, I bring her back for another kiss.

When I pull back, she's staring at me with dilated eyes. "You're kind of a dick."

"I know," I say, almost laughing, because it's as if she's read my mind. Again. "I want you too."

"I know." She's stealing my line, and I'm tempted to tell her so, only she grinds against my cock again, taking more blood from my brain.

"You're driving me crazy," I say.

"That's the idea." She rubs up against me again, making a little low hum in her throat that makes my dick even harder.

"I don't have a condom."

"Oh," she says, sounding disappointed.

This time I do laugh, even though it's literally painful how much I want to fuck her. "You thought I was the kind of guy who walked around with a party pack of condoms, and you still wanted to have sex with me?"

She looks hurt, and I don't like myself for having put that look on her face, so I release her hair and lift a hand to her jaw, tipping it up slightly. "There are other things we could do."

"Oh?" she says again, this time warm and interested.

I let my hands slide down to her hips, then lift her up and set her on the edge of the pool.

"Take off those shorts," I say. "I've been wanting you to all night."

"Really?" she asks, sounding pleased. Then she lifts up slightly to slide them off. I didn't ask, but she takes her panties off with them. Her legs are closed, but when I stalk closer, she opens them to me.

A sigh escapes me, because it's a moment of pure happiness, being here with this woman, her pretty pussy on display for me—her eyes alight with invitation and wanting.

I'm stealing this moment. I'm stealing *her*, from the men who flew across the country to win her favor, but I couldn't give a shit. The only thing that matters is that she wants it too.

"I guess there's something an empty pool is good for," I say, smiling up at her. Then I spread her legs wider and tug her closer to me. "Lean back, Princess. Let me make you feel good."

She does as I asked but leans back on her elbows so she can still watch me. I like that she wants to watch, that she wants to see my head descend as I touch and lick and taste her.

I lean in to kiss her thigh, near what I want but far enough away to give her a little tease, then run a finger through her folds, swearing internally when I feel how wet she is for me. "You're beautiful, Kennedy," I say as I trace my finger around her clit.

She bucks her hips, and I replace my hand with my mouth, sucking as I curl a finger inside of her, trying to find the spot that will make her buck harder. I do, and I smile as I continue to suck her clit, curling my finger and then pulling it out so I can sweep my tongue through her folds. She tastes musky and sweet, and I could do this for hours. No, I could stand here in this empty pool in a house full of people I hate, pleasuring this woman, for days. But it's not long before she reaches down to touch my hair, not pushing my head down but running her fingers over my head like she wants to have her hands on me.

"Rowan," she says, and I've never been so happy to hear my name. "Rowan, I'm going to come."

"Come for me, Princess." I lift my head slightly so I can look at her, still working her with my fingers. "I want to feel you pulse against me when you come. I want to taste it."

"Oh my God," she says as I bury my head between her legs again, and I get exactly what I want, what I *need* when she says my name again as her body lifts to my mouth. She shudders against me, her whole form going stiff and then relaxing, her taste a balm to my senses.

When I look up, she's staring down at me, her eyes soft and full of wonder. "Come here," she says. "Come here."

So I lift up onto the rim of the pool and then lie down beside her, turning toward her. I lean in and kiss her, soft and sweet, even though my dick is pissed the hell off at me right now.

She leans down and tries to capture it through my jeans, but I move her hand away, thus pissing my dick off even more.

"Not tonight."

"Then when?" she asks, a frown forming between her perfect brows.

"Never," I say. "We both know we can't do this for real."

She sits up, that frown deepening, and I have a feeling I've fucked up again. Still, I have the presence of mind to present her with her shorts.

"I thought you wanted me to take them off."

"I did. I do. It's just—"

There's a noise from beyond the door, and it takes me only half a second to recognize what it is. The door at the top of a stairway has opened.

Alarm beats through my veins, even more powerful than the boner that's demanding I get my act together so it can get in on the action.

"Kennedy, put them on," I say in an undertone. "We have to hide."

Hide, because we clearly can't leave the way we came in. We'd be seen. Maybe it's a shitty attitude, since she's not mine, but I'm not going to let anyone else see her like this. Not while I'm around.

Her eyes widen, and she slides the shorts on and goes for the towels, which I'd forgotten.

"Where's your shirt?" she asks in a whisper.

Fuck. I don't have the first clue. After she took it from me, I stopped caring that it existed. Now, it seems to have disappeared.

"Doesn't matter," I whisper back, even though it might. "I need to shut off the light, and we need to duck into the changing room. Now."

The room is against the back wall, with a small window embedded in the top that looks onto a seascape mural painted on the wall directly across from it.

"Go," I say.

She gives me a look I can't decipher, but I suspect she's not happy with me, this interruption notwithstanding. It's not entirely unexpected. I seem to have an unparalleled ability to piss off women. But she heads for the changing room, much to my relief. If one of the guys comes down, better for him to see a handyman messing with the empty pool than to see a handyman with their television love inter-est. Or, worse, their love interest alone and by herself in a pair of shorts no larger than a postage stamp.

I'd have to step out if that happened, obviously. No way would I leave her alone with one of those assholes.

Thinking about it, I'm scowling as I switch off the light and pad back into the room, noticing my light-footed approach more now that Kennedy called me on it. I hadn't even realized I could still walk like that—undetected. At the fire house, or out on a job, there's never a need to be covert. We all bang our feet around, almost as if it's a competition.

I step into the changing room, and Kennedy instantly grabs me and pulls me in. When the door swings shut, she doesn't let go. I'm glad for it. I didn't like the way things were going before the interruption. She lifts up onto her toes and whispers in my ear. "If you think you're off the hook because of this, you're wrong."

I almost laugh, but she whispers, "I wonder who they are."

There's no longer any doubt that this is indeed their destination. There's the padding of feet from people who don't feel the need to go undetected. A murmuring of voices.

I can feel Kennedy staring a hole into my head because we both recognize one of the voices: it's my grandmother's cold, clipped voice. What's she doing awake at this hour, let alone wandering around the Labelles' house?

The door opens, and a light switches on in the room beyond us.

"Why'd you make me wear my bathing suit if there's no water in the pool?" a whiny voice asks. I'd know that whine anywhere. It's Jonah. It's clearly Jonah.

Kennedy and I exchange a *what the hell is happening?* look as my grandmother scoffs, "If you win, you'll need to do plenty of photoshoots, including one at the beach. I needed to know you were swimsuit ready."

It's a load of bullshit, especially since the show will be airing in March, and there's no way in hell Kennedy would go to the beach with that tool, even if she chooses him because Harry and my grandmother convince her it's what's best for the show and thus for her business. I don't care to think too long or hard about why my grandmother would lie about something like that.

"I'm cold," Jonah says stubbornly.

"Be a man," Nana retorts. "Did you bring her the basket earlier?"

"I did," he says, perking up. "And I added a framed photo of myself." He seems pleased with himself, as if doing so clinched him a spot in the top two.

"You what?" she asks, clearly pissed by this. "It was supposed to be the best gift, *Jonah*."

"Exactly, I made it the best," he says steadfastly. "I even included a biography of the first Jonah Highbury."

"Well, no matter," Nana tells him. "Harry tells me food poisoning usually passes in twenty-four hours. I'll have to give Kennedy tomorrow off. But we'll do the horseback riding date on Tuesday or Wednesday, at the latest. Marcus thinks he's pulling one over on both of us because he went to horse camp when he was a teenager and didn't disclose it, but there's nothing I don't know about *all* of you." There's a smile in her voice as she continues, "Just like how I know *you* like older women."

Then there's something that sounds like...

Fuck. Fuck. *Fuck.*

Kennedy squeezes my hand, looking at me with eyes that shine in the dark, but I can't even meet her gaze, because *fuck.*

I knew my grandmother was a bad person. I've known since I was a little boy, when she used to make us play ten to fifteen rounds of the silent game in a row, slapping the hands of the kid who broke first with her ruler. But this is a new low. It's obvious she's giving Jonah insider information and help in exchange for...

I lower to the floor and spear my hands into my hair, willing this day to end already. Maybe this is my just punishment for being here with Kennedy when I know I should be at the hospital with Jay, or at least at home with my sisters, talking about Jay. It was shitty of me to walk out on him like I did, especially if Kerry has already left him. But even so, what man should have to listen to his grandmother attempt to seduce a man who's at least forty years younger than her in exchange for professional favors?

Kennedy sits beside me and silently wraps an arm around me. I clearly haven't learned my lesson because I lean into her, grateful for the comfort she's offering.

The kissing noises on the other side of the door stop, thank fuck, and I hear Jonah say, "Are those footsteps?"

"They are, you idiot. Put your clothes back on."

"I didn't wear anything besides the suit," he says in a panic.

"Then what's that shirt under the deck chair?" she asks, frowning.

I can hear some furniture shifting, and he must've held it up because she hisses, "Who's been leaving the house?"

"Well, some of the people on the production team are allowed to come and go," Jonah says pragmatically. "And you and Harry. And all the guys have snuck off at some point or another."

"There isn't supposed to be any sign of Christmas on set," she says, sounding like she wants to off the entire population of Whoville. "What are you doing?" she snaps. "Put it on. Quick."

"But it's not mine," he says in obvious disgust. "What if I catch a disease from it?"

"You can't catch a disease from a shirt, you nitwit. Put. It. On."

I feel a scowl twisting my face because I don't want that asshole wearing the shirt Kennedy bought for me, but it's my own damn fault for leaving it out where it could be seen.

"Should we go into that locker room?" I hear Jonah asking, and my back stiffens in preparation to... I don't know. I'd be perfectly fine with punching him, but I'm not going to uppercut my grandmother. She's no sweet little old woman, but she's still family.

Kennedy's obviously worried—I can *feel* her worry—but she runs a soothing hand up and down my back. For some reason, it really does make me feel better.

"No, you fool," my grandmother snaps. Someone switches off the overhead light in the other room. "Then we'd be stuck. Come with me. The children used to break into this house through a window. We'll break out the same way."

Kennedy shoots me a glance, and I'm guessing she's as surprised as I am. My grandmother's going to climb out a fucking window?

I'd be impressed if I weren't so disgusted.

There's some complaining from Jonah, but I can very clearly hear the window opening, some scuffling, then the window closing.

Kennedy turns to me on the floor of the changing room, her arm slipping off my back. "Rowan..."

I run my hands through my hair. I curse. "I'm traumatized for life," I tell her. "I...I have no words."

There's a keening sound from her, and I swivel on my ass to look at her, worried that I've offended or upset her, but she's laughing. Laughing so hard, in fact, that I'm surprised she can also breathe.

Then the light switches back on in the adjoining room, and I only have a few seconds to get myself—and Kennedy—to our feet before the door swings open.

Chapter Fourteen

Rowan

My sister Holly is standing in the doorway, gaping at me. Harry is next to her with a flashlight that he obviously doesn't need in the bright room, only he's holding it by the base like a weapon. To be fair, I'm pretty sure it's my Maglite from home, and if you bashed someone over the head with it hard enough, it would absolutely do damage.

"What the fuck are you two doing here?" I ask in bafflement. I'd expected it to be one of the guys coming to check out the noise.

"What are *you* doing without a shirt on?" Holly asks archly, her eyebrows rising as she looks behind me at Kennedy. I hadn't even realized I'd stepped in front of her, which was sort of pointless since I'm the half-naked one. "Ah," Holly adds. "Eeenteresting."

"It's not what it looks like," I say, which we all probably know isn't true. "Kennedy and I thought we'd go for a swim, but the Labelles must have drained the pool before they left. We heard someone coming, so we ducked into the changing room because we didn't want her to get caught."

"Get caught doing nothing?" Holly says, lifting her eyebrows. I don't care for the amount of insinuation she's pouring into her voice.

"Maybe she was worried about getting caught out of bed," Harry says, giving Kennedy a look that's part worried, part pissed. "Because she's supposed to have aggressive food poisoning."

"Yeah, thank you for that," Kennedy says as she steps out from behind me. "All the guys seemed to think I was having non-stop diarrhea, and it's obvious they're making it a plot point for the show."

"Was that not a good idea?" Harry asks, flustered. "It seemed like a good idea at the time."

"You didn't like it when someone thought *you* had an upset stomach," Kennedy says significantly.

I have no fucking clue what she's talking about, but *he* clearly does, because his cheeks turn pink. "Yes, well, but I *did* have an upset stomach. Yours was just pretend." She doesn't respond to this with anything more than a look, but he bunches his lips to the side and says, "Yes, I see your point."

There's a lull in the conversation, and Holly doesn't miss the opportunity to step in. "Do you realize how worried we've been, you prick?" she asks me. "You went off grid after telling us Jay had a heart attack. You should have checked your phone."

"It's been a hell of a day," I concede. "How'd you find me?"

Holly shrugs. "I tracked your phone. I'd apologize for turning on your find my friends app—"

"You did what?"

"—but I'm not actually sorry," she continues as if I hadn't spoken. "I did it after you went off hiking that one time and didn't come back until after dark. You need to call our sisters. They're all worried."

Of course they are. A feeling of dread courses over me, but I don't need to tell them what Jay told me. Not yet. I don't want to believe it, but somewhere inside, I know it's true. I guess maybe he did too because he was always taking me places when I was a kid—bringing me hiking or to the river to fish. He hung out with the other kids too, but it felt like our bond was special...until it didn't.

"Yeah, okay," I say. "Can you give us a minute?"

"Who, you and Harry?" Holly asks, but the hint of slyness on her face tells me she knows exactly who I'm talking about.

"Me and Kennedy, smartass."

"Sure," she says, waving at the changing room door. "Your love nest awaits."

"Maybe you guys could wait outside that door," I say with a gesture to the door on the other side of the pool room.

She rolls her eyes, then says, "Don't even think of trying to escape through the window." Like me and the rest of the delinquents who grew up here, she did the Labelle Pool Challenge too.

"I won't, but Nana did," I say, because it's at least a little funny.

Her eyes narrow. "I'm going to want to hear everything about that...in a minute."

Harry gives us a jaunty wave, Maglite in hand, then follows Holly from the room, leaving me and Kennedy alone together. They shut the door behind them to give us some privacy. I still don't have a shirt on, and although I'm not particularly self-conscious about it, I know it's cold outside. It's always chillier at night and in the morning in the mountains, and tonight it's dipped into the thirties. So I grab one of the big towels from the floor to wrap around myself.

"Make sure it's not the spider one," Kennedy says.

When I look at her, she's giving me a sad smile. Something like regret blossoms in my chest because our night was cut short, and the next time we see each other, I'm going to have to pretend I don't give a shit about her, other than as the star of this ill-thought-out show. I don't like that. I like it even less that she's here at my grandmother's mercy, when it's obvious Nana has none. She's messing around with the male contestants, throwing around promises and favors like she's some sort of magnate.

The sooner the show is shut down, the better.

And yet...Kennedy's so passionate about her work, so sweet and driven and genuine. I don't want her mission to promote Leto's Hands to fail—I just want my grandmother to.

"I thought you liked men who attract spiders," I tell Kennedy, smiling slightly. Maybe I'm trying to bring some lightness back to us.

"You were going to push me away before they got here," Kennedy says, giving me a lofty look that's all princess. Her hair is mussed and her lips are swollen from my kisses, which only make her more appealing. I want to sweep her away from here, to claim her as my own—which is such a stupid thought it sends fear pumping through my veins.

I've seen where that kind of thing leads, and I want no part of it.

Jay must have been infatuated with my mother when he cheated with her. I was born of such an infatuation.

"I was," I admit staunchly. I wrap the towel around my shoulders because I don't want to have this conversation half naked. "You know this can't lead anywhere, Kennedy. You're here to find someone *rich*," I say, referring to the title of the show. "I don't know how to break it to you, Princess, but I'm just this side of broke. You're going to have to pick another horse to ride. Although after what we just heard, I'm hoping you throw off my grandmother's boy toy at the first opportunity."

She looks at me with the contempt I absolutely deserve. "So that's how it's going to be, huh? You're pushing me away."

"I..." But the words dry up because I don't really have any.

"Go, then. Go if you want to."

"It's not that I want to, Kennedy," I say, reaching out to touch her arm. I'm not sure why I'm objecting. She's giving me the dismissal I need. Maybe it's because I can still taste her on my lips and my balls are telling me that I'm going to be feeling an ache for her all fucking night. Touching her arm was a mistake, though, because I can instantly feel an electric pull to touch her more.

"So what *do* you want?"

"I don't know," I tell her honestly. "Today was a mindfuck."

"Seeing your stepfather like that." She nods. "It's not the first time I've seen someone have a heart attack."

Her words surprise me. "Really?"

"Olive's grandmother. She came over to help with us one day, and..." She swallows, her elegant throat contracting with it. "She didn't make it."

"Christ," I say, rubbing my hand up and down her arm. "I'm sorry that happened to you. I'd wondered if today was the first time..."

"No, but it's not the kind of thing that gets easy." She touches my hand, still on her arm. "It's okay, Rowan. I wish things were different, that we'd met some other way, like you said, but you're right. This could never work. We were crazy for letting ourselves believe otherwise."

It's what I thought I wanted her to say, but suddenly I don't want to hear it. Maybe that's why I blurt out, "Jay told me something at the hospital."

"Oh?" she says, perking up.

"He...he says he's my father." Her expression is confused, so I add. "My actual father. I guess he had an affair with my mother while she was married to the man who I thought was my father."

Her gasp is so sweet, so concerned for me, that I nearly buckle on the spot and kiss her. I want to swallow that gasp. I want to take a piece of her away with me, like a thief in the night. "Oh, Rowan. I'm so sorry...except...maybe this is a good thing."

At this, my face slips into a scowl. "I don't see how it could be a fucking good thing."

"Well..." She tightens her grip on my hand, spreading the electric feeling, and then says, "You told me your father wasn't a nice man. That he left you. You seem to think a lot of Jay. Maybe this means..."

"*Thought* a lot of him," I say harshly, not entirely sure I mean the reversion to past tense. "He messed around with a married woman. He suspected I was his son for years and did jack shit about it. The

141

only reason he knows now is because my mother finally confirmed it." More bitterness slips into my voice as I add, "To him, mind you, not to me. And she only told him because she wanted to reveal the truth on this show. She figured it was her big chance to get some airtime."

She releases my hand, and I'm seriously getting weak for this woman, because I'm sorry for it. Her hand lifts to her throat. "I'm so sorry, Rowan. Oh my God. I can't even..."

"It's not going to happen," I say. "He refused her. But he figured he should tell me, especially since...."

To my horror, I feel heat gathering behind my eyes. I haven't cried since I was a kid...since the day my dad left and told me I'd need to be a man and take care of my little sister, Willow, because he wasn't going to be around anymore. Now I'm on the verge of tears for a different father. Seeing him collapse like that earlier...I thought he was gone. I thought I'd have to call Ivy with different news. I thought I'd have to say goodbye to the one parental figure who'd meant a damn thing to me. But the day had shaped up so differently. It had hollowed me out in a different way.

I hear again what Kennedy just said—*maybe this is a good thing*. But she only thinks that because she's sweet and innocent.

Then, to my surprise, she's wrapping her arms around me, the towel crinkling between us. "Oh, Rowan," she says into my ear, and in that moment, with the two of us wrapped together, I can't imagine giving her up.

The door opens.

"Chop, chop," Holly calls out from beyond the opening. "This is your thirty-second warning."

Kennedy's arms drop. The moment ends. I shore my emotions up, back into the deep pit where I usually keep them. "Thanks for the distraction, Princess," I say, lifting a hand and chucking her chin. "I won't be forgetting it anytime soon."

"Neither will I," she says, staring into my eyes. "Talk to Zach about this...he'll understand."

My brow furrows. "What? You want me to tell your brother—"

"No. Not about us. About your dad. He's been through something similar."

I know he was disowned by his father. Everyone and their dog knows, but no one knows why. I nod, although I don't have any intention of bringing it up. For one thing, I'm not so sure I could look him in the face right now, knowing he'd want to smash mine in if he had any idea what I'd done with his sister. For another, that's a man's private business, isn't it? I wouldn't much like it if he asked me about mine.

Still, she's waiting for a response, so I give a nod.

"You're not going to do it," she says, smiling slightly.

"We'll see."

"I know that means no. You come and see me again, all right?"

"Okay," I say, even though I don't mean that either. The look on her face, sad but knowing, suggests she's well aware of that. I guess she can read me like a book. That's part of why I need to stay away. I already feel a deep-seated need to claim her for myself—and, worse, to let her stake a claim on me. I've never let anyone do that before, and I'm determined not to start making bad—or worse—decisions now. I'll be Cupid only in name, not in action. "Let me see you to your room."

"That's okay," she says with a thread of sadness in her voice. "I know the way, and you already dealt with the spiderweb. It's probably best if you all just leave."

I know she's right. After all, my grandmother and Jonah are creeping around somewhere on the grounds, but I don't like the thought of leaving her.

The door opens again and Holly calls out, "Time's up."

Kennedy starts to walk toward the exit, and I follow. "I'm going to go back up to my room," she tells them.

"I can—"

"Alone," she says. "I'll be fine."

"Here," Harry offers from the open doorway. He takes several steps forward, Maglite extended. "Take this. It can double as a weapon if one of the guys sees you and tries to get fresh."

The thought of this possibility, however unlikely, makes me want to growl, but Kennedy just takes the light and thanks him.

"I wish you'd let me take you up there," I repeat.

"I think you need to go," she tells me. It's said firmly, like she won't be allowing any arguments. "You need to talk to your family now."

She's right.

I take her hand and squeeze it, resisting the temptation to kiss it, to kiss her mouth one last time so I have some sweetness to carry away with me. Then Harry hugs her, and he and I both turn to leave, joining Holly at the door. Holly waves in at Kennedy, "Bye, Kennedy! Merry almost Christmas! Harry told me all about the Christmas tree outing."

I scowl at Harry, who shrugs but looks a little shame-faced. "She needed to know for context. Since I was a first-hand witness of what happened with Jay."

"I'm so glad you were there with them," Holly says firmly to Kennedy. "These jackasses need all the help they can get." Then she grabs the end of my towel and leads me along. After she and Harry get me to the back exit and we step out into the cold, she gives me a level look and says, "Lucy, you have some 'splainin' to do."

Do I ever.

Chapter Fifteen

Kennedy

It's Wednesday morning—three days since Rowan Mayberry made me come next to an empty swimming pool.

He hasn't returned to see me. Nor has he visited the set. The only glimmer of him is in the little contraband Christmas tree that I take out of my closet every time I lock myself into my room. In fact, I'm looking at it now, remembering the slightly petulant expression on his face when he gave it to me—like he thought I might accuse him of sentimentality for doing something nice for me.

It's ridiculous, but I miss him. I even miss the sight of him on the sidelines of the show, watching with a scowl or smirk.

There's a knock on my door, and I jump out of bed to hide my Christmas tree, taking it down from the low bookshelf beneath the shuttered window and carefully tucking it into the closet, before calling out, "Who's there?"

I already know it's not Rowan. He'd come by at night, if he came at all, under cover of darkness—a thought that shivers through me. So I hope to God it's Harry. Although I managed to put the horseback riding expedition off until today, every single guy in the house came to visit me again on Monday, and then for a third time on Tuesday. I know they're getting bored because Colton actually wrote a poem for me. He compared me to a profitable investment portfolio. I should be spending time with them, obviously, but the only man I'm thinking about is Rowan.

Also, it's really hard to look Jonah in the eye after what I overheard in the pool room. Is he actually attracted to Nana...er, Maeve? Or is he just giving her favors in the hope of getting more screen time?

"It's me," Harry says, and relief flows over me.

"Come in." When I open the door, I find him in a pair of brightly checkered pants, a white button down shirt, and his usual beanie. I beckon him over to the fainting couch arranged at the side of the room, and we both sit. "Do you have any news?"

He blushes. "How did you know?" He lifts a hand to his face. "Could you tell because I trimmed my nose hair? I wondered if it was overkill, but there was one really long one, and I didn't want that to be the only thing he fixated on over dinner. It could really kill the atmosphere, you know?"

"You're having dinner with Oliver after filming wraps today?" I deduce. The only things on the docket at the house are the horseback riding date, followed by a picnic with Jonah and Marcus, one-on-one interviews, and then quiet time.

"Yes," he says, turning toward me. "We're going to a place called Salt and Bone. I don't want to order anything though. We already know I have an issue with dairy, and I don't think I've ever eaten a salad without getting something caught in my teeth. You know, I read a statistic that forty-one percent of respondents judge a first date by what they order." He pulls off his beanie and worries it with his hands. "Would it be weird if I didn't order anything?"

"Yes," I say. "Besides, don't you want to enjoy a nice dinner? Don't worry what he thinks. He's not much of a catch if he loses interest because you got something in your teeth."

He sighs. "I really want this to go well."

"So do I," I say with a smile. My mind makes a leap to Rowan potentially giving Oliver a pep talk about the same date. He's partially responsible for this happening. He engineered the whole Christmas tree outing, which only endears him to me more. "When I asked for news, though, I meant about the whole Jay thing."

"Oh," Harry says, his eyes widening. "Of course. Well, Jay's still in the hospital, but it sounds like he's going to be released soon. Their sister, Ivy, is in town." His gaze narrows on me. "Are you ready to tell me what happened between you and Rowan the other night?"

He's already told me that Rowan refused to say anything about it, other than that he'd come by to give me an update about Jay and we'd decided on a late-night swim. I know Rowan doesn't see himself as Prince Charming. He'd probably claim not to have a noble bone in his body, yet here he is, trying to protect me. It's enough to mess with a girl's head.

I sigh, leaning further back on the couch. "It doesn't matter," I say, even though it feels like it really does. "We both know I shouldn't be thinking about him."

Harry sits up, slapping his hat down on the couch's one and only arm. "Of course it matters. You're my friend. He's my friend. What kind of a matchmaker would I be if I ignored the sparks between you?"

I'm tempted to tell him that he's not a matchmaker at all—that's supposed to be Nana Mayberry's schtick, but Harry's earnest and sweet, and it's honestly nice to have someone to talk to about this.

"I like him," I admit. "But he seems pretty determined to stay away from me, and he's right. Nothing *else* can happen between us. Even if I wasn't on this show, I live in Chicago, and he lives here. Anything that happens would have to be temporary."

Harry looks offended by the suggestion. "When I met Oliver for the first time, I lived in Asheville, and he lived in Highland Hills, and look—now we're both here. You never know what's going to happen in the future."

My mouth lifts up slightly. "So I should start hoping they're going to fire me from Leto's Hands?"

He makes a face. "They should really reconsider that name."

"So I've heard."

"And no, that's not what I meant."

"Aren't you worried I'll ruin the show?" I ask, surprised. According to Tina, he left a really good job to accept this gig as Nana's co-host. "Tina said working on a dating show is your dream."

"Oh, it is," he confirms. "And it's every bit as thrilling as I thought it would be. I mean, imagine how ah-mazing it would be if you end up with the handyman instead of any of the rich men Nana Mayberry has paraded in front of you. Now *that* would be a season of TV that people would want to watch. It's the kind of thing they'd talk about for years. Centuries! Okay, maybe I'm getting carried away, but it's exactly what would make the show memorable. Like keeping Jonah around even though he—" He makes a face because while I didn't tell him everything, I did tell him about Nana Mayberry.

"Harry," I say, "I'm pretty sure Rowan wants nothing to do with the show. He basically admitted he's just helping on set because he thinks it's his duty to watch over his grandmother."

Actually, now that I think about it, Rowan's explanation doesn't totally square. It's obvious there's no affection between Nana Mayberry and her grandchildren, and I completely understand why after the behavior I've observed from her and what I've been told. Rowan's eldest sister is marrying a billionaire. If their grandmother needs help and they feel obligated to provide it, surely they could hire someone. So why has Rowan, who holds contempt for the show and his family's matchmaking history, spent so much time here?

He isn't coming anymore, a voice in my head whispers. *He's staying away because of you.*

Harry and I sigh at the same time. "Still," he says, "it would make for memorable TV."

"You're right," I admit, because I've seen plenty of dating shows too. "But it's not going to happen. It seems like he wants to stay away from me."

"For now," he agrees. "But you never know what the future might hold. Maybe we should have Tina read your tea leaves when she visits the set. That would be good for the cameras."

"Are they still going to be here on Friday?" I ask greedily, because I'm sick of being here by myself. I'm lonely. I know the guys have been hanging out in the brandy room most afternoons, and I got six separate invitations to join them yesterday evening, but I found myself making excuses.

"Yes," he says. "They're set to arrive a few hours before the Rolex ceremony." A feeling of relief wraps me up like a hug. I want them. I want to be around people who like me for me, not for the five minutes of fame they might get if I let them keep their Rolex watches for another week. (The watches are returned to the polished wood box prior to the ceremony, and the eliminated guys' watches are removed. Jonah was very disappointed to learn he wouldn't be getting a new one each week, and also that the winner is the only person who will walk away with one at the end.)

"Are you going to send Jonah home?" Harry asks, pursing his lips.

"Wait, you don't want me to?" I ask in disbelief. "He was making out with Nana Mayberry."

He lifts his eyebrows. "And you were *you won't say*-ing with *Rowan* Mayberry. So maybe you have something in common. You both have a thing for the Mayberrys."

I mime throwing up. "That's vile, Harry."

"My point is that you're not in it for the right reasons either, or at least I hope you're not. I've spent a little more time with the guys over the last couple of days, and..." He scrunches his nose as if he smells something unsavory. "Let's just say, I couldn't in good faith try to push you toward any of them. I thought Colton was okay, but then he told me a story so boring that I felt resentful about the two minutes of my life it stole from me. And I'm going to be totally honest with you, Marcus seems more interested in Jonah than he is in you." He tilts his head. "Another good reason to keep Jonah around. He makes for good TV. Even better TV if someone finds out he's seeing someone else." He wiggles his eyebrows up and down.

"You want Nana Mayberry to get fired?" I ask, because I'm surprised he'd be so vicious.

"I didn't say that. And I'm not saying that you or I should be the ones who tattle on her. If we're lucky, it'll all come out organically. But yes, obviously I want her to get fired. She calls me Sweet Tea because she spiked my drink at our first one-on-one meeting, and I passed out on her couch. Holly and her boyfriend had to save me."

"What?" I ask in disbelief. "And you still came to work for the show?"

He picks up his hat and starts messing with it again. "I really did want to work on a dating show, and what was I supposed to do? Leave you here alone with her? No one deserves that." He cocks his head. "Well, maybe Jonah would deserve it, but we're not altogether sure he wouldn't like it."

"Huh, well, this is all certainly some food for thought."

"Good talk," he says, putting the hat back on and getting to his feet. He gives me a skeptical look. "You were just pretending to be sick, right?"

"I haven't been sleeping well," I admit.

"I'm going to ask Tina to bring you some of her sedative tea." He pauses. "I don't know how to say this and make it sound nice, but you're not wearing that on the riding date, are you?"

"I'm still in my pajamas, Harry," I say dryly. "I have the outfit that was selected for this outing, but I have to tell you, I think it's ridiculous." It looks like something an equestrian would wear in a Victorian novel.

"You should see what they have Jonah and Marcus in," he says with a grin.

Then, because he's a good friend, he gets me coffee while I change.

* * *

Jonah and Marcus are wearing identical equestrian outfits, only Jonah's is white and red, and Marcus's is white and blue. Their pants are baggy around their crotches and tight at their calves. We were supposed to take a nice, pleasant ride through the valley, but they've spent the past hour racing each other, although they've each circled back twice to pretend they wanted to talk to me.

The cameramen have been following us in an all-terrain van. Harry's inside too, and every time the van careens past me to catch up to the guys, he gives me a wave of solidarity, his mouth in a grim line that speaks of motion sickness. Nana Mayberry is there too, sitting back with a dour look on her face. Maybe she was up late with Jonah.

The third time the guys gallop off, leaving me and my borrowed horse, Lady, in the dust, they don't come back. The van follows them, and I'm left to make my own way to the valley where the picnic has been set up.

I'm annoyed, but it's much more pleasant to ride alone through the towering pines—and if that doesn't say it all about my feelings, or lack thereof, toward Jonah and Marcus, I'm not sure what does.

When I arrive at the valley, cameramen are crouched on either end of a long white-and-red-checkered picnic blanket, filming Jonah and Marcus, who've apparently been making themselves at home. While Marcus is sipping from a crystal flute, Jonah has piled a plate high with what looks like caviar. It's not what I was expecting from a picnic, but I've learned Nana Mayberry has very pointed opinions about what we should eat, drink, and wear to pull off the premise of the show.

As soon as I ride up, both of the guys set down their things and hurry toward me. The cameras follow their movement.

"I'll help you down," Marcus says.

"I got here first," Jonah tells him, sulky, trying to edge him out of the way. Marcus is bigger and doesn't budge. I dismount on the other side of them because I'm sick to death of their never-ending game of one-upmanship.

"Oh," Jonah says sadly, as I walk my horse over to one of the production assistants.

"Would you like some champagne?" Marcus asks, trailing me. He's as handsome as ever, even in the ridiculous costume, but I feel another surge of annoyance. Couldn't he have just trotted along with me and let Jonah posture?

Still, I nod as I hand over the mare's reins. "Sure, that would be nice." There's a scuffle of quickly moving feet behind me, and the production assistant and I share an amused glance before I gather myself and turn back around.

As I approach the blanket, I watch Jonah heap caviar messily onto a plate as if it's a casserole while Marcus pours me champagne from a bottle in a bucket of ice.

When I reach them, they both practically shove their offerings at me, like whoever gets there first will be given a prize.

"Thanks," I say, even though I don't really feel like champagne, and the pile of caviar, without any crackers or silverware to eat it, doesn't seem all that appealing.

I take a seat. For a second, they both stand there scowling at each other, but then they sit too, one on either side of me. I take a long sip of the champagne to settle my nerves, because I suddenly feel hemmed in.

"Did Marcus bring you a gift while you were sick?" Jonah asks.

"Yes," I say with a sigh. "All of the gentlemen did."

"Whose was your favorite?"

"Jeff's," I say quickly, and if it's a mark of bad character that I'm pleased to have disappointed both of them, then guilty as charged. "He gave me a Christmas book."

"Ah," says Jonah, his voice slightly contemptuous. "You're one of those Belle women."

"Bell women?" I ask in confusion.

"Yeah, one of those chicks who'd sleep with a beast just to get at a good library. You know, *Beauty and the Beast.*" He gives me a significant look. "There's a very large library in Highbury Manor. We even have one of those swinging ladders."

This is the first thing I've found to like about him, although it would be poor form to say so. Odds are, it's not even his library. "Really, do you have a photo?"

Jonah goes to reach for his phone before remembering. He lifts his hands. "I don't have my phone."

"I have three hundred leather-bound books," Marcus interjects.

I'm not sure how I'm supposed to respond to that, so I just nod and say, "That's nice."

"I'll bet you bought them in bulk," Jonah says.

The wounded look on Marcus's face, plus the ease with which he recalled the exact number, suggest that's true. "I'll bet you haven't read a single book in that library," he snaps back. "You probably only went in there to fuck around with the swinging ladder."

Also probably true.

I drink more champagne.

There are a few moments of awkward silence and snacking, and then Harry and Nana come over. The cameras follow them, so it's obvious they're not coming over just to chat. There's a plan.

"We thought you three might enjoy playing some ice-breaker games," Harry says with unearned enthusiasm.

"Like Truth or Dare," Nana Mayberry says, the words so frosty they almost burn.

I suck in a chill breath of air.

How does she know? *What* does she know?

Her face tightens. "Such a pity you got so sick, Kennedy. We were originally planning a larger game with the other gentlemen."

"Yes, well, bad fish eggs will do that to a girl," I say, pushing the plate away woodenly.

Harry's eyes widen. Speaking to the camera, he says, "She's not speaking about these fish eggs, obviously. *These* fish eggs are lovely and crunchy, and...I don't know what caviar taste likes. I have an aversion to fish eggs. I'm sure they're lovely, though, if you enjoy that sort of thing."

He's obviously trying to shill for whatever brand gave us free food, but he's flubbing it worse than I did. His look of utter panic says he knows it. I pat him on the arm. "That's what post-production is for."

"Oh, thank God, you're right."

"Keep it together, Sweet Tea," Nana says primly and pats her perfect snow-white bun. "You're more tightly wound than a snake in a watering hose." Her cold glare moves to me. "Well, Kennedy, who would you like to go first? We wrote out some suggestions for you."

Meaning there's already some sort of script for this. Interesting. Hopefully that means the whole Truth or Dare thing is a coincidence, because I hate the thought of someone spying on us or, worse, of there being a camera in my room. I already know I'll be searching the whole place, top to bottom, when we get back.

Harry fumbles with his leather messenger bag, then mouths, "Sorry," at me, which isn't a good sign.

I scan the list after he hands it over, my attention snagged and held by the first item on the "suggested dares" list.

Meet me in the pool to go skinny dipping.

Horror knifing through me, I glance up sharply. Nana Mayberry observes me without comment.

Rowan didn't tell her about our night, did he?

No, he wouldn't. Never. He's not the kind of man who shares personal information easily, which makes it that much more meaningful that he was so open with me. But if he didn't tell her, then who? I know Harry wouldn't have betrayed me willingly.

"Thank you, Nana," I say. Then I tear up the paper and pocket the pieces, because a lady doesn't litter. There's a gasp from someone, but I don't know who, because my eyes are fixed on Nana, hers on me. "But I think I'll be going off-script for this one."

"By all means, *dear.*" She pats her perfectly coiffed hair and sits on the blanket. Harry lowers down next to her.

"Who wants to go first?" I ask the guys cheerfully.

"Why don't we all tell each other when we first lost our virginity?" Jonah offers, apropos of nothing.

A distasteful suggestion. I'm not exactly surprised since he's the one who made it.

"Fine," I say, even though I don't like thinking of Brandon, and I like speaking about him even less. "I was nineteen."

Marcus grins at me. "Fifteen," he says proudly. His gaze shoots to Jonah. "Think you can beat that?"

Ugh.

Jonah shoots him a victorious look, then surprises both of us by saying, "I'm a virgin."

Chapter Sixteen

Kennedy

"I don't believe you," Marcus scoffs.

I don't believe him either. Jonah's made several comments that suggest he's far from chaste, and then there's what Rowan and I overheard between him and Nana Mayberry. And yet...why would he say something like that on camera if it weren't true?

"We should respect his decision," I say, waving at Jonah, who's beaming proudly at the cameras. That's when it hits me—he's lying because he wants to draw attention to himself and keep it there.

"I'm saving myself for you, Kennedy," Jonah says, shifting his gaze to me.

"Uh, let's not get ahead of ourselves. Why don't we carry on with our game?" I scrunch my lips to the side. "Let's see, do either of you have pets?"

"No," Jonah says instantly. "And I don't think any civilized person would willingly pick up someone else's waste."

Marcus huffs a laugh. "I don't," he tells me. "But my friend has a Great Dane."

"Disgusting," Jonah says, and he clearly means it.

I think again of that dog I wanted as a kid—*still want*—the little imagined bulldog with its underbite and rolls of furry flesh. I feel a pang of longing, although it's not just for the dog, but for the innocence of the girl who thought she could ask Santa for her dearest wish and get it.

Mind you, my needs were always met, and my parents would have given me anything I wanted, as long as I wanted the things they wanted for me.

The problem was that I almost never did.

"You like dogs, don't you, Kennedy?" Marcus asks.

"I do," I admit with a small smile. "Love them."

Jonah has such an obvious *I just messed up look* on his face that I almost laugh.

"You seem like a dog person," Marcus says.

A smile crosses my face, because I feel seen for the first time all day. When Marcus forgets about the TV show, he's a nice guy. "How'd you decide that?"

"You're warm and kind. Compassionate."

"I'd get a small dog if you wanted one," Jonah says quickly. "We could hire a dog walker. And a pooper scooper."

"That's an implement," Marcus says. "Not a person."

I take another sip of champagne. "Are you guys up for a dare?"

"What would you dare me to do, Kennedy?" Marcus asks, his eyes on my lips. He's such a beautiful man, all golden hair and big blue eyes, but I wouldn't ask *him* to go skinny dipping. That thought inevitably leads to another—who told Nana about Rowan and me? Because I'm fairly certain she didn't know we were at the pool the other night. She must have found out after the fact.

I consider for a moment and then snap my fingers, because as ideas go, it's pretty much perfect. "Why don't both of you make a PSA about Leto's Hands? We can have a contest for who does it best."

"Do we get to judge?" Harry asks with obvious delight.

Nana snaps into a dry cracker, shooting me a look that suggests she'd prefer it if she were snapping my spine.

"*You* do," I say. I give Nana Mayberry a smile that would give a person sugar shock. "His nickname is Sweet Tea. Seems like he's the right audience."

She chews, swallows. "A bleeding heart, you mean?"

"The best kind," I say brightly.

"Am I supposed to know what Leto's Hands is?" Jonah asks with confusion. Then he nods to my untouched plate of caviar. "Are you eating that?"

I give it to him without comment.

Marcus stares at him in disbelief. I'm pretty sure *he* remembers where I work. I've talked about my job every day, even on most of their sick room visits. His gaze shifts back to mine, his bright blue eyes turning mischievous. "What about you?" he asks. "Do we get to give *you* a dare?"

Discomfort uncoils inside me. Rowan didn't ask me to do anything I might not want to—even though I *very much* wanted to. But do I trust Marcus and Jonah to do the same?

No, especially not Jonah.

Still, I want them to do the PSAs. This could be exactly the funding breakthrough we need.

"Sure," I say, waiting until Jonah has a big mouthful of caviar. "What did you have in mind?"

Jonah looks like he's struggling to swallow—you can't choke on fish eggs, can you?—but Marcus has the upper hand, and he's not about to lose it.

"Why don't you film the videos with us?" he asks with a bright smile. He's sucking up, but I'm so relieved, I don't care.

"I'd be delighted to!"

Jonah, who's just swallowed, adds, "And kiss us on camera."

My face wants to crinkle in distaste, but I remind myself that he didn't specify *how* I was going to kiss him. A cheek kiss will do perfectly well, and I do need to act like I'm interested in the guys. That's the only way people will be invested in the show.

My mind skips back to what Harry said, to the possibility of creating a different sort of narrative, but Rowan would have to be open to it, and it's very obvious that

he's not.

At least he's not like Brandon, I guess, interested in me only because of my family's status and the money in my trust fund. If anything, Rowan seems put off by those things.

"Fine," I say. "Shall we?"

"So what is Leto's Hands again?" Jonah asks. "Is it some kind of sexual thing you're interested in trying?"

"Said like a true virgin," Marcus deadpans.

* * *

It took dozens of takes for us to film the spots. I'm pretty sure Jonah kept flubbing his lines on purpose so I'd have to keep kissing him on the cheek. He has smooth skin, at least, but I don't feel even the smallest hint of attraction toward either him or Marcus.

I was pleased with how the spots turned out, though, even more so because they're going to be a major part of the plot for this episode. Based on her expression, which soured more with every take, Nana Mayberry knows it too.

"You're kissing them like you would your brother, Kennedy," she told me halfway through. "Who's going to believe you're falling in love?"

I didn't like that she was right. I especially didn't like the implications. Everyone's going to expect me to act like I'm in love with someone by the end of this thing. And I'll be honest, I can't imagine simpering over any of these guys, on camera or off.

By the time we finish, it's late afternoon. The production assistants pack up the picnic and, to no one's surprise, the guys race each other home while Lady and I walk back at a more sedate pace. Both of them are waiting for me outside the house when I arrive, the camera van preceding me as if we're some sort of a parade of two.

Once again, the guys argue over who gets to help me dismount.

Once again, I do it by myself.

Marcus and Jonah both offer to see me up to my room.

"I'll be doing that," Harry says, stepping forward. He's such a sweet man, accommodating and funny and neurotic, but there's something harsh about the way he says it.

Nana Mayberry just sniffs and walks off, but not before giving Jonah a significant look. What it means, I can't guess, and I don't particularly want to.

Harry takes my elbow and leads me up to my room. Once we're inside, he glances both ways down the hall, then closes and locks the door. "Are you thinking what I'm thinking?" he asks.

"I literally have no idea."

"Candy cane," he says, referencing our safe words, so I nod, because I have a feeling I know where he's going with this. Nana Mayberry knows things she shouldn't know, and if he didn't tell her, and I didn't tell her, who did?

My mind flashes to Rowan again, but I still don't believe he'd share intimate details about me with anyone, let alone his grandmother.

"Let's see," he says loudly in a voice that's clearly meant for someone else, someone who could be watching and listening. "We need to find the flickering bulb so we can replace it. It may take a long time."

It does. The two of us work silently and thoroughly, going through every square inch of the princess room, which is a bigger deal than it sounds like considering how many tchotchkes grace its shelves.

"I'm about ninety-three percent certain there's no camera in here," Harry says, sitting back on the fainting couch, "so that's good."

His eyes narrow. "Rowan's future brother-in-law is that tech billionaire, of course, but there's no lost love between him and Nana Mayberry."

I can't help but be interested. "It doesn't seem like any of the Mayberrys are fond of her."

Sighing, he runs a hand over his head. "Can you blame them? It would be like being fond of a piece of furniture. A straight-backed metal chair with spikes on the seat."

"Vicious," I say with a laugh. "And accurate."

I make my way to the closet and take out the tree, propping it in my favorite spot for it, on the shelf in front of the curtain-covered window. I turn on the battery-powered lights with a happy sigh and then join him on the fainting couch.

"You'll have to leave the room to get dinner," Harry says nervously. "Someone might see it."

"I'll ask one of the production assistants to bring me something."

"No, I will," he says. Then he gives me a significant look. "But you should be spending more time with the men for the cameras. As much as I hate to say it, Maeve is right about that. You'll need to act like you're interested in getting to know a few of them. Otherwise it's not going to be much of a show."

I sigh again, trying to focus on the tree with its pretty lights, but I get that sinking feeling again, like I'm a balloon that's slowly but steadily turning back into a flattened rubber tube.

"They're horrible," I say flatly.

"They're horrible," he agrees. "Maybe I'll get to pick the guys next season."

"That doesn't help me."

"No." He gives me a sympathetic look. "Want me to leave my phone in here so you can call Olive?"

Everything inside me brightens at the suggestion. "Yes, oh my God, yes." I pause. "But don't you need it? You're going on your date tonight."

"And Oliver and I already set the time and location," he says firmly, taking out his phone and handing it to me. "Just be sure to pretend you're talking to yourself if anyone hears you and knocks."

I laugh, because I don't hate the thought of the guys thinking I'm insane. Maybe it would keep them from coming on too strong. "Thank you, Harry. You're a godsend."

"Don't thank me yet," he says, his lips thinning.

There's something ominous about the words, so I give him a searching look.

"Please don't ask me what I know. I hate it when people ask me what I know."

My mind conjures up an image of Rowan. He'd probably say something like, "Would you prefer for them to ask for information you don't know?" So I say that.

"Yes. No. I don't know," Harry says nervously and then runs a hand over his hair. "I promised Tina that I'd take care of you, but I'm doing a pretty shit job."

"Maeve Mayberry is a wily woman," I tell him. "No one could blame you for not always being two steps ahead."

"I guess," he says with a sigh. "Just try to be flirty with a few of the guys tomorrow. For my sake."

The thought chafes, but it's why I'm here, and I haven't forgotten that.

"Thanks, Harry," I say. "I'm going to want to know everything, literally everything, about your date."

"Good," he says, getting up. "Because I was going to tell you whether you wanted to know or not."

I wrap him up in my arms because I'm desperate for a hug. He pauses for a second, hopefully from surprise and not disgust, and then hugs me back hard. "It's going to be okay, Kennedy."

"Is it?"

I can feel him laughing as he pulls away. "It has to be, doesn't it? For you and the show. And maybe even for me and Oliver. I mean...

it can't go as badly as the first time we hung out, right?" He starts tapping his fingers together. "Actually, I'm probably jinxing myself by saying that. I'll be honest, I'm sweating in places I didn't know I could sweat." He grimaces. "No, that's a lie. I make a habit of sweating when I'm nervous. I hope he won't want to shake my hand. Or touch me at all."

"I think you *want* him to touch you," I say. "And if he gets to, he won't care about a little sweat."

Harry laughs, nods, then carries himself resolutely to the door. "Get ready for some massive oversharing."

"I was born ready. I'm already looking forward to it."

He turns and leaves, and a gaping emptiness seems to open in my room.

Loneliness wells in my stomach, in my brain, in my toes. I could go down to see the guys. Maybe I should. Both Nana and Harry are right—I have to seem more excited about being around them. No one's going to want to watch the show if it's a bunch of stiff conversations over caviar and champagne. But Harry left me with his phone, and...

The tree's sparkle catches my eye.

Rowan's number is on that phone.

Would it be pathetic of me to call him, when he's made it clear that he wants to keep his distance from me and the show? I should call Olive, or maybe my brother, but I know who I *want* to call.

Chapter Seventeen

Rowan

"Why are you being so weird?" Holly asks, giving me a searching look. We're in our house, sitting on the couch across from the bare tree—a reminder, as if I need one, of everything that went down last weekend.

"I'm not being weird," I snap at her. Weirdly.

It's Wednesday, and I still haven't told anyone what Jay told me. Well, anyone except for Kennedy Littlefield, and I threw that burden on her just before ghosting her.

Yup, I'm a real catch.

I'm guessing that Jay hasn't told anyone either because none of my sisters have asked me any leading questions about my parentage.

"You're being super-duper weird, actually," Holly says, her eyes calculating. "Is this about Kennedy? Or lingering psychological damage from listening to our grandmother make out with a thirty-year-old."

My mouth automatically twists with distaste. I did tell her that much, mostly because I wanted to take the heat off myself. My sister had plenty of questions about why I was half naked in the changing room with Kennedy when everyone in my family knows I'm trying to derail her TV show. Dammit. Holly even asked if I'd seduced

Kennedy to fuck up the show, which made me feel like a real piece of shit, even though it wasn't true.

Truth is, I didn't put much thought into it at all. I touched her, tasted her, because I wanted to. Because I couldn't, in those moments, think of anything else. And I can't lie. Even though my life has been transformed by the events of the past several days, I've been thinking about her. My mind keeps going back to that empty pool, to the way she opened her legs to me. To the way she looked at me after I told her about Jay.

My sister's still staring at me, though, waiting for an answer, and she's not the patient type. "It's not about Kennedy," I tell her through my dry mouth. I'm not sure whether or not it's a lie. "And I will always be disturbed by overhearing Nana making out with that asshole."

"I don't believe you," she says, tapping me on the nose. I grimace at her. She rolls her eyes. "Oh, your grumpy expressions don't faze me. If you insist you're not acting weird, then how come you didn't go visit Jay with us last night?"

They all went—Holly and Bryn; Willow, who drove up from Asheville and is staying with Bryn; and Ivy, who arrived from Charleston on Monday and is staying at Jay's.

I told them I had work to do.

I hid in my room.

Willow was particularly pissed because she and I have always been so close. We've had the bond of knowing we had the same piece-of-shit dad, only now I know he isn't *my* piece-of-shit dad. In some ways, I fear telling Willow most of all because maybe our special bond will disintegrate.

If I told Kennedy that, I bet she'd say that I wouldn't treat Willow any differently if the situation were reversed, so I shouldn't expect worse from my sister...and also that Ivy and me might get closer. Maybe she'd be right...if I could bring myself to tell either of them.

Coward.

Willow's still in Highland Hills, but she's leaving for Asheville later this evening. Ivy's going to stay for a few weeks, maybe into the new year, depending on what the doctors say about Jay. After she arrived, she confirmed what I already knew from Kennedy—Kerry left, and she is not, in fact, a nice woman. I guess Jay didn't tell anyone because he was trying to delude himself into believing she'd come back.

I can understand that. I'm all about believing unpleasant truths will go away if I avoid them well enough.

"Why don't we talk about Oliver and Harry?" I suggest.

Holly skewers me with a suspicious look. "You never want to gossip."

Shit, she's right. "Well, our roommate and my best friend are going out on a date tonight. That's a thing. It seems like the sort of thing women like to talk about."

She snorts. "Are you asking for a matchmaking medal? Because I'm pretty sure Willow would make you one. She's all about celebrating false accomplishments."

"Hey," I say, my tone turning harsh. "Don't talk about her like that."

She gives my shoulder a shove. "I wasn't saying it's a bad thing, dipstick. She'd do it because she's way nicer than the rest of us, which most people would agree is a good thing."

I give her a pointed look. "Most people, not including you."

"Correct," she agrees. "Being too nice is a definite failing, but it just makes her more loveable." She gives me a sly look. "Cole and Jane are coming over in twenty minutes to decorate the tree. Are you going to stay and help? I made cookies."

I can't help but laugh at that. No one taught us how to cook or bake when we were kids, so only the motivated ones learned how. Holly and I did not. "You don't know how to make cookies."

She laughs with me. "Okay, fine. So Cole made them. What's the point of dating someone if you can't take credit for their hard work?"

"I *will* take a cookie, since you had nothing to do with making them, and then I'm going to clear out," I tell her. "I acquired the tree, and it's on you and your crew to make something of it."

She gives me a naval salute, which seems particularly wrong since we're in Western North Carolina, a good seven hours from the water, and says, "Aye-aye, Skipper."

I'm about to complain about the whole naval thing, when my phone rings. My heart instantly starts racing in my chest, but a quick glance at the screen reveals it's Harry's number.

"Harry," I say, lifting it. "You think he got lost?"

"Surely he has GPS on his phone." She makes a face. "Unless he's still in that thought spiral about people using it to track him."

We've learned Harry takes dips into the toxic waters of conspiracy theories now and again, especially the ones related to possible misuses of technology. It seems to happen mostly when he's stressed, and he's understandably very stressed working with our grandmother. And living with us.

Nodding to my sister, I lift the phone and answer. "What's up, man? You get to the restaurant okay?"

"It's me," a woman's voice says, and it takes me only half a second to register that it's Kennedy. She says her name, but it's unnecessary.

"Shit, did Harry lose his phone?" I ask.

"No," she says softly. "He lent it to me. I've been feeling a bit lonely, so he figured I might want to call someone."

I hate the thought of her being lonely. She's someone who exudes light. She's a bit like Willow, actually—too sweet for a world that likes to throw people around just for fun. I shouldn't like that about her, but I do. In fact, I've spent more time than I should admit searching for bulldog puppies in the county because (a) she doesn't even live here, and (b) I'm not certain she'd be allowed to keep a dog in the Labelles' house.

"You should have called Olive," I say, like a dick. I can feel Holly watching me, so I get to my feet and pace into the kitchen. Sure enough, there's a big tub of cookies that look much too good for a Mayberry to have made them. My only hope for avoiding uncomfortable questions after this call is that Holly might think I said Oliver, not Olive.

"Probably," Kennedy says. "But I wanted to call you. Have you been avoiding me?"

There's something so sad in her voice when she says it, and I instantly feel like the biggest jerk on the planet.

"Yes," I admit, grabbing a paper towel. I take one cookie, pause, and take another. They're decorated to look like Santas, which would normally make me roll my eyes, only it's obvious that Jane, Cole's daughter, must have done the decorating. "But to be fair, I've been avoiding everyone. I've made an art of it." I head outside to the car, ignoring Holly's searching gaze. I'm on call tonight, anyway, so I figure I'll go hang out at the firehouse.

"That's not the kind of thing you should brag about," she says. "I take it you haven't told anyone about Jay?"

I sigh as I slide behind the wheel of my truck. "No. I don't really know what to say."

"Maybe you don't have to say anything," she says, warming to the subject. "Maybe you just need to tell them and let them say what they want."

Something inside me knows she's right. It'll come out at some point, especially if my mother has decided it might get her some of the attention she craves. It would be better for me to do the telling.

"We'll see," I tell her. "You throw Jonah out yet?"

"I don't get to cut anyone else until Friday," she says. "Are you going to come back?"

"Do you really want me to?" I ask, placing the cookies on the passenger seat.

"I really do," she says. "I know it's not a great situation that we're in, but I want to get to know you better. I want to spend more time with you."

My heartbeat kicks up, because I can't deny that sounds fucking great. There are just two problems with her plan. One, if I have to watch those assholes romance her, I'll lose my mind. Two, I felt on the verge of losing control with her, and I've seen what happens when people let themselves lose their minds for someone. I want no part of it.

"I don't know if that's such a good idea," I tell her.

"Oh," she says. It's such a simple word. Not even a word, really, but it carries the weight of the world. And I feel like complete shit for having put it there.

"I want to see you, Princess," I admit, because it's true, and I can't have her thinking otherwise. "But I don't think I can sit back and watch—"

"*Oh*," she says again, and this time, it's an altogether different sound, almost breathy. My cock twitches. Shit.

"There's something else," she adds, and from the way she says it, it's obvious this isn't a good something else. "Your grandmother...she knew things she shouldn't have known about last weekend. She made me play Truth or Dare with the guys today, and there was a list of suggested dares that included skinny dipping in the pool."

I say "fuck" with feeling. I hate the thought of anyone witnessing any part of what we shared. It was private. It was *perfect*. And what if it's one of the guys who's spying and not my grandmother? What if some pervert is watching her while she undresses at night? While she touches herself?

"Did you search the room for a bug?" I growl.

"Harry looked, and he couldn't find anything," she says. "You know he's really paranoid about stuff like that, but would you like to..."

I've already put the truck into drive. "I'm on my way."

It's not until I park outside the house that I realize I grabbed two cookies because I wanted to give one to her.

* * *

Kennedy's eyes light up when I shove the cookie at her. "Here, it's for you."

"I love it," she says as I shut the door behind me.

"Let's not make a big deal out of it," I say, even as my eyes catch on the Christmas tree she has displayed in front of the closed window. I like that she has it up, although she probably loves it because it makes her think of Christmas, not because it makes her think of the man who got it for her on an impulse he didn't fully understand. "I didn't bake them."

Her lips twitch with amusement. "I didn't assume you had. But I'm no less grateful. I love Christmas cookies."

"I'm not surprised."

She's wearing that damn Christmas tree farm shirt again, which makes me remember, with a pulse of regret, that I lost mine. This time it's paired with yoga pants, probably because there's a cold bite in the air. Ray's Weather Center says there'll be snow this weekend, or early next week at the latest, and Ray knows his shit.

"Is that the only thing you have that's not an overpriced gown?"

"One of the only things," she says with a slight smile. "I also have a ridiculous equestrian outfit that I think you would have enjoyed very much." Her nose wrinkles. "The horse smell was less enjoyable."

She looks down at the cookie and then lifts it for a bite, her full lips closing around it. Santa's one lucky man to be consumed by her. And there's your proof that falling for a woman can make you lose your ever-loving mind.

"Where'd Harry look in your room?" I ask.

"Everywhere," she says. "He was pretty thorough."

"We'll be more thorough."

We start by the bedroom door and work inward from there. I can already tell it's going to take a while with all the crap arranged around the room. The Labelles really have a thing for collecting dust in a variety of different ways. I move one piece of junk, then another. There are no listening devices or cameras, or at least none I can see. Kennedy trails me with the cookie.

"You're good at this," she says. "Look for bugs often?"

"No," I say. "But it's not the first time. I told you I'm a handyman. One time, this woman had me check her house for bugs because she thought her husband was trying to spy on her. They were going through a divorce."

"Was he?" she asks.

She must be interested in the story, because she hasn't taken another bite. It's sort of...well, it's cute.

"I didn't find anything. So either he wasn't as much of a shit as she thought, or I really suck at finding these things." I smile at her. "Let's hope it was the first."

She laughs as she checks the area by the window where she's set up the Christmas tree. Putting in front of the window is a bold choice, but the curtains are thick.

"Why do you like Christmas so much, anyway?" I ask, shooting a glance at her as I continue the search.

"It's magical," she says, taking another bite of the cookie, her teeth sinking into it in a way that shouldn't feel sexual but does. Maybe it's because my mind keeps going there with her, and I don't know how to make it stop. "It's a time where it feels like anything can happen."

"If you have enough money to make it happen."

Kennedy finishes the cookie and wipes her hands primly on the napkin before throwing it into the pumpkin-shaped trash bin. I swallow a scoff.

"The reasons I like it have nothing to do with money," she says,

171

meeting my eyes and holding them. I feel a weird stirring inside, like I missed her, and now that she's here, I don't want to step away from her. There's a sudden, sharp awareness that we're in a bedroom, and even though it looks like a kid's room, there's still a bed. A big bed. I'll bet it's soft.

I clear my throat and pick up a ceramic horse. The head falls off.

"Shit." I say, dropping it. It shatters on the floor. "Fuck."

Kennedy surprises me by laughing. "So you prefer Halloween and the headless horseman to Christmas?"

"What are the odds that was priceless?" I ask.

She waves to the little figurines all around the room. "What are the odds that they'll notice?"

"Probably a lot lower if we hide the evidence," I say, smirking at her.

"Put it in the dresser." She smiles back at me.

I bring it over, and she comes with me. When I tug on the handle for the top drawer, she opens her mouth to say something, but she's not quick enough. I've already slid it out, and it's full of silky panties, green and gold and red, like her obsession with Christmas has slid into her underwear drawer. This woman obviously brings out something strange in me, because I want to bury my face in them. I want to stick a pair in my pocket. Instead, I look at her mutely.

"They won't find it there," she says.

"No, I guess not," I tell her. Then I swallow and nestle the pieces of the horse inside, setting a few pairs of underwear on top.

She watches me do it, her pupils dilated, and I know without asking that we're both thinking of the other night, of the way I pulled off her panties and made her come. I'd like to do it again. I'd like to throw her onto that princess bed and show her something truly magical.

Instead, I swallow and shut the drawer. "Why is it magical then, Princess?"

She takes a step toward me, then another. I feel my will crumbling like one of those cookies. "Remember what I told you about my parents' Christmas Eve party? It's a whole event. They spend a ton of money on caterers, gift bags, that kind of thing."

"Yeah, sounds like a good time," I say, my lips twitching. She takes another step toward me. I don't think I've ever been so aware of someone's presence...of the space they take up in a room.

"It's terrible," she says. "But one year, when I was six, I had a cold. My mother refused to share the same air as me because she wasn't going to cancel her party for anything. My dad either. But they didn't care about Nanny Rose or Olive getting sick, so they sent me home with them a few days before Christmas. And that's when I realized what Christmas was supposed to be like. When I was feeling better, we went caroling with these big travel mugs of hot chocolate Nanny Rose made for us, and then we went to see Santa Claus at one of the big box stores." She smiles in reminiscence. "My mother had never let me do that. She would have been scandalized. And we baked cookies together. We knew Santa came to visit us on Christmas Eve, because the next morning the cookies we'd set out were all gone." She shrugs. "It was the best Christmas I ever had."

"Your parents chose a party over you?" I ask, irrationally pissed. It wasn't like my parents were any better, but I hated the thought of her being sent away so they could hold some stupid fucking party.

She smiles at me, but there's plenty of sadness in it this time. "They always do, Rowan." She takes another step toward me. "I have my brothers, though. Both of my brothers, but Phillip has always tried to follow in our father's footsteps. Zach never fit into them." She worries her lip in her teeth. "I shouldn't be telling you this. I'd rather you heard it from him, but I think it might help you."

"What?" I ask, interested in spite of myself. I'm spellbound to the bit of floor beneath me, like I can't move away, but I also can't move toward her.

"Our parents disowned Zach because he found out that our father wasn't his biological dad. Our mother had an affair."

A surprised "Oh shit" tears out of me.

Her mouth lifts slightly. "Exactly."

"The fact that they disowned him isn't exactly making me want to tell my sisters about all of this," I say wryly.

"*I* didn't disown him," she says fiercely. "In fact, we've become much closer since he told me. It changed our relationship and put us on equal footing." She lifts her eyebrows. "Because you can't be on equal footing with someone if you don't trust them with your feelings."

I laugh and adjust my weight, my feet still frozen. "Fuck, if that's true, then I'm not on equal footing with anyone."

That look of hers drills into me. "But you could be. They're your sisters. They'll want to go through this with you."

I think again about Willow and how she'll only be here for another few hours. "My sister Willow's in town," I say numbly. "And Ivy. They're the ones I should tell first."

"Why don't you invite them out for coffee or a drink?" she suggests, just this side of bossy. It's enough to make me scowl, because I grew up with a natural disinclination to do what I was told, but she blushes and slinks back a step, which I didn't want.

"Okay," I say.

"You'll do it?" she asks, as excited as if I'd announced I wanted to go caroling in costume.

"Sure," I say, one corner of my mouth hitching up. "Because you twisted my arm. But why do you care so much?"

"My mother would say that I care way too much about other people's business and too little about my own."

I'm close enough to touch her, and I don't deny the desire any more. I tell myself I'm just doing it because she needs cheering up, but only a fool believes his own lies. Tipping up her chin slightly, I look into her big blue eyes. "And what would *you* say?"

She doesn't flinch or look away, her gaze soaking into mine, her proximity making my skin feel like it's buzzing. Her skin is warm and soft against mine, and I have a moment of self-consciousness. I know my hands are callused from building cars. From odd jobs. I try to pull away, but she lifts her other hand to mine, keeping it there.

"I'd say that I like you, even if I shouldn't. I've been worried about you."

"You don't need to worry about me, Princess," I say, but I don't try moving my hand from her jaw. I find myself tracing the shape of it, the rest of my body inching closer. "I'm the last person you need to worry about."

"I think you're exactly the person I need to worry about," she says. "If you don't open up to anyone, who helps you carry the weight?"

I smile at her because I can't help it. "Right now, I guess you are. Why go to that much trouble for someone you barely know, Kennedy?"

"Because I'd like to know you," she says, as my fingers reach up to stroke her cheeks, to soak in a little more of her. "Truth. What's your passion, Rowan?"

Right now, my passion is Kennedy Littlefield. But I know that's not what she means. "Making model cars." I curse as soon as the words come out, immediately feeling like an idiot. "It's stupid."

"It's not. You mentioned it to me the other day, but you didn't tell me much. I'd like to know more."

"They're toys."

"I didn't know you liked kids," she says with delight.

"I don't," I blurt, letting my hand drop. Then I instantly shrug. "Okay, I sort of do. I like the way kids see the world. I like that they haven't been put into boxes yet, like the rest of us."

She smiles. "I'd like to see some of your cars."

I don't plan on it. I just do it, which is maybe the story of my life. I lean in and kiss Kennedy, because even though I don't want to need her, something inside of me does. She lets out a little gasp of surprise, and I swallow it, but it only takes her a second to wrap her arms

175

around me and draw me closer. She's sweet like that damn cookie, and I want her so much it physically pains me. I can't remember ever wanting another woman this much.

It's because of what happened while she was around, I tell myself. But I don't really believe it. I deepen the kiss, because I want to forget the stupid voice in my head, and I really want to forget the six men competing to marry her. Hell, I want to make her forget it too, so I deepen our kiss, weaving a hand into her long hair so I can bring her closer—and because I have a bone-deep need to feel the silky strands wound between my fingers again.

Her breasts are pressed to my chest, the sweet sensation adding to my fire, making me want to strip that shirt off of her, because there's no way in hell she's wearing a bra. I feel like a fool for not doing that last time, when I had her splayed out before me. I could have had something else to think about at night.

She pulls away, her lips pink. "Is this a way to avoid showing me your cars? Because I still want to see them."

"Maybe," I say with a smirk. But to my surprise, I want to show her the damn cars.

I take out my phone, flinching when I see there are two missed calls from Oliver. "Shit," I say, showing her the screen.

Her eyes go wide. "Harry."

She checks the phone he left her with shaking hands, then shows me the screen.

Oliver: *Hey, man, did you get held up?*
Oliver: *Where are you?*
Oliver: *Okay, Harry. I can take a hint. You could have just said no, you know.*

"Rowan," she says, her voice full of terror. "He was looking forward to this date. A lot. He never would have stood Oliver up."

Chapter Eighteen

Rowan

"What do you mean I can't go with you?" she asks, looking somewhere between pissed and sad. "Of course I have to go, Rowan. You can't expect me to stay cooped up in here by myself, possibly with a bug, while Harry is out there lost or hurt or—"

She lets out a sob, and I hate that I made her cry. It twists something inside my chest, almost like there's a key in a skeleton lock somewhere in there, down deep, holding back everything I want to keep contained, and the key is being jarred. Fuck.

I wrap my arms around her and pull her to my chest. Even though it's me she's pissed at, at least partially, she leans into me, her tears soaking my shirt. I run a soothing hand down her back, because that's what my sisters do when they hug each other when they're upset. "It's okay," I tell her, even though I'm not totally sure it's true. "It's okay. I'm not going to rest until I find him and make sure he's all right, and we're not going to leave you here in the dark, Princess. One of us will get a message to you tonight. I guarantee you that. I'm not going to make you try to fall asleep without knowing he's okay. I wouldn't do that to you, especially not after—"

In my head, I see Jay clutching his shoulder again. I see him collapsing to his knees. The stab of pain is unexpected and unwel-come, and it leaves my heart racing. I find myself clinging to Kennedy a bit tighter because her warmth and scent are surprisingly calming.

But I *do* want to find Harry, so I pull away slightly and tuck her hair behind her ear. "I'm going to find him, but I need to leave now. Okay?"

"I don't want to be in here alone," she says softly.

I don't want that either, but what am I supposed to do in the short term? The answer comes to me in half a second, but I don't like it. "Where are the guys?" I ask gruffly.

"You want me to go spend time with them?" she asks. There's something terse about her voice. I've pissed her off, I realize, and for at least half a second, I'm glad for it.

"No, I don't want you to spend time with them," I say. "I want to take you with me. I want to pretend that my grandmother never dreamed up this show, and that you're—"

Mine.

It's a stupid thought. I mean, I've known this woman for all of a week. So I shake it off and say, "And that you're free to do whatever you want. But we both know that's not the case. You won't be helping Harry if you're seen looking for him outside the house. You'd both get in trouble."

It doesn't escape my attention that this would bring me closer to my end goal of getting the show canceled early—a goal I've done diddly squat to pursue over the past several days—but I don't want it to happen like that. I don't want anyone I care about to bear the burden.

"Okay," she says sadly. "I don't like it, but I guess you're right."

I kiss the top of her head, and because that's definitely not enough, bend down to claim her mouth. "You won't be alone in here for long, Kennedy. I promise this will be fine."

She nods and hands me Harry's phone. We figure he might try to call it at some point, knowing it's a way to get in touch with Kennedy.

"Keep checking the room," I say with a grimace before I step out. "Make sure you've looked everything over. We didn't finish."

The look she's giving me suggests we left a lot of things unfinished, and she's absolutely right.

But I leave anyway, my heart thumping, because I'm not sure I can take any more bad news today. I like Harry, and I don't want to think something bad might have happened to him, but I've worked as a parttime fireman for long enough time to know that the thing with Jay wasn't an aberration. Bad shit does happen, and it doesn't care whether it's convenient for someone's schedule.

Still, I see my grandmother walking through the hallways like a wraith on my way out, and I stop her. There's an idea I need to plant in her head. I want her to think it's hers.

"It's about time you showed up," she sneers. "I have a list of things for you to do. There's a strange smell in the men's wing. It's been very upsetting to Jonah. He has a delicate constitution."

Yup, that's my bad. I tucked a dead fish into the back of the toilet.

"Tomorrow," I say. "There's something I need to do right now. But, hey, I had a thought."

"Color me surprised," she says, putting a hand on her hip. "You're not known for thinking."

"And you're not known for listening," I say. "But this show needs seem livening up. Maybe an animal sidekick."

"There were horses today," she says defensively.

"I was thinking about a puppy."

"Dogs are dirty," she says loftily.

"Yes," I say. "And most of the guys will hate it, but Kennedy will love it. I heard her telling someone she's always wanted a puppy. Used to ask Santa for it."

The way she tilts her head with interest tells me she's not aware of everything that passed between Kennedy and me the other night, thank God.

"A bulldog puppy," I continue.

"You want me to get her a dog?"

This is the part I don't like so much. This is the part that's going to get her the dog. "I can locate one, if you want. You could have one of the guys take credit. Your frontrunner."

Her expression is contemplative, but I know I've got her on the hook. I can't sound too interested or invested now; it would put her off. "Anyway, just a thought. I figured it would add something to the show."

"So you have half a brain after all," Nana says, patting her bun. "Up until now, your mother is the only one who's shown any interest in the show, and her suggestion was preposterous."

I stiffen, because I have a pretty damn good idea of what she suggested. I can't believe she asked Nana about it even after Jay told her no. Actually, shit, I *do* believe it. It's precisely in her nature.

"Goodnight, Nana."

"I'll let you know what I decide," she says. "But in the meantime, see if you can source one."

As if a puppy were a side of meat or a bag of grain.

I walk off without a wave or a feigned gesture of affection, and she does the same.

Once I'm outside, I dial Oliver. "Hey," he answers, sounding like a guy who's just been stood up.

"Hey," I tell him as I make my way to the truck. "We need to find Harry. I was just with Kennedy, and from what she said, he was pretty excited about meeting up with you. He even left his phone with her because he already knew where to go and when. I'm hoping he got lost, but..."

"Shit," Oliver says, his mood transforming in an instant. "I figured he'd stood me up. That he ran away like the last time some-thing...anyway, that doesn't matter. Goddammit."

"Yup, that's what we were thinking." He doesn't ask why I was with Kennedy, probably because his mind is busy working on the problem of where Harry got off to. I'm good with that. I don't have any sensible answers, and I want to find Harry too.

"Meet me at...where were you supposed to meet him? I never asked."

"Salt and Bone."

"I'll be there in ten."

I drive faster than I should because I'm getting more and more agitated.

My phone rings when I'm a minute and a half away, and I pick it up in case it's Oliver. It's not. It's the fucking emergency room.

I answer halfway through the first ring. "What's going on?"

"Sir," a woman says in a calm, measured voice. "We have a man here who says he's your roommate."

"Harry?" I blurt. "What's happened to him?"

"He'll be perfectly fine, sir. There's really no reason for him to be here for something—"

"Let me talk to him," I hear Harry say, his voice practically bouncing with nerves.

"No, sir. You will *not* use my phone."

"I'll be right there," I say.

"He's perfectly fine to drive ho—"

"No, I'm not, I'm a *mutant*," I hear Harry wail.

Well, shit, I'd better get over there. "I'll be right there," I repeat.

Instead of trying to find street parking, I call Oliver and tell him to meet me outside the restaurant because Harry's in the hospital.

He's there when I pull up, his face drawn with worry, and it's obvious that he likes Harry. A lot. I shouldn't take any satisfaction in that—I've done almost nothing to help throw them together other than suggest the Christmas tree outing—but I'm surprised to feel almost...excited by the possibility. Fuck. Kennedy is clearly messing with my head, because that's not like me. At all. I've always run away as fast as I could from my family's matchmaking legacy.

"What's happening?" he asks, as I drive toward the hospital. "Car accident? Shit, was he involved in a hit and run?"

"No, I don't think it's anything like that," I say, then share the weird exchange I overheard at the hospital.

He frowns. "What could have happened? Especially within such a tight timeframe?"

I pull into the hospital parking lot. "I have a feeling we're about to find out."

And we do, fifteen minutes later. Or rather Oliver does. With the flu running rampant through Highland Hills, they have a one-visitor policy, and I tell him to go. He doesn't fight me on it, not that I thought he would. I send him back there with Harry's phone too.

I pace the lobby, nerves prickling, until Oliver calls me on my cell.

"Well, they're releasing him," he says. "But you know how long all the paperwork can take."

I nod before realizing he can't see me. "I know. So what the hell happened?"

"*Your grandmother* happened," he says, sounding mad as hell. It takes a lot to piss Oliver off this much—leave it to my grandmother to manage the impossible.

"What do you mean?" I ask, catching his anger like it's a flame to my paper. "What did she do this time?"

"I guess she ran into him when he was on his way out of the house, and she told him his skin looked dry. Offered him some of her special cream. He's allergic to lavender. We think she knew."

"Fuck, of course she knew. I'm so sorry, man. How does he look?"

"His face is covered with hives. His hands and arms too. They say he's going to be fine. He doesn't need anything but topical treatment. He keeps talking about the past repeating itself, but I have no clue what he means. He took a few CBD gummies for the nerves."

"She needs to be stopped," I say, anger thrumming through my veins. "She's trying to make sure he misses shooting so she can be the star. That *bitch*."

"You're right," Oliver says. "I wasn't on board with your pranks in the beginning, but you're goddamn right. There's something missing in that woman, and now she's rolling other people into her schemes. She's power tripping."

"Will you take him home?"

"Of course."

We hang up, and I'm left more unsettled than when I started the drive from the Labelles'.

I hate the thought of Kennedy being stuck in that house like a princess living with an evil stepmother. My grandmother might not live in the Labelles' house, but for the next month, it's her territory, no mistaking that, and she will take every last advantage that role affords her. Over the past several days, I've felt my will to destroy the show crumbling because Kennedy wants this, even if her reasons for wanting it have nothing to do with the supposed purpose of the show. But I can't let this go. I can't. I turn to keep pacing and almost run smack into my little sister, who's wearing a pair of overalls that suggest she's ready to tackle some kind of dirty task, even though I'm pretty sure she's never changed a tire.

"Rowan," Ivy says, her lips turning down, and I see it now. Ivy has always looked different from the rest of us kids because she got Jay's light coloring. But we also look more alike than I ever registered. It's there in the shape of our eyes, the similarity of our noses. The evidence has been there all along, and it's disconcerting to see.

I shake myself, because Ivy looks fucking pissed, and she's not going to give me the luxury of a stroll down memory lane.

"You're finally here, huh?" she says, lifting one eyebrow. Her ability to do so is a gift, according to Holly, who always complains that she can't manage the trick.

I didn't come to see Jay, of course, but I can hardly tell her that.

My mind skips to Kennedy, to how I promised her that I'd tell my sisters the truth, Ivy and Willow first of all.

"Is Willow here?" I ask, and something falls in Ivy's face, like she's hurt that I asked.

"Can't talk to me for two minutes without backup?" She says it like it's a joke, but it doesn't sound like much of one. I've barely said anything, and I've already upset her. That has to be some kind of shitty brother record.

"We talked the other day, didn't we?" I object.

She makes a sound of disapproval. "Willow's not here, but she wanted to put in one more visit before she heads home to Asheville. She's coming in fifteen minutes." Her expression sharpens. "From what I understand, you haven't seen *her* either. Who pissed in your cornflakes? I know it wasn't my dad because he's not exactly in corn-flakes pissing form."

"Nana," I say deadpan, but my heart is racing in my chest. I'm still not ready to talk to him, but maybe I'll never be ready. Maybe it's the kind of thing you just need to do, with the hope that you can manage it because you have no choice.

She laughs before she schools her expression. "I'm mad at you."

"You're probably the only Mayberry who'd say it so directly. I was expecting one of those bullshit lines, like I'm not mad, I'm disap-pointed."

The corners of her mouth creep up. "Oh, I'm both. I guess it's a good thing I'm not a Mayberry."

My heartrate kicks up a notch. She's the only one of us kids who doesn't go by Mayberry. "Let's get some coffee, huh? Wait for Willow together?"

She looks half-tempted to turn me down, but she nods. "Fine."

We do, and then we're sitting at a little table in the lobby with cups of coffee, the silence between us awkward and a little antagonistic.

"So you're pissed at me," I finally say.

"Obviously," she tells me. "You're the one who told me about my dad, but for the past several days you've been off doing God knows what while we're in here trying to cheer him up because he just had a heart attack that's going to force him into retirement years early, and his bitch wife left him for a podiatrist."

"Seriously? A podiatrist?"

"The only one in Highland Hills," she says, her lips twitching. "He treated her bunions. She posted on Facebook that it's the most romantic thing to have ever happened to her."

"What did *you* say?" I ask, because I know her enough to know she said something.

She laughs. "I commented with a video from her wedding to my dad, where she said meeting him at the Christmas tree farm was the most romantic thing to have ever happened to her. She commented that she's not surprised I'd take his side, as if there's any other side to take, and then defriended and blocked me."

She says it offhandedly, as if it doesn't matter, but I can tell it does. That woman was in her life for years, and it sucks that she'd throw her away so carelessly, as if she's nothing. Maybe Ivy's not so different from the rest of us Mayberrys after all.

"I'm sorry, Little Bit. Goddamn. I thought she was different. Jay always seemed so happy with her."

She grins at me, but there's a hint of sadness in it. "He's always like that. I think he's worried that if he ever stops acting happy, he'll figure out how he really feels and won't like it." Then she laughs. "Kind of like how you act like an asshole three-quarters of the time so no one will know you have a bleeding heart."

"Bite your tongue," I say, teasing, but the words burrow into me.

"I've been trying to talk him into getting a roommate. He could use the extra money, especially if Kerry's going to take him to the cleaners, and he's the kind of person who does better having someone else around." I don't miss her meaning. She's staying, but not forever. "I'm going to write an ad for him."

"You think that's necessary?" I ask with a laugh. "You tell one person what he's looking for, and suddenly everyone in town will know."

"True," she acknowledges with a bob of her head. "Besides, I'll be around for a while. I can help him find someone who won't take advantage of him."

"Have you talked to Holly about working at the brewery while you're here?"

"A bit," she says. "I'm not ready for that yet, though. Dad really does need someone around."

Guilt slings its arms around me and hugs.

"I didn't mean to guilt trip you," she says, giving me some side-eye that slips into a grin. "But if it gets you off your ass, I don't hate it. Now, what's this I hear about you and the bachelorette?"

"That's a different show," I say.

She nudges my shoulder. "I obviously want to know everything."

"Don't you dare put this in a book someday," I say. "The guys are still handing your fireman romance around at the firehouse, calling me Cupid. If you write about me and Kennedy, I'll never live it down."

She gives me another shoulder nudge. A guy sitting at a table across from us is checking her out like she's dessert, and I scowl at him until he turns away.

"The Cupid nickname has as much to do with our big sisters as it does with me," Ivy says. "And how would they even know it's about you and Kennedy unless something happens between you and Kennedy?" she asks, watching me carefully. They see too much, my sisters. They see through me, certainly.

"Rowan?" I look up and see Willow walking toward us, and it's like someone's reached into my chest and squeezed. I can tell she's been crying, and I'll bet some of that's because of me. I've been an asshole, icing her out when she needs me. They all need me, and I've been off moping and daydreaming about the bit of heaven between Kennedy Littlefield's legs.

Both Ivy and I get to our feet, and I wrap my arms around Willow when she reaches us. I can practically hear Kennedy telling me to let them in—both of them—so I pull Ivy into our embrace.

"Ho-ly shit," Ivy says, giving each syllable some play. "Rowan Mayberry just initiated a group hug. Sometimes life really is stranger than fiction."

But I can tell she kind of likes it.

I kind of do too.

"I need to talk to both of you," I say, still holding them. In that moment, I need to be anchored to them. I *need* it. "There's something I have to tell you. Can we go sit somewhere private?"

Chapter Nineteen

Kennedy

I'm awakened by a light knock on the door. My first fuzzy thought is to be surprised that I managed to fall asleep. I spent the whole evening a big bundle of nerves, unable to do anything other than finish searching the room. There were no visible bugs, although would I even know what to look for? I flipped listlessly through the holiday romance Jeff gave me, followed by the biography of Jonah's similarly named relative. I wasn't surprised to discover he was a horrible man—the kind historians write cautionary tales about.

I was physically exhausted, so I finally lay down on the bed and studied the little tree, counting the lights as if they were sheep jumping over fences.

The knock lands again, and terror rips through me. It's clearly very late. Does this mean something awful happened? Something so bad Rowan couldn't get away until this very second?

The door cracks open before I can say anything, just an inch or so, and I see his face through the opening, his strong jaw, his short beard, that turbulent intensity in his eyes that made me half afraid of him when we first met.

"Rowan," I say, sitting up in bed.

"You were sleeping." He shuts the door behind him. "I didn't mean to wake you, but I knew..."

"Harry," I say, as worry snakes through me like toxic vines. "How—"

"He's okay, Princess," he says, sitting on the edge of my bed and running a hand down my hair. "He's okay. He was in the emergency room, but—"

"What?" I squawk.

His mouth firms into an angry line. "My grandmother's a bad woman, Kennedy. She'll do anything to get what she wants. The sooner you realize that, the better."

"What'd she do to him?" I ask, horrified.

"She gave him a cream he was allergic to. I guess he slathered it on his face and arms, and he broke out in hives. Oliver went to the hospital with me, and he drove him back to my place. I talked to them both just now, and Harry's fine."

"Oh, thank God," I say, but it registers that Harry's first romantic encounter with Oliver ended with the gas situation, and their first official date was interrupted by hives. "Poor Harry."

Rowan strokes my hair again, his fingers brushing my scalp and sending tingles of awareness through me. It suddenly dawns on me that he's here in my room. Sitting on my *bed*.

"My sister's decorating the tree with her boyfriend and his kid, so I guess they helped. Now, they're watching a movie," he says, still touching me, like he can't help it or doesn't want to. "Oliver's good at making people comfortable. It's his gift." He gives me a wry smile. "One I'd like to borrow from time to time."

"You make me comfortable," I say, even though it's slightly untrue. He unsettles me. He makes me want things. But right now, with his hand in my hair, I'm exactly where I need to be. I pause, soaking him in, then say, "Did you talk to your sisters?"

"I did." He lowers his hand, and the loss of his warmth feels almost criminal until he leans down to remove his shoes. Once they're off, he shocks me by lying down on the mattress and pulling me to him. Snuggling me close so my head is tucked under his chin, my back to his hard chest, and his strong arms around me. "Is this okay?"

"It's more than okay," I say, because it feels like bliss. I was so alone tonight, so worried and scared. And now I'm engulfed by Rowan's warmth and scent. I feel safe. I feel cherished. I clear my throat. "How'd it go?"

"It was awful," he says gruffly, then laughs. "But I guess it was okay, too. Willow..." He doesn't say anything for a moment, and I can practically feel the emotion he's suppressing, a great big cloud of it trapped in his chest. I want to tell him that the people who say men —and "proper little ladies"—shouldn't express their feelings are full of crap. Those same lessons were poured into my ears ever since I was old enough to understand language, and they never served me or my brothers well. The opposite. If I weren't afraid he'd stop talking, I'd assure him that he can always be himself around me.

I want to look at him, so I nudge him slightly. He releases me, and I roll onto my side next to him, tugging his arm until he turns to fully face me, our bodies still pressed together.

Lifting a hand to my cheekbone and tracing it, sending out pulses of warmth like sugar dust, he says, "Willow said she wishes it had come out sooner so that I could have gone to live with him like Ivy." I feel his chest shaking a little, and tears press against my eyes, because I know his sister's words snarled through him. He swallows. "I told her that of course I wouldn't have left her. I never would have left her. Then Ivy seemed upset." He swallows again. "I can't seem to stop hurting people, Kennedy."

I lean forward and kiss him because I have to. Because I've never wanted to soothe someone so much, to give back to them what they've given to me. "*You* didn't hurt them. None of you are responsible for what your parents did. You were just left to deal with the fallout."

He nods slightly and pulls me closer. Even as he does it, he says, "I shouldn't be here, Princess. I know I shouldn't be here. But I can't bring myself to regret it."

"Good. Did you see Jay?"

His jaw firms, but he gives a slight nod. "Yeah, I saw him for a few minutes with my sisters. I...he seems like he's doing okay. He's going to make it, but Ivy says he'll have to retire early. He can't do site visits anymore. He does environmental site inspection, so that's his whole job."

"That'll be a hard transition," I say. I know nothing about Jay's job or his attachment to it, but I'm certain my father will die in his desk chair. It's the only thing he knows or wants to know. And when he finally passes, my big brother Phillip will step in for him. He's the type who'll probably die on the job too, although I wish more for him.

"Ivy's going stick around for a while," he says, his voice almost plaintive.

"You don't have to be there for Jay, Rowan," I say, rubbing his back, registering the cords of muscle as I do. Who knew a back could feel like this? "You don't have to. But I think maybe a part of you wants to be."

"You're too sweet for your own good," he says, but in a way that suggests he's happy to take me as I am, just as I'm happy to take him as he is.

Maybe that's why I slide my hands beneath the hem of his shirt, looking into his eyes, soaking in the surprise and then the flash of hot wanting, and say, "So let me be sweet to you."

"Kennedy," he says, his voice shaking slightly. I know what he's going to say, and I don't want him to, so I kiss him—it's a soft kiss, but when he kisses me back it's fierce, like he *needs* to kiss me, like kissing me is giving him air rather than stealing it away.

A little hum of pleasure escapes my throat because no one has ever kissed me like this. No one. Brandon made me believe he loved me, before I discovered the truth about him, but he never made me feel *wanted*. Rowan's making me feel like I'm a glass of water discovered by a man in the desert. His mouth is hot and possessive as it arcs over mine, his hand spearing through my hair.

I pull away slightly, but only because I really want him to take his shirt off. I haven't been able to stop thinking about what he looks like without one, the stacked ridges of thick muscle, the sprinkling of chest hair that he hasn't waxed away like other men I've dated.

"Your shirt," I say, my voice breathy and strange to my ears. "Take it off."

"There's my princess, telling me what to do," he says, but his tone is warm. Fond. "I've never been good about following instructions, though." He lifts me to sitting before tugging off *my* night shirt, a desperately unsexy gift from Olive that says *Is it too late to be good?* over a drawing of the Naughty List.

Yes, it's *definitely* too late to be good.

A groan escapes him when he sees I'm not wearing a bra underneath—that, in fact, I only have on a pair of silky green underwear—and he lobs the shirt at the floor, his mouth lowering to my nipple. As he sucks and nips at it, sending sensation uncurling toward my core, he reaches up and palms my other breast, his warmth engulfing it, his fingers tweaking, and I'm so ready for him. I've *never* wanted a man this much. I don't think I've ever wanted *anything* this much. Maybe it's selfish, but I don't care that there are six other men in this house who are supposedly here *for me*. I only want this one.

He switches his mouth to my other breast, but his hand reaches down between my legs, dipping under the silky panties. I feel the sound he makes—a rumble from his chest—when he discovers how desperately turned on I am.

"Fuck," he says, with feeling. Stroking his fingers through my folds and then circling my sensitive spot, he elicits a gasp from me. "You're so wet for me, Princess. I need to taste you again. I haven't been able to think about fuck all else for the past week."

I want that too, obviously, but I need him to be naked. I need to see all of him. I need...

"I don't just want your mouth on me," I say in a stranger's voice. Because there's no control left in the woman who's speaking, no hint of propriety. "I want more of you." And I reach down to touch him through his pants. His hardness is straining to escape, and the feel of it against my hand sends a shiver through me, because I can hardly think beyond getting him inside me. Getting all of him. I reach for the button of his pants.

He swears again, but he moves my hand away.

I frown. "I want you. I want your—"

"I don't have a condom," he says. "We can't. I can't—"

"You can," I say. "I'm clean, and I have a birth control implant." Self-consciousness nips at me, and I look down. "I mean, as long as you—"

"Oh, I fucking want you," he says, grabbing my chin and pulling it up so I'm looking into his intense eyes, beating into me. I can see that he *does* want me, and the sight only makes me wetter. "And I'm clean, but Kennedy...I can't do this and then watch you flirt with the seven dwarves. If they touch you—" There's a hint of menace in his voice, of possessiveness, and I'd be lying if I said it didn't turn me on even more.

"There are only six of them," I say, earning one of his grumpy looks. "Besides, what's the difference? If you go down on me, it's still sex." I'm pretty sure I know the answer, but I want him to say it. If he makes me come with his mouth and his hands, I'm the only one relinquishing control. If he takes me with his dick, then he will have relinquished some measure of control too.

He gives me one of his grumpy looks. "If we cross that line, if I come inside you, then there won't be any coming back from it for me. I won't be able to watch from the sidelines as those assholes touch you."

Judging from the way he's avoided the set, I'm guessing he

already has a problem watching me interact with them, but I don't argue. I like the thought of him feeling possessive of me, because I feel possessive of him.

I reach for his pants again, undo the button. This time, he doesn't stop me. "I'm not going to flirt with them," I say. "I don't want any of them. I wouldn't be interested in them even if you weren't around to always make them come up short." I undo the zipper, savoring the sound he makes as I free him. "But we can talk about all of that later. Right now, there's only one thing I want."

He's looking at me with something like wonder. "Are you telling me you want my cock, Princess?"

I've never talked like this before, so directly, so crudely, but I like the feeling of naughtiness when I reach down and touch him again, this time with only his boxer briefs in the way, tracing his hard length from root to tip before pushing the band of his underwear down so I can feel his hot flesh in my hand. He's long and thick, not that I'm surprised. Everything about him is big. "I want your cock, Rowan. I want all of you."

A growl escapes him, and he gets up, and in one rough move-ment shoves down his pants and his underwear. His shirt goes next, dispensed with as if it offended him. He pauses only to take off his socks.

He's glorious like this, and if I had my choice, I'd spend several minutes just admiring him—touching and kissing him everywhere, from his Adam's apple down to his muscular thighs. But he's only still for an instant before he's on the bed again, shoving my under-wear to the side, his fingers curling up into me. Surprise and then something deeper roils through me when he finds a spot inside me, just a couple of inches in, that sends waves of pleasure coiling up and out. He pulses his fingers there, and when my lips drop open with a moan of pleasure, he leans in and captures it in his mouth, giving me those thirsty kisses again as he continues to pulse his fingers, pressing the palm of his hand to my clit. My mind is consumed by him, my body owned by him, and I feel myself—

He pulls back slightly, staring at me with that intense gaze. "You're going to come for me, Princess. I can feel your sweet pussy clenching around my fingers."

And hearing him say that is enough to send me over the verge.

"Rowan," I call out as pleasure spirals through me, and he kisses me again as if needing to swallow his name from my lips. I can feel him pushing down my underwear. I help, using my legs to get them the rest of the way off, and then, while pleasure is still pounding through me, I feel his tip pressing at my opening.

Oh my God, yes. Yes.

He pushes in slowly, as if he knows he's big even though I'm so ready for him. There's a delicious tightness that sends fresh pleasure coursing through me as he finally bottoms out. His mouth is still on mine, giving me soul-sucking kisses that make me feel like I can never go a minute without kissing this man, but he pulls back slightly, his eyes on me.

"Are you okay?"

Am I okay? I've never felt better—fuller and more satisfied, yet filled with the need for more. "Better than okay," I say on a gasp. "You feel amazing."

He's propped on one elbow, looking down at me, but he lifts his thumb to my lips and traces them. "You feel so fucking good I can't stand it," he says. I capture his thumb in my mouth and suck, mesmerized by the way it makes his pupils dilate. When he pops it out, he kisses me again, his hard length pulsing inside of me, his tongue in my mouth.

He starts moving again, slowly, the friction driving me insane, and I wrap my legs around his hips to bring him in even deeper. I still need more of him. He's moving slowly, consciously so, and the thought flits into my head that this isn't sex, it's making love. I tell myself to stop being delusional, because I've only known this man a week, and he'd probably laugh at the term "make love." But the slow rhythm is driving me insane, hitting me exactly where I need him to —until it's not enough either.

I break our kiss. "I need you harder, Rowan, faster."

His grin is radiant. "As you wish," and I feel his muscles contract as he pushes into me hard, pulling a surprised sound out of. I reach back and grab one of the fancy swirls of metal from the bedframe, tightening my grip as he keeps up the faster rhythm.

He sucks in a breath and grabs my hand with his, pinning it, and it turns me on even more, making me buck up to meet him. "I like seeing you splayed out for me," he says in a harsh whisper. But he thrusts into me only twice more before grabbing my hips and rolling onto his back, putting me on top of him.

Still inside of me, he cradles my hips with his hands. "Take what you want from me. I want to watch you ride my cock."

And as I start to move over him, setting the pace, reveling in the sensual power he's given me, he props himself up and starts kissing and sucking on my breasts. "That's it, Princess," he whispers. "You feel so damn good."

"So do you," I say, gasping as he thrusts his hips up, hitting the perfect spot. "There, there."

He listens, his face knit with concentration. He hits that spot again and again, sending bolts of pleasure through me. It's never been this easy for me before, this good.

He's watching my face as I come, his hand palming my butt, and then he urges me to lower my upper body to him so our chests are pressed together. He keeps moving inside me, his movements intense and fast now, urgent, and fresh pleasure spirals through me. To be needed and wanted by him is a joy like nothing I've ever known.

"Kennedy," he says, his voice guttural. "I'm going to come."

"Come for me," I say, like it's the most natural thing in the world. Like I'm the kind of person who says things like that. If I am that person, it's only for him—for this man who's sensitive, even if he doesn't want to be, and sweet, even if he'd never admit it. For this man who brings out a different side of me.

He kisses me fiercely and thrusts one more time, his hand pushing my butt to him, so he's even deeper, and I feel him come inside me. We stay like that for a long moment, pressed as closely together as two people can be, and then he rolls us onto our sides.

I immediately want him back inside me after he pulls out, which is stupid, because I know we can hardly go about our days connected to each other.

"I need to go wash up," I tell him, because Olive told me she once got a horrible UTI because she didn't pee after sex. No thank you. I'd prefer to keep my illnesses in this house fake. I take care of business in the connected bathroom, pausing only to look in the mirror. My cheeks are full of color, and I look happy. Something I haven't felt a lot of in this house other than in this room, where I can celebrate Christmas and be with Rowan and Harry, the only two people here who care about me.

Are my feelings about Rowan so intense because I've been stuck here, unable to see anyone else or work or do the things that usually fill my life with purpose? Would we have hit it off if our paths had crossed in a different way?

It doesn't take me long to dismiss the thought. I may not have given Rowan any serious thought if I'd met him a different way, but that's only because I wouldn't have been given the opportunity to form any intimacy with him. He's not someone who gives himself away to just anyone. Most people would look at him and see a grump, an old man living in a young man's body, but he's so much more than that. And I never would have known if not for this stupid show.

I leave the bathroom and take a moment to admire him. He hasn't gotten dressed, but the white sheet is pulled up to his hips, and the Christmas lights from his gift are casting multi-colored light onto it.

"Come here," he says, smiling at me. I'm so relieved there's no regret in his eyes that I do it without thinking, lying beside him and snuggling close like it's where I'm supposed to be.

Like I'm not the star of a TV show who's supposed to be engaged to another man inside of a month.

Good thing I have an idea for how to fix that.

Chapter Twenty

Rowan

I didn't mean to fuck her. I specifically didn't bring a condom because I wasn't going to fuck her...and because I would have felt like a creep to sneak in here in the middle of the night with a condom in my pocket to give her the news that our friend is all right, but, oh, my grandmother basically poisoned him. I definitely didn't mean to fuck her like *that*, like it meant something. But I can feel deep in my bones that it did.

If I'm in trouble, and I'm pretty damn sure I am, I can't bring myself to care. Kennedy is like an elixir restoring me. A balm to my wounds. When I'm with her, it's easy to forget all my failings.

She looks up at me from where she's nestled in the crook of my arm. "You said you'd show me your cars earlier," she says. "I'd like to see them."

Something warm unfurls in my chest, but I tell myself I'm just pleased she remembered. Many people wouldn't.

I get up and locate my pants, pulling out my phone.

I'm not surprised to see I've missed texts from Holly and Bryn, but I'll look at those later. I pull up photos of my two latest projects and pass the phone over.

"You made those?" Kennedy asks, her eyes widening. I can tell she's actually impressed.

That warmth in my chest spreads, feeling dangerously like pride, but I insist, "It's just a hobby. I work on them when I have time and donate them at Christmas." Delight fills her gaze, and I laugh as I slip back into bed beside her. She burrows into me, and my smile widens. "I know what you're thinking. It's definitely not because I have a thing for Christmas."

"Then what is it, you pretend grinch?" she asks, still beaming at me.

I draw the blanket up and over us, not wanting her to get cold. It's an old house, drafty even when I'm not messing with the radiators. I pick up a lock of her long, glossy hair and run it through my fingers. It's grounding in a strange way. "I know what it's like, is all. To live in the house where Santa doesn't stop. I might think it's bullshit now, but it's not bullshit to those kids. I don't want them to feel like they don't matter because Kris Kringle didn't stick the newest iPad in their stocking."

Her face stricken, she puts an arm around my waist, her grip stronger than I'd expect. "Oh, Rowan."

I laugh. "No need to *Oh, Rowan* me. It's bullshit that kids are taught they'll get gifts if they behave a certain way, when the truth is, some kids aren't going to get them at all. It makes them think they're no good. That's why I do it. They shouldn't have to think they're worth less than anyone else."

"That's beautiful," she says, but a crease forms between her eyebrows. "Is that a problem here?"

This time my laugh is harsher. "Poverty? Last I checked, it's a problem just about everywhere, but yeah, there are a lot of families below the poverty line in Heber County."

A look of determination steals over her face. "I'm going to talk about it on the show. There must be a local organization that I can get the producers to donate money to."

I don't like her mentioning the show. It sours my mood like milk left out too long. Because as much as we've been pretending otherwise, our situation hasn't changed. She can't be my woman, and I sure as hell can't be her man.

"We can't let my grandmother get away with this shit."

"I agree," she says. "I have some thoughts about what we can do."

I should let her tell me, but suddenly the truth is pressing at my lips, demanding to come out, because fuck, if ever there's a time for honesty, it's now. "I'm going to do what I can to stop this show from happening, Kennedy," I blurt.

"What?" she asks, pulling the blanket up. I feel a pang of regret, because I can tell I've damaged something between us. "Why?"

I start to get a little pissed. "You're seriously asking why I want to stop the show?" I ask, sitting up abruptly. "For one thing, I don't want those assholes following you around, trying to lure you into—"

She lifts her eyebrows.

"Well, I don't. You said you understood that."

"I do," she says with consternation.

"And for another, my grandmother has obviously lost what little sense she was born with. For fuck's sake, she basically poisoned Harry."

"That'd be twice now," she says with a nod.

"He told you about the sweet tea incident, huh?" I run a hand through my hair, then grab my shirt off the floor and tug it on.

"He did."

Kennedy's watching me with these sad eyes that make me feel like I punched a puppy, but it feels wrong to be naked for this conversation. I don't want her to feel vulnerable too, so I hand her the cutesy nightshirt she had on, which is a desperately sexy thing for a grown woman with curves to wear, it turns out. The way it clings to her breasts and hips makes it a masterpiece.

She takes it without comment, pulling it over her head as I locate my underwear and work jeans and pull them on.

"I guess there's something I should tell you," I say, shoving my phone into the pocket of my jeans."

"Oh?" she asks. She's sitting up on the bed, watching me from it, and I feel a pang of regret because minutes ago we were nestled there together, pretending the rest of the world didn't exist—or that it could go fuck itself. I wish I could rewind the clock, but I know from experience that it's impossible. Pointless to even think about. I try not to take part in pointless things whenever possible.

"I've been trying to get this show canceled since the beginning." I didn't mean to say it defensively, but it sounds defensive. "This isn't good for my family. What Jay told me about my parentage...my mother wanted my grandmother to talk about it *on air*. And my sisters and me...we've gone through enough with our grandmother. We don't need her to have a platform for her bullshit. No one in this town does. She's always caused more harm than good. *Always*."

Something flickers on her face, but I can't read it. What I can read is her body language. She's crossed her arms over her chest. She's not happy, not that I expected otherwise.

"What have you been doing, exactly?" she asks.

I suck in a breath and rock on my heels. I don't like the way she's looking at me, but I probably deserve it. I know this show is important to her, and I was trying to fuck it up. Those are facts. I nudge the floor with my foot. "The radiator malfunction. The power going out. The hole in the fondue pot."

"The beeping alarm," she continues. "The leaking sink. The howling noise."

I shrug self-consciously, because it all sounds pretty stupid when it's listed out like that. "A dead fish in the back of the toilet tank in a bathroom near the guys. I guess Jonah's complained about the smell."

One corner of her mouth lifts up, and she gives a little shake of her head. "You lack your grandmother's killer instinct, you know. She'd have had half the guys holed up in bed by now, nursing injuries."

"I know," I say, because she's right. "I didn't want to hurt anyone, but I figured if there were enough annoyances they'd give up. People like them aren't used to putting up with shit like that. They're not patient with it."

"You mean people like *me*," she says, tightening her arms over her chest.

Christ, I really didn't, but I can see how it sounded like that.

Then she gasps and shoots an accusatory look at me. "Did you turn me orange? The makeup artist said she'd used that tanner before and it had never had that result."

I swear under my breath but nod, because the truth is out now. Might as well be fully honest.

Her eyes look glassy now, like she's holding in tears, and I feel like a prize asshole. First, I upset Willow, then Ivy, and now Kennedy. I can't do anything right.

"Are you really doing this for your family, Rowan, for your town? Or is it because you're sick of being called Cupid?"

I clench my jaw, because there's a grain of truth in what she's accusing me of. Defensiveness rises up within me like toxic sludge. "Don't you see? My grandmother's lost her mind. She's spying on you, poisoning Harry. She needs to be stopped." Then I remember what Kennedy said after—

Don't remember what it felt like to be inside her, don't remember the feeling in your chest when she fell apart around you.

It sounded like she had an idea for stopping my grandmother.

"Didn't you say you had some thoughts about how to deal with Nana?"

"I did," she says, her arms still wrapped across her chest like they're armor. "But I'm not so sure it's a good idea anymore. You've made it clear just what you think of me, Rowan. You should leave."

But I can't leave her like this. I *can't*.

"I didn't do any of that shit after our evening at the pool,

Kennedy," I say, sickened by the note of pleading in my voice. Has it come to this?

Maybe I'm like my father after all, my real father, consumed by a woman.

Maybe I don't care.

"Okay," she says.

"Okay?"

"I need to figure out a way to make this work without getting the show canceled," she says firmly. "Leto's Hands needs this to work." She lets her arms drop, and I'm happier about it than I probably should be. There's still a severe look on her face, one that reminds me of that first day, when she came off as regal and cold. Like she was better than me and knew it. Now, I guess she does know that she's better than me. "Those kids you help, Rowan. I'm trying to do the same thing on a bigger scale."

She probably didn't mean for that to make me feel like shit.

"I'll leave you to it, then," I say. "You don't need help from someone with such mediocre ambitions."

I turn to leave, catching sight of the stupid Christmas tree as I do. Another dumb thing for me to have done, especially when Christmas has always served as a reminder of all the things I don't have.

She says my name as I'm leaving, but I don't turn around. My blood is pumping in my ears, and I feel fucked up and wrong, like everything I do is a mistake. Even this, leaving now, feels like a mistake. But I don't know how to do anything differently. I don't know how to do things the way they should be done—if I did, I'd do them right the first time.

I don't want to see anyone. I don't want to talk to anyone. But I have the misfortune of living with two roommates, and when I arrive at my house, the overhead lights are on in the living room—the Christmas lights too. Seeing them feels like being knifed in the gut, but I swallow back my emotions. I hope to God Cole and his daughter are gone by now. Maybe that's a shit thing to think, but I guess I'm a shit person.

I try to go in quietly, but the house is old, and despite all the time I spend tuning it up and oiling the hinges, it creaks like a casket in a horror movie.

Fuck.

The three people on the couch in the living room turn toward the door as one, preventing me from escaping up the stairs like I was hoping.

Oliver. Harry, with pink welts all over his face. Holly.

They're sitting by the tree, which looks much better than you'd think, considering it was decorated by an eight-year-old. They all have mugs of something. It's a cozy scene, and I feel a little prick of loneliness because I'm not a part of it. My mind returns to Kennedy, shut up in her room in that cavernous house, with only those assholes and some production assistants and cameramen to keep her company.

I shouldn't have left her like that, but I can't even call to apologize. And what would be the point? I *did* turn her orange. Is there any coming back from that?

"Want a drink?" Oliver asks, lifting his mug.

I'd prefer to climb into my bed and forget everything for a while, but that feeling of loneliness intrudes.

Kennedy is alone. Maybe you should be too.

But I ask, "Is there alcohol in it?"

Harry laughs this time. "Your friend makes very stiff drinks." He pulls a face. "Your grandmother too, but at least I knew this one was alcoholic going into it. That makes a difference."

"Should you really be drinking after—"

"He was only given a topical cream," Holly says in an undertone, as if it's a sensitive subject. Judging by the unhappy tilt of Harry's lips, I guess it is. Oliver gets up to fix me a drink, thank God.

"They refused to take me seriously," Harry says. "The same

thing happened to Willow one time, and they gave her a steroid shot."

"Huh," I say. "Yeah, I remember that." Back when Harry lived in Asheville, he and Willow were roommates, and they made the mistake of using some cheesy unicorn face masks that triggered an allergic reaction in my sister. "Maybe the ER is more reactive there."

"I wish she hadn't left tonight," Harry says mournfully. "But I also didn't like her seeing me like this."

I jolt a little. "She came by the house after visiting Jay?"

Holly studies me and nods. Is that the nod of someone who knows I'm the product of an affair?

"She seemed upset by something," she tells me. "Any idea what that's about?"

"You assume it was my fault?" I snap.

She sets down her drink, cocoa, I can see now, and lifts her hands palm outward like I'm a feral dog. Apparently, I'm not the only one who thinks so, because she says, "No one said it was your fault, Cujo. She just mentioned she'd seen you at the hospital, so I figured you might know what's up."

Oliver chooses that moment to return with the drink, thank God. I take it from him and then take a big slug because right now, I couldn't give a shit if it burns my mouth. It does. But it's not a bad burn because it's chased by the taste of whiskey, and the burning in my gut is not unpleasant this time.

I lower into a chair across from where the three of them are nestled on the couch, Oliver and Harry on one side, Holly on the other.

"You decorated the tree," I say.

"Yes," Holly says. "We like to make merry around here."

"Jane told me it was hard to look at me," Harry says sorrowfully. At another time I would have laughed. Cole's daughter is nothing if not direct, but I can't muster any humor. My mind is Willow's visit. Had she wanted to tell Holly about the Jay thing?

Probably. She's gotten more into talking about her feelings lately.

I should just get it over with and tell them he's my father. Except Bryn might get offended if she finds out last.

I scrub a hand over my face. "Let's FaceTime Bryn," I mumble.

"Are you okay?" Holly asks with genuine concern. She's eyeing me like she's no longer certain I'm her brother.

"Oh, for Christ's sake," I say. "I know what FaceTime is. I don't live in a cave."

"No, you'd just like to," Oliver rebuts. Despite the smartass comment, there's a look of concern on his face too. He's trying to keep things light because he thinks I need him to. Maybe he's right. I'm not really sure what I need right now, but my mind is conjuring images of a princess room with a discount tree in front of the shuttered window.

I take another mouth-burning gulp of the hot chocolate. "Just do it, okay?"

"Is it okay if I hang out in the background?" Harry asks, lifting a hand to his welts. "No one else should have to look at me right now. I probably gave Jane nightmares."

Oliver gives him a fond look. "I don't know. I think they're kind of cute."

"Okay, enough flirting," Holly says, pulling out her phone. "My brother is clearly going through some sort of personal-slash-existential crisis. The next thing I know he'll be asking us to use TikTok."

"What's TikTok?" I ask.

"There he is," Holly says with a grin as she clicks away at her phone. Despite Oliver's assurances, Harry gets up. Since I'll presumably need to be seen, I get up from my chair and gesture for him to take it, then steal his place on the couch.

The video call rings twice before Bryn picks up. I feel like crap when I see her rubbing her eyes, the headboard of her bed in the background. It's past eleven on a weeknight. She's pregnant, and her fiancé is the CEO of a billion-dollar company. Multi-billion dollar. Of course they're fucking asleep.

"What happened?" she asks frantically. "Is Jay okay?"

I hear her fiancé, Rory, muttering in the background.

"Shit. I'm sorry," I say. "I just. I wanted to tell you and Holly at the same time because our other sisters already know. I..."

"Are you sick, Rowan?" Holly asks, her face ashen.

I almost laugh. Almost.

I'm very aware of Rory in the background, listening whether he'd like to or not. Of Harry and Oliver. But secrets haven't done anyone in this family any favors, and they certainly haven't done *me* any favors—I see a flash of Kennedy's hurt face—so maybe it's time to unburden myself of mine. "No... It's just. Jay told me something the other day, after his heart attack. I guess he's my real dad. Turns out, he and Mom started an affair after she married my dad, but I guess they called it off for a while after she got pregnant with me. Until Willow was a couple of years old." I clear my throat, feeling awkward now. "I guess Mom wanted to bring it up on the show. She figured it would get her some screen time, but Jay refused to cooperate, and Nana didn't like the idea anyway. I'm guessing she thought it would take attention away from her and her boy toy."

"Oh, fuck," Holly says, dropping the phone on the table. She leans over and wraps her arms around me, engulfing me in a hug. Oliver shrugs and gets in on the action.

"Hey, what's going on over there?" Bryn asks. "Are you hugging?"

"You want me to drive you over there so you can hug them?" I hear Rory ask. If another man had said that, I would have assumed he meant it sarcastically, but I'm pretty sure he really would drive her over here if she said yes.

"I'm hugging you in spirit," Harry says. "My skin itches too much."

My eyes feel hot, and shame cascades through me. I was taught from a very young age that real men are stoic and strong and they absolutely do not, under any circumstances, cry. My father told me so...or at least the man I thought was my father. My grandmother taught me the same thing. Now, here I am, on the verge of it again. My emotions, usually so willingly stuffed away, have been engulfing me lately. My mind shoots to Kennedy again, to the way I left her, and my eyes feel hotter.

I break free of the group hug and grab up the phone. "No need to come over," I tell Bryn, who stares at me with all the concern of a big sister who'd like to solve everyone's problems. "I just wanted to let you know at the same time so you wouldn't feel left out."

Her lips tip up. "Thank you, Rowan. That means a lot to me."

There, I got something right. I'm obviously messed in the head, because I'd like to tell Kennedy about this, but I won't be talking to Kennedy, will I? I should stay away because I hurt her. I should stay away because she makes me feel like I'm veering out of control, and I already feel that way most of the time.

"Now, what are we going to do about Nana?" Holly asks. "She has to be stopped. She tried to poison Harry twice!"

Bryn's brow furrows in her worried look. "Should we press charges?"

"No one can prove she poisoned Harry," I say. "She'll just claim she didn't know he was allergic to lavender."

Holly guffaws. "Anyone who's met him knows. He tells literally everyone inside of two minutes."

"Do not," Harry says sullenly. "It just tends to come up sooner or later. That's not my fault. It's part of the natural flow of conversation."

"I like your natural flow of conversation," Oliver tells him with a smile. "It's unlike anyone else's."

"We don't do anything," I insist, earning me surprised looks from all of them. "We leave the decision to Kennedy."

"Way to bait and switch, Ro," Holly tells me. "You're the one who's been gung-ho on the sabotage mission from day one."

"Wait, what?" Harry says, frowning. Half a second later, his eyes widen and he points an accusatory finger at me like Donald Sutherland in that peapod people movie. Yeah, it's old. We only owned about five movies as kids. "It was you. You turned Kennedy orange."

I sigh and hand the phone over to Holly, who takes it with a look of contrition in her eyes. "Yeah, I did," I say. "She knows already, so I'm not going to ask you not to tell her." He still seems upset, and I remember that he's dreamed of hosting a dating show for years. So I've been shitting on someone else's dream. Fantastic. "I'm sorry man. I fucked up. I just...my grandmother shouldn't be in a situation of power. She's not a nice person. I thought it would be best for everyone if I could pull that out from under her while it was still possible."

"So your solution was to turn Kennedy orange?" he sputters in disbelief.

"Yeah, it sounds like a pretty shit plan when you put it like that." I rub my beard. "Turns out I'm not very good at sabotage."

"No, your grandmother's much better at it. Still, I wish you'd told me." His mouth twists to the side, then he flinches, so maybe the sudden movement aggravated the hives. "I actually thought you liked Kennedy. I told her—" He cuts himself off and shakes his head, miming that he's zipping his lips. "You know what, I've gotten into too much trouble from opening my mouth when I shouldn't. I'm going to mind my own business for once."

Shit. Does he need to start now? I'm suddenly desperate to know every last word he said to her.

"Harry...I *do* like her." I swallow, thinking of the disappointment and hurt on her face. "A lot."

Holly's eyes immediately widen, and she looks gleeful.

"Yes. *Yes*," she says with feeling. "I knew this was going to happen. You were such a Debbie Downer when I fell for Cole. You said you'd never let yourself fall in love, and now look how the mighty have fallen."

"Are you calling him mighty?" Oliver snorts.

I simultaneously blurt out, "No, I'm not in love with her. That's not what I meant."

Except...I might not be all the way in love with her, but I can't totally lie to myself. I'm partway there.

"Maybe I should come over," Bryn says from Holly's hand, surprising me because I'd forgotten the FaceTime connection was still open on the phone. "It feels like a lot of significant things are happening over there."

"No, don't," I say, but it came out too harsh, so I add, "I'm going to bed soon. I'm really tired. Why don't you go back to bed too, Bryn?"

"I like that plan," I hear Rory say in the background. "But, hey, if you need anything, let us know, Rowan."

Again, I know that he means what he says.

I hate asking my future brother-in-law for help. He's beyond rich —he's loaded. Which also means he has people asking him for favors every minute of the day, probably every second. I don't want to be one more person holding out a hand. But some things in life don't come cheaply, especially if you need them quickly.

So I sigh and bite the bullet. "Do you think you can get me a bulldog puppy?"

Chapter Twenty-One

Kennedy

"Stop glowering at them," Tina tells Zach, but from the way she's beaming at him, it's obvious she kind of enjoys the glowering. Turning to me, she says, "So which one is he, Kennedy? It's that Marcus guy, isn't it? He's pretty."

Zach shifts his glower to her. "*Pretty?*"

"What? He is!"

It's Friday, family day, thank God, and Zach and Tina are here. Tina, at least, seems pleased about it. Zach, who's usually the life of any party, looks like he wants to be the death of this one.

Then again, he's made it very clear what he thinks of me doing this show. Unlike our parents, he isn't worried about how the publicity will reflect on him. His objections are twofold. He doesn't think much of Maeve Mayberry—join the club—or of the kind of man who would willingly appear on a dating show—fair enough, as I've come to realize. We're at a happy hour in the ballroom, enjoying appetizers and another champagne tower that Jonah hasn't learned enough to stay away from, and Tina and Zach have hustled me over to a corner of the room to discuss the various guys. It would feel more intimate, more like a real family meeting, if there weren't a cameraman hunched on his heels across from us, soaking in every moment and making it belong to *Matchmaking the Rich.*

I keep looking at the doors as if Rowan might stroll right in, but there's no sign of him, of course. I haven't seen or heard from him since he left, and even though it makes me feel helpless and angry and sad to admit it to myself, maybe I won't. I tell myself it's for the best. Yes, I feel a deep connection to him. He's gorgeous and intense and soulful and so much more than the front he puts on for the world. But he's also the man who turned me orange.

The room is warm tonight because he isn't downstairs messing with the radiator, but I can't deny that I want to be here about as much as Zach does. *I don't want to do this anymore.* I *do* want Leto's Hands to survive—I need it to—but it's starting to feel like I'm no better than these guys. None of us are here because we believe in the show's premise.

Worse, Harry has been giving me knowing looks for the past two days, but he refuses to tell me anything. Admittedly, I haven't gotten a good chance to try to pry anything out of him. Yesterday, we all went to a chocolate factory, which sounds amazing, but Nana Mayberry convinced me to wear a white dress, of all things, saying I'd look like an "ethereal snow angel." If I'd known about the chocolate, I would have refused, but she didn't tip me off. So I only got to try a few non-messy things, although Jonah kept offering to feed me every thirty seconds. Two of the other guys, Quinn and Ray, got into a lengthy discussion about the subpar quality of the cocoa beans.

The cameras kept following me around, obviously hoping to catch some act of physical affection on tape, but I couldn't bring myself to act my part. I kept seeing the look on Rowan's face when he told me that if we really did this, if we really had sex, he couldn't bear to watch me flirt with the guys.

He's not here. He walked away from me. But even so...

"I have eyes," Tina continues, gesturing to Marcus in a way that is sure to attract the attention of every single person in the room. I'm still getting used to her overenthusiastic physical gestures. She claims it's because she's Italian American and was taught to communicate in hand gestures before she learned to speak. "You definitely can't send him home, Kennedy."

"I like your eyes," Zach says to Tina. "You have fine eyes."

"Fine?" Tina quips. "As in adequate?"

"I meant it in the Regency sense."

They've been on a Regency and Victorian movie kick since they run the Highland Hills branch of Tea of Fortune, and Tina has become obsessed with stories that include tea service and high tea.

"Well, my fine eyes have informed me that Marcus over there has a nice ass," Tina says.

"It's not him," I blurt, without having meant to say anything.

The look of excitement on Tina's face—and dourness on my brother's—tells me what a big mistake I've made. Crap.

"Colton?" she asks, tipping her head. "He has a certain *I'm a banker* something." Zach's glower deepens. "Or maybe." She snaps her fingers once. Twice. Makes a face. "Eh, I'm hazy on the others' names."

"Tell me it's not Jonah," Zach says, taking a gulp of his champagne. "For the love of Christ, tell me it's not Jonah."

I can practically feel the camera narrowing in on me, and my stomach feels sick. I was so looking forward to talking to Tina and Zach, to unburdening myself to them, but I can't tell them anything real, because whatever I say will eventually end up on millions of television screens.

"Jonah has really nice hair," I say flatly, recycling the line I used with Meathead.

"You know what, he really does," Tina says, nodding adamantly. "I'd already decided to ask him about his conditioner."

"You're not going to ask him about his conditioner, Tina," Zach says with a scowl. "It's probably made out of the tears of virgins."

Tina snorts. "Your sister's almost thirty. She's not a virgin. She's safe from becoming part of Jonah's conditioner."

"Jonah claims *he's* a virgin," I interject, unable to help myself.

Zach chokes on the champagne he was downing but still manages to empty the glass. A production assistant hustles over with a silver tray to collect it and gives him a replacement. Zach takes it so quickly he almost knocks the tray over. Something sparks in Tina's eyes, and she gestures for the PA to come closer. The production assistant looks like a cornered fly, but he takes a couple of steps toward her.

"I need some privacy with my future sister-in-law," Tina says in an undertone. "She has a surprise visitor."

"Oh, did they bring in Phillip?" the guy asks with interest. "I heard he refused."

Zach swears under his breath at the mention of our brother. Of course Phillip refused. He's our father's second-in-command, and my father's made it very clear that he is displeased with me and my refusal to walk the line that's been painted for me.

"No, not that kind of visitor," Tina says with another overeffusive wave of her hand. "The kind that comes once a month and ruins very expensive gowns." She gestures to my blue silk dress. "You can see our predicament. Luckily, I always walk around with tampons in my purse. Never go anywhere without at least six, so I got her covered. We just need some alone time to get her all settled and ready to come back. But you can understand why we wouldn't want to get all that on camera. Men can be a little squeamish when it comes to blood."

Zach looks like he's on the verge of laughing. But the PA, who doesn't know it's a ruse, looks liable to pass out.

He glances at the cameraman, as if hoping the other guy will bail him out, then returns his gaze to us. "B-b-by all means. It's just...we were going to do some thirty-second waltzes in a few minutes, so try to come back quickly."

"What the fuck is a thirty-second waltz?" asks Zach, whose look of horror is back.

"It's a thirty-second waltz," the PA says slowly, as if my brother's a fool.

"Isn't a waltz, by definition, longer than—"

Tina grabs my hands and waltzes me to the door.

"What on Earth?" I hear Nana Mayberry snap, to which the PA very loudly announces that I have my period.

Fantastic. My ears are burning, and I feel like the little girl who had to ask Nanny Rose what a period was because my mother had never told me.

But Tina has us out and through the door in seconds. "Okay, let's find a bathroom. Do you know where we can find one? I haven't spent time in this part of the house, and this place is laid out like one of those murder houses in movies where everyone gets killed but none of the other people hear it happening."

She's not wrong. I lead her to a bathroom, even as I say, "Do we actually need to go to one? I don't have my period, obviously."

"They don't know that," she says. "And yes, at least we can be pretty sure the bathroom's not bugged." She makes a face. "Reasonably sure."

My heart beats faster, my mind dredging up that night down at the pool. Rowan, with his head between my legs. Rowan, without a shirt on. *Rowan.*

"You've got that lovesick look again," Tina says as we reach the bathroom. She drags me in and turns on the lights. It's not until she shuts and locks the door that she takes in the room's theme—gnomes. There's a gnome toilet paper holder, and the toilet is designed so the bowl looks like it's being held up by two gnomes. The water dispenser in the sink is shaped like a gnome's mouth.

"Seriously?" she says, making a hand gesture that bumps into my arm. "What the hell is wrong with these people?" After giving herself a full body shake, she skewers me with her gaze. "Okay, spill. You're into someone, I can tell. Who is it? I have to warn you, though, I'm pretty sure Zach would challenge, like, ninety percent of these guys to a duel to the death rather than let them marry you."

I laugh at the thought of Zach challenging Jonah to a duel. I'm pretty sure Jonah would tuck tail and run, or maybe he'd blurt out that he's a virgin so Zach has nothing to worry about. Then I feel tears tracking down my cheeks.

"Oh, shit," Tina says, instantly drawing me into a hug. "I didn't mean it. Well, okay, I sort of meant it, but I'll keep him from doing anyone bodily damage. Plus, let's be honest, Zach's not the type of guy who'd get into a physical brawl. He's more likely to poke holes in a guy's ego or order him a shitty drink on purpose."

"It's not that," I say, pulling away. "It's just..."

"What?" Tina asks, then tilts her head, studying me. "Wait...it's not one of those guys, is it? To be honest, they all seem..."

"Like stuffed shirts?" I offer, because I'm sure that's how Tina sees them. She's one of the most light-hearted people I know.

"No," she says. "They seem like they're not for you. Is it one of the PAs? Crap. Was it the guy I told the period lie to?"

Sighing, I close the lid of the gnome toilet and sit. I probably shouldn't tell her. There's obviously no future with Rowan, the only man who's ever turned me orange. Truthfully, though, the whole orange debacle doesn't hurt nearly as much as the way he walked out on me. It made everything we'd shared, which had felt so special, feel cheap and meaningless. Like a one-night stand, not that I'd ever had one of those.

But the words pour out anyway, like maybe they need to.

"It's Rowan Mayberry," I say on an exhale. "He's been working on set as a handyman. Or at least that's what I thought. He acted like he was helping out, but he admitted that he's been trying to sabotage the show."

"Oh, *shit*," she says with feeling, then gives a nod. "I can see it.

217

He's hot in this severe mountain man way. I guess you fought about the show?"

"Of course," I say, getting worked up by the memory. "He knew why I wanted to do the show, why Harry wanted to do it, and he was still trying to mess things up."

Tina nods again. "So what'd he do, anyway?"

I tell her, and she gives me an unreadable look. When I finish, she says, "Those aren't the actions of a ruthless man, Kennedy."

I kick at the base of the sink, a gnome, of course, with one foot. "I know that."

The thought kept recurring to me last night, right when I was on the verge of falling back to sleep.

He has a heart.

In fact, it's his warm heart, the secret tenderness he buries down deep, that has endeared him to me from the beginning.

"Tell me more," she says, her eyes shining, as she perches on the edge of the sink.

"What about Zach?"

She waves a hand dismissively. "I told him I'd drive. He can get drunk on champagne and insult all your suitors." A grin stretches across her face. "It only makes it funnier that he won't be making jabs at the real one."

I can't tell her everything. I'll keep Rowan's secret about his parentage for as long as it *is* a secret, and my future sister-in-law *definitely* doesn't need to know that I slept with him, or opened my legs to him that night at the pool, but I find myself telling her about most of it. The Christmas tree farm. Jay's heart attack. Rowan bringing me the tree. His visit the other night...

When I finish, I pause, waiting for her response. I realize I don't know how I *want* her to respond. I'd like her to be fired up on my behalf, definitely, but part of me also wants to know that she doesn't judge Rowan too harshly for the role he's played. I'm mad at myself for feeling that way—he left me as if I were nothing to him—but like most people, I'm not always logical.

"Okay," she says slowly. "I ship it."

"What?" I ask, but I'm laughing. Tina has that effect on me. From the moment I met her, I knew my brother had found the right person for him, the person who would be his partner and other half. One thing's for sure, she will absolutely tell him whenever he's being an idiot. Which is why I'm relieved she's not calling me one now, I guess.

"You heard me," she says.

I did.

"By the way, how freaking amazing are Harry and Oliver together?" she asks.

A smile stretches across my face. "Very. Harry seems really happy. He hasn't even mentioned his hives today." They're barely hives at all at this point, just slight bumps that Nana Mayberry, of course, commented on several times, calling them everything from pimples to welts to warts.

"They're coming by the tea shop tomorrow," she says. "I can't wait to tell them both they're going to fall madly in love."

My smile widens. What sets Tea of Fortune apart is that its servers are taught to interpret their guests' tea leaves. "You're not supposed to pretend, you know."

She waves this off. "I won't have to. Most of the tea leaves people leave behind look like hearts anyway." With that, she takes my hand and tugs me up off the gnome toilet. "Now, let's get back in there before your brother finds out Jonah's not really a virgin."

Laughter bursts from me again, but I go with her. We link arms on our way back to the ballroom. Being with Tina and Zach is so different from the gaping loneliness I've felt since Rowan left that I'm almost giddy from it. Or at least I would be if I didn't know they're going to be leaving soon, and I'll still be here.

Before we go back in the room, I turn to her and ask in an undertone, "What in the world am I going to do, Tina?"

She smiles at me, and for all her lightheartedness, there's an edge of sadness to it. "You're going to put on a show." She tilts her chin to the side. "And you're going to make that man grovel. I think this situation calls for some good old-fashioned groveling."

"I don't even know if he—"

"Oh, he wants you," she says knowingly. "If he didn't, it would have occurred to him that the very best way to interrupt the show would be to steal the star out from under it. But he never tried to make what was happening between you public, did he?"

I consider it. Nana Mayberry knew things she shouldn't have known about our night down at the pool, but Rowan had seemed pissed as hell about that. In fact, he'd stormed over to check my room for bugs.

"No, he didn't." I tell her, thoughtful. It feels like I'm missing something important, a revelation that's hiding just beneath the water like a fish that won't surface. It's chased away by a rumble that comes through the thick doors. Is someone shouting?

"Well, there you go," she says—and swings the door open onto chaos.

Zach is laughing his ass off, tears in his eyes, while Jonah and Marcus try to scale the trellises nailed to the walls of the ballroom. The cameramen are capturing it all on tape—they've split up, each focusing on one of the guys, who are at about the same place in their climb. Nana Mayberry, it looks like, is directing them. Harry and the other guys are watching with no small amount of interest, half of them clustered near Jonah while the other half are around Marcus.

We walk over to Zach. "What the hell's happening?" asks Tina, who has a way of getting to the heart of things.

"I told them I'd give my approval to whoever can climb a trellis the fastest," he says through laughter. "I said my sister needs the best in everything, including romance, and they're not romantic enough if they can't climb a good trellis like in *Romeo and Juliet*."

"Gee, I'm glad you're taking this so seriously," I tell him, kind of aggravated. He was acting overly protective earlier, and now he's pretending he'd hand me over to the highest bidder.

"You told me to have fun," he says through more laughter. "This is me, having fun."

"What if they hurt themselves?" I ask, but I'm the only one who seems particularly concerned. Everyone else is getting in on the action. Colton is even collecting bets from the other guys about which of them will reach the top first.

It's Jonah. Of course it's Jonah.

When he gets back to the bottom, victorious, I reach out to shake his hand, and he pulls me in for a kiss. It's chaste, it's dry, and we have about as much chemistry as two alkaline substances. He pulls away from me and pumps a fist into the air. My brother no longer looks all that amused, and Harry's making a face that suggests the kiss looked about as inspiring as it felt.

"Do you like winners, Kennedy?" Jonah says to me in an undertone. Maybe he means it to be sexy, but it's off-putting. Gross.

I glance at Marcus, who's sulking. His foot went through part of his trellis, so I suspect the production team will be getting a bill from the Labelles. Luckily, he made it down safely. I spoke to him briefly before Jonah swept me into that unwanted kiss, and he begged me not to eliminate him tonight. He said Jonah brings something out in him, which is clearly true, and that he'd love the opportunity to bring me on an individual date. I'll be doing a lot of that next week—going on individual or two-on-one dates with the four remaining guys.

Colton is chatting with Marcus now. Between their easy camaraderie and the cocoa beans conversation between Quinn and Ray, it seems like most of the guys have managed to make nice with one another.

What other choice have they had, Kennedy? a voice inside me chastises. *You've ignored them to moon over a man who is actively trying to sabotage you.*

Except Tina's right. If Rowan had wanted to use me, I'd given him the perfect opportunity to blow the show to smithereens. He hadn't used it.

"I'm going to go get changed," I mutter, my mind elsewhere. Apparently, it's not enough for me to wear one expensive gown in an evening. I'm supposed to change before tonight's Rolex ceremony.

"I'll help you," Tina immediately offers, stepping forward.

"Me too," Zach says, though he grabs another flute of champagne from a production assistant before joining us.

"You're going to help your sister change?" Jonah asks.

"No, I'm going to convince her to send you home." His eyes are twinkling as he says it, but that's because Zach could twinkle in his sleep. He very clearly means it, and Jonah can tell.

Jonah glowers at him. "Your suit is a knockoff."

"No," Zach says, uncaring. "You know it's not."

The three of us go upstairs, Zach casually sipping his champagne. "I hate this house," he says. "Did I mention that? The show's even worse because it's taking place in this godforsaken house."

"Yes," I say with a sigh. "You did mention that. You know, they asked us to refer to it as Labelle Manor," I add, because I know it will make him laugh.

It does, and he adds,

"Every ghost and poltergeist in the county is probably drawn here."

I shiver at the notion, even though I'm pretty sure the only ghost is Nana Mayberry, skulking about and spying on people.

There are cameras following us, of course, so we stick to small talk all the way to my room.

By the time we get there, I feel drained and depleted. I want to lock the door behind us so we can finish the rest of Jonah's Scotch. I want to forget about the guys gathered downstairs. I definitely want to forget about Rowan.

But when I open my door, a tiny little bulldog puppy with an enormous red ribbon around his neck trots out to greet me.

My heart explodes in my chest.

"Well, shit," Zach says. "It looks like there's a note on his collar."

Then my heart explodes again, for a different reason. The note reads *A princess for a queen. Love, Jonah.*

"You think anyone told him this dog has a dick?" Zach asks conversationally.

Chapter Twenty-Two

Rowan

"She didn't send Jonah home?" I ask Harry, my hand squeezing hard enough to break the car part I'm holding. I'm in my workshop in the garage, trying to finish the third car this week because I can't banish Kennedy's words from my head. Suddenly, messing around and finishing a few of them before Christmas doesn't feel like enough. I want to do more. I want those little kids to believe in magic the way she does. The way she makes me want to. Except that's obviously bullshit because, based on what Harry's saying, she didn't send Jonah home when she had the chance. Instead, she sent home Quinn and Ray. "Why the fuck not?"

He shrugs and then scratches his head. He does it with feeling, like there's an itch he can't get out, something I understand well enough. It's Sunday afternoon. I haven't seen him since Friday morning. I guess the last couple days have been busy at the Labelles' house. My grandmother's been sending me multiple texts, asking me to "pop by" to do everything from snake the drain in one of the bathrooms the guys have been using to teaching the puppy how to do tricks that would look good on camera. I haven't answered, but I feel a phantom itch on the back of my neck every time I ignore one of her texts—not because I feel bad for ignoring her stupid tasks, but because she's giving me an excuse to see Kennedy, and turning her down feels like taking a shot of battery acid.

"He claimed he gave her the puppy," he says, keeping his voice pitched low, like he's afraid I'm an animal that'll pitch a fit if he's not careful. I don't like that I'm coming off that way, but I can't deny that I want to break something. I set down the mangled car part and grab a piece of waste wood to squeeze instead. The little splinters bite me, but I couldn't give a shit.

"So she obviously would have looked bad if she sent him home after that," he continues, "plus she..." Scratch. "We think it'll give her a better chance to reveal the truth about your grandmother if we keep her..."

Boy toy? Fuck stick?

"Paramour around."

"That's a fancy way of putting it," I growl, throwing a piece of waste wood into a bucket. "But she knows that I really—"

"She knows the puppy's from you," he finishes. Then his eyes brighten and he rummages in his pocket, coming up with a sealed letter. "She asked me to give you this."

I just barely stop myself from lunging for it. Truthfully, these last few days have been hell. I've gone about my business, preparing the light display at the mayor's house, helping put out a kitchen fire that started at an old guy's house because he tried to microwave a packet of pop tarts, and working on the cars. My sisters all went to see Jay again last night, but I couldn't bring myself to go. He was discharged from the hospital earlier today, and Ivy is helping him settle in at home. Holly is with Cole at the brewery. Oliver is helping his mother reorganize the house now that his father's sleeping downstairs. His dad's new meds make him dizzy, and going up and down the stairs multiple times has become a health hazard.

I'm...here.

None of the things I've done have made me stop thinking about Kennedy— what she's doing, what she's wearing, who she's talking to, and whether she loves the puppy.

Of course she fucking loves the puppy. She's probably knitted it hats and written it sonnets. Am I jealous of a dog?

I *am* jealous of a dog.

Which makes me have even more mixed feelings about the fact that I'm holding a letter from Kennedy *in my hand*.

"I need to read this," I say.

"Yes," Harry nods, then frowns and scratches his head again. "You do." He studies me for a long moment. "I have something to say."

I give him a pointed look. "Okay. You can talk to me."

He looks around, and I realize he's searching for somewhere to sit. There aren't many options, because every available surface is covered in tiny car parts. There's no system, no order, and the look on his face suggests this is his own personal horror story. I'd laugh if I weren't so hung up on the letter in my hand.

Harry settles for leaning against the wall. "Did you set me up with Oliver? Kennedy thought you did."

Well, shit. I don't particularly want to cop to it, but I don't want to lie to him. "I thought Oliver was interested, and he's had a shit time of it lately. So yeah, I invited you to the tree farm hoping you two would hit off. I was just trying to help him out. And you."

He nods as if this is what he expected me to say, and I'm glad that I didn't piss him off. I don't need another person I care about to be pissed at me.

"Thank you for that," Harry says, studying me.

"Seems to be going well," I say evenly, feeling suddenly embarrassed. I know they had a late dinner last night, after Harry was released from his duties with the show. They both made it to the restaurant this time, and Oliver told me he owed me a bottle of whiskey, which suggests he's happy with the way things went.

"It is. Finally," Harry says, giving his head a scratch. "I was starting to think I was cursed. But no animals jumped on my head last night, I avoided dairy like the poison it is, and everything went okay. Better than okay."

I only understand half of what he said but nod anyway. "Good. I'm glad. You know, Oliver's like a brother to me."

"He's said the same about you," he tells me, and a warmth spreads through my chest. I knew as much, but Oliver and I are both the kind of guys who'd tell someone else that but not each other.

"Is that what you wanted to talk to me about?" I ask when Harry makes no move to leave. "Yeah, but not just that. You like Kennedy."

I could object, but we both know it's true. Even if I hadn't admitted as much in front of him and everyone in my family, they would have known. I wouldn't ask a favor of Rory for just anyone. I like her. It's an established fact.

"I meant what I said. I'm not going to mess with the show anymore, Harry," I tell him with a sigh. "I shouldn't have done that in the first place. Especially not without talking to you."

He nods. "If you'd told me, we could have worked on it together."

I nearly drop the letter in my hand. "What do you mean?" I ask when I've recovered enough to speak. "You *love* the show."

"Yes," he says, his expression souring. "That's exactly why I don't want to see it ruined by your grandmother. She's carrying on with one of the contestants. She's recording Kennedy's private conversations. She's a menace. A disgrace to reality television!"

A laugh slips out of me. "You really think most people on reality TV have higher moral fiber than Nana?"

"They should!" he says crisply. "Everyone should!"

I don't disagree with him, so I settle for a shrug. "I'm not sure what you're getting at there, bud."

"We need to take Maeve Mayberry down," he says firmly. "We

need to make sure she's never allowed within ten feet of a camera. Ever. I'm staging a coup."

I can't deny that I like the thought. Harry staging a coup. My grandmother booted off her own goddamn show. She deserves it. *He* deserves it—if anyone can pull off working in reality TV while not being a garbage person, it's him.

"Okay," I say, tapping the letter against my hand. "I'll bite. What do you need me to do to help?"

"Can we sit down in the house and talk?" he asks. "It's cold out here."

I hadn't even noticed, but now that I've stopped working for five minutes, I can see that he's right. I give a nod, and we both head into the house, shutting the door behind us.

"I can help you organize out there, you know," Harry tells me as we walk into the living room.

"You're as allergic to my workroom as you are lavender, aren't you?"

"Yes," he says with a shudder.

"Sorry, bud," I tell him. "The chaos suits me. It lends to my creativity."

"But wouldn't you be more creative if all the different parts were sorted into bins where you could immediately find what you need?"

"Nope," I say, gesturing for him to sit on the couch. "Want a beer?"

"Please."

I pop the tops on two beers from Ziggy Brewery—now that Holly is with Cole, all our beer is from Ziggy Brewery—and hand one over to him before sitting.

"There's a recording device in the pool room," Harry says as he takes it. "Kennedy and I found it the other night. She got the idea it was in there, and sure enough."

Shit, they really have been busy.

"That's how Nana knew about Truth or Dare," I say, rubbing my whiskers. Fuck. It makes me feel physically ill to think that my grandmother might have a video of me going down on Kennedy. That was *our* moment. "Audio or video?"

"Audio," he says.

I breathe a sigh of relief, although this whole thing is still seriously fucked up. Yes, Kennedy and the others agreed to be taped for the show, but they didn't agree for their every moment at that house to be watched and taped. "You destroy it?"

"Nope," he says. "We don't want her to know that *we* know."

His expression turns crafty. "Think about it. This is our in, Rowan. Kennedy and I can give Maeve bad information, and she'll sway the show around it." He pauses, then grins and adds, "I also suggested that *we* plant a camera down in the pool room. We know they meet down there. The next time they do, we'll have it on tape."

They're not bad ideas. In fact, they're pretty damn good ones. Still, I snort. "We've already established that I'm bad at sabotaging things. Why are you telling me this? If I got involved, I'd probably mess everything up worse." I take a swig of beer and rub at my chest. It's not that it hurts—I don't think I'm on the verge of a heart attack, thank God—but something feels *wrong*. Like I'm a puzzle with a crucial piece missing. The face of the dinosaur, the nose of the princess, King Kong's leg.

What can I say? All my puzzles were missing pieces when I was a kid.

"You like Kennedy," he says significantly. "That's why you're involved, Rowan. Do you realize that the absolute best possible TV that could come out of this show would be if we take down the evil witch..."

He means my grandmother, obviously. I don't object.

"And find the princess real, lasting love," Harry adds.

I feel a twinge of something—possessiveness, sadness, anger—at the thought of any of those assholes making a move on her. They can't, my heart and head both insist, because she's mine. It's not true, and my sisters would probably tell me I'm a sexist jerk for calling any woman *mine*, but I can't deny that's the way I feel—a way I've never felt before.

Worse, I'm pretty damn sure I'm hers. There's this warmth that's uncracked in my middle, and every time I'm with her, it seems to take over. To guide me. I'm not sure I like it, but I don't know how to shut it down.

"Let's get real with each other," Harry says, and something about the way he says it tells me I'm not going to like what comes out of his mouth next. He hunkers down, his elbows on his knees, as if to show he means business. "That's not going to happen with any of the assholes on this show. None of them. A couple of them are okay, but do you really think Kennedy is the kind of woman who should have to settle for okay?"

No, I don't, which is why she deserves better than a handyman who makes toys. I open my mouth to say so, but he lifts a hand, looking surprisingly bossy for a man with such a nervous temperament. "Please don't say anything self-effacing. No one's saying you're perfect. Trust me, no one's saying that."

"Do you need to sound so adamant about it?" I grump.

Suddenly, I'm not so sure I want to open the letter that's currently burning a hole into my hand. Despite what he's told me, I'm worried about what I'll find inside of it. What if she sends me away? What if she tells me that she's decided to throw her everything into the show? What if she's in love with Marcus or Colton or one of the others whose name I don't remember?

"Well?" Harry asks, as if to tell me he doesn't have all day to sit around and watch me not opening the letter. Fair point.

I tap it on the table once, suck down a gulp of beer, and open the handwritten note.

Dear Rowan,

I know that you arranged for me to have the puppy. I've named him Jester after the name you used the night we met. I know you got him for me because you know how alone I feel in this house. Thank you. <u>Thank you</u>. Both he and the tree have been such a comfort. I turn on the lights every night. You'll be happy to know that he's already peed on Jonah's leg twice. They say dogs can sense evil, but I'm convinced this one can sense BS.

I'm not angry with you anymore. You shouldn't have turned me orange (obviously), but I understand why you did. Your grandmother's not a nice person, and she's made life hell for you and your sisters for years. I don't blame you for wanting to stop her. You didn't know me personally then, so even though you knew why I wanted to do the show, I get why you didn't ditch your plan. Still, I want to share a little more about Leto's Hands with you, so you can see how special their mission is. I've enclosed a pamphlet I wrote for them before coming here.

I hope you'll come see me again, Rowan. I miss you. I want you. I know why I'm here. I know I'm supposed to pretend to be happy with one of these guys, but I don't want to do that anymore. I still want to help Leto's Hands, but maybe I can figure out a different way. If you come to see me, maybe we can do that together.

Love, Princess

"I'm an asshole," I say, glancing up at Harry.

"I mean, I'm not going to tell you no," he says, though he has the grace to look a bit sorry about it. "Are you going to look at the pamphlet?"

I do, and by the end I have tears in my eyes. Again.

"I don't know what's happening to me," I say out loud.

Harry looks at me with something like fondness. "I think you're falling in love."

"I need to go to her."

He pulls a face. "Yeah, there's just one problem with that. The house is on lockdown. Jonah's fault. He bribed one of the PAs to use his phone and ordered stuff from five stores downtown. Delivery. Obviously not the kind of attention we want. No one in or out at night."

Chapter Twenty-Three

Kennedy

I'm restless.

My tree is glowing with muted light in its place by the window, and Jester is at my feet, following me as I pace the room, back and forth, back and forth. Has Rowan read the letter? Will he respond?

I hate being cooped up in this house. It's Monday night. On Friday, after I eliminate one more bachelor, I'll be leaving for the ski cabin with the three remaining guys and the PAs, but that thought doesn't comfort me because it means I definitely won't be seeing *him*. Of course, even if Rowan did try to visit me here, one of the PAs would turn him away. It's Jonah's fault, and I can't help feeling bitter toward him—and the necessity of letting him stay. It was the right choice because now Harry has a chance to stage his coup, but I still don't like it. I definitely didn't like the smug look on his face while he gave a five-minute speech on purity at dinner last night. It was him, me, and Colton, and none of us had much to say afterward. I mean, what is there to say after a man who's obviously not a virgin has told you, at length, why everyone should be one?

Jester gives my ankle a sloppy kiss, and I pause in my pacing and pick him up, feeling a surge of joy from the sight of his adorable, crinkly face. His short fur is like soft velvet under my fingers.

"I'd be lost without you, buddy," I tell him, and he licks my nose, wildly shaking his little nub of a tail.

He needs to go out several times a night, but with the new lockdown, I'm told that I can only let him use his puppy pads. I can't help but wonder if Nana Mayberry did this purposefully—not just to keep Jonah where she can control him but also to keep *all of us* in assigned spaces and firmly under her control.

I set Jester down and sit on the bed. Maybe I'll read my holiday romance again. Maybe I'll give the Labelles' Mary-Kate and Ashley collection a go. Heck, maybe I'm bored enough that I'll read Jonah Highbury the First's biography in full. Last time, I stopped after he divorced his first wife for gaining weight.

She was pregnant.

Jester gives a little yelp, his version of a bark, and wags his nub of a tail as he approaches the window where I have the Christmas tree displayed.

"You like Christmas as much as I do, bud?" I ask.

His response is to whimper.

That's when I hear a tapping on the window.

Fear spikes through my blood. I live in Chicago, and even though it's in a nice building—the kind with a doorman—I know it's not good news when someone shows up at your window in the middle of the night.

There's that slight tapping again.

Is an intruder trying to break in?

I glance around wildly, looking for anything I can use as a weapon, but there's nothing. Then my eyes alight on the star on the little tree. It's small but spiked, and it certainly wouldn't feel good if I jammed it into someone's eyes.

"Get back, Jester," I tell him, then pluck the star and move the tree. The sound is coming from just behind it.

Putting the star in my knuckles like I learned in the self-defense class I took before moving out of my parents' house, I pull the curtains aside, and gasp, mouth agape.

The person on the other side seems shocked too, and I watch with terror as he rocks back.

I drop the star. *Oh no, no, no, no, no, no.*

I unlock the window, my hands shaky, and tug Rowan in by his collar before he can fall to his death.

Okay, probably not his death. We're only on the second floor. But I don't want him to be maimed either.

"You came," I say on an exhale as he tumbles in, landing half on top of me. My whole body lights up in greeting. Jester starts prancing around us, making those little yips, his tail nub moving excitedly.

"Were you going to attack me with that star?" Rowan asks.

There's a feeling of instant contentment, because his warmth and smell have engulfed me. Even though Jester's made me so much less lonely, it's still felt like something's been missing these last several nights.

He gets up, peers out the window, then shuts it and draws the curtains. I watch as he eyes the tree, and my heart expands when he returns it to its spot and even places the star back on top.

"You shouldn't have risked climbing up here," I say, even though I'm glad he did. I'm still sitting on the floor, watching him. Soaking in the strong line of his back, his messy dark hair, the bulk and height of him.

His mouth hitches up as he comes to me. "I strung lights on the mayor's house this weekend. I got up much higher than this." He lowers down next to me, and Jester clambers over and plops into his lap, as if I'm not the only one who's been hoping Rowan would visit.

"There are guards at the doors," I blurt.

"I heard," he says. "I've never let something like that stop me."

I can't help but smile, because my mind's conjuring an image of a teenage Rowan, sneaking out and getting into trouble. Drinking in a barn and making out on hay bales.

Actually, that last thought makes me scowl.

"I'm sorry," he says, misinterpreting my expression. He takes my hand and stares into my face, his gaze heated. "I'm so fucking sorry, Kennedy. I was a coward to leave you like that, after what we shared. I was..." He swallows, his eyes still on mine. "I was scared."

It's a bit stunning to hear a man like this, who climbs the sides of houses, say he was scared, and I know him enough to understand what the admission cost him.

He looks down, pats Jester with his free hand, and my heart swells in my chest at the easy affection he's giving him. For a man so gruff and big, he's gentle too.

When he glances back up at me, he forces a smile. "That's right. You *scare* me, Kennedy Littlefield. It's like...my entire life I've tried not to feel things, and it's never given me much trouble, but these last few weeks, it's all come up to choke me."

"It's not just me," I say. "It's your father. That situation would be enough to scare anyone, Rowan. I—"

"Maybe so," he says, running his calloused thumb over the back of my hand, sending a shower of sparks through me. "But if you hadn't helped me through it, I would have closed back down harder than ever. Thank you for that." He pulls a face. "And what did I do to repay you? I tried to get your show shut down."

"That was before," I say, refusing to relinquish his hand when he tries to pull it back. "And I understand why you felt you needed to do it. Did you read the pamphlet?"

"I did," he says, smiling. There's a slight sadness to it, though, and I'm not sure why. "You're remarkable."

"That's not why I sent it to you," I say, feeling my cheeks flush. "I just wanted you to see—"

"I know what you wanted me to see, Princess," he says, releasing my hand and lifting his fingers to caress my blushing cheek. "And I see it. I see *you*." He swallows, and without really meaning to, I reach up to touch his Adam's apple. Before meeting him, I hadn't realized a man could have a sexy throat. He smiles and captures my hand. Kisses it and sets it down on Jester's head. "But we're still in the same situation, aren't we?"

I let out a sigh and give Jester a good rub. "Yes, I guess we're pretty star-crossed."

"Star what nowed?"

"You know, like in *Romeo and Juliet*."

His mouth quirks up. "Leave it to you to turn to Shakespeare. I was going to say we're well and truly fucked."

I laugh. "You have a way with words."

"Not a good one."

"It's a good one," I dispute, setting my hand on his knee. I feel this weird urge to have a hand on him, like he won't be able to disappear on me if I'm always touching him. "Our situation isn't ideal," I say. "But...what if we just...I'd like to spend time with you, Rowan. Can we do that without thinking ahead? Can we keep getting to know each other?"

He leans in and touches my chin, tilting it up to him. "I'm a simple man, Kennedy. There's not much else to know."

"You're wrong," I object. "I want to know everything."

His mouth quirks, and I feel the desire to lean in and kiss it, to memorize it with my lips. "You might change your mind."

"I won't."

"I want you," he says, his throat bobbing. "I want to taste you. I want to feel you come around my cock." He pauses, his eyes burning into me, his gaze and words making me wet for him. "And then I want to play truth with you in bed until dawn."

"What?" I ask, showing that I certainly don't have a way with words where he's concerned. "Truth?"

"No dares," he says. "We don't want you to get caught. But I want to know everything about you too, Princess."

He gently sets Jester aside, and my little puppy, God bless him, must realize we want to consume each other, because he trots off and curls up on his little plaid bed. Something Rowan must have picked out for him. In my mind's eye, I can see him doing it. Seeing that plaid and thinking, *Kennedy's a Christmas nut. She'll like this,* even as he internally rolled his eyes.

I don't think. I just climb into his lap and wrap my legs around his waist, humming with pleasure when I feel that he's already hard for me. He spears a hand through my hair and claims my mouth, his kiss almost vicious, and I kiss him back just as hard, because I've spent so many hours now wanting to kiss him. My chest feels warm, and after a few seconds of his lips on mine, his beard tickling at my face, his tongue in my mouth, it's not enough.

I pull back, panting, and attack his shirt, because the maniac is wearing a long sleeve flannel, no coat, even though it's winter and cold.

"There are too many buttons," I say. "I'm going to need some help."

"No," he says, giving me a slow smile, his eyes appreciative. "I like watching you do it." He pulls away slightly. "But I'd like watching even more if you were naked. And I'd *really* like watching you get naked."

I'm wearing a nightshirt again, no bra underneath, only a pair of gold underwear. When he doesn't reach forward to take my shirt off, I do, inching it up slowly because I like that spark of heat and need and humor in his eyes. Like sex can be hot and fun, something I've never experienced with anyone else. I throw the night shirt to the ground, but when I go to lean in and keep unbuttoning his shirt, he stops me.

"What is it?" I ask.

"You're fucking beautiful," he says. "I want to admire you. I want to remember you just like this."

I don't like this talk about remembering, as if I'm going to be just a memory, not part of his life. But I don't say so. I don't want to destroy the moment. Instead, I tell him, "I'd rather you admired me with your mouth, like you promised."

His grin is almost painful, and the feeling of need it stokes in me is more so. "As you wish."

"But let's get that shirt off first," I tell him. "I'd like to have a good view too." So I unbutton it, pausing every now and then to press a kiss to the ridges of muscle on his chest, to admire him, because he's indescribably beautiful to me too.

Once his shirt is off, he takes off his boots and socks.

"Your pants too," I say, my mouth dry, and he smiles at me as he undoes his belt and steps out of them.

"And my underwear, Princess?"

"No," I say, approaching him on my knees. "I'll take care of those."

He swears gutturally as I slide a hand under the band of his boxer briefs. I touch him, loving how hard he is for me, and then push his underwear down his legs. He steps out of them.

Still on my knees, I reach for the base of his dick and stroke him up and down once, twice. Gazing up at him, I lower down and slowly lick the tip before taking him in my mouth. His eyes soak me in, but he leans his head back, his Adam's apple bobbing, as he watches me. His hand reaches down and lightly grips my hair.

"You're going to kill me."

I respond by taking in more of him, swirling my tongue around the tip as I suck. I cup his muscular butt with one hand, using the other to hold him at the base.

The sound he makes as I bob my head fills me with satisfaction, with heat, because there's a heady power in bringing someone this kind of pleasure.

"That feels so fucking good," he says, pulling my hair slightly, just enough that the nerve endings light up. "I like watching you take my cock."

His words shiver through me. I love that this man treats me like a princess but can also be dirty with me. He makes me feel so sexy, so free, like I can do and be anything I want with him. I use my hand on his butt to push him in deeper, gagging slightly, but it's worth it for the satisfied groan he makes, for the flexing of his fingers in my hair. Then he's pulling me up, looking at me with those glittering eyes that make me feel like he sees something in me that no one else has—that maybe no one else never will—and he kisses me, sucking on my bottom lip. "You were going to make me come," he says gruffly. "But I'm not ready for that. There's so much more I'd like to do to you."

Pleasure pulses between my legs. Anticipation.

"You seem like a man of action," I say, barely recognizing my voice. It's so full of need for him.

He smiles at me, the smile of a wolf, then leads me over to the bed. He lies down, then says, "Sit on my face."

"What?" I say, the word coming out like a squawk.

"Sit on my face."

"I can't do that! I'd crush you," I say, even as the insinuation slithers through me, heating me.

"Most of your weight will be on your thighs, but even if it wasn't, you could never crush me," he says through a slightly amused smile. "Even if you tried."

He reaches for my thigh, letting his fingers play over my butt, tracing circles on my skin that send bursts of hot-cold shivers through me.

"I've never done this before."

"Good," he says through another of those wolf smiles.

I go to him, and I climb onto the bed, feeling awkward as I sit over his face, but the feeling only lasts for half an instant because his mouth is on me, his hands reaching up to cradle my breasts. He caresses them and tweaks my nipples as he sucks on my clit and then circles it with his tongue. His hands keep moving as he pleasures me with his mouth, his tongue sweeping through my folds and then spearing inside, pulsing, before he goes back to my clit. The waves of sensation shooting through me escape my mouth in breathy sighs as I feel bliss working through me—building, building...

"Oh my God, Rowan, oh my God."

It's too much as he sucks on my clit again and then returns to pulsing with his tongue, his hands still on my breasts, every part of me consumed by him even though it's me sitting on his face. The thought of him wanting to do this for me, of him being turned on by it, only spirals my pleasure higher. So does the tickle of his beard against my skin and the heat of his breath, of his mouth, the slight nip of his teeth, and then—

"I'm coming. Rowan, I'm—"

He only works harder, pushing me over the edge as he circles my clit again and sucks. I collapse to one side of him, not wanting to actually crush his head, and he gathers me up to him, my back to his front. I can feel his hardness pressed against me, and even though waves of pleasure are still cascading through me, I whisper, "Now. I need you now."

He kisses the side of my neck and reaches down, finds my wetness with his hand, sucks in a breath, and then moves himself into position.

I cry out when he thrusts into me—one hard thrust that puts him exactly where I need him, and even though I just came, I feel the rumbles of pleasure coursing through me again, already, as he moves into me, his hand reaching around to play with my clit as he thrusts. His lips are hot on my neck. "You feel so good, Kennedy," he says in a breathy growl. "Like your pretty little pussy was made for me."

And it feels like his cock was made for *me*, because it's never been this good before, even with Brandon, when I was so blinded by infatuation that I thought he was my soulmate. It never felt quite right. It never felt like this—like someone was giving pieces of me back to myself. It always felt like he was taking something away.

Rowan lightly bites my neck as he thrusts in deeper, moving the top of my leg over his legs to change the angle, and it feels so good, so impossibly good. One of his hands is still caressing my breasts, the other on my clit as he rubs slow circles around it, timing them with his thrusts.

I look back at him in wonder, and find him staring at me the same way, his eyes free of any shutters. They're full of emotion, and it's for me. He leans in and kisses me, his thrusts slowing, and suddenly I need to face him—I need to be looking into his eyes as we finish this, so I pull away.

"I want to look at you," I blurt out. Normally, I might feel self-conscious, like I'd said something needy or stupid, but I don't feel any of that because he's gazing at me with such liquid warmth.

He doesn't say anything. He just pulls out, and turns me so I'm on my back, then slowly, so slowly the anticipation might very well kill me, thrusts back in. We take each other like that, slowly, looking into each other's eyes, kissing slowly too, and the combination drives me indescribably wild. It's not long before he pulls another orgasm out of me, leaving me gasping with pleasure.

"I can't do slow anymore, Kennedy," he says, breathing jaggedly. "Seeing you fall apart like that, I—"

"So fuck me fast," I say, the words a surprise to me as they fall out of my mouth.

He thrusts in fast and hard, almost pushing me over the peak again. He finishes in seconds, and after I clean up, we lay together, me nestled in his arms, my head on his chest.

It feels amazing, and we both laugh when Jester, who's been snoozing on his bed, paws the side of the mattress to be let up. Rowan picks him up so gently it almost brings me to tears, and he nestles in next to us.

"Let's play truth," Rowan says after a few minutes, running his fingers along my jaw and then down the bridge of my nose like he wants to memorize me.

"Truth. What's your favorite part of living in Highland Hills?"

"Being close to my sisters," he says, and I can't deny that a pang of sadness unfurls inside me. I'd like that too. Phillip's still in Chicago, of course, but he never spends time with me. He treats me with the same blank affection you'd feel for a Golden Retriever—it's more for the role of little sister than it is for me.

It's always been different with Zach. He can be annoying and overbearing, but he's also my friend. He knows the adult I've become, not just the little girl stuffed into a series of uncomfortable but pretty dresses.

"That must be nice," I admit, running my hand up his chest, saying hello to each delicious ridge of muscle. "But is there anything you like about Highland Hills itself?"

He looks down at me, grinning. "You ask the hard questions, don't you?"

I can't help but laugh. "If there's nothing you like about it, why don't you go somewhere else?"

"Because nowhere else would have the iron-grip of a home I didn't ask for or want but can't leave because it would kill me."

My laughter fades a little, mostly because I've never felt that way about home. Like it was a part of me I couldn't quit. The only place that's come close is Olive's apartment, where she still lives with Nanny Rose and her brother.

"Plus, my sister just started dating the bartender at Ziggy's, so I drink there for free. Can't complain about that."

"I've never been to Ziggy's," I say with a sigh. "I've hardly been anywhere in Highland Hills. I only got a day to wander around before they said I had to stick to the house. It's so beautiful, though. It's like a winter wonderland."

"You're not missing much," he says, blunt as ever, but there's a gleam in his eyes that suggests he actually loves this town, for all his complaining. He loves it and hates it.

"Tell me more about what I'm not missing."

"Well," he says as he runs his fingers through my hair again, the repetition of it soothing, like I'm a cat basking in the sun. "The worst place in town is Christmas All Year Coffee. You'd love it."

Laughing, I bat at his chest like I'm that cat I was imagining. "Why do I sense you mean that as an insult?"

He smiles at me with wry amusement. "Because you're one smart lady. They've got a Christmas tree in that place from January 1 to December 31, but they decorate it differently for each holiday."

"Tell me more," I say, tipping my head to get a better look at him. "I want to know *everything*."

"I thought maybe you did. They play only Christmas carols, and they've got a drink called the Three Wise Men that tastes like honey going down and gives you a hangover that lasts two days, easy."

"It sounds wonderful." I sigh, letting myself think about going there with him, out in the open—two people with nothing to hide. We'd bring Jester on a leash, and if this place is everything Rowan's made it out to be, then maybe we'd be able to buy my canine baby an ugly Christmas sweater, and—

"It's hell on Earth," he tells me, his fingers stroking gently through my hair again. "But I'd take you there and be happy for it. I'd feel like the luckiest man alive."

My heart cracks open, because I know he means it. Going there *would* be hell for him, but he'd do it...for me.

"You're really something, Rowan, you know that?"

"Does this mean I'm going to get laid again?" he asks, a twinkle in his eye.

I sit up and straddle his waist, feeling a surge of womanly power. "I think we could arrange that."

Chapter Twenty-Four

Rowan

"Where do you see this going?" Holly asks, gesturing toward me with a fry. I'm reminded of eating here at Ziggy's with her a couple of weeks ago, undergoing a very different interrogation. Then, I was trying to destroy the show from the inside. Now?

I'd still like to destroy that show, don't get me wrong, but I won't do it if it fucks things up for Kennedy.

"I don't know," I grumble. Because I don't like to be reminded that the woman I'm enraptured with is technically being courted by other men. That's the kind of thing that's a real blow to the ego. "It's only been a couple of days since we started talking again."

"If that's what you call it," she says with a huff.

I scowl at her. "We're taking a wait and see approach."

Holly guffaws and drops the fry. I deepen the scowl.

She throws a gesture toward Harry and Oliver, who are eating in a booth a few tables away. Harry looks happy. Relaxed. Like he's not constantly writing a mile-long pro/con list in his head, even though I'm guessing that's exactly what he's doing. "Harry took a wait and see approach after he crop-dusted Oliver in Asheville," Holly says, "and look what happened there. They could have started dating months ago."

Harry had one too many of Holly's chocolate peppermint schnappsicles last night after getting home from a long day at the house, and he spilled the whole story. I snuck into the Labelles' house to see Kennedy afterward, just like I'd be doing right now if she weren't out on a one-one-one date with Marcus.

Marcus is the one who bothers me the most. Jonah's no threat to anyone but the gene pool, Colton's too stiff to interest someone who's as in love with life as Kennedy is, and I can't even remember the name of the other dude who's still on the show. But Marcus looks like a goddamn movie star, and despite his stupid rivalry with Jonah, he actually seems like a decent guy most of the time. Which makes him one dangerous asshole.

"You look constipated," Holly says, throwing a fry at me.

"I'm angry."

Her mouth pulls to the side. "You're angry because your woman's out with someone else. What are you going to do about it?"

"Are you trying to piss me off?"

"No, I manage that very well without trying," she says. "But I can tell you really care about this woman, Rowan. *What are you going to do about it?*"

"Wait and see," I repeat, popping the fry she threw into my mouth. I've already polished mine off.

She gives me a look of distaste, although I'm not sure if it was prompted by the dirty-fry eating or the fact that I'm an idiot. Either would be a fair enough point. I reach forward and steal another of her fries.

"So you think you're going to win this woman over by sneaking into her room every night and—"

"*Holly,* watch yourself."

She lifts her hands up, palms out. "Far be it from me to call you out for being a slut, but I will point out that you were a real buzzkill when I told you about my enemies with benefits plan with Cole."

"Well look how that turned out," I say with a smirk.

"Yeah," she says, lowering her hands. Her expression is almost sad, although I'm pretty sure she's not sad for herself. No, this expression is dangerously close to pity. For me. "I'd say it turned out pretty well."

"Don't look at me like that."

"Like what?" she asks with fake innocence. "All the same, maybe fill me in on how you'd like *your* complicated situation to turn out."

I'm almost grateful when our little sister comes around with a couple of beers. She's been working at the brewery for the last couple of days. I guess Jay sent her out of the house because she's an extrovert, like him, and he could tell she was desperate for company. Meanwhile, he's been getting near hourly visits from neighbors and friends and friends of friends, many of them divorcees and widows who have heard about Kerry's defection. So Ivy figured she might as well get going with her research. She sets the beers in front of us, and Holly gives her a mock-serious look. "Excuse me, ma'am, but we didn't order these. This is most irregular."

"Ma'am, your ass," Ivy says, claiming the chair next to Holly. "And Cole told me to send them over. He said you looked like you could use them." Her gaze shoots to me, and I'm struck again by her resemblance to myself. By the knowledge that we have more in common than I ever thought possible. "Are you talking about Rowan's love life? Because I've only heard bits and pieces from all of you. Harry told me some stuff too, but I'd like to know more. This is the kind of juicy shit you don't stumble into every day."

"Jesus, does Harry know how to shut his mouth?"

"Not when he's been offered peppermint schnappsicles." She gives a jaunty wave in his direction, and when he glances over at us, he has the decency to look slightly ashamed. Oliver's laughing. I haven't seen him look so happy in a long time, definitely not since he was sucked back into Highland Hills's orbit.

I didn't sit Ivy down for a heart-to-heart talk about Kennedy because I'm still not altogether sure how to talk to her, now that I know. I'm also genuinely worried she'll use this as inspiration for a romance novel that other people are going to read. I've never liked having my personal business put out as a party platter for strangers to eat. I've never liked getting knowing looks from people I don't, in fact, know. I'd much prefer for people to mind their own business and leave me to mind mine.

"Harry wouldn't need to tell us stuff if you would," Ivy says intently, her gaze fixed on mine. "So why don't you?"

Holly bumps her side into Ivy's in the booth. "It's because he has the emotional constitution of a constipated guinea pig."

"Fuck, I have no idea what that means, but is this what's going to happen now that Ivy's back in town for a while? Are all of you going to gang up on me?"

"Alas, poor Rowan. We knew him well," Holly says.

"While we're on the topic," Ivy says, staring at me, "Harry says you've been sneaking into the mansion every night."

"Goddammit," I say, glaring at him. "It's only been two nights." He must sense my attention, because he darts a panicked look at me, his earlier cool fading. He points at himself as if to say, *who, me?* I glare back. He's had his last schnappsicle.

"He also tells me that he hasn't gotten anything on Nana yet."

"It's only a matter of time," I bite out. "She'll slip up. She can't help herself."

Ivy lifts an eyebrow. "You mean she'll be sexually harassing men forty years her junior in no time?"

My face slips into a very natural frown. I never thought I'd see the day when I wanted my grandmother to seduce someone my age, but I'll admit that I'm very annoyed she hasn't. I want Harry's plan to work.

Ivy grins at me. I don't grin back. "You're worried Kennedy's going to fall for one of those rich bachelors."

I snort. She doesn't need to sound so excited about this whole mess.

Holly shrugs. "Well, it *is* a valid concern."

"Traitor," I tell her.

Another shrug. "I've heard that one of guys looks like a Greek God."

"Not helping," I say, just as Ivy says, "Ooh, who told you that?"

"Harry."

"Let me guess?" I say on a sigh. "*Schnappsicles*."

"Obviously," Holly says. "So this brings me back to the question I've already asked at least twice. What. Are. *You*. Going to do?"

"I'm starting to think schnappsicles are the answer no matter what the question is."

We all laugh, but by the time we get to the end of it, both of my sisters are giving me pointed looks. I have no idea why, and I say so.

"You need a plan," Ivy says. "A good one."

"I got her that dog, didn't I?" I ask. "She loves that dog."

"Yes, the dog was good, but the dog is not a plan."

"Let me guess. You have one for me?"

"You said she loves Christmas," Holly says, smiling at me, then Ivy. They're obviously in on this together, and while I'm happy they've been talking, I really wish they hadn't done their bonding over me. "You need to show her a real Highland Hills Christmas."

I expected to hate whatever plan they decided to roll out for me, but I'm surprised by how little I hate this. I think of Jay and the tree farm. Of what it felt like when he brought me there as a kid, before so much shit went down that it buried me. I think of that tiny tree, winking in Kennedy's window.

It's just—

"How's this going to end?" I ask them. "She lives in Chicago, and I live here. She loves her job. She's helping people. This non-profit she works for helps single mothers and women leaving abusive relationships. How can I ask her to leave that behind?"

Ivy lets out a humph. "Why does she have to leave *her* life?"

Because I want to get to know Ivy better. Because I want to spend time with Jay and figure out what the fuck all of this means. Because this town is a part of me in some intangible way that doesn't necessarily feel good but is undeniable.

At the same time... "You're right. But I'm a handyman who makes toys in his spare time. I'd probably be homeless if I lived in Chicago."

"I think there's someone who might take pity on you," Holly says with a twinkle in her eye, but here's the thing. Maybe I'm old-fashioned, but I need to be able to stand on my own two feet. I need to be the kind of man who can take care of the people I love. I don't want to be a shackle on Kennedy's leg, weighing her down, making her unhappy because I'm a hick stuck in a city that doesn't want me.

I shake off Holly's suggestion. "I wouldn't be any good in Chicago. You know I hate big cities."

She gives a half shrug, because she does know that. I visited her once when she was living in New York, and I nearly got run over by not one, not two, but three taxis. Then we went into a bar, and within five minutes someone had challenged me to a fight.

I won. We were invited to never come back.

I rub my chest, feeling an unpleasant burn there. "I can't see any happy ending for us." Saying it puts a deeper burn in my chest, because I'm starting to realize I *want* a happy ending. Actually, I don't want an ending at all. I want to keep following this bit of string to find where it goes, and I hope to fuck I don't end up with nothing but an unraveled sweater.

"Oh, Rowan," Ivy says, giving me a sympathetic look. "Did I soak up all the imagination in our gene pool?" She pretends to sprinkle me with something. "I'll give you a fairy dusting of it."

"Hey," Holly says as she points a fry at our sister this time. "I imagine plenty of things. In fact, I was telling Bryn just the other day that we need to have our Matchmake Me app play songs for the user after a relationship doesn't work out. You know, like 'Cry Me a River.'"

"You want your app to taunt people too?" I ask. "You don't get enough satisfaction from doing it in person?"

The fry hurtles at me, and I catch it in my mouth. I'm chewing it, enjoying the textures and the burst of salt, when Ivy says, "You need to show her the magic of Highland Hills, you dipshit. Show her that she wants to stay."

I nearly choke on the fry, so I leave it to Holly to tell her she's insane.

"Did you just say magic and Highland Hills in the same sentence?" Holly asks, laughing.

"You don't live here," I say after swallowing the fry. "Seems to me you left this place first chance you got."

"I'm here now," Ivy says. "I'm working at this bar. You don't get more Highland Hills than that."

"It's a brewery," Holly says, narrowing her eyes at her. "And we're all assuming you're going to leave after the New Year."

"I wouldn't be so sure about that," Ivy says. "I may want to stick around until I'm done with the book. I usually like to live the part while I write, and I just started *Beauty and the Bar*." She lifts her chin at Holly. "I might even try dating someone who hangs out here, really fall into the role."

"As long as you stay away from Cole," Holly teases.

"What about his brother?" Ivy asks with a smirk. "He's always here, and he is sexy as hell. I heard he punched some jerk in here a couple of weeks back for being too forward with a woman."

"Nope. Nuh-uh. No way," I tell her. "Logan is a total man whore. Everyone knows that. You will not under any circumstances flirt with him."

Ivy rolls her eyes and puts a hand on her hip, her blond curls bouncing. "Did it ever occur to you that I might *enjoy* being involved with a man whore?"

"Oh, for fuck's sake," I snap. "This is why earplugs were invented. The inventor clearly had little sisters."

Holly shrugs. "Wouldn't bother me. You can bang-bang-bang away with Logan if you want. Hey, maybe you'll fall in love with him, and we can be sisters-in-law *and* sisters!"

"My ears are bleeding," I complain.

"Nah, not what I'm looking for," Ivy tells us. "I just want a little fun to help inspire me."

I can feel my eyes go round. "Do you find special inspiration for all of your books?" Because she's written at least twenty. It's not that I'd judge any woman for finding as much "inspiration" as she pleases, it's just that I'd rather not think of my sisters' sex lives.

"Is that any of your business, Rowan?" Ivy asks with plenty of attitude. "From what I've heard, you're not exactly virginal."

"Can we put a halt to this conversation? Please? I think my brain is going to explode."

"Well, anyway, I think I'm going to stick around a while," Ivy says. "I mean, Bryn tells me that she and Rory might want to get married before the baby's born. Why bother going all the way back to Charleston if I'll just have to turn right back around for the wedding?"

Holly and I exchange a look. Who's this person, and what did she do with our wild little sister who lives in Charleston but is constantly traveling anywhere other than Highland Hills?

"Are you going through something?" Holly finally asks.

"Obviously," Ivy says. "My father had a heart attack, and I found out that my half-brother's my full brother. That'd be some shit for anyone."

We both nod in acknowledgment, because, yes, that'd be some shit for anyone.

She makes a face. "Plus, I guess I have my reasons for not wanting to go home right now."

Holly leans toward her like she's a shark that smells blood in the water. *"What happened?"*

"I'm not ready to talk about it," Ivy says, making a face. "But I don't think I'm going through something in the way Rowan is going through something. He's going through a sea change, don't you think?"

"What the fuck's a sea change?" I ask.

"The kind that leaves you a different person," she tells me, eyes twinkling. "That's what's happening to you. I can see it happening."

These words are still soaking into me, settling down deep just like what Ivy said about showing Kennedy the good parts of Highland Hills, when Zach and Tina walk into the brewery. He's dressed up like he should be going to a yacht party somewhere, and she's more casual in a sweater dress and boots.

I try to look away, but I'm not quick enough, and Zach catches my eye.

Does he know?

He can't know.

Shit, though, there's something in his gaze that tells me he does.

Schnappsicles.

Nerves twist through me like tree roots as he approaches our table.

"Zach's here," I say through my teeth.

"Who's Zach?" Ivy asks loudly as she plays with one of her blond curls.

From the way Zach angles his head as he approaches the table, he clearly heard her. I grimace at Ivy. She gives a shrug.

Zach and Tina reach the table.

"Hey, guys, can we join you?" Tina says as she lowers into the chair next to mine. There are no chairs left, but Zach murmurs something to the table of women next to us, and it's no one's surprise when they cough up a chair. Wouldn't surprise me a bit if they just gave up the chair of someone who's in the bathroom, because according to Holly, Zach's the kind of guy who has charisma. Holly has also said that I lack any.

Thanks, Holly.

My whole body tingles as Tina gives me a significant look.

"Hi," I say, at a lack for words.

"Hello, stud," she says, taking one of the fries Holly wordlessly offered by shoving the plate across the table.

I get to my feet. "I need to..." I start, hoping an acceptable excuse will filter in. "I'll be right back."

It's not really an acceptable excuse, but it is, at least, a statement of some sort. I leave the table without any real destination. For a second, I consider crashing Oliver and Harry's date to yell at Harry about the Schnappsicles, but they both look like they're having fun. There are no squirrels tonight, no dairy, no lavender-based creams—just the two of them. It looks like they're all they need.

I think about bringing Kennedy here, about eating fries with her and Holly. About the glint of happiness she'd get in her eyes if I brought her to Christmas All Year Coffee. The discomfort I felt earlier drifts away, replaced by a kernel of happiness in my chest. I can see the image so clearly because part of me feels like she *belongs* here. I like that thought a whole lot. Of course, I might be lying to myself, but the picture in my head is clear and crisp, so perfect...

I wander toward the bathroom and use it since I'm there. When I leave, Zach Littlefield is waiting for me in the hallway, leaning against the wall with a wry look on his face.

"Hey, man," I say.

"Hey," he says, standing up straight. "You got my sister that dog, didn't you?"

So we're doing this, then...

"Technically, Rory got him," I say with a shrug. "I don't have those kinds of connections." *Or that kind of money.*

He studies me as he nods. "Yeah, I wondered."

I feel myself bristling internally, although I couldn't say why. Maybe because I'd like to be able to do something like that for Kennedy without having my soon-to-be brother-in-law's help. Maybe because I feel a little inadequate, honestly, when stacked up against her rich suitors. They have enough money to buy her a fleet of bulldogs. I have a creaky old family home I share with my sister and Harry, a workshop, and a bank account that's never exceeded four digits.

I cross my arms, realize it probably makes me look antagonistic, and drop them at my sides. "She was lonely," I say defensively. "She said she's always wanted a puppy."

"You did good," Zach says with a grin that slides into a grimace. "She was lonely there. Those guys are all assholes. Big shock. It took me all of two minutes to get them climbing ornamental trellises to compete with each other. They're not there for my sister. They're not looking out for her needs. They just want to be on camera, you know?"

He's studying me as he says it, like I'm a book he wants to read, which is hilarious for any number of reasons, including that neither of us are probably big readers.

"*You* looked out for her," he says.

It's a searching remark, and I know that I could handle this one of two ways: I could tell him it was no big deal and suggest we go back out there and drink a beer together. Or—

"I'm falling in love with your sister," I say, shocking both of us. My heart starts beating too fast in my chest, adrenaline riding my blood as it pumps through my veins. At least I didn't tell him that his sister sat on my face the other night, or that last night I fucked her against a shuttered picture window next to a Christmas tree.

Zach lets out a jagged laugh and runs a hand through his slightly too long hair.

"Well, shit," he says. "I thought maybe you had a thing for her, but I wasn't expecting that."

"If you want to punch me, can we get it out of the way now?"

He studies me for a second, then claps me on the back. "I don't want to punch you. *Yet*. You keep being good to her, and you and I have no problem. You fuck up or start climbing trellises, and I *will* punch you, even though you and I both know that you could beat the shit out of me. I'll still do it. It'll have to be a sly punch, delivered when you're least expecting it, but if you mess with my sister, it'll happen."

"Fair," I say.

"Now let's go get drunk. I think that's what you're supposed to do when your friend tells you he's dating your baby sister."

"Are we friends?" I ask, lifting my eyebrows.

"I really fucking hope so, or else I might have to renege my approval."

"I don't know how this is going to work," I admit. "I don't see myself moving to Chicago."

A corner of his mouth lifts. "Tina already has half a dozen plans to get Kennedy to move here. I'm sure she'd be more than happy to share them. She's confident Kennedy's boss loves her enough that she'd let her work remotely."

Something lifts in my chest, or at least that's the way it feels. Oliver works remotely, so I know it's possible for some people.

"Would your parents be pissed off?"

He laughs with honest amusement and gives me another back clap. "Good God, I hope so." It's then that I remember that his situation isn't all that different from my own.

"But wouldn't they take away her trust fund?" I know she has big plans for it, once the money is hers to do with as she wishes.

The amusement drips from his face, and a different look enters his eyes. "You wouldn't want her without it?"

Horror rips through me. "No. Fuck, that's not what I meant. I just don't want her to get it taken away because of me. I know she wants to use it to help fund her non-profit."

He studies me, as if looking for signs of honesty, and God, I hope he finds it. Because I've never meant anything more. I don't want to be the man who takes anything away from Kennedy—I want to be the man who gives her things.

"Okay, I believe you," he says. "You know, there was someone she dated before, a little slug named Brian or Brutus or some shit. He was in it for the money, and it took her a long time to get over being used like that."

Anger replaces my horror, because I want to find this Brian or Brutus and tear him to pieces for using Kennedy. "Did you make him pay?" I growl.

An almost delighted laugh emanates from him. "Not in the way you're implying, I'll bet. But I got him banned from all the places he wanted to network. Made sure plenty of doors were closed to him."

"I still wish someone had punched him," I say.

"Yeah, me too," he says with a sigh. "But there's always tomorrow. As far as the trust fund goes, no, I don't think my father would take it away. He's already shunned one of his kids...wouldn't be great metrics for him to suddenly have one less Littlefield running around, especially if she's everyone's TV sweetheart. Besides, she's going to mention the company she works for every chance she gets on that show. The last thing he'd want is for everyone to think he's the kind of asshole who'd disinherit the daughter who's devoted to public service."

"And your father cares what other people think?" I ask, reflecting on what I know about the man, including that he's not Zach's real father.

He laughs as if I've made a rip-roaring joke. "It's the only thing he cares about. Besides, the only reason he cut me off is that he figured out I'm not his. He won't cut off his own blood."

I'm shocked he told me so easily, because from what Kennedy told me, it's a secret that not many people know. I say as much.

He shrugs it off. "I used to care. Not so much anymore. I've got everything I want in life. I don't need the approval of a man whose opinion I never much cared for or a mother who never stood up for me or my sister and brother."

I smile at that. "You know, I think maybe we have a lot in common. Let me pretend to buy you a drink."

"Pretend?"

"Cole gives us everything for free now that he's with my sister."

He grins. "By all means. I'm all for a pretending you bought me a drink, and you know that Tina and your sisters are dying to tell us what to do. Let's let them."

It's then that something new burns in my chest. Hope.

Chapter Twenty-Five

Kennedy

It's Thursday, the day before the next Rolex ceremony. Dinner with Marcus last night was...okay. When he's not around Jonah, he's a nice guy—confident but approachable—and he told me about his parents and his sister, a single mom. He said he has a special appreciation for Leto's Hands' mission after watching his sister go through a messy divorce with her emotionally abusive husband. I told him a bit about my family too. Olive and my brothers. Nanny Rose. But he kept trying to steer the conversation back to Littlefield Bank. To what it was like to be part of a dynasty, and I just felt this bone-deep wanting for Rowan. For his touch and his taste. For his laughter and conversation. For *him*.

Nana Mayberry, who was my "handler" last night, gave me a big talking-to about my failure to flirt with Marcus, whose attempt to lean in for a kiss was rebuffed when I flinched back like he had scabies. My response was to agree to smile more for the cameras today.

"If you think it's the cameras you need to be smiling for, you need to have your head examined," she said with pursed lips.

I gave her a smile as sweet as saccharine.

She called me surly and stalked off.

I can't *wait* until Harry catches her on camera with Jonah.

Speaking of Jonah, I went on a group date with the four remaining guys this afternoon. We went berry picking at a local farm. Obviously, there's nothing on the vines, so we had to pretend to pick from the plants, and the next shots were of us having a picnic with big buckets full of berries that were probably flown in from Mexico. There was nothing charming about it, other than a short visit to the shop, which sells homemade blackberry jams, apple butter, and hot chocolate with whipped cream. There was even a rogue bit of garland hung up by the register that the production assistants and Nana Mayberry had obviously missed.

I bought several jars of the jam and apple butter, along with a huge hot chocolate, figuring I could give the jam as gifts.

Maybe Rowan would like some.

I brought Jester with me on his little leash. He's clearly no judge of character because he kept trying to approach Nana Mayberry, who holds clear disdain for him. To be fair, she might just smell like beef jerky or bacon. Who knows what she does when she's not in Labelle Manor trying to control everyone like a tyrannical queen? Maybe she has a jerky addiction and watches those Olsen twin movies when no one's watching.

I'm supposed to be getting ready for a one-on-one date with Colton tonight, but instead I'm lying on my bed, Jester reclined on my chest, staring at the ceiling and thinking about Rowan.

I'm in love with him.

I'm desperately in love with him.

He's the person I think about in the morning, the one I'd like to wake up to.

He's also the person I think about at night.

He's the person I'd like to build a life with.

But there's no denying some essential facts. Although we've been brought together for this short period of time, our lives are in different places. The thought of dating someone who lived somewhere else didn't bother me much when I signed on for this show. Because I wasn't doing it with the real hope of finding love. I figured that if I did, whatever, we'd work it out. Or maybe I'd get lucky and fall madly for some doctor or whatever who lives in the Windy City.

It's possible Rowan would be willing to go to Chicago with me to see where this connection takes us. Only...I know without asking that he wouldn't like it. He's a small-town guy, and he's already told me this place runs through his veins.

We could try long distance, I guess, but it's such a very long distance, when all I want is for him to have his arms around me.

"What are we going to do, buddy?" I ask Jester, who rouses from his snoozing for long enough to lick my shirt.

You could stay here, a voice in my head whispers. *You could stay in Highland Hills.*

There's a wrenching feeling in my chest because I really do love my job. It was the first thing in my life I ever felt like I'd chosen for myself, not because someone had steered me to it. It was the first thing I felt good at. The thing is, I know my boss, Gayle, is willing to compromise with the people she likes. She let me come here, didn't she?

Would she let me stay?

What about Olive? Although I don't mind the thought of leaving my parents several states away, I hate the thought of being permanently separated from Olive and Nanny Rose. They'd visit—I know they'd visit—but it wouldn't be the same.

I pet Jester, who licks my hand.

"I don't want to go out with Colton," I tell him. "I definitely don't want to go out with Jonah. Or Marcus. Or Jeff. Rowan's the one I want."

Jester offers a little half bark, and I decide that he agrees with me. "He's our guy, Jester."

Something stirs inside me, and I recognize it for what it is—that

Littlefield problem-solving gene. I sit up, moving Jester to my lap, where he cuddles happily enough.

"Harry was right," I tell him.

He wags his nub of a tail.

I set him down and get up, starting to pace.

"Rowan needs to be part of the narrative for the show," I tell Jester.

I know in my heart that he will want to do no such thing, but it's the perfect solution—the perfect *compromise*.

He doesn't want me to flirt with the guys on the show, and I absolutely don't want to do that either, but if there's no flirting, there's no show, and if there's no show, then Leto's Hands won't get the boost it so desperately needs.

But if the show subverts people's expectations...if I end up with Rowan, the grandson of one of the hosts, instead of one of the "rich" men she chose for me...

Well, Harry's right...it would be highly entertaining.

There's a knock, and then an envelope is pushed under the door. I sigh, because yesterday Colton slipped another poem under my door, and it was truly awful. He rhymed "kiss" with "piss," and I'm not looking forward to pretending I enjoyed it over dinner.

Jester shocks the life out of me by scrambling over to the door and picking up the envelope in his mouth, then bringing it to me.

"You're a genius," I tell him, in serious wonder. And he pees on the floor.

After I clean it up, I open the envelope, steeling myself for poor rhyming and worse attempts at iambic pentameter.

To my surprise, it's a note from Harry.

Kennedy—

I can't risk being seen going into your room right now. Tensions are very high in the house. I've told everyone your stomach's acting up again. Sorry. I couldn't think of a better excuse. Be prepared, though, Colton wants to talk to you—at length, I'm sure—about the possibility that you might have ulcerative colitis. He has discussed his bowel movements with me for the last hour.

They wanted to check on you, like last time, but I told them you had some serious thinking to do before tomorrow's Rolex ceremony, and that's what set off the drama. Colton and that guy Jeff started fighting about which of them is more boring—I thought it was Jeff at first, but it's DEFINITELY Colton—and then Jonah said he'd be a shoe in for the final three because he's pledged to give you his virginity, and the others all agreed that he wasn't in fact a virgin. Anyway, there's a lot of controversy out here. Be grateful you're tucked away with a stomach complaint. ;-)

Xoxo, Harry

P.S. Dispose of this note. No one will think twice about you flushing the toilet a lot.

Laughter slips out of me, and delight fizzes in my body because surely this means...

Rowan's coming, isn't he? Harry knows I want more time with him, and he's arranged for it to happen, the dear man.

I kiss the top of Jester's head, dispose of the note as Harry suggested (something tells me he's waiting outside to hear that flush), and then settle into the cozy chair by the window.

While I wait for him, I try reading the biography of Jonah Highbury the First again, then set it aside for another reread of the holiday romance novel. Jester lies at my feet, his warm fur brushing my skin. It feels like waiting for a pot of water to boil, but finally a light but insistent tap lands on the window, and I jump from my chair like a jack-in-the-box, prompting Jester to grunt and give me a grumpy look before he settles back down.

"Sorry, Jester," I murmur as I race to the window to let Rowan in.

When I open the blinds, he's there, and I'm aware of how much I've missed him over the past forty-eight hours. It hasn't taken very long, but he's slipped into my soul. It makes me think again about the distance between Asheville and Chicago.

I open the window to a waft of cold air and Rowan scent, and he smiles at me. "Harry told you?"

"He didn't tell me much," I say. "But I hoped you were coming. He said I didn't have to have dinner with Colton tonight because everyone in the house thinks I have explosive diarrhea. Again."

He smirks. "I shouldn't laugh."

"Oh, you can laugh. Everyone else probably is, except for Colton. He's apparently preparing a speech on ulcerative colitis."

He surprises me by leaning in and kissing me with cold lips, which instantly warm when they're pressed to mine.

I'm struck with the knowledge that he's still halfway out the window.

"Rowan, come in," I say, fear twining around me. "I don't want you to fall."

"I thought maybe you'd want to come out, instead," he says with shining eyes.

"Come out?" I ask in shock.

"I have something planned for us."

My heart beats faster. He has something planned for us. He wants us to leave the house, together. *I get to leave.*

"What if we're caught?" I ask haltingly, because even though Rowan is the boy who never followed the rules, the boy who never had any, I've never been like that. Yes, I balked my parents' expectations by taking the job I wanted instead of becoming a socialite, but he's talking about the sort of rule-breaking that might get us in trouble.

"Harry promised to create a distraction," he tells me with a grin so radiant I feel it in my toes. This is no exaggeration, they *curl.*

"I need to get changed," I say, tugging on the collar of his coat. He climbs into the room with the practiced movements of a rule-breaker and sits in my chair, bending to pet Jester as if it's the most normal thing in the world. The sight of them together gushes warmth through my chest, but I don't say anything for a moment. I just soak it in. "What should I wear?" I ask.

"Nothing fancy, Princess," he says. "This is Highland Hills, after all, and I want you to be comfortable."

"But what if someone notices me?" I ask. My photo was released to the press earlier this week, so I can no longer expect to be fully anonymous. Rowan knows this, not because he saw the press release —I imagine he actively avoids such things—but because I told him the other night.

He snaps his fingers, then pulls a bag out of his jacket, handing it to me.

I look inside and see a red wig, a pair of eyeglasses, and some bright makeup that I would never normally wear.

"Where'd you get this?"

"Ivy," he says. "She says she dresses up while she's researching different fields for her writing. I'd rather not overthink it. I guess the glasses are non-prescription."

"It'll take me a minute," I warn.

"It won't feel like long if I'm in here petting Jester," he tells me. "But I won't be following you into the bathroom to keep you company. If I watch you change, I'm going to get ideas, and we have a schedule."

"We do?" I ask with delight. Rowan's not really a schedule kind of guy. He told me that's why he prefers the work he does—it's different every day.

"For you, we have a schedule," he says, and I can't help it, I lean in and kiss him, just once, but I make it count.

"There you go again, giving me ideas," he says with a grin. "But I won't be distracted. This is happening."

"Well, all right, sir," I say, and he groans.

"I think that's the first time anyone's ever called me that, and I like it more than I thought I would."

I'm laughing as I make my way to the bathroom.

It's fun, changing into someone else. I decide my name is Daphne. Nanny Rose used to play old cartoons for me when I was a kid, even though my mother insisted I should only be allowed to watch educational programs, and *Scooby Doo* was my favorite. I look different. I *feel* different.

When I come out to put on my shoes and grab my winter coat, Jester's lying on his back in Rowan's lap, and Rowan's petting his tummy, saying, "You're a good boy." The feeling of love and abundance in my chest surges.

"*You're* a good boy," I tell him.

He smirks at me. "Huh. I didn't know I had a praise kink."

"And I don't know what a praise kink is, but if it involves me telling you when you do good things, I'm all about it." I smile. "Also, I should introduce myself. My name is Daphne, and my biggest personality flaw is that I prefer slow jazz to any other sound."

He sets Jester down, watching me, and then says, "You look fucking hot, but you don't look like you. I like it for tonight, but I like you as yourself best of all."

"See, you *do* know the right thing to say," I tell him, because I'm pretty sure it's the best compliment I've ever received. He lifts from the chair and kisses me, capturing my bottom lip between his teeth for an instant. If he were to suggest staying here all night and forgetting his idea, I wouldn't hate it, but he pulls back, rueful.

"We're sticking to the plan. I'm not messing this up for you." He says it with such conviction, and something inside me softens, even though I wasn't aware there was anything left in my heart that could become softer toward him.

"By all means," I say, pulling on my coat and watching as he tugs his back on.

Jester gives a mournful little cry, obviously realizing we're going somewhere and he's not.

"I'm sorry, bud," Rowan says, then pulls something out of his pocket and gives it to him. Jester takes it greedily, already gobbling it up.

"You brought him a treat?" I ask, feeling that soft space in my heart again.

"As a distraction," he insists, because he doesn't like to have his goodness commented on. Then, his grin turning a bit wicked, he says, "Are you ready to break some rules, Princess?"

Am I ever.

* * *

Climbing down the side of the building was easier than I'd feared. There's a large trellis nailed to the side of the building, and it was almost like using a ladder. It reminded me of Jonah and Marcus's inane competition from the night Rowan got me Jester. In fact, it's so dangerously easy that I'm tempted to write the Labelles an anonymous letter, warning them of the danger.

Afterward, we slipped into the woods by the house so we could circle around the to avoid the guards who've been posted at the front door after Jonah's mistake. It felt clandestine, and kind of hot, and we're going to be a few minutes late for whatever Rowan arranged, because I told him that it was Daphne's fantasy to be taken against a tree.

He gave me what I wanted. Sort of. It was much too cold for us to take our clothes off, but he used one arm to pin me to the tree and the other to make me come.

It took us several minutes to hike to the car, parked in a little clear patch of land off the long driveway. We're sitting in it now, a little disheveled from our stop in the woods, but in a *good* way.

"This is for you," he says, handing me a travel mug from the cupholder. He has an identical one, I see, but he doesn't move to open it.

The smell is out of this world fabulous, like spiced eggnog mixed with rum and butter and goodness. "Is this a Three Wise Men?"

"The very same," he says with a grin. "Drink slowly and with caution."

I take the first sip of the boozy drink, and it's so delicious that I understand why it's notorious for creating hangovers. Who would drink one of these and say, *I've had enough?*

"What are we doing?" I ask with excitement.

"You'll see," he tells me, giving me a sidelong glance. "But I can tell you with confidence, Daphne, that it'll be horrible."

Chapter Twenty-Six

Rowan

"I warned you," I say, glancing at her. She looks so damn happy, it's like I can't help but catch some of her happiness and keep it. Except that's not quite right, because the reason I'm happy is that *she* is—that I was able to make this happen for her.

Even though the only thing I've given her is atonal caroling in the town square.

That's no exaggeration—one of the carolers is so tone deaf, the screech she issues during "All I Want for Christmas is You" sounds like it's made by a murder victim. Worse, four of them are in costume. One is, randomly, a bear, another is dressed to look like a nutcracker, a third is wearing antlers with jingle bells (Kennedy says this isn't a costume, but I argue that if a person were to wear such a thing at any other time, they would be considered eccentric, if not troubled), and a fourth is dressed as Jolly Saint Nick himself.

If left to my own devices, I would only attend this particular event if one of the carolers accidentally lit a fire. Or if someone suffered from a medical emergency, like Jay, and they had to wait for the EMTs to arrive.

But I can't deny that I'm having fun. Standing here with my arm around Kennedy, both of us holding drinks from Christmas All Year coffee, although I'm the DD, and mine is non-alcoholic, there's a lightness inside of me. With her, I can watch this absurdity unfolding and be slightly amused and entertained by it, not annoyed by the loud and badly performed music or the mildew-scented costumes several of the singers are wearing.

From the looks Kennedy keeps giving me and the way she snuggles closer, I know she's enjoying herself too.

Still, there's only so much a man can take, and when a true asshole shouts out encore for "All I want for Christmas is You," and they actually start singing it again, I slip my hand down to take hers and nod.

"Next stop."

She shoots me a sly look, like she understands exactly what I'm all about, and steps away with me.

"You didn't want to hear that high A again, did you?" she asks in a lowered voice.

"Did you?" I ask, giving her side a playful bump.

She giggles and takes another sip from her to-go mug as I lead her away. I watch as she soaks in the holiday scene—the wreathes hung over the street, the holly and pine decorating each of the old-fashioned lamp posts, the white fairy lights, and the brighter multicolored ones in the shop windows. It's always struck me as over-the-top, commercialized, and geared toward the tourists who rip through our town like locusts. And to be honest, I still feel that way. But I suck in her joy like it's the drink in my mug.

She glances around as if worried she'll be overheard over the sound of the carolers, who are still loud even though we're retreating from them, then says, "I can't believe all this has been going on around me, and I didn't even know. It's like all the Christmas was stripped from Labelle Manor and brought here."

I snort. "It's like this every year, Kennedy. They do it for the tourists."

"But you get to enjoy it too," she says, grinning at a small girl who's stepped up to a shop window to check out the display of stuffed horses. Her mother is beside her, one hand on her hair, but she has a tired look, and I wonder if she'll be able to afford one of the stuffed animals her little girl's ogling. "I always liked horses too when I was a little girl."

"Your father got you a pony, didn't he?" I ask, unable to help myself.

"How'd you guess?" she asks with a self-aware smile. "Her name was Buttercup, and I regret nothing."

"Wait here," I say on impulse, squeezing her hand.

She gives me an inscrutable look but nods and points at her feet. "Waiting here."

I come out a few minutes later, hand one of the bags I'm holding to the little girl's mother with a nod and an "it's from Saint Nick." Before she can stutter out more than a thank you, I return to Kennedy and give her the other.

"It may be the only pony I can get you," I say with a half-smile. "But I came by it honestly." I flinch when I see the tears in her eyes. "Did something happen?"

Was she pissed that I'd been away for so long?

"That little girl," she says, nodding toward her. I don't look back, because I'm concerned the girl's mother might have tears in her eyes too, and then I'll have made two women cry in as many minutes. "I saw what you did, Rowan. That was...that was so beautiful." She cradles the shopping bag to her chest. "And I'm going to treasure this forever."

Self-consciousness claws at my chest. I didn't do it to come off as a good guy. I did it because I wanted to, but now I feel uncomfortable. I scratch my chest through my coat. "Well, if you react like that to me giving out a couple of little gifts, maybe I should play Santa all night."

Her eyes light up with excitement, never far off for her, which is one of the things I love about her. "Yes," she says with emphasis. "Let's do it. Exactly that."

Her words surprise a laugh out of me. "What? You want to buy a bunch of gifts at the toy store and give them to people who look like they need a pick me up?"

"*Yes*."

"What if someone thinks we're perverts for giving presents to kids?"

She considers this for a second, but nothing will put her off now that she's attached to the idea. "We'll only give them to kids who have an adult with them. And we'll give them to the adult."

I scrunch my nose. "There's a good chance I'll know some of these people, and you're supposed to be keeping a low profile."

She glances around before saying in an undertone, "I'm not Kennedy. I'm *Daphne*."

It's true that she doesn't look like herself. I wouldn't be surprised if her own brother did a double take before he added one and one and got two. Still, I don't love the idea of approaching a bunch of strangers with gifts. I'm even less partial to the thought of going up to people I haven't had the misfortune of talking to since high school. But that look in her eyes...

Maybe this will help her fall in love with Highland Hills.

Maybe this will make her want to stay.

I sigh. "Okay."

"Okay?" she asks, giving a little jump on her feet, like her body can't contain her joy.

"Okay," I say, laughing. "How much of that Three Wise Men did you drink, anyway?"

"Enough that it's empty," she says with a shrug, and slips the closed canister into the bag with her pony. Mine is in my jacket pocket.

"Let's go play Santa Claus."

So we go inside, buy dozens of presents, and ask for them to be wrapped.

* * *

One man spat at us, and a woman I vaguely remember from high school claimed that I'd never called her back after we hooked up, an accusation that made my ears turn red. But there've also been a lot of smiles, a lot of joy, and so much of it has been from Kennedy that I feel drunk on it.

"We're running behind schedule," I say. "But this is what's next." We're just outside the bookstore, and Kennedy lights up when she sees the name on the awning—Read Me—which I've always thought was stupid until right this moment. "I'm going to buy you some new holiday romance books so you don't have to keep reading the same one over and over again."

She immediately lifts up onto her toes and kisses me. My heart swells in my chest because tonight was supposed to be all about her, but somehow, it's become about us. She pulls away but takes my hand. We walk in together, and I help her choose several books, laughing my ass off at the descriptions but getting kind of into the whole thing since it becomes a game to see if I can choose something that holds her interest.

When we leave the bookstore, she shoots me a sidelong glance.

"What?"

"What's next?"

I laugh and put my arm around her. "We're about to go to the worst place on Earth. Brace yourself."

Seven minutes later, we walk into Christmas All Year Coffee.

Her gasp is so adorable I can barely take it, even though I feel an equal measure of horror. This place has always struck me as a night-mare tourist trap—somewhere I'd rather not go, thank you very much

—but tonight there's something magical about it. It's as if I'm seeing it through Kennedy's eyes.

The Christmas tree is all decked out, there's Bing Crosby playing over the speakers, and the whole place smells like coffee and chocolate, with a hint of spice and liqueur. The tables are packed with people eating desserts and drinking coffee or hot chocolate or hot alcoholic beverages, but the small square two-top closest to the tree is empty.

"That's for us?" Kennedy asks with awe as I head toward it. "Who'd you have to kill?"

"Friend of a friend."

"You killed a friend of a friend?"

I smirk at her. "Smartass. A friend of a friend set this up. It's no big deal."

She slowly shakes her head as we sit at the table, the chairs upholstered with red velvet and brass tacks because everything in this place needs to beat you over the head with Christmas.

"This is amazing," she says, leaning across the table as if she's sharing a secret. "Rowan...this is maybe the best day I've ever had."

"Me too," I say, taking her hand, and I mean it. I wouldn't have chosen to do any of these things on my own, but with her, they were okay. No, they were more than okay. They made me fall a little bit in love with this place too—they helped me see it with the blinders that tourists wear whenever they pop in for their weekends away.

I let Kennedy order whatever she wants for me, with the disclaimer that I won't be drinking alcohol because I'm her driver, and we end up with hot chocolates covered in so much whipped cream that the sight of one of these suckers would probably give Harry a panic attack from all the dairy. We talk easily, the way we've been doing all night. About Highland Hills. Leto's Hands. And at one point, she laughs herself into near hysterics over the coincidence that my best friend is named Oliver and hers is named Olive.

When we're done, I take her hand, and we walk to Ziggy's. "My little sister wanted to meet you," I say, rubbing a thumb over the back of her hand. I've already told her why Ivy's been helping out at the brewery. "She's going to bring us some food."

Actually, I wouldn't be surprised if everyone I know is lying in wait in the tap room, hoping we'll come in so they can see how it's going. We're barely through the door of the modern-industrial style tap room when Ivy descends on us.

"Right this way," she says, without even introducing herself. She leads us to a booth in the back, where we'll be relatively tucked away. Once we're seated, she beams at Kennedy. "The red wig suits you. I loved wearing the red. I got a job at the zoo wearing that wig." She pats her chest. "I'm Ivy, by the way. I know *your* name."

Kennedy's cheeks flush slightly, then something sparks in her eyes. "You're the romance novelist! That's amazing. I'd love to read your books sometime."

Ivy winks. "I'll hook you up. Don't wait on this guy to bring you any. Rowan Mayberry likes to pretend I write children's books."

She says it so casually, but there's a pinch of hurt to it, and I suddenly feel like an asshole. It's not her fault that the guys at the firehouse are dicks about her writing. Or that someone made a sign with "Cupid" on it on Valentine's Day and tacked it up on my front door. I'm proud of Ivy, and if you're proud of someone, it's best to tell them, isn't it? I've spent so much of my life not telling people how I feel—not even acknowledging my feelings to myself. Where has it gotten me?

I swallow. "I'm proud of you, Ivy. We all are."

There's a pleased twinkle in her eyes as she cuts a bow. "Now let me get y'all some food. I'd bring over menus, but let's be frank, the burgers are the only food worth having here. That sound okay?"

We both nod, and Ivy hustles off. As she leaves, I see a solo man at a table near us look up and watch her, and there's a frank appreciation in his gaze that makes me bristle. I glare at him; he doesn't notice. He's wearing glasses, and there's a stack of paper in front of him, like he decided a brewery was a good place to get some work done. But he's a stranger, and the most beautiful woman in the world is across from me, so my attention doesn't stick to him for more than half a second.

"Have you spoken to Jay?" Kennedy asks, leaning over the table, and I have another moment of discomfort, of feeling like I've done something important wrong. I *did* see Jay at the hospital last week, after I spoke with Ivy and Willow, but we weren't alone together. He gave me plenty of significant looks, which I ignored. I asked him about his health. He asked me about my toy cars. That was that. I haven't gone by the house since he was released from the hospital. Nor have I asked him about Kerry and the podiatrist. I need to do those things, but I haven't felt ready for them.

"No," I admit. "Not really."

"Would you like help practicing?" she asks. "Sometimes it helps if you practice all the different ways a conversation could go."

I feel the corners of my mouth lift. "So you're gonna be Jay?"

"If you want."

I don't, not really. I'd rather sit here with her, eat a burger, and enjoy being with her out in the open. Of not hiding how I feel. But she's right. I do need to confront this thing with Jay head-on, and I don't know how to do that. Maybe practicing will help.

"Okay," I say. "How do we start?"

"*Rowan, I am your father,*" she says, her expression deadpan.

I laugh again, but it cuts off when I realize it's my turn to speak.

"Yeah," I say. "I got that part. I can even understand, I guess, why you started seeing Mom while she was still married. Love makes a man to do stupid things. The part I don't get is why you left me when you thought I might be yours. Why you never told me about any of it until now."

"Maybe I was scared it would change things," she says softly. "Maybe I was scared you wouldn't look at me the same way if you knew about the affair. That you wouldn't respect me anymore. And even if a part of me suspected you were mine, I didn't know for sure. I wanted it to be true, and I worried it wasn't."

"You stopped treating me like a son after you divorced my mother," I say, my voice trembling. "You may have still asked me to hang out now and again, but I didn't feel like I was family to you anymore. I felt like an afterthought."

Fuck, it feels like something inside me is tearing open. Like all my fears and worries and inadequacies are tumbling out and biting into me. I don't like it. *I don't like it.*

Kennedy reaches across the table and takes my hand, squeezing it.

"I didn't know what to do," she tells me. "Your mother made it clear that she didn't want me around you kids, except for Ivy, so I honored that. Because I worried she'd take you away from me completely if I didn't keep my distance. Whether you were my son or not, my name wasn't on your birth certificate. She had all the power."

"Kennedy," I say, her name jagged on my lips. "I don't think..."

"We're practicing how it might go," she says, squeezing my hand again. "And remember that I've met Jay. I've spoken with him. He *loves* you."

I feel someone staring, and when I look up, the guy with all the papers is watching us. I scowl at him. He looks away.

"He loves you," Kennedy continues. And then, looking into her bright blue eyes, so intent in their desire to make me feel better, I do something truly stupid.

"And *I* love *you*," I say.

Chapter Twenty-Seven

Kennedy

"Wait," I say, "are you talking in character?" But I already know the answer. Everything in me is hot and gooey, like the middle of a barely done chocolate chip cookie. I want nothing more than to fold into this man and this moment because this is as close to perfect as real life gets.

"No, Kennedy," he says, lifting my hand to his lips and kissing it. "I'm not. I'm an idiot, and I don't know what I'm doing at least three quarters of the time, but I love you. These past weeks...the only reason I haven't fallen apart is because of you. Because I want to be the kind of man who's good enough for you."

"You don't need to try to be that man," I say, my heart pounding, a ball of raw emotion lodged in my throat. "You *are* him." I'm suddenly not nearly close enough to him, and I get up from my side of the booth and move over to his, sliding in next to him, and his arm slips around me, cocooning me in his warmth. "You gave me the best day I've ever had, Rowan. The best...and playing Santa Claus for those kids tonight..." I feel tears pushing at my eyes. I know he did it for me, but he enjoyed it too. I could see the goodness in him tonight, from handing the pony to that little girl's mother to giving out those gifts to passersby. I lean in, taking in his woodsy scent, and kiss the rasp of his bearded cheek. "I love you too."

His eyes glint with warmth, with *love*, and he leans in and kisses me, soft and sweet. "Thank God for that," he says, cupping my cheek. But his hand falls too soon. "Kennedy, would you ever consider...would you consider staying in Highland Hills?"

I think of Gayle, of my job at Leto's Hands, of Olive and Nanny Rose. I don't want to leave all of them, but I don't have to, do I? I'm pretty sure I can work something out with Gayle, and I have the resources to visit Olive and Nanny Rose or fly them out here whenever I want. Plus, there's an idea I've been working on in my head, something Rowan and I could work on together if he has a mind to. A project we could both pour ourselves into.

I'd also be with Zach and Tina, with Harry. I *want* that. I want this little town that I've experienced tonight, with the caroling, and Christmas all year, and people working together even though they don't always like each other.

"I think so," I tell him, and the joy in his face is so real, so potent, I almost weep. "But, Rowan," I say. "We need to talk about the show." I start telling him about Harry's idea, about how we can hijack the narrative of the show and make it our own, but his lips set in a hard line, and the softness that was there moments ago is fading. Panic grips me.

He's going to say no.

What will I do if he turns me down?

This is the only way I can finish the show without pretending to get engaged to Jonah or Marcus or Jeff. (Let's be honest, Colton's poetry and obsession with stomach conditions sealed his doom.) It's the only way we can be together now, on our own terms.

It's the only way I can still help Leto's Hands *and* Harry.

"Kennedy," Rowan says, his voice sad, resigned. "I can't do that."

Panic weeds through my arms and legs, my head. When he

shrugs his arm off me so he can scrub his beard with both hands, I feel the loss of his touch, and my panic grows.

"It's the only way," I tell him. "It's the only way we can be together now, without me pretending—"

"Don't you see?" he asks, his tone beseeching. "The thing I hate most about this town is the way people talk, the way they've always looked at me—like they know everything about me because they know about my past. If we did this, they'd never let it go. I'd always be *that* guy. Worse, people across the country would be looking into our business, our lives. You think my mother would let this go? She'd see it as her chance for the spotlight, and she'd find someone to interview her about it."

"So you want me to choose one of the guys?" I ask, horrified. "If I did that, I'd have to pretend—"

"No," he says emphatically. "No. Can't we just..."

"What?" I ask, pushing away on the bench, suddenly pissed. Partly at him, and partly at this situation we've backed ourselves into. "What? You want me to shut down the show so we can be together? Don't you see what a big F-U that would be to Leto's Hands? To Harry? To all the people who have poured themselves into this production? You wouldn't only be screwing your grandmother, Rowan. You realize that, right?"

"I—"

But I'll never know what he was going to say, because there's an epic crash close to us, followed by a slew of swearing. I look over and see a tray full of food has fallen to the ground, creating an enormous mess, and Ivy and a guy at the table closest to us, who had a sheaf of papers in front of him, are standing in the middle of it. His crisp white shirt has ketchup and some liquid splashed over it, and several of the papers have scattered across the floor. He's handsome, I realize, the kind of good looks that are hard to miss—dark eyes and tousled dark hair—but I didn't even notice earlier because my attention was so thoroughly fixed on Rowan. I'm unmoved by this stranger, just as I am by Marcus's beauty.

Ivy looks apologetic, until the man turns on her, his full lips pursed. He removes his glasses and sets them on the table. "You screwed up my manuscript."

"Excuse me," she says, putting a hand on her hip. "You tripped me. Who puts a bag out in the middle of the floor?"

"It was next to my chair," he says wryly. "I figured I was allowed to set things down next to my chair."

Rowan gives me a slight nudge and, taking the hint, I get up and let him out. He approaches the guy like a bear who's been poked. "Don't talk to my sister like that," he grumbles. Then, "I don't like the way you were looking at her earlier and watching me and my girl."

My heart does a stupid little flip...because he called me his girl.

I'm not sure how much longer I'll get to keep that title.

He asked me to move to Highland Hills with him, but he won't do any of the things that will make that happen. He wants me to change my life for him—without him changing anything for me.

The guy lifts his hands to indicate he's no threat. "I heard you saying your last name, is all. I wondered if you were related to someone I know."

Rowan shoots me a look as if to say *this is what'll happen, Kennedy, don't you see?* But the guy continues, "Willow."

So it's not Rowan's grandmother or mother this guy knows about. He's not here because of the show.

Rowan flinches. "You know our sister?"

"I'm Lou," the man tells him, his gaze shooting from Ivy back to Rowan. "You're her brother and sister."

"Yeah, but your name doesn't clarify who *you* are," Rowan says. "She's never mentioned a Lou."

"You and I have crossed paths before," the guy insists. "I'm a friend of her fiancé's. I was there when he proposed to Willow back in the spring. They told me about this place, you know. Highland Hills, I mean. Not the brewery. They said small town folk are nicer." There's a dryness to the remark.

"Why didn't Willow say anything?" Rowan asks suspiciously.

"She doesn't know," Lou says. "I've been trying to keep a low profile. Keep to myself. It's just...I heard your name, and I wondered if you knew her."

"Well, let's pick up this food," Ivy says, giving Lou a dirty look that suggests he's at fault for the whole thing. To be fair, his bag *is* jutting into the aisle between the tables, and something tells me she was watching the fight between Rowan and me more than she was the ground at her feet.

"I'm going to go back to the inn to change my shirt," Lou says, his mouth in an expression of distaste. He starts stacking his papers, even grabbing the few saturated ones on the floor. There's something a little jumpy about his movements, like he doesn't want anyone to take too close of a look at those pages.

"It would be the gentleman-like thing to help," Ivy tells him.

"Good thing I'm not a gentleman," he says. "Plus, as far as I can tell, you're the one who works here."

Rowan glowers at him. "You say you're a friend of Willow's. Willow would stay and help."

"Yeah," Lou says with an almost wistful expression. "She would." And then he takes out his wallet, slaps down some cash on the table, grabs his things, and leaves in his ketchup-smeared shirt.

I slide out of the booth, clutching the bag that holds my pony. It's time for me to go too.

"What are you doing?" Rowan asks, looking at me with wide eyes when he sees me take a step away from the booth. I'm suddenly aware that everyone is staring at us. Everyone.

Part of me recognizes that this is what Rowan doesn't want—to be watched, to be studied, to be interpreted by people who don't know him. And I can understand that. Even so, I'm crushed by the knowledge that he won't do it for me when it's the only way we can be together without any pretense.

"I'm going to help Ivy," I say. "And then I'm going back to Labelle Manor."

"It's okay," Ivy says. "That jackwad was right. I do technically work here, and I *did* technically create this mess. I'll clean it up." But she gives Rowan a censuring look that suggests he should clean up his own messes.

Too bad I'm starting to think there's no cleaning this one up.

"I'm going to take you back to the house," he says. "Of course I'm going to take you."

But then his phone rings. His brow furrows, his whole body going to attention, and he pulls it out. "Shit. Fuck," he says after checking the number.

"I hope you don't say that when *I* call," Ivy quips.

He looks up at us. "It's the firehouse. I'm on call."

* * *

Ivy, who's been borrowing her dad's car while she's in town, gives me a ride back to Labelle Manor. Apparently, Cole, the owner of brewery, was happy to give her a break, possibly because the tray of food she spilled all over the ground wasn't her first mishap for the night. I hope she's better at writing than she is at serving.

Before he left us, Rowan looked me in the eye, his expression pleading, and said, "We're not done talking about this." Except it feels like we *are* done. He still doesn't want to be on the show, and I don't know where that leaves us. I'm also worried, in spite of myself, about the fire. I know the majority of his calls aren't even about fires —most are from people who've locked themselves out, or can't get their cat or dog or child down from a tree, or have started a kitchen fire. But I still hate thinking of him walking into a blaze with little protection besides his suit. He's such a big man, seemingly unbreakable, but we're all breakable in the end.

"So, men are stupid at least ninety percent of the time," Ivy says after a stretch of silence. Her mouth twists. "Maybe more like ninety-five. They need a lot of help realizing what they actually think and feel. Like it would be great if each of them had a pocket therapist, you know?"

"Are we talking about your brother?" I ask, feeling a smile surface.

"Yes," she says. "He's possibly the most stubborn man alive, but don't let that put you off. Because he's also loyal...and sweet...and very, very talented. You should see those little cars he makes. I'm not even into cars, but I can tell they're special. He's just...he's a quiet guy, and he thinks he wants a quiet life."

"I think he really *does* want that," I say thoughtfully, hugging my pony through the bag. "And being with me would really mess things up for him."

"So what?" Ivy says flippantly. "So, things will be a little louder than he'd like for a while. People will pay him more attention than he cares to receive. So what? They'll stop caring. People always stop caring after a while. They'll move on to someone else, and he can go back to being a hermit crab."

"I don't think he sees things that way," I tell her.

"That's okay, Kennedy, because he has several pocket therapists. We're called sisters, and we're gonna screw his head on straight for you. We'll try to get him down to being stupid only ninety percent of the time."

I laugh, but there are still tears behind my eyes, because I don't really believe it. I don't believe anyone could convince him to be on the show—and even if he did, I think he'd regret it.

I don't think I'm enough.

"Tell me more about the book you're writing," I say. I just...I can't talk about Rowan right now. I can't think about him.

She gives me a quick sidelong look as she steers the car, then tells me that she doesn't know what's going to happen yet because she's a fly-by-the-seat-of-her-pants kind of girl, and she knows as much about what will happen in it right now as I do.

Talking to her, I think of Rowan and the maybe-fire.

"You don't think it's a real fire, do you?" I ask worriedly.

She reaches over and taps my hand. "If it is, he'll help put it out. It's emotions he struggles with. He's never had any trouble being brave."

She probably meant for that to make me feel better, but it doesn't.

When we get closer to Labelle Manor, I hear sirens behind us, and I glance at her in surprise. Her eyes leave the road for a fraction of a second to meet mine.

"You don't think—" I start.

But they're already getting louder. It's obvious they are going in the same direction, maybe even to the same place.

"Ivy...Harry's in that house. And my dog Jester...and everyone else."

"Fuck," she says with feeling. "I really like dogs."

Nervous laughter pours out of me as she steps on the gas. I'm not sure why she's speeding up when the fire truck is behind us. What the heck are we going to do if we get there first? But I don't tell her to slow down. Those vines of worry are squeezing me.

It doesn't take long for the truck to catch up, and Ivy pulls out of the way for it to pass us. I watch it, my heart in my throat, looking for some sign of Rowan, but of course there isn't one.

"I don't like this," I tell Ivy.

"Me either," she says, following them like a speed demon.

There's another alarm, another truck.

Then a third.

If there had only been one truck, I'd think maybe it was a false alarm. But three? This means Rowan's with them, definitely, and there's almost certainly a fire or some other sort of emergency.

It occurs to me that I'm not supposed to be out of the house, and now I'll definitely be caught, but what does it matter if there's a fire at the house?

Some things are more important than the rules.

Those vines of worry grow tighter. What if no one remembers Jester's in there? What if they leave him to get hurt by the fire? What if *Rowan* is hurt in the fire?

"They're going to be okay," Ivy says, but from the way she's saying it, it's as if she thinks she can will it to be true. I know that's not the case. I remember seeing Olive's grandmother collapse as if it were yesterday. Nanny Rose told us it would be okay too, and it wasn't.

But I don't say any of that. Rowan might be...well, I love him, but he's her brother.

Both of us are tense as she zooms up the long driveway. The sirens are no longer blaring, signaling that the trucks have reached their destination, but now that we're closer, smoke is drifting in through the car's air system. I don't think I've ever been this afraid before in my whole life.

When we reach the point where the driveway widens, Ivy pulls to the side, out of the way, and parks. We're at a distance but more than close enough to see the house is smoking like a burning birthday cake, and several uniformed firefighters are hustling about, spraying it with water. A window on the second floor breaks, and flames lick out of it. A frightened gasp escapes my lips. *No, no, no.*

There's a group of people gathered to the right of Ivy's car. A fireman stands with them, in uniform except for the helmet. I can make out Harry, thank God, rubbing his head as if he has lice and a good brushing with his hand might chase them out. There's Jonah, dressed in red flannel pajamas, and Colton, wearing a reindeer pullover that must have been sent by his mother. Jeff. Marcus.

There's no sign of Nana Mayberry, but then she's usually not at the house this late. I do make out all of the production assistants, plus the cameramen. They're okay. *They're okay.* Their faces are pale and full of panic, but they're unharmed.

There's no sign of Jester.

If Rowan's one of the firemen who's bustling around, I can't tell. The uniforms they wear cover their entire bodies and faces.

Ivy leaves the car with purpose, and I stumble out after her. She grabs my arm and marches up to the group of people. The fireman instantly steps forward to intercept her, even as Harry breathes out, "Oh, thank God, you're okay," and wraps me into a smoky hug. I'm trembling, I realize, and so is he.

"Harry, what happened?" I ask him.

Jonah says, "Who are you?" looking straight at me, and I realize he hasn't caught on to the wig. I tug it off. Then the glasses. I left my pony bag in the car, so I shove them into the pocket of my coat. He reacts with as much shock as someone in one of those makeover montage movies. "It's you."

A couple of the other guys address me too, but I don't process what they're saying. My gaze is on Harry.

He opens his mouth to speak. Then both of us divert our attention to Ivy as the fireman sidesteps to stay in her path.

"You can't go any further, ma'am," he says gruffly.

She scowls at him. "Don't call me ma'am. I'll have you know we were in Algebra II together, and we're very much the same age. I'm looking for my brother."

The guy swears under his breath, studying her, then says, "Shit. I didn't know you were in town."

"Where's Rowan?" she insists, clearly not in the mood for questions. Neither am I, come to that. I need to know Rowan is safe. I need it more than I've ever needed anything in my whole life.

"He's in the house," the fireman says. "Says there's a dog in there."

Worry tightens around me to the point where I can barely breathe. What if I lose them both? What if Rowan dies but Jester survives, and I know it's all my fault?

"Damn it, Rowan. Damn it," Ivy says, and I can tell she's jumping in her skin, same as me. Neither of us are wearing coats. We took them off in the car and didn't think of it when we got out, but I can barely feel the deep chill. I'm numb. I'm full of excruciating pain. I'm *terrified*.

"This is all my fault!" Harry bellows.

"What happened?" I ask, vaguely remembering that he'd promised Rowan to provide a distraction so no one would go looking for us. If it's his fault, I guess it's partially ours as well.

"It's not his fault," Marcus says calmly. "We were all worried about you, obviously"—he eyes me curiously, probably wondering about the wig and glasses disguise—"and Harry suggested a cookie baking competition to keep our mind off things. But Jonah here..." His mouth firms. "Misread the recipe and set the oven to 523 instead of 325 and then forgot to set the alarm. We're guessing the fire started in the kitchen."

"It could have happened to anyone," Jonah says in a sulky tone, watching as more flames lick through the broken window.

Rowan is in there. He's *in there*.

Ivy eyes that window too before saying woodenly, "I doubt that could have caused a fire like this. Are you sure nothing else happened?"

"I'll never make a cookie again," Harry says. "I'll never eat one again as penance!"

Colton gives Jonah a lingering look. "You were gone for a long time before we started the cookie thing. You never explained where you went."

"The pool room," he says, sounding annoyed. "Don't the rest of you get bored and wander around?"

Jeff shrugs in agreement. "The rooster room's my favorite," he offers.

"That's because you're a dick," Jonah says, snickering.

"Can you stop it?!" I shout, my voice louder than intended. "Rowan is in danger. Doesn't anyone care?"

"Who's Rowan?" Marcus asks, his brow wrinkled. Something flashes in his eyes, a connection being made, and then he says, "Is he the guy who said you were already out of the house?"

I can feel myself breaking because I'm not supposed to act like Rowan is important to me. I'm not supposed to act like my heart is in there, in danger. To them, he's no one, someone who tinkered around on set for a few days before leaving—the relative of a woman they don't much care for. To me, though, to me...

A figure bursts through the door in a cloud of smoke, and tears instantly fall from my eyes, because it's *him*. It's him. He's *okay*. And there's a little bundle cradled in his hands that can only be Jester.

My heart beating hard in my chest, I take a step toward him, then another. The fireman who was blocking Ivy tries to sidestep in front of me, but I can't let him. I can't. Other people shout at me, and I hear Harry, in particular, but I don't pay them any attention. I run to Rowan as he steps away from the burning building, Jester in his arms. I run to him.

Someone stops me before I get very far, but I don't even look to see who it is. Because I'm crying too hard, my arms are extended toward them.

I need to know they're okay. I need to see Jester breathing. I need to see Rowan's face.

The next thing I know, Ivy is taking me from whoever stopped me. She's hugging me hard.

"They say the building's going to go, Kennedy," she says into my ear. "We need to get Jester and get out of here."

"But...Rowan," I say through sobs.

"He's okay," she tells me softly, running a soothing hand through my hair. "He's going to be okay. We're going to get Jester from him so we can bring him to the emergency vet, and then we'll let him do his thing. He's not in any more danger."

She says something to the man who was holding me back, and he signals to someone, who signals to someone else, and we're led over to the back of one of the fire trucks. Rowan's sitting there with his helmet and mask off, his face red and streaked with soot. He's drinking water from a straw someone gave him, and there's a medic next to him, taking his blood pressure.

Jester is in his lap. He looks groggy, but he's awake.

Rowan saved him.

I want to race across the distance between us. I want to cover him in kisses. I want to take him back to his house and make love to him for hours.

But he takes a look at us, emotion washing over his face, his eyes brimming with it, then says, "I think he'll be all right, ma'am, but you'll need to take him to an emergency vet for smoke inhalation. No one else was harmed in the fire."

The blood in my veins turns to ice. He's pretending he doesn't know me. He doesn't want any of these people to know we mean something to each other. Part of my mind recognizes why he's doing it—I don't want the show to end and he doesn't want to be on it—but I figured that this situation—an emergency—would supersede all that. I figured that he, like me, couldn't give two shits about the show right now. I guess I was wrong.

I stiffen my back, wipe my cheeks, and pretend right back.

"Thank you, *sir*," I say, looking into his eyes. "I was really worried about him, but I can see that he's doing just fine without me."

Then I scoop up my dog and turn my back on Rowan.

Chapter Twenty-Eight

Rowan

They're waiting for me in the living room when I open the door to my house. Holly and Bryn. Ivy. Harry and Oliver, who gives me a nod. I guess my sisters felt bad enough for me that they left their gooey other halves home.

"An all hands on deck meeting, huh?" I ask, walking past them to get to the fridge. I'd hook myself up to a beer IV if I could. What started as the best night of my life quickly devolved into one of the worst. Then again, that's always been the way my luck has swung— one side of the pendulum to the other.

They let me get a beer and pop it, then Holly clears her throat and says, "Take a seat."

"Is this an intervention?" I ask dryly, "because, last I checked, I don't have a drug problem, and I'm pretty sure anyone would have a beer after the day I had."

"You walked away from Kennedy," Harry accuses. Oliver gives me an apologetic look over his shoulder.

"You were a contributing cause to a fire that wiped out a multi-million-dollar house," I shoot back. The Labelles' house is totaled. It's gone. The roof crashed in. The damage is so complete no one other than squirrels will be living there anytime soon. "I hope they had some good fucking insurance...the show too."

"The show insurance is airtight," Harry says. He waves a hand. "Apparently, there were some trust issues involving your grandmother, so they locked into the highest plan possible."

If regret tickles at my throat, then it's because I'm a selfish asshole. I guess part of me was hoping this meant the show would definitely end. Because earlier, when Kennedy was weeping, trying to push her way to me and Jester, it killed me—absolutely killed me—to act like she meant nothing to me. Like I hadn't stomped into that burning house, knowing it might be the last thing I did because the puppy she loved was shut up in her bedroom. Like she wasn't the woman I want to spend the rest of my life with, something I didn't know I was capable of wanting until I let her in.

I scratch my throat, cringing at the pain it causes. My whole face is pink from the fire, although I avoided getting burned any worse. The medics wanted me to go to the hospital for smoke inhalation, but I refused. I've needed treatment before, but I feel fine. Chalk it up to a Christmas miracle, I guess. Kennedy probably would.

Okay, I *don't* feel fine. That's a damn lie. But it's not the smoke that's making me feel shitty—it's only a contributing cause.

"Where's Kennedy?" I blurt. "What happened with the dog?"

"You did good, man," Oliver says, and there are a couple of nods around the room.

"He needs to stay at the vet to get oxygen for a couple days," Ivy says. "But he's fine. You rescued him."

"Kennedy's at the inn with the rest of the cast and crew," Harry says. "They kicked out all the people staying there so they could maintain secrecy."

I huff out a laugh as I lower into the only empty chair with my beer. "Good fucking luck with that. That fire's all anyone's going to talk about for months. *Years*. The Labelles might try to sue." Either that, or they'll be secretly thrilled. They'd been trying to unload that house on the downlow for at least two years, but no one wants a bizarre mansion with themed bedrooms, shocker of all shockers. This way, they'll get the insurance payout and they'll get to move. Win–win for them and for the town, I guess, if a fire that almost killed people can be called a win.

It strikes me that Zach and Tina have probably already heard about the fire. Shit. Are they worried? I'm surprised Zach hasn't barged in here demanding the full story. Unless...

"Do Zach and Tina know about this?"

Harry nods. "They were here earlier. They already know everything. Zach said he needed a stiff drink, and they went to Ziggy's."

"You think he'd know by now they only serve beer," Holly says. "But on the plus side, Cole keeps a bottle of whiskey behind the bar. I texted him and asked him to hook Zach up."

"I wasn't a contributing cause to the fire," Harry adds.

At first, I think he's just being defensive, but there's something almost victorious about the way he says it.

"We have something to show you," Holly says, twitchy in the way she always gets when she has a particularly good secret to share. She grabs her laptop from the coffee table and cues it up, then gestures for me to come closer. I don't particularly want to see whatever it is or do anything besides obliterate this emptiness I feel inside. But they all seem eager for me to look, so I head over to join them.

It's a camera feed from the pool room. It's paused, but it very clearly shows two figures: my grandmother and Jonah. My gaze instantly lifts to Harry, who's leaning over the computer, Oliver beside him. "You got something."

"We got something," he says excitedly.

Holly makes a *dun-dun-dun* sound, Bryn gives her a nudge, and then the footage is playing.

"You need to step it up, Romeo," my grandmother tells Jonah. "The next Rolex ceremony is tomorrow night."

"I'm doing the best I can," he complains. "My virgin strategy is working."

"It's not," she snaps. "It's feeble." Then she reaches out and plays with one of the buttons on his sweater. "Anyone who looks at you can tell you're not a virgin." There's something flirtatious about the way she says it, and I cringe, glancing at my sisters to see them do the same.

He grins. "Yeah, I guess I didn't think that part through. But she thinks I gave her the dog. We're golden."

"You need to reveal, on air, that Marcus has a girlfriend."

"He *does*?" Jonah asks eagerly.

She shrugs. "I've hired someone to say she's his girlfriend. It comes down to the same thing. It'll ruin his chances, and I'll convince Kennedy that choosing you will make for the best narrative. But I expect you to come through with your end of the bargain." She gives him a shrewd look and hands him a file folder that looks like it's full of oversized photos. "Or else I'll be sending these directly to Jonah Highbury the Fourth."

He flips the folder open, winces. "Maeve," he says, "I thought we were *friends*."

She snorts. "I don't have friends. I have people who are useful to me and people who are not."

"Fuck," I blurt. Every time I think my grandmother couldn't possibly be a worse human being, she goes and surprises me.

"Indeed," Ivy says.

"Indubitably," Holly adds.

Bryn, who's always had a thing for having the last word, says, "Precisely."

We watch as Nana turns and leaves the room, as Jonah continues to flip through the photos.

"It's a smoking gun," I say in wonder, because Harry could have hardly hoped for a better indictment of my grandmother. Although it pains me to admit it, it'll also make for some good TV if they can figure out a way to use it. Then again, I'm betting both my grandmother and Jonah have already signed releases for video footage for the show. This is video footage made for the show.

"It's not over," Holly says with great pleasure. "Keep watching."

Sure enough, Jonah sits down by the empty pool, looking through those photos, then pulls a lighter out of his pocket and flicks it on, feeding it one photo and then another. They all catch. He sets them down on the tiles next to the empty pool, so he probably thinks what he's doing is safe enough. Still, he stays until they're smoldering, no longer in flames.

Then the fucking idiot walks away.

He slams the door, probably pissed about getting blackmailed by my grandmother—not as rare of an event as one would hope—and the curtain rod tumbles down, taking the curtain with it. The curtain doesn't catch fire immediately, but I can see where this is going.

"Holy shit," I say.

"See," Harry tells me a little smugly. "You maligned me. Jonah's the one who started that fire. I had nothing to do with it."

I'm shocked, blown away, but I still have to laugh. "Whichever way you look at it, he's the one who started it. Either with shitty cookies or burning evidence." One of my buddies at the scene told me the cookie story after the flames finally died down. I lift my eyebrows. "You think those were pictures of him and Nana together?"

"I watched it frame by frame," Harry says. "They were."

Part of me is disappointed by what this means. The show will go on, obviously. They have a narrative that's sure to excite people. This means that Kennedy will have to—

"I feel it's important for us all to be honest with each other, right?" Holly asks. "Didn't we decide that?"

Ivy lifts a hand. "I was not present during that discussion, but I agree that we should, in this instance, be brutally honest with Rowan."

Holly rolls her eyes. "You're temporarily off the hook for telling us about what's going on with you, but only because we're busy speaking our truth to Rowan."

Our sister nods. "I'll take it."

"You're in love with Kennedy," Harry tells me. It's not a question.

"Did she tell you that?"

"No one needs to tell us anything, you dipshit," Ivy says. "We see it. You're a changed man. Hell, before all of this went down tonight, I saw you smiling and laughing in that booth with her at Ziggy's. Despite all the shit that's gone down with Dad, you've been happier lately. Lighter. Don't you think that's worth fighting for? Don't you think *she's* worth fighting for?"

"Of course," I say, annoyed. "I went in there to get her dog, didn't I?"

"So what the hell are you doing? She was crying earlier, trying to run to you, and when she finally got to you, you acted like you didn't know her."

I swear and look down. "I did it for her," I tell the floor. "She wants to keep doing the show. She doesn't want to let everyone down."

"I don't think you're telling them the full story," Harry says knowingly.

"Jesus, did you get into the schnappsicles again, or are you just naturally this chatty?"

I look up at him in time to see his shrug. "Both."

"Okay, fine," I snap, irritated because I'm starting to realize how badly I've messed all this up, and like most people, I don't like feeling like a screw-up. "She asked me if I'd go on the show. If the show could tell the story of how we ended up falling in love instead of her choosing one of those dipshits. I said no." I rub my chest.

"Rowan," Bryn says in that *you've disappointed your big sister* way.

I bristle. "I hate all the attention this is bringing to us. I didn't want any part of this. None of us did."

"But it's changed," Harry says, gesturing to the computer. "It's still changing. Admittedly, this will bring a lot of publicity to your family, but it's not going to reflect badly on anyone other than your grandmother, and maybe you can use the publicity in a good way."

"Yes," Holly says. "This will actually be pretty amazing for our dating app...and Cole's brewery...and your handyman business."

"What about your cars?" Bryn says. "Have you ever thought about making that a business? Maybe this is your chance."

"I don't care about any of that," I grumble, feeling overwhelmed by the suggestions because my mind is one on thing—Kennedy and the way I've screwed up with her. "I just want to make this right with her, but I don't want the attention. I don't—"

"Was she open to the idea of staying in Highland Hills?" Ivy asks with arched brows.

"Yes," I murmur, her words like a stab.

"Ever heard of compromise, Ro?"

That *you're an asshole* feeling is fast becoming a *you're an asshole and an idiot* feeling. I see another flash of Kennedy's face from earlier. Of the tears tracking down her cheeks because she was worried about me and Jester. Other than Willow and the people in this room, no one's ever cared about me like that before. No one.

"You're right," I tell them through numb lips. "I...I love her. I don't want to lose her. I can't. I just...I feel like I'm too fucked up for her. Doesn't she deserve someone better?"

"Who?" Harry asks with a snort. "Jonah Highbury the Fifth? I'd rather see her marry a toilet bowl brush."

Ivy pats me on the shoulder. "It's nothing some talk therapy won't cure."

I cringe. She swats my shoulder. "Can't I just talk to all of you?" I ask.

"Maybe," Holly says. "But you'll have to do a whole lot better at saying the things you'd normally bury six feet under with a shovel."

"And then salting the scene and adding a cross," Ivy adds.

"I think that can be arranged," I say. Then I nod at the computer. "What are we going to do about Nana?"

"I think I can safely say that none of us want anything to do with her," Bryn says. We all nod. "I suggest that we leave her to be miserable alone. Rory has graciously offered to pick up the tab if she ever needs to live in a retirement facility or get a home nurse. I'd say that's where our responsibility to her ends." She rubs her slightly rounded belly. "I know I don't want her to have anything to do with the baby."

"Thank God," Holly mutters.

I nod thoughtfully. "Okay, yeah. Although I don't think Rory should have to do shit for her, I'll admit it takes a load off."

"So let's get back to the subject you're avoiding," Ivy says. "What are you going to do about Kennedy? Because if this were a romance book, it would really fizzle out if the guy decided his privacy was more important than his love life."

This makes me flinch. I never, not for one second, wanted Kennedy to feel she's less important than my desire to be a hermit. But I guess that's exactly what I did.

"I'm going to stop being an asshole," I say. "I need to fix this."

"Good," Oliver says, speaking for practically the first time this evening. He always has had a better gauge on when to shut up than I do. "Because I don't want to get stuck matchmaking a grump. That's something you Mayberrys are supposed to do." He puts his arm around Harry as he says it—a silent acknowledgement that I did something else right. Maybe it's time to make a habit of that.

"What do I do, guys?"

Chapter Twenty-Nine

Kennedy

The inn is beautiful—an old Victorian building, with crown molding and a tower bedroom for me, as if I'm truly a princess. It's also decked out for Christmas, with a huge tree in the lobby and garland everywhere. One wall hosts an enormous hearth. The production team asked them to strip the decorations, and they replied that they'd already kicked everyone out to make room for us—the decorations were staying. Harry says they'll cut them out in post-production.

It's nice and cheerful, but I don't feel the joy of it. My little tree was lost to the fire in Labelle Manor, and my heart is in tatters.

It's Friday evening. We're about to hold the Rolex ceremony, even though my one-on-one dates with both Colton and Jeff, which was supposed to take place this morning, were canceled because of my supposed stomach complaint and the fact that the entire house we were staying in was engulfed in flames. That kind of thing will create a delay or two, I guess. Honestly, I'm kind of surprised the show wasn't canceled on the spot, but Harry tells me it'll actually be fantastic for the story arc, and the producers are, and I quote, "excited" by the fiery destruction Jonah wrought on Labelle Manor.

This means I can finally cut him, right?

Admittedly, he was trying to make *me* cookies, but he nearly killed my boyfriend and my dog while doing it.

Rowan is most definitely not yours. He made his decision.

I smooth my hands over the front of my silky red dress, looking in the mirror, and I'm forcibly reminded of that first night, when Rowan slowly slid up my zipper. A production assistant did it tonight, and I just sent her on her way so I could have a few minutes alone.

I sigh and walk over to the bed, slumping onto the mattress. The stuffed pony Rowan got me sits against the pillow, and tears prick at my eyes. Both because I miss him and because the pony, however cuddly and adorable, is not much of a substitution for Jester. My baby is still at the emergency vet, but I'm told he'll almost certainly pull through. He'll be okay because of Rowan.

I'm tempted to use tonight's ceremony to announce that I'm leaving the show, but I don't have it in me to ruin things for the production assistants and producers, for Harry, and even for three-fourths of the remaining guys.

Jonah Highbury can go stuff it—and Maeve Mayberry with him. I'm sure she's going to have some choice words for me tonight, what with the fire and the fact that I was caught sneaking out.

I glance at the door. If there's someone waiting behind it, I can't tell through the small strip at the bottom. I take a chance and reach under my pillow to grab the contraband phone Harry let me borrow. I don't have to call my brother—he and Tina stopped by earlier and demanded to talk to me, and Zach slung around the perfect combination of threats and flattery to be allowed access to me. I assured them that both Jester and I were alive, thanks to Rowan, and they exchanged a significant glance that poked at my sore heart.

I dial up Olive, who answers on the first ring. "Kennedy?" she asks. "Tell me it's you."

"It's me," I say, feeling a rush of joy upon hearing her voice. "Boy, do I have a lot to tell you."

"Good," she says. "Tell me everything. Spoiler alert—they're going to ship me out there next week to hang out with you on Christmas Eve. My mama too."

I want them here *now*. I want them here yesterday. "Oh, thank God," I say, and I tell her everything. Everything.

"Holy shit," she says when I've finished. "That's gonna be some show."

"Yeah, I guess," I say, but I can't muster any excitement right now, not even for her.

"I look forward to meeting him."

"Who?" I ask, surprised, mostly because I haven't made much of a case for Jonah, Marcus, Jeff, *or* Colton. I could understand why she'd want to meet them, from a morbid curiosity viewpoint, but there's actual excitement in her voice.

"Rowan, obviously."

"I don't know if you will meet him." My heart sinks at the thought because I like thinking of the three of us hanging out. Olive would give him grief for being such a grump, and he'd give it right back. Nanny Rose would be there, of course, and knowing her, she'd insist on cooking for all of us even though the show has chefs on staff.

"Oh, I will," Olive says knowingly. "I can tell."

My heart tries to buoy up from the mire in which it has sunk, but I don't want to let myself hope. I used to think there was nothing bad about hope—only an upside—but hope can be dangerous. It can lead to the kind of disappointment it's hard to bounce back from.

"He doesn't want to be dragged into any of this," I say.

"We'll see," she says knowingly, and I'd be annoyed with her if she weren't saying something I'm desperate to believe. "I'll see you soon, Kennedy. It's almost over. We're gonna get crunked when you're finally finished shooting. And we're still going to watch half a dozen Christmas movies. I don't care if that's almost over too."

We hang up, and one line keeps running through my head—*It's almost over.*

She's right, but what will my life look like once it's done? Should I call Rowan and ask to talk this through? At the same time, he knows what I want—I've made that very clear—so it's on him to reach out to me, isn't it? Still, I find myself looking through Harry's contacts to find his number.

A knock lands on my door, and I shove the phone under my pillow.

"Are you ready?" Harry asks from behind the door.

No. Yes. As ready as I'll ever be.

I give my stuffed pony a pat, feeling a pinch of nostalgia for last night...before the fiery doom that engulfed Labelle Manor, obviously. Then I grab the phone, get up, and open the door.

"That dress is fantastic," Harry tells me as I glance around and then hand him the phone. He sounds like he means it, but I don't miss the way his face catches on mine. Despite turning me orange, which we now know was Rowan's fault, the makeup artist is very good at what she does, but she couldn't totally conceal that I'd spent half the night crying instead of sleeping. "This is going to be good...*great*. This show is going to blow everyone's expectations out of the water."

I nod because I don't trust my voice not to waver. "Are we still going on the skiing trip tomorrow?"

"Some people will be going, yes," he says enigmatically. Maybe he put it that way because I haven't told anyone who I'm planning to cut. To do that, I'd have to know myself. I'm still on the edge of quitting, of telling them I can't do this. Because even if I can't have Rowan, even if he doesn't want to be at the center of this shitshow with me, I'm still in love with him. Isn't it morally wrong of me to pretend that I could have feelings for someone else? Shouldn't I at least talk to the other guys openly about it so they know that I'm not interested in them? I've made no promises, and Nana Mayberry told me I flirt as badly as a block of ice, but even so, I don't want to disappoint anyone.

"It's going to be okay, Kennedy," Harry says kindly, his eyes warm. "It really will. Just don't ask Jonah to make cookies." He makes a face. "That was my error." Then he glances behind me into the room. Maybe it's my imagination, but I think his gaze lingers on the pony. "Are you ready?"

"As ready as I'll ever be."

"Let's go, then," he says.

The couple who run this place have half a dozen wonderful rocking chairs, each equipped with its own thick plaid blanket, arranged around the lobby, so that's where we'll be sitting instead of the thrones from Labelle Manor. There's a big screen TV mounted to the wall across from them, near the tree, and the sweet lady who runs the place told me that they're going to be playing holiday movies every night. She even offered to fix me hot chocolate and cookies if I'd like to join her. Better yet, there's a little reading room next to the lobby filled with hundreds of books.

"Most of them are romance," she'd told me with a conspiratorial look. "Something tells me you won't mind that a bit."

I love it here.

I wish I were here under different circumstances.

I wish I were here with a different person, no offense to Harry.

He leads me downstairs, neither of us talking.

A cameraman is waiting at the foot of the stairs, taking footage of me descending.

I can see that someone has set up a little bar down below, near the fireplace, and there's a tray of champagne glasses, another nod toward where we began.

The guys are all dressed in ill-fitting suits, which Harry tells me was the cause of much consternation earlier today. While Tina lent me one of her dresses, the guys weren't so lucky. (My brother, understandably, felt no interest in lending his nice things to the production, and no one else came forward with any offers.) There are only two suit shops in Highland Hills—one of them run by a man who claims his artistry would be offended by attempting to fit suits to four men in a matter of hours, and the other a discount shop. The producers opted for the latter. They say it will add to the shock value of the fire, although I'm unclear on why the fire needs to seem more shocking.

Colton and Jeff are sitting on the rocking chairs, rocking and chatting as if they could care less about the outcome of this Rolex ceremony, but Marcus and Jonah are each putting sticks in the fire from the collection gathered next to it, as if to prove to each other that they're capable of being outdoorsy. Nana Mayberry is watching them with pursed lips, standing a distance away from everyone. She's wearing a red sweater and a skirt with green stripes, but she couldn't look less merry if she were wearing a Krampus costume. A few of the production assistants are hanging around too, and a couple of them are having an intense whispered conversation. Maybe they're worried about Jonah being so close to the flames.

"Should he be allowed near the fire?" I ask hesitantly.

Harry blanches. "Away from the fire, Jonah," he shouts. "Step away."

"But Marcus and I have a little—"

"*Away.*"

Surprisingly, he listens. Maybe even Jonah Highbury the Fifth is capable of being chastened by the fact that he just singlehandedly destroyed a mansion.

When we get to the bottom of the steps, Harry nods to the fast-talking PAs, and one of them beams back at him and pulls a laptop out of his bag. Harry nods for me to take a seat. I do, and Marcus and Jonah sit down too, one on either side of me. I'm freezing despite the fire but I suppose that's the downside of wearing formal wear in the winter.

Harry, still standing, waves to the flat screen TV mounted on the wall across from the rocking chairs, and I'm vaguely aware of the cameras, soaking us all in.

"We have a special surprise prepared for you," he says, and the way Nana Mayberry sharply cranes her head, like one of those velociraptors in *Jurassic Park*, tells me that she's had no part in this. Even though I still want to be anywhere but here, my interest is piqued.

"Here we go," the PA says, giving Harry a thumbs up.

The TV flickers on, and a video shows up on the screen. It's the PA wearing a Santa suit with a scantily clad female elf on his lap.

"What the—" someone says, just as Nana Mayberry screeches, "What is this about, Sweet Tea? You did not run this by me, and I'm the official co-host. Put a stop to this nonsense *at once*."

"Just wait," Harry says, although it looks like some of the wind has been taken out of his sails. "It's not the right video. When you see the correct footage, you'll all be blown away."

The PA hustles to fix the problem, blushing furiously, and a new video appears on the screen. I recognize the pool room from Labelle Manor. Nana Mayberry's voice blares over the speakers, and our mouths gape as we listen. I glance at Nana just as she launches herself at Harry, whose eyes bulge in horror.

"Not again," he shouts.

"You've ruined *everything*," she shouts back, grabbing onto his shirt and shaking him.

"She's going to kill me!" Harry yells. "Help! Help! There's murder in her eyes!"

Jonah lets out a yelp, and the other guys look like frozen deer, but I nearly fall over my feet trying to get up in my dress, which wasn't designed with sitting in mind. I don't need to, though, because someone steps out of the reading room, and a strangled sound escapes me because it's him. It's *him*.

Rowan pulls his grandmother off easily, restraining her. He's dressed in one of his flannel shirts, the sleeves snug around his big arms, and his mouth is pressed into a serious line. Someone else might find him foreboding, from his intense expression to the bulk of him, but I've never been happier to see another person. It feels like my body naturally arcs toward him, like it's reaching out for him without my explicit permission.

"You idiot," Nana shouts at him, her face contorting. "How *dare* you turn on me after everything I've done for you. You've never been worth—"

"How dare *you!*" I seethe, finally managing to get out of my chair. For some reason it feels insane to be sitting through this. "He's helped you his whole life, and for what? You're an *awful* woman."

Admittedly, he was trying to mess up her show, but it seems like she did a pretty good job of that herself. I can feel everyone staring at me, but my eyes are on her calculating, narrow-eyed expression.

"I chose poorly in you," she says spitefully. "You're a foolish, bleeding heart—"

"Finish the video," Rowan says flatly. His eyes are on me, but the words aren't for me. It's then I realize the PA paused it on a particularly unflattering still of an eyes-half-closed Jonah gripping a folder of what must be incriminating photos.

My gaze instantly returns to Rowan, and I find him staring at me, his eyes hot.

What does it mean that he's here, that he's part of whatever Harry's doing? Hope is kindling inside me, but I don't want to let it get out of hand. I've seen what fires can do.

"I'm leaving," Nana Mayberry says sharply, pulling to release herself from her grandson's grip. He lets her. They both know he could stop her without raising his heart rate if she were to attempt another grab at Harry or anyone else. "I don't need to put myself through this abuse. All of this was my vision, and—"

"You said you were leaving?" Harry asks, now almost cocky. "Because that would be for the best. I've already shown this footage to the producers, and you're fired, of course. Old Sweet Tea over here is the new host of this show, no co-host necessary."

I grin at him because I'm proud of how far he's come. He's not afraid of her anymore. He's not afraid of Oliver anymore either, and that's a beautiful thing. Part of me wishes he'd warned me about all of this—about Jonah's role in the fire, about Nana, about *Rowan*—but I understand why he didn't. Harry has sharp instincts for what makes for good TV, and I'm guessing my genuine shock was part of his plan. Given everything he's been through to get to this point, I don't blame him one bit.

Nana Mayberry gives us one more withering look, pausing to make it extra *freeze you to your soul* when she reaches Jonah. Then she walks out the door without retrieving her coat, as if she can't be bothered to get cold.

"It's time," Rowan says again, nodding to the PA.

I keep my attention on Rowan, not the video broadcasting on the screen, but I glance back at it when I hear Marcus croon, "No fucking way."

We all watch as the curtain falls onto the smoldering photos. As the fire starts.

"We don't know that's what made the house burn down," Jonah says defensively, squirming in his chair now.

"No," Harry says, more confident now that his nemesis has been ruined. "The other option is that you burned it down by making cookies. Either way..." He tilts his head to the side and lifts his shoulder. "No one will ever enjoy the rooster room again."

"He has a good point," Colton says. "Not about the rooster room, but about the cookies." His gaze flicks to me. "You know, you really shouldn't eat cookies anyway if there's a chance you have ulcerative colitis, Kennedy. They say—"

"She doesn't have ulcerative colitis, you dimwit," Jonah says, his face red. He finally gets up from his chair. "She's been tricking us. I'm not the only one who's been up to something I shouldn't have." He points an accusatory finger at me. "Kennedy snuck out of the house in a disguise."

"Spoiler alert, Jonah," I say. "You're not getting your Rolex back in the ceremony tonight."

"Well, this is *just great*," he says, kicking the leg of his rocking chair. It rocks back and then forward sharply, hitting him. He starts hopping on one leg, then scowls at me as if it's my fault. "I pretended to be a virgin for you."

"Called it," Marcus mutters.

"I got you a puppy," Jonah continues.

I wonder if he's about to admit to making out with Maeve Mayberry "for me," but before he can say anything else, Rowan rumbles, "No, you didn't."

Then he's walking toward me, and I forget everything else. I certainly forget Jonah and whatever he's muttering about Jester.

"You don't have to do this," I say as Rowan comes closer. Because I know what this means, and I know very well what it will cost him. His privacy, so dear to him. His anonymity, even dearer. As he takes my hands, the warmth of him instantly dispels the chill I've felt all day.

"No, I don't." He swallows. "I should probably do the noble thing and say that I want to. But we both know I don't. You're worth it, though, Kennedy, a million times over, and I'm sorry if I'm such a stubborn jackass that I made you feel for one second like you're not."

Tears burn behind my eyes, and maybe I'm the jackass, because I don't care that we're in front of the four guys I was supposed to be dating, or that no one other than Harry knows that we're together, or that we haven't properly talked things through...

I put my arms around his neck, lean up, and kiss him.

He kisses me back as if he's unaware of the cameras taking it in—as if he really doesn't care so long as he can be with me.

When he pulls back, I keep holding his hand, because I don't want to stop touching him.

"Well," Harry says with a look of victory. "It would seem you two have *quite* the story to tell us."

Epilogue

Rowan

It's Christmas morning. Kennedy and I spent the last several days on the mountain, just the two of us...and Harry and the filming crew. I won't pretend I haven't hated being filmed, having our private moments pulled from us. We're not done, either. We have today off, but we're supposed to film the big finale next week. It's when she would have traveled home with one of the remaining dipwads. There's only me, though, and she's already met my entire family. In fact, we're going over to my sister Bryn's house later today, where she'll be buried in them. Willow and her fiancé, Alex, will be driving up from Asheville. Cole and his daughter, Jane, are coming, and so are Harry and Oliver, although Oliver's mother is probably going to curse me in at least twenty different ways for taking her son away on Christmas, even if it's only for a little while. Tina and Zach won't be there, but only because she has a big Italian family, and she claims they'd both be murdered if they didn't show up for Christmas.

I have big plans for Kennedy and me before we go over to Bryn's. Right now, though, I'm content to just lie with her, Jester snuggled between us.

I feel grateful.

I'm not going to pretend I've started believing in the holiday spirit or miracles, or any of that bullshit, but life is good. Better than good. Kennedy's boss has agreed that she can work remotely, with once-monthly trips to Chicago to check in, and she's moving into this house with Holly, Harry, and me. It won't feel empty anymore, the way it did when it was just me, the echoing walls, and the dust bunnies that Harry later banished. I doubt it'll be long before Holly up and moves in with her boyfriend, and fuck, it sounds like Harry and Oliver are moving fast, but for now it's going to be a full house. No one's as surprised as I am that I actually *like* that idea.

"You're awake," Kennedy says, curling into me. Jester gets up, moves around until he's found a comfortable spot in the new alignment, then circles in place until he curls up too.

"I'm awake," I confirm, putting an arm around her waist.

"Oh, you're *really* awake," she says as she pushes into me.

I laugh at the little grumble of complaint Jester makes when I lift him from the bed and lower him softly to the ground.

"Let me prove to you just how awake I am," I tell her, sliding my hand around and beneath the band of her underwear. She's wet for me, and I feel the same thrill I do every time.

I push her underwear down, and she helps me. Mine go next. I keep working her with my hand slowly, enjoying the little responses her body makes, the sounds that come from her mouth.

"Now," she says, her voice demanding in a way that makes me grin. "*Now*, Rowan."

"I want you on top," I say. "I want you to ride my cock so I can watch your tits bounce."

She rocks back against me, then turns and mounts my hips, her eyes sparkling. "You have a mouth on you."

"You like it. You especially like it when it's sucking your sweet pussy."

"I do."

She lifts up, then adjusts my cock, and slowly sinks down. It feels so good, my eyes almost roll back. "Merry Christmas, Kennedy," I say, then lean forward and capture her nipple in my mouth.

She grinds against me, my cock buried deep, gasping as I move to her other nipple. "*Merry* Christmas, indeed."

All in all, it's not a bad way to close out the year, balls-deep in the woman I love, looking up at her face and knowing that this year will be better than the last—a million times better, because I've finally let myself love and be loved.

It's not long before I pull her down so her breasts are pressed to my chest, and I can kiss her mouth while I thrust up to meet her movements. I want all of her, always, and for some unholy reason that I can only thank my lucky stars for, she feels the same way about me.

After, we get dressed, but I tug her back by the hand before she can leave the room. "I'd like to give you your present first. Just the two of us."

"You already got me Jester," she says, stunned. "Rowan, you didn't need to get me anything else."

"It's nothing," I say, self-conscious. Because it *is* nothing, or next to it. "I made it. It's not something I bought."

"You made me something?" she asks with the same look she got in her eyes when I told her about Christmas All Year Coffee. I feel a pleasant ache in my chest.

"I did."

She clears her throat as I pull out the package from my closet. It looks pretty good, but only because Bryn wrapped it for me. "I got you something too," Kennedy says.

"Did you get my shirt back from Jonah?" I ask. "I have fond memories of that shirt."

"I have fond memories of you having it off," she says with a slight smile, although I detect something nervous about her. "But no. That one went down in the blaze at Labelle Manor, unfortunately. This isn't something I can actually give you, although I did get you something little. It's just…" She pauses, looking at me, like she's worried about what she has to say, which makes *me* a little worried.

"Well?"

"I get access to my trust fund a little over a year from now. I was thinking maybe we could start our own little nonprofit, here in Highland Hills, to make sure all of the kids get Christmas presents, like we were talking about. I thought maybe we could sell your cars as part of it. Step up production."

My mouth gapes open. Here she goes, thinking big, when I've always been a small-picture kind of guy, but I don't hate this plan. In fact, it's a pretty fucking good plan, except…

"Kennedy, you can't spend your money on me."

"I won't be," she says firmly. "We'll both be spending it on kids who need help."

I slowly nod. "This would be a good time for you to open your present, so you can see if your plan is shit."

She lets out a tinkling laugh, then sifts through her suitcase and comes out with a small package, which she hands to me.

We both tear in, and I laugh when I reveal a little blue pony similar to the one I gave her last week. She's more of a *let's carefully remove the wrapping paper* type, so she slowly disassembles the paper on the package I gave her, pulling aside the flaps.

When she gets to the box, she opens it, and the slight gasp she makes is adorable. It's a bright purple, two-door coupe, made of painted wood. I use recycled plastic for the windows, since I usually give them away to kids, and the last thing you want to hear is that you're responsible for little Danny losing an eye. "You *made* this?"

The way she says it, I feel special, like I'm not some two-bit handyman-slash-fireman without any real ambition or talent. That's her talent, though—making people feel special. I'm just the lucky so-and-so she chose.

"I did," I say, looking down at the car. "You told me purple's your favorite color, Princess."

"And it works?"

"It does," I say with a grin.

"Want to try?"

"First, I think you ought to open the car door and look inside."

"The door opens?" she asks in wonder, and hell, if she's that easily impressed, she's really going to be blown away when she—

She looks up at me, her lips parting, a plain white gold band on her palm.

I scratch the back of my neck, suddenly feeling like an idiot. I should have taken Rory up on his offer to help me with a ring. I shouldn't have—

"Rowan, is this what I think it is?" she says in a whisper.

I take her other hand. I get down on one knee. "I know we're supposed to playact getting engaged next week for the cameras. But I don't want it to be pretend, Kennedy. Maybe you'll think I'm crazy, but I want to marry you for real. This past month has been hell...and it's also been the best month of my life. It's not much of a ring, but you can use the one the production gives us if you prefer."

"I want this one," she says, her eyes glistening as she slips it onto her finger. Because I ran her ring size past her brother, who had no fucking idea, and Tina, who put forth an educated guess, it fits. "I want this. I want *you*."

"Thank God for that," I say, letting out a breath as she wraps her arms around me and squeezes. She kisses me, and I kiss her back thoroughly, so grateful I can't put it into words.

I pull back slightly and say, "I didn't ask your father for permission."

She laughs. "Good. We both know he wouldn't have given it."

That, and he doesn't deserve to be treated as if his opinion matters. He's never paid Kennedy that compliment. She's always been told to do things, never asked.

Her parents *do* know about us, however. Zach was right about them. They haven't disowned her, but they've made it very clear that I'm not allowed to attend any family events or even visit their house. Suits me. I want upper crust parents-in-law about as much as they want a blue-collar son-in-law. Kennedy has other relatives, though, including a great aunt, who made sure to call to wish us a happy Christmas Eve. Her other brother, Phillip, did the same. It was awkward as hell, but I appreciate that he made some kind of effort. Although I don't want to drive a wedge between Kennedy and her family, she insists that if her parents had approved of me, she'd have been worried. I get that.

My own mother doesn't know we're together, or at least she doesn't know from *me*. I was done with her before I found out the truth about Jay, and now I'm more done with her than ever.

"I didn't ask because it's a ridiculous tradition," I tell her, "and yes, he would have said no. It's always better not to ask if 'no' isn't an acceptable response. But I did ask Zach for his blessing." My mouth hitched up. "He gave it, and he seems pretty pleased you'll be staying in Highland Hills."

She gives me a broad smile. "As it happens, I'm pretty pleased too."

"I also asked Olive and Nanny Rose for their blessing."

"You did?" she says, her heart showing in her eyes.

"They said no."

She pushes my arm. "No, they didn't."

"No, they didn't," I confirm. I reach up and trace her bottom lip. "They seemed pretty pleased." They'd come up to see us for a couple days after the ski trip, and we'd brought them to Christmas All Year Coffee...which was shut down for us so there weren't any gawkers. Although the production team didn't want to include anything related to Christmas on the show, I made the argument that the place always looks like that, mostly because I knew how much Kennedy wanted to share it with Olive. I could have happily spent the rest of my life without stepping foot in it again...if it didn't make her so damn happy.

"I love you," she says, and I'll never get tired of hearing those words from her. If that means I'm exactly as much of a sap as Holly and my other sisters have always accused me of being, then so be it. I'll hear I told you so five million times or more, but I'll develop selective deafness. She's worth it.

"I love you too."

We spend the next twenty minutes playing with the car, which Jester does *not* like. We really are like kids on Christmas morning, and Kennedy tells me at least three times that we have to pursue her business plan because every child in America needs one of these. I'm not so sure about that, but I like the idea of bringing joy to kids. Kennedy's brought joy to me, and now I feel like everyone could use a little more of it.

After we get coffee from downstairs, which is empty because Holly is with Cole and Jane, and Harry is in Asheville with his mother for the morning, we put Jester's leash on and leave for our next destination—Jay's house. Because there *is* one parent I'd like to share my news with.

I expect Ivy to answer the door, or maybe Jay himself, so it's a shock, to say the least, when that guy from Ziggy's opens it. Leo. Or maybe Lou.

"What the fuck are you doing here?" I burst out, because my initial reaction is that he must have broken in or roofied Ivy or something. I'd intended to ask Willow about him after our dinner at Ziggy's, but what with the fire and the Rolex ceremony and the ski trip, it escaped my mind. Still, I'm fairly sure he has no place in my father's house, on Christmas, no less. I don't like it, and I have a strong suspicion I don't like him.

"Merry Christmas to you, too," he says with a slight upward

movement of his lips. Then he steps aside, holding the door open wider.

"Your sister's a late sleeper, and your dad is lying down in the living room," he says. "I offered to get the door."

I notice, distantly, that he said dad and not stepdad. Does he know? Did Jay tell him?

"You still haven't said what you're doing here," I grumble, adjusting where I'm standing so I'm in front of Kennedy and Jester.

"I live here," he says, laughing. "When everyone got kicked out of the inn, the innkeepers let me stay with them for a couple of nights, but Moira said she knew of someone who was looking for a roommate. That someone turned out to be your dad." He waves a hand. "You know what they say about small towns."

"What do they say?" I ask, still confrontational. I don't like that I didn't know about this, but I suppose it's my own fault for being so wrapped up in Kennedy. Actually, I wonder when Ivy found out. She flew back to Charleston last week for a few days to grab some things, so she must have been gone while all of this went down. Something tells me she would have told Jay to say no.

"That there are no strangers in them. So I probably shouldn't have come here to escape my problems. Go figure. There are no bad ideas, just dumb people who come up with them."

He seems like he's talking to himself more than me. "*Excuse* me?"

He shrugs. "Come on in. Don't worry. I'll make myself scarce." He steps back to let us in. Kennedy enters the house first, unclipping Jester, who immediately rushing up to Lou as if they're long-lost best friends. I'd be more moved by his approval, but he treats everyone as if they're a long-lost best friend. I take some satisfaction from the thought that he's probably drooling on Lou's socks, if only because Lou looks like the kind of guy who wears, I dunno, cashmere socks or some shit. Cashmere socks deserve to get dog drool on them, if you ask me.

"Are you coming to Bryn and Rory's house later?" Kennedy asks him. "Rowan says Willow's going to be there."

"She and Alex invited me," Lou says, nodding, and I feel a spurt of annoyance, but then he adds, "but I'm not going to go. I'm not good company right now. Obviously. I'll see them before they leave."

Kennedy's expression says she's intrigued, but I couldn't care less what secrets this guy has tucked up his sleeve. I'm thinking about Jay...about what I came here to say to him. I'm thinking about forgiveness and the promises it holds.

I take her hand and squeeze it, then nod to the temporary addition to the household. "Thanks for letting us in. Merry Christmas."

"Is there anything merry about it?" he asks with a laugh, and it strikes me that he's slightly drunk. At ten a.m.

He walks off, and Kennedy and I exchange a look as I close the door behind me. "Something's going on with him," she says. "Poor guy. We should ask Willow what she knows."

"You're right," I say, leading her into the living room. Jay's been in this place ever since he and my mom divorced. I've only been here a few times, but they were memorable enough. "I've meant to, but I've been otherwise engaged. He's shady, if you ask me."

"I wouldn't go that far." Her gaze is shrewd. "You have a bad impression of him, but it's not because you thought he was rude about those papers."

"I noticed the way he was looking at Ivy," I admit. "I could tell he liked what he saw."

She smiles at me, her eyes as warm as lake water at the peak of summer. "You sound like Zach."

"I'll have you know that I offered to let Zach punch me, and he turned me down."

Her smile widens. "Of course he did. You'd have obliterated him."

"Nah," I say, reaching down to scratch Jester's head. He snorts and leans into it. I'm so damn happy that he's alive that his snorts are music to my ears. "I would have let him get one in for free."

"You're such a guy," she says, scrunching her nose. Truthfully, though, she doesn't seem too upset by it.

"Does this mean I'm a gentleman, after all?"

"Yeah, I think maybe it does." She takes my arm, hooking hers through it. "Now, are you ready, *sir*?"

I give her a look, soaking in this woman who wasn't supposed to be mine—this woman who has changed everything for me. I was so sure that I wanted to be the last man standing, alone, while everyone else found a partner, but it turns out that was another thing I was being bull-headed about. "Yeah, I think maybe I am."

Because, with her, I'm ready to face anything.

* * *

Want more Kennedy and Rowan? Find out what happens when Rowan meets Kennedy's best friend, Olive! You can get the bonus chapter here:

Ivy and Lou's story, Matchmaking a Roommate, is

coming out in February! Turn the page to read the first chapter.

You can also check out Bryn's book, Matchmaking a Billionaire, and Holly's book, Matchmaking a Single Dad!

Join our Facebook group, Angela and Denise's Laughing Hearts, for releases parties, giveaways, and fun content!

Matchmaking a Roommate
sneak peak

Chapter One
Ivy

"I don't need to do the New Year, new you thing," I say. "A new me is always around the corner."

Brittany gives me an *if you say so* look. She's the chief bartender at this establishment, other than my sister Holly's boyfriend, Cole, who owns Ziggy Brewery but is spending New Years with Holly. Brittany is also one tough bitch. I don't say this in a judgmental way —it's why I like her.

"That's bullshit," she says.

See? I meant it about the tough bitch thing.

Tucking a lock of dark hair back into her tight ponytail, she waves to a man down the bar, signaling he's been seen and will be served. Eventually. It's New Year's Eve at nine-thirty, and the place is packed full of people looking to get drunk. Dozens of them are flocked around the bar, while others are eating and drinking at tables in the tap room. It's probably not the best time to chat, even though this particular party will be ending at eleven-thirty, before the ball drops in New York City, but I'm feeling in a reflective mood. Maybe

Brittany is too, because she says, "People don't change that easily, like slipping on an outfit. You're the same person whether you're working at a brewery"—with this she gives me a pointed look, as if to say that working at *her* brewery is no game—"or a zoo or a firehouse or whatever else you've done."

"I really enjoyed working at the zoo," I say conversationally. "There was this one animal handler who, I shit you not—"

"Why don't you take the rest of the night off?" Brittany asks, popping a hand onto her hip. Her gaze shoots to the tasting room floor, where a few servers are running around with trays. It's hard to balance those trays. I know this because I've dropped three in the past week. "You clearly don't feel like working."

"I'm sorry," I say, feeling a sprinkle of contrition. "I'm just a talker."

"Well, less talking, more pouring."

For a while I do just that. I'm here to get a feel for the job, after all, and a big part of working at a brewery or bar is, inevitably, pouring alcohol. It's also about picking up on the personalities gathered around you, which is something that comes naturally to me. Of course, I'm perfectly capable of making up stories if none present themselves. That's what I do as a romance novelist. The man sitting in the corner, who has his phone propped in front of him and keeps glancing back at the door and around the tap room, is about to realize he's been stood up for an internet date. The woman whose chair is approximately seven inches away from her date's is angry with him because he ate the last of their Christmas candy without asking if she wanted any. (Okay, that's definitely made up, but wouldn't you be pissed too?) The—

Brittany taps my shoulder as she passes me to grab someone a drink. "You're spacing out," she calls over her shoulder. "No one wants a beer that's half foam."

Shit, she's right. I shrug and set it down, then refill another glass and bring it to the man who asked for it, who is old enough to be my dad.

I love my dad, but that doesn't make me feel more kindly to this guy when he leers at me and says, "Aren't you a sight for sore eyes?"

"Why, are your eyes sore?" I ask, tilting my head. "You spend too long on the computer? Because that always gives me eye strain. You might want to try those blue-light glasses. Target's running a special on them."

His mouth gapes open a little, and I give his hand a friendly pat before moving on to another customer.

It goes on like that for another hour and a half, at which point we start trying to herd the mostly drunk people out the door as if they're cats. We pretend we're closing up shop, but that's not why they need to vacate the premises. My brother, Rowan, and his fiancée, Kennedy, are about to show up with a couple of cameras in tow—along with the rest of my siblings. Rowan and Kennedy's love story is fantastic, the kind of thing even I couldn't hope to make up. She was the lead contestant on a travesty of a dating show concocted by my wicked grandmother, and he was the on-set handyman who was trying to sabotage the production. But hijinks ensued, he got the girl, and my grandmother has (unwillingly) retired. Can I get a hallelujah?

Truthfully, I'd like to scrap my current kernel of a book idea and write about them, but despite the fact that he's well on his way to being reality TV famous, my brother hates attention. He would not be pleased, and I *do* want to please him.

I'd rather not feel that way—it's so much easier to only want to please yourself—but there you go. He doesn't want to serve as inspiration; I don't want to annoy him, and thus I'm here being a shitty bartender and annoying Brittany.

The other servers depart with the guests, and the last drunk patron, Mr. Blue Light Glasses himself, is pushed out by Cole's sex-on-a-stick brother, Logan, Brittany takes out a bottle of whiskey from behind the bar and fills two glasses. Logan comes back and reaches for one of them, but she pushes it toward me. "That's for Ivy."

I grab it. "Don't mind if I do."

"Where's mine?" Logan asks, almost sulky for such a big bearded hunk of a man.

"In a shitty bottle in your apartment, I'm guessing," she says, lifting her eyebrows. "You can't stay here, Logan."

"Cole's going to be here in half an hour," he complains. "He invited me to the afterparty."

"So come back in half an hour if you want. *I* didn't invite you."

He gives her this seriously sexy glower that probably works wonders at disintegrating other women's panties, but she just gives him her bad bitch glare, and *it works.* I can practically see the man's dick withering. He nods at me, says, "Happy New Year, Ivy," very pointedly not including Brittany in the sentiment, and then turns and leaves, the door almost smacking him on the ass.

Damn it. I'd been hoping to corner him at midnight.

Turning to Brittany, I hoist up the glass of whiskey and tap it to hers. "I'm impressed, Britt. Can I call you Britt?"

"No." I shrug, and she starts laughing. "You call me that, and I'll start calling you Little Bit like your brother Rowan does, because Britt's what my daddy called me."

"Fair enough." I take a sip of the whiskey, then ask, "What gives? Why don't you like Logan? I'm going to be frank with you, he's one fine piece of ass."

She laughs harder, pressing a hand to her chest. "And I thought your sister Holly was sassy."

"If you don't tell me the real story, I'm going to make one up in my head," I warn.

"I don't doubt you will." She runs a finger around the rim of her whiskey glass. "There's no story. He just reminds me of my ex-husband. I prefer not to be reminded of my ex-husband whenever possible."

I hoist my glass in an air salute. "Say no more. I'm a child of multiple divorces. My mother's been married four times, and my dad's about to get his second one in the bag. Hell, from the way the widows and divorcees of Highland Hills have been crowding around him over the last week or so, I'm guessing he'll get around to divorce number three in no time."

"So you can understand why I don't want to repeat old patterns," she says.

"Hell, yes, I can." I'm all about avoiding patterns of any kind. Hence my habit of dipping into different jobs, even though most romance novelists do their research on Google like normal people. Hence my avoidance of Highland Hills like it's a plague.

People think it's cute when I tell them that my family used to run a matchmaking business. There are the usual requisite jokes because I'm a romance author from a family of matchmakers. Mayberry Matchmakers. Truth is, matchmaking hasn't been good to this family. My grandmother is basically every fairytale stepmother, and if my mother should have used birth control. I mean this. There are five of us kids, from three different fathers. Admittedly, I'm person-ally happy that she did not, but let's just say her parenting skills are on par with that of a rabbit. Rabbits give birth and then immediately hop off, only to return for a few minutes every day with some food. Our mother would have pulled that off if she could. (I learned a lot about animal habits while writing my zoo romance; go figure.)

I've recently gotten another lesson in what a shitty mother she is. Apparently, my brother Rowan, whom I thought was my half-brother, the way my other siblings are, is actually my full brother. In other words, she had an affair with my dad before divorcing her second husband and making him her third. How messy is that?

"How's your dad, by the way?" Brittany asks, shooting me a sympathetic look.

"Shockingly good for someone who just had a heart attack and had to retire early," I say, trying to keep things light. I almost had a heart attack when I heard about his health emergency, and to be honest, it's just about the only thing that could get me to stay in Highland Hills for more than a few days. Except a little voice in my head, which insists on being honest with me, however much I'd prefer otherwise, reminds me that's not the only reason I'm here. "I imagine he's doing way better with early retirement than Nana Mayberry."

"I guess so if he's already got women lining up to be his third mistake."

I'd just taken a sip of whiskey, and I nearly sputter it out. "I like you, Badass Brittany."

She lifts a finger. "Now, *that* can be my nickname. Are you going to be on camera for the show?"

I make a face. "Nah. I'll leave the spotlight to Ro. He'll hate it, of course, but that's what he gets for romancing the star of a reality TV show."

We drink our whiskey, and by the time Holly knocks on the locked door, which is a bit of pure impatience on her part because Cole obviously has a key, we're a little bit toasty, just the way anyone should be on New Year's Eve. "For God's sake, Holly," I hear him say as I throw open the door, but it's said fondly, and there's this delightful energy between them.

"We didn't burn the place down!" I announce. "Behold"—I sweep a hand around the tap room—"it is only the usual amount of dirty."

"Good, because this town doesn't need any more fires to put out," Holly says, pulling me into a hug. They hustle inside, and Holly brightens at the sight of the whiskey bottle on the counter. "Tell me you have more glasses, Brittany."

Brittany meets my eye, winks, and says, "I do," before taking out glasses for Cole and Holly. She doesn't say anything about sending his brother away. Neither do I.

"We have an announcement to make," Holly says, and Brittany covers her face with her hand.

"You're getting married?!" she says.

Cole swears under his breath and rubs his beard. Holly bursts into laughter. "No," she says. "I'm going to give him a test run first. If we move in together, and Jane and I don't murder him, then maybe I'll take pity on him."

"You're moving in together *upstairs?*" she asks, surprised. It's a valid question. Cole and his daughter Jane have lived upstairs, on the brewery's second level, for years, I guess.

"We're gonna figure that out later," Cole says, but he and Holly exchange a glance that piques my interest. Is there a story there? Something tells me there is, but it's obvious they're not ready to tell it.

My pregnant sister, Bryn, and her fiance, Rory, arrive a few minutes later, followed by Rowan and Kennedy and the cameras.

Rowan seems a bit pissed by the presence of the cameramen, possibly even by the invention of the camera, which is extremely amusing, but Kennedy has an unreal ability to soothe his prickles. Rory and Bryn have a special connection, too. I mean, he's drinking sparkling apple juice with her so she doesn't have to be the only one not getting crunked.

They've done all right for themselves, my siblings. Our other sister, Willow, lives in Asheville, about two hours away, but she's engaged too. Which leaves me the last Mayberry standing. Or it would if I didn't go by my father's last name.

I'm happy for them. I'm amused by the filming for the show, even though I don't want to be in it (my publicist would probably shove me in front of the camera, but she lives in California, so she's not in prime shoving position).

I'm also feeling a little off-kilter tonight. Maybe what Brittany told me earlier is right. Maybe we don't get to constantly reinvent ourselves. Maybe I'm like a cat embarking on its ninth life. Maybe it's all going to catch up to me.

Which is probably why I drink too much whiskey with Brittany, followed by too much champagne with my sisters after we filmed a New Years Countdown three times, something that would make anyone punchdrunk, and sent the cameramen home. Logan doesn't show up, not that I really expected him to after the welcome Brittany gave him.

My sisters and I are laughing wildly about something, probably a dick joke, when Cole announces it's time for us all to clear out.

"I'm not saying you have to leave," he tells us, "but you have to leave."

"Then you're a liar," I say, "because you just told us to do what you said you weren't going to do." I get lost in the logic, or illogic, of my own sentence and start laughing again.

"I should have said that everyone except for Holly has to leave," he says, and Brittany snorts and starts grabbing the remaining glasses, including a full glass of champagne from one of my sisters.

I figured my sister Bryn would have the unenviable task of driving us all home, given she's pregnant and didn't drink, but her rich fiancé arranged for each of us to get a car. Good going, fiancé. Good going, Bryn.

I say goodbye to everyone, throw a salute to Brittany and say, "See you soon, Badass Brittany," and stumble into my car.

The driver and I get into an argument about the correct spelling of the word *coitus* —don't ask—even though I'm obviously right, then he leaves me off outside the door of my dad's house. It's a pretty house, yellow with a cherry red door, because my dad asked me which colors we should paint it when I was eleven, and that was my color scheme for the week, but I don't want to go in.

It feels a bit like a trap.

It makes me want to gnaw my leg off and run.

But it *is* massively cold, so I'm soon rummaging through my bag for my key.

Oh, shit. I didn't bring my key. Now, I'm feeling less like a rat in a trap and more like a hairless cat caught in a snowbank. I hop on my feet, willing myself to be warmer, and consider my options. I don't want to wake up my father. He just had a heart attack, and the last thing he needs to do is let me inside when I'm smelling of booze.

The answer is obvious. I could wake up his—*our*—roommate, the man who started staying with him just before Christmas.

My face slips into a scowl.

I don't want Lou to open the door for me either. Although I don't know the man well, I do know the following things: he is a literary agent for "real" authors (i.e. not me because I'm both independently published and a romance novelist); he lives in New York and has come to Highland Hills for reasons undisclosed, and he is friendly with my sister Willow's fiance but hasn't even told either of them what the hell he is doing here. I also know that he is judgmental and condescending, because even though we've exchanged no more than a handful of remarks, most of them have annoyed me. If I asked him for a favor now, he'd probably give me a wry look and say something cutting about young people these days, even though he's just seven years older than me.

He'd probably—

"The window!" I say to myself, probably speaking louder than I intended.

I hustle to the back of the house and open the trick window, the one that never locks.

Hell, yes, my father never fixed it, because I can feel it giving when I tug up. Maybe I should make him fix it, but for now I'm grateful for the oversight.

"Come on, baby," I say to myself, giving it a harder push. "Give it to me good." The windows in this house are so old they look like candy glass and would probably break as easily, but it would totally be worth it if I don't have to talk to Lou right now. The window gives without cracking, and I do a little dance on my feet before putting my head and arms in, like I'm really feeling the hokey pokey, and pulling myself up. Except there's a shouted "oh, fuck" on the other side, and then someone's shoving my shoulders. It only lasts a fraction of a second, but I nearly tumble out on my ass. Then there's a breathed out sigh and the voice says, "Oh, it's you."

The hands that tried to push me out tug me in, and Lou looks down at me like I'm a naughty child, caught sneaking out rather than sneaking in. He's wearing pants with a drawstring and white T-shirt, the kind of clothes I didn't think he'd wear since he comes off as a stuffed shirt who'd go to bed in a button-down. His hair is mussed, and it strikes me for literally the first time that this fusty man who's moved in with my father—against my will, let the record show—is actually sort of cute.

Then he lifts an eyebrow and says, "Aren't you a little old for this sort of thing?"

See. Called it.

Get *Matchmaking a Roommate*!

330

Also by Angela Casella and Denise Grover Swank

Highland Hills

Matchmaking a Billionaire

Matchmaking a Single Dad

Matchmaking a Grump

Matchmaking a Roommate (coming in February!)

Bad Luck Club

Love at First Hate

Jingle Bell Hell

Fraudulently Ever After

Matchmaking Mischief

Bringing Down the House (prequel) by Angela Casella

Asheville Brewing

Any Luck at All

Better Luck Next Time

Getting Lucky

Bad Luck Club

Luck of the Draw (novella)

All the Luck You Need (prequel novella) by Angela Casella

About the Author

ANGELA CASELLA is a romcom fanatic. Writing them, reading them, watching them—she's greedy, and she does it all. She writes the Fairy Godmother Agency series solo, and she's lucky enough to collaborate with Denise Grover Swank on multiple series, writing as Angela Denise.

She lives in Asheville, NC. Her hobbies include herding her daughter toward less dangerous activities, the aforementioned romcom addiction, and dreaming of having someone else clean her house.

Visit her website at www.angelacasella.com or Angela Denise's website at www.arcdgs.com.

About the Author

DENISE GROVER SWANK was born in Kansas City, Missouri and lived in the area until she was nineteen. Then she became a nomad, living in five cities, four states and ten houses over the course of ten years before she moved back to her roots. She speaks English and smattering of Spanish and Chinese, which she learned through an intensive Nick Jr. immersion period. Her hobbies include witty Facebook comments (in own her mind) and dancing in her kitchen with her children (quite badly if you believe her offspring). Hidden talents include the gift of justification and the ability to drink massive amounts of caffeine and still fall asleep within two minutes. Her lack of the sense of smell allows her to perform many unspeakable tasks. She has six children and hasn't lost her sanity. Or so she leads you to believe.

For mystery and romance: denisegroverswank.com
For urban fantasy: dgswank.com